Dedication

This book is dedicated to my friends at Long Island Romance Writers for their love and unyielding support. And for my sister, Mindy Paticoff-Weinman, forever in my heart.

"Heller? Are you with me?" a feminine voice asked.

Heller? The word sounded familiar yet somehow wrong. Is that my name? How was it possible to have no memory of one's own name? His head throbbed in time with the pounding of his heart. At least he had a heartbeat. He cracked his eyes open, but a blinding light forced his lids to shutter back in place.

A soft hand rested in his. *Zephyr*. He may not have recognized his own name, but even with his eyes closed, he recognized her. He inhaled her seductive fragrance, a spring breeze, sweet and floral. There were many things he couldn't remember, but Zephyr wasn't among them. A stunner, her hair fell in dark, shiny waves down her back, and her eyes sparkled bright blue in a vivid hue he'd never seen before. Long legs and soft curves completed the package of what had to be the most beautiful woman in the world.

His body gave a restless twitch, and her warm breath whispered in his ear. "Did you say something?"

There was a pause, and then another puff of heated air grazed his neck. Throat dry and tight, he was unable to answer the simple question but commanded his eyes to open. A shadow filtered the glare, and he blinked, adjusting to the change in brightness. Zephyr's gorgeous face came into view, and what a face it was.

Praise

In "The House of Air," the next installment in the acclaimed Guardians of the Elements series, M. Goldsmith once again plunges readers into the beauty and mystique of Aether, a world where magic, fueled by the elements, endows its citizens with powers their enemies will do anything to acquire. With its magic and intrigue, intense characters, and action-packed battles, Aether is a lushly-drawn world readers will want to visit again and again.
—Patty Blount, award-winning author

"The House of Air" will keep you on the edge of your seat from the very first page. Ms. Goldsmith has created a mystical, authentic world where Guardians and Protectors are to die for delicious. Dark secrets, sexy, badass heroines, and powerful heroes—what's not to love?
--Heather Alexander, author

The House of Air

by

M. Goldsmith

Guardians of the Elements, Book Three

The House of Air

Contact Information: info@thewildrosepress.com

Cover Art by *The Wild Rose Press, Inc.*

The Wild Rose Press, Inc.
PO Box 708
Adams Basin, NY 14410-0708
Visit us at www.thewildrosepress.com

Publishing History
First Edition, 2024
Trade Paperback ISBN 978-1-5092-5268-8
Digital ISBN 978-1-5092-5269-5

Guardians of the Elements, Book Three
Published in the United States of America

Prologue

Zephyr Anani, Guardian of The House of Air

Ashlyn and Hawk's beautiful Joining ceremony resembled the final scene in a Hollywood disaster movie. Too bad this wasn't a movie.

Caustic clouds of smoke floated around the edges of the Outdoor Chapel. Even through the hazy air, Dr. Charles Barrington's maniacal voice was clear. Spit flew from his mouth like a rabid dog as he shouted and waved a gun at Brooke Sanders, Aether's newest Water Guardian. The poor woman had believed this lunatic was her father until recent events revealed her to be half Aetherian. The man had been stalking Aether for years, coveting the power of the Elements, and when Brooke's true identity came to light, it only served to inflame his hate.

Zephyr stood frozen in place, her heart pounding. One tiny misstep could set the unhinged man off the rails even further than he'd already fallen. If only she had her crossbow, she could dispatch Barrington with a single shot. She didn't like to brag, but Zephyr's Guardian powers gave her arrows a little extra something. Sliding her feet inch by inch, she'd barely taken a step when the blast of a gunshot stopped her dead in her tracks.

Cassy Sanders crumpled to the ground at her granddaughter's feet. She must have shielded Brooke with her own body, taking Barrington's bullet in the chest. Before Zephyr or the others had time to blink, a dark figure leaped through the murky fog. Rapid-fire gunshots showered Barrington and his mercenaries with bullets, bringing them down like metal ducks in a carnival game. Adrenaline churned inside Zephyr. *Who the hell is this guy, and where did he come from?*

Red bloomed across the front of Cassy's dress, and blood gushed between her fingers. Brooke sank to her knees and overlaid her grandmother's hands to stave off the bleeding.

Tears streamed down Brooke's face. "What did you do, Gran?"

"Saved you," Cassy's words rasped out, her blood-stained hands falling to her sides.

Zephyr blinked, unable to process what she was seeing. Barrington's own henchman, the one with the blank look in his eyes, the one who was supposed to be under guard in the Medical Center, lowered the matching SIG Sauers clutched in each of his hands. She had to be imagining things; he couldn't be the same man. Zephyr squeezed her eyes shut tight and prayed that when she opened them again everything would right itself. She waited a heartbeat and then took a long, hard look at the man.

Yup, it was definitely him. Mr. Heller. Everything was the same, all six foot four inches of roped muscle, thick blond hair, and broad shoulders—everything except for his blue eyes. Once steely and vacant, the soldier's gaze now held an expression of pure hatred. Charles Barrington, the man bent on destroying Aether, was face down, swimming in a pool of his own blood. Zephyr stared at his unmoving form, waiting for the slightest twitch, but he didn't budge.

"Good riddance, asshole," she whispered under her breath.

Brooke cried out, and a cold chill ran through Zephyr. Blood continued to pour from the wound in Cassy's chest, and her granddaughter's efforts to get it under control seemed futile. The loud rumble of an ATV broke through the Guardian's panic, and Cassy was whisked away into a cloud of dust.

Zephyr's gaze shifted around the pavilion, bustling with activity, until a nearby scuffle captured her attention. Her stomach lurched as she watched a young Protector grab Heller by his shirt and throw him to the ground. The big man hit the wooden floor with a resounding thud. A second Protector stood over the soldier, cocked his weapon, and pointed it at the defenseless man.

For the second time tonight, Zephyr's hands itched for her crossbow. Hadn't they seen what she had? Heller killed Charles Barrington, dead, as in no more. What was wrong with her people? Couldn't they tell the good guys from the bad guys?

She stalked toward the dead bodies of Barrington's mercenaries. With Heller fixed in her sights, she reached the closest man sprawled on the ground, held her breath, and pried the weapon from his grip. The weight felt foreign resting in her palm, and she opened and closed her fingers around the cold metal. It wasn't her crossbow, but it would do in a pinch.

The Protector who'd taken Heller down shoved the subdued man with a booted foot. His partner taunted the soldier, jamming his gun into his back. Heller's body went limp, and he laced his fingers behind his head.

Despite his acquiescence, one Protector continued to harass him with jeers.

Zephyr lost it. A strong wind swirled around her head like a halo, lifting the ends of her long, dark hair. Her gut clenched with the surge of her Guardian powers, and the Air around her grew hot on the cool spring day. Steam rose in vaporous clouds. She positioned the gun above her head and pulled the trigger. The shot rang out, echoing in the acoustics of the amphitheater. Everyone stopped moving, and the silence which followed whispered in the breeze.

Snarling at the two men through gritted teeth, she spat her words in sharp command. “Let…him…go…now. He saved us all.” She leveled her stolen weapon on the Protector pointing his gun at Heller.

Hawk, lead Protector of Aether, came up beside her, placed his hands over hers, and lowered the gun before removing it from her white-knuckled grip. “What the hell, Zeph?” His deep voice rumbled with surprise.

“These guys are acting like he’s the enemy.” Zephyr’s breath was ragged. “Heller is the one who took out Barrington. You can’t do this to him, Hawk. He didn’t ask for any of this. Look at him. He’s not even fighting.”

Brooke came up beside her. “I agree with Zephyr. I’d be dead right now if it wasn’t for Mr. Heller. We all would.”

Hawk nodded to his men. “Ease up there, guys. Let’s show some respect to our guest.” He faced the two Guardians, his tone authoritative. “I’ll tell you what’s going to happen. We’re going to get out of here and head to the Medical Center to get checked out by Kai’s staff, including Mr. Heller. You have my word; he will be treated kindly. And, Zeph, no more guns. Do you hear me?"

"Yes, sir. Next time, I'll make sure I have my crossbow," Zephyr grumbled.

He stepped in close. She should've been threatened by the large man hovering inches from her face, but in truth, Hawk had always been on her side, and Zephyr wasn't the least bit intimidated.

"Watch it. I'm pretty sure we've discussed this issue *ad nauseum*. You can't be a Protector unless the Elders give the go-ahead." Hawk dropped a beefy hand on Zephyr's shoulder. "Listen, you know if it were up to me, it would be a done deal already, but it's out of my hands. So, can you please give me a small break here?"

Zephyr kicked at the dirt beneath her scuffed dress shoes. "Fine, but I'm going with those guys to make sure they don't hurt him."

She pushed past the Protectors, helping the soldier to his feet. Heller's gaze met hers, and the confusion in his eyes broke her heart. Zephyr had always been attracted to bad boys, but maybe this was taking things a bit far…or maybe not. Gentling her tone, she addressed Mr. Heller, "My name is Zephyr." She conjured a warm smile and continued, "Don't you worry. I've got your back."

Chapter One

Zephyr

Zephyr was not the type of woman who sighed, yet one slipped out all the same. She had no idea why she'd been glued to the soldier's side since Barrington's attack, but even after three solid days, she found it impossible to leave. Her head ached, and her eyes burned. She thrived on a challenge as much as the next Guardian, but the man known only as Mr. Heller had become a source of endless frustration, an enigma Zephyr couldn't unravel. Opposing images fought for center stage in her head. Each scenario she analyzed shared one common component, the soldier asleep in the hospital bed beside her. The question remained; was he the mercenary sent to destroy Aether or the person who saved their world from Dr. Charles Barrington?

Heller moaned softly, and Zephyr reached for the washcloth on his nightstand. She brushed a few stray blond hairs from his forehead and leaned in, the aroma of cinnamon filling her nose. Dear Goddess, the man smelled amazing. Shaking off her intense reaction, she pressed the cool terrycloth to his heated skin. He thrashed from the initial contact but settled when she whispered a quiet *shh* in his ear. Tossing the cloth back into the bin, she glimpsed the mark embedded in her left palm. Most Aetherians believed being born with the symbol of a Guardian was the highest honor. And though Zephyr treasured her role, she couldn't deny it had controlled her life from the moment she'd taken her first breath.

According to the village Elders, a Guardian's destiny was preordained by the God and Goddess, but as soon as Zephyr understood what Protectors did, she longed to trade her mark for the colorful tattoo of its membership. She didn't care about fate. Zephyr was of the new generation and believed in taking control of her own destiny.

She trained with her fraternal twin sister, Skye, and her best friend, Bracken Beck. The two Protectors taught her everything they could about their ways. Zephyr's skills developed with a natural ease, and soon she was every bit as good as the seasoned Protectors. But the Elders were impossible; they couldn't see beyond the scope of her position as a Guardian. Stubbornness was a dominant Aetherian trait, and she'd have to search for a way to open their minds to the possibility of her being more…much more.

Heller mumbled something unintelligible, and Zephyr picked up his large hand, turning it over in her own. She traced the lines of his palm with a finger and imagined all the things this man's hands had done—both good and bad. Unlike the pigheaded Elders, she vowed to give Heller a chance. It had nothing to do with the fact that he was an off-the-charts hottie. He looked more like a movie star than a soldier. Thick lashes framed incredible blue eyes that were memorable even though she'd barely seen them open.

There was no law against finding someone attractive, and yet, no matter how she tried to reconcile it, consorting with an enemy of Aether was a definite no-no. Zephyr was determined to figure out who the true Heller was and win the Elders over with her resourcefulness. Once she proved worthy, they'd have to reconsider and allow her to enter the Protector trials.

The soldier's full, red lips parted slightly as his chest rose and fell. Zephyr placed her palm over the thin material of his hospital gown. His heart thrummed beneath her fingertips, and she didn't move for a long while, contemplating the situation. If the man didn't regain consciousness soon, it wouldn't matter what plan she devised.

After Heller and Barrington had been taken into custody two weeks ago, the soldier drifted in and out of consciousness. During his brief periods of alertness, he hadn't uttered a single word; he merely stared into space. It made his awakening and attack on Barrington even more shocking. Heller may have done some horrible things in his past, but Zephyr's gut told her it was the doctor's drug-induced mind control at work. There had to be more to this complicated man than anyone suspected, and she was determined to fill in the missing pieces.

Since the violent attack, darkness clung to Aether, seeping into every crevice. Zephyr had developed a serious case of insomnia, and it was beginning to take its toll. Her heavy eyelids shuttered down, and her chin hit her chest. As she drifted off, the quiet room erupted into a dream world of utter chaos. *Grenades exploded. Thick acrid smoke filled the air. The Outdoor Chapel echoed with the shrill shouts of her people, followed by the coppery smell of blood in the air.* Zephyr woke with a start, sweat dotting her forehead. Would these nightmares plague her forever?

Heller bolted upright and captured her forearm. He clamped down hard, his fingers biting into her flesh. Zephyr's heart pounded, but she calmly placed her free hand on the soldier's. His gaze flew to hers, and he instantly loosened his grip but didn't let go. He reached out and caressed her cheek with a feather-light touch. She froze and held her breath.

"Zephyr," his voice rasped out, breaking the tense silence.

She offered him the smallest of smiles. "Yes, that's my name," she said, keeping her tone reassuring, but inside, her Element rushed through her veins.

His return smile was fleeting, and his eyes rolled back in his head. Any happiness she felt fizzled in an instant. Heller's hand slipped from beneath hers, going slack and falling to the bed with a heavy thud.

Hands shaking, Zephyr clutched the front of his hospital gown. "Can you hear me?" Her heart thundered. "Someone," she yelled. "Help!"

A nurse poked her head into the room. "What's going on?"

"He passed out." The panic inside her raged like a storm.

The nurse put a stethoscope on Heller's chest. "His heart rate *is* a little fast, but I'm sure it's nothing serious. I'll try to reach Kai, but he may be out of calling range. Hang in there. I'll be back soon." She gave Zephyr's shoulder a squeeze.

The woman's effort to reassure her was a nice touch, but since her parents' untimely deaths years earlier, Zephyr's support system started and ended with one person. She pulled out her phone, hit Skye's contact, and waited only one ring for the sound of her sister's voice to come over the line.

"This better be good. I'm—"

"Stop talking. You have to come to the Medical Center right this second." Zephyr cut the call before Skye could answer.

She picked her cuticles raw—waiting and wondering. What if the Elders kicked the soldier out of Aether? What if she never saw him again? The what-ifs were beginning to stack up when Skye burst through the door six minutes and thirty-two seconds later.

"I'm here." Her sister huffed, flinging one of her long, dark braids over her shoulder. "What's the big freaking emergency?" Skye stopped just inside the doorway, her assessing blue gaze, so similar to her own, landing on Heller's unconscious form. "Oh, shit. I'm sorry. What did Kai say?"

"He's not here."

"Um, hello, I'm a Protector, not a doctor. Why would you call me? Isn't there a nurse or someone more qualified around?"

Zephyr's voice wavered. "The nurse is trying to reach Kai. But Heller hasn't moved. I'm at the end of my rope. I haven't slept in three days. I don't think I can handle it if something happens to him."

"You're acting a little nuts. Why don't you tell me what happened right before he passed out?"

"He said my name and then…nothing," Zephyr said. "The nurse told me his heartbeat was fast. I'm worried that he's not going to make it."

"It wouldn't be the worst thing in the world if he croaked," Skye contended. "In fact, if you want, I can kill him, and we can tell everyone he couldn't handle

Ashlyn's stolen Guardian powers and burned out. No extra charge for my story embellishments."

"Do you have to turn everything into a joke?"

"Who says I'm joking?" Skye's tone grew more emphatic. "Listen to me. I've said it a million times. *This guy is trouble*. The kind of trouble you need to stay far away from. Don't let this innocent act lull you into a false sense of security. Heller, if that's even his real name, has danger written all over that pretty-boy face of his."

Zephyr narrowed her eyes. "Heller is not a pretty boy. He's…he's—"

"Wait." Skye's palm shot up. "Let me stop you right there. He's not any of the things you're thinking."

"How do you know what I'm thinking?"

"Duh, we're twins. We may not be identical, but we always know what each other is thinking. Which is why I want to remind you that Commander Coma, over there"—Skye tossed her head toward Heller's bed—"is Barrington's muscle. He was probably a killer before the bat-shit crazy doctor took control of him and enhanced him with Ash's powers."

The very same thought had gone through Zephyr's mind, not that she would ever admit it to Skye. A couple of weeks ago, when Heller and the doctor crossed into their lands, the Protectors believed they'd gotten the upper hand in capturing the two trespassers. The duo had shown up weeks before Barrington's contingent of mercenaries descended on Aether. Their people had no way of anticipating the intruders would be leaving so much death and destruction in their wake.

She couldn't deny the possibility that the soldier had been a willing participant in Dr. Barrington's plot to control the Elements. But her instincts were powerful and nudged her in another direction. When Heller and Barrington confronted Cassy and Brooke in the woods, the soldier appeared drugged. He'd yielded to the doctor's orders like a trained animal.

Zephyr crossed her arms over her chest. "That's some pretty heavy speculation. Kai is a brilliant doctor, and even he doesn't have a complete picture of what's been done to Heller." She seared her sister with a burning gaze. "Why are you being so negative? And suspicious? I don't get it."

"Because I'm a Protector, and besides, someone has to. You're too blinded by the guy's hotness quotient."

Zephyr attempted to look abashed, but instead, her cheeks heated. She opened her mouth to defend herself, but Skye stopped her with a nasty scowl.

"Oh, don't think I haven't seen you checking him out," Skye accused. "But I wish you'd remember your boy Heller practically strangled Cassy the day he and that psycho, Barrington broke through Aether's barriers. You were there."

"Anyone could see Heller was under the doctor's mind control, and the operative word here is, *was*. He isn't under anyone's control anymore," Zephyr insisted.

"And you know that, how?"

"I saw it in his eyes."

"Now, you're messing with me." Skye laughed. "The only thing in that man's eyes was murder. Probably, the slave trying to become the new master."

"Don't be ridiculous."

"Fine, tell me what I'm doing here in that case?"

"I was scared. My first instinct when that happens is to call you," Zephyr admitted.

Skye's gaze softened. "Believe me, I always want to

help you, but I have zero desire to be involved with soldier boy who is only pretending to be asleep." She hiked her thumb over her shoulder and glared at Heller. "And not for nothing, but Kai's bound to notice the guy can talk now."

"He didn't talk…he…he said my name and that's all." Zephyr's half-hearted rationalization did nothing to convince Skye—or herself.

The nurse swept into the room at the perfect moment. "The doctor is on his way."

"Thanks," Zephyr said with a mix of relief and trepidation.

"No worries. I'll be by the front desk if you need me." She slipped back out the door with a nod.

Once the woman left, the sisters stood on opposite sides of the room. While they waited for the doctor, each stared at the floor, frozen in stubborn silence. It was amazing that twins could resemble one another so strongly yet have such different personalities. They both had long dark hair, their mom's vivid blue eyes, and tawny brown complexions, but their physical attributes were where their similarities ended.

After five minutes, Zephyr broke. She met her sister's gaze and whispered softly, "I wish you'd give him a chance."

Skye groaned and perched a hand on her hip. "Fine, for argument's sake, let's say Heller is a good man who's been forced into a bad situation. When you get all doe-eyed looking at him, it's hard to be confident that you're thinking straight. What if this guy isn't right in the head? Please, promise me that you'll keep your guard up."

"Fine, I promise." It didn't matter if Skye was right; Zeph had been drawn to Heller with a magnetic pull she couldn't explain.

Kai burst into the room. All of Aether was anxious to uncover the information hidden inside Heller's brain, especially the doctor. Charles Barrington's experiments, and of course, whatever else he'd been planning before his death, could be crucial to Aether's survival.

"What happened?" Kai dropped a hand to her forearm. "Tell me everything he said and did."

Hawk sauntered in before she could answer. Zephyr shouldn't have been surprised to see their lead Protector. The guy knew everything that went on in the village. He was dressed in head-to-toe black, wore a gun on each hip, and had a fearsome-looking knife strapped to one of his thick muscular thighs. His menacing expression stated, *don't fuck with me.* Yet, beneath the mask and bravado was a sweetness that still took her aback.

"Hey, Zeph. You look wrecked." Hawk pulled over a chair and gestured for her to take a seat. "Please, sit and tell us what happened?"

She shook her head and remained on her feet. "I'm good. It's really not that big a deal." They were suspicious enough about the man. She didn't want to add to their distrust by making it seem like he had attacked her. "He touched my arm and said my name. That's it. Heller isn't the bad guy anymore. In fact, I don't think he ever was."

"Sorry, Zeph, but I'm afraid we're going to have to agree to disagree here. The only thing we know for sure is that Heller is an unknown. I refuse to speculate. Kai, since you're our medical expert, I'd appreciate it if you could assess his condition." Hawk spun the chair around he'd offered Zephyr and straddled it.

Kai continued the examination he'd begun the

moment he entered the room. He prodded and poked the unconscious man until he seemed satisfied. He draped his stethoscope around his neck and addressed Hawk.

"His heart rate, which had been elevated to a dangerously high level, has returned to a normal rate. It seems the drugs are making their way out of his system, and his Aetherian healing powers are finally kicking in. I'll do an EKG and some blood work to confirm." The doctor turned to Zephyr. "He's going to be all right. Rest is the best medicine we can offer him right now."

"I'll stay with him…you know…in case he, um, wakes up," Zephyr answered without thinking.

Hawk's booming voice rang out. "Is that so?"

"Well, he might be…confused, and since he said my name, I'm guessing he remembers me somehow. It seems I'm the best person for the job."

Hawk laughed. "I like your style, kid, but I'm afraid now that he's conscious, we're going to be placing a twenty-four-hour armed guard outside Heller's door until we know more about his frame of mind." Zephyr opened her mouth to argue, but Hawk stopped her with a pointed look. "Before you start giving me shit, I want to remind you who this man worked for."

"But, Hawk, it's not his fault. Heller won't hurt anyone."

"Really?" A condescending smile spread across Hawk's face. "And you're sure enough about this man, you're willing to risk your life on the notion?"

She didn't need to ponder anything. "Yes. Yes, I am."

"Too bad, kid. *I'm* not willing to risk your life. You may stay in the room with the door open and the guard in sight."

"Wow, our father used to say the exact same thing," Skye interjected.

Two years ago, they'd lost their parents in a tragic hiking accident, and they'd never quite recovered from the heartbreak. The memories washed over Zephyr. Skye caught her gaze and gave her a subtle wink. Following the death of their mother and father, the young women's bond grew impossibly close. There was no other reason Zephyr would have called her sister, considering Skye's distrust of the soldier.

"There's one life goal to mark off my list." Hawk glided over the mention and shook his head. "I'm only eighty-three, and I already sound like someone's father. Fantastic."

Kai clapped a hand on Hawk's shoulder. "Buddy, you've sounded like someone's dad for a long time. Get over it."

Hawk flung Kai's hand off. "You're right. I'm over it." He shot his friend a dirty look. "And because you're so helpful—" He extracted a Glock from his holster and tossed it to Kai. "You get to keep an eye on him until I get one of the Protectors over here. If he so much as sneezes wrong, don't hesitate to shoot." Hawk turned his gaze to Skye and pointed to the door. "Go, now."

As her sister headed out, she mouthed to Zephyr, "Be careful."

Kai grabbed one of the metal folding chairs and banged it out into the hallway. Grumbling, he took a seat. "All my years of medical training, and I'm a babysitter." He poked his head in and called to Zephyr, "I'll be right here if you need me because, clearly, I have nothing more important to do."

"Exactly." Hawk clapped Kai on the back, tossed

Zephyr a wink, and walked out behind his friend.

The quiet room reverberated with the sounds of Heller's rhythmic breathing. Zephyr tugged a chair beside the bed, picked up his large hand, and entwined their fingers. "I want you to know, you're safe with me. I'm not going to let anyone hurt you." Heller didn't open his eyes, but his grip tightened around hers.

****

Heller

"Heller? Are you with me?" a feminine voice asked.

Heller? The word sounded familiar yet somehow wrong. *Is that my name?* How was it possible to have no memory of one's own name? His head throbbed in time with the pounding of his heart. At least he *had* a heartbeat. He cracked his eyes open, but a blinding light forced his lids to shutter back in place.

A soft hand rested in his. *Zephyr.* He may not have recognized his own name, but even with his eyes closed, he recognized her. He inhaled her seductive fragrance, a spring breeze, sweet and floral. There were many things he couldn't remember, but Zephyr wasn't among them. A stunner, her hair fell in dark, shiny waves down her back, and her eyes sparkled bright blue in a vivid hue he'd never seen before. Long legs and soft curves completed the package of what had to be the most beautiful woman in the world.

His body gave a restless twitch, and her warm breath whispered in his ear. "Did you say something?"

There was a pause, and then another puff of heated air grazed his neck. Throat dry and tight, he was unable to answer the simple question but commanded his eyes to open. A shadow filtered the glare, and he blinked, adjusting to the change in brightness. Zephyr's gorgeous face came into view, and what a face it was. The rich tone of her light brown skin glowed in the dim light. The combination of her coloring, the slim slope of her nose, and her full red lips pursed into a pout made his stomach do a flip. Runway and magazine models looked like amateurs next to this extraordinary beauty.

"Are you with me?" she asked.

Worrisome, dark circles rimmed her striking blue eyes. How long had he been out? Even through his fog, her sleep deprivation was obvious. Why was she still here with him? Surely someone like Zephyr had better things to do.

He cleared his throat, intending to question her, but his vocal cords tightened like rubber bands ready to snap. The only sound he managed to produce was a low rumble. Instead, he reached out and ran his thumb across her plump bottom lip.

She didn't pull away but rather gifted him with a warm smile. "I guess that's a yes." Her voice had a husky quality he found sexy as sin.

He would have given anything for the strength to pull her into his arms, but even sitting up was a struggle. The world needed to stop spinning, so he could get off this maddening ride. Zephyr rushed to his aid, stuffing a bunch of extra pillows behind his back. Her efforts were wasted as the room continued to whir by in sweeping circles. Giving up the fight, he sank into the soft pile and closed his eyes.

A cool cloth flattened out on his forehead, followed by the addicting voice he couldn't get enough of. "Don't rush it. It takes time to heal. Barrington's drugs are making their way out of your system. Your…um…powers should help expedite your recovery. Please, rest. I'll be here to watch over you."

Powers? Maybe he'd hit his head or something because everything the beautiful girl said sounded crazy. Before he could process her last statement, a strange and intense blast of heat washed over him. It coursed through his veins like flames making their way across a kerosene-soaked rope. The cloth on his forehead shifted, dabbing his cheeks, neck, and chest, soothing his fiery flesh.

Zephyr leaned in close, her lips mere inches from his own. "Relax. What you feel is the energy of your Fire. It's healing you. Trust me."

What the hell is she talking about? He opened his eyes and paused, staring at her lips before it hit him. The girl was beautiful, but unfortunately, she was also quite delusional.

A low hum crackled in his ears, drawing his attention away from Zephyr. He gazed down and caught a flash of orange before red sparks shot out from his fingers. *What in the ever-living fuck?* He raised his shaky hands in front of his face, and flames flickered atop each of his fingertips like candles on a birthday cake. *This can't be real. Breathe. Not happening. Breathe.* The fire blasted away all rational thought, leaping several inches and then receding. His heart rate kicked into high gear. Someone had to be messing with him.

Zephyr doused the tips of his fingers with the wet washcloth. They hissed and sizzled, a steamy cloud rising in the air.

"Take a deep breath," she announced, unflappable confidence spilling over into her sweet smile.

He wanted to believe her, but he wasn't quite sure she was all there. Removing the cloth, he inspected his fingers with wary eyes. No redness. No blisters. No pain.

His mind had to be playing tricks on him. There was no other explanation for flames bursting from his fingertips. He closed his eyes, and distant images flashed in his head. The more he tried to make sense of the strange visions, the more searing pain stabbed behind his eyes. Digging his fingers into his temples, he squeezed his eyes shut tighter.

"Dear Goddess, you're hurting." Zephyr jerked to her feet. "I'll get the doctor."

He snagged her hand and halted her movement. Running his tongue across his parched lips, he swallowed hard and searched for his voice. "Please…don't…go," he croaked out in a hoarse whisper.

She took a seat next to him on the edge of his hospital bed. "No worries, I'll stay," she said, the corners of her mouth lifting.

Her expression warmed him more than the odd fire now smoldering inside his body. Nodding was all he could manage. She placed her hand in his again. The simple touch of her skin infused him with vigor, and he managed to scratch out a few more words.

"Where…how…what—"

"I'll try to explain things to you as long as you're sure you're up to it." Zephyr threw him a questioning look, and he flipped her a mini salute. She smirked and then glanced back at the door standing ajar. "You're in Aether."

His brows knitted.

"I guess I'd better start from the beginning." She crossed one leg over the other and leaned back. "Aether is a world tucked away among the trees and mountains, cloaked in magic. The people here answer to the four

Elements: Fire, Water, Air, and Earth."

She paused as if it were the end of the story, but he gestured for her to continue.

"This lunatic doctor named Charles Barrington penetrated our borders and kidnapped Ashlyn, our Fire Guardian. Her control over her Element is off the charts. Our best guess is that Barrington somehow created a drug replicating her powers." Zephyr's gaze fell to the floor. "You...you were with him. We assume that's how you got your new powers."

The muscles in his chest constricted. How could he have no memory of any of this? This girl had to be pranking him. The things she was saying made no sense. Magic and evil doctors only existed in books, not in real life. Once again, flames burst from the tips of his fingers, shutting down the internal argument he was having. Immobilized, he couldn't speak, and his breath went shallow. All he could do was sit there like an idiot with his mouth hanging open, mesmerized by the orange and red dancing up and down his forearms.

"Shit, too much, huh?" She cringed. "You look totally freaked out. Should I get Kai? He's our doctor."

Zephyr's question hung in the air. In truth, he had no idea if a doctor could help...unless he was a shrink, of course.

Chapter Two

Skye

Skye half groaned, half whined, fully aware of how ridiculous she sounded. Hawk's extra patrol shifts were driving her insane, but since Barrington's attack, every Protector was expected to step up. Skye's responsibilities took the form of suffering through a guard duty rotation joined with Bracken Beck. Her sister's best friend and the word *Joined* had no business in the same sentence. To make matters worse, Aether's forest was stifling hot on the late spring day. Today was going to be a long one, for sure.

Sweat trailed down Skye's back as she emerged from the thicket. Propped against an oak tree, Brack took up a casual pose, his long legs crossed. No one as obnoxious as him had a right to be that good looking. His jet-black hair was perfectly coiffed, and his tanned face was covered with the perfect amount of stubble to be sexy. A tight, gray T-shirt clung to his defined pecs, showing no signs of perspiration. She, on the other hand, was sweating buckets. The man irked her by simply standing there, and instant tension drew her muscles into tight coils. She sank her teeth into her lower lip and vowed to resist her violent urges where he was concerned. From the smug look plastered on his cocky face, she feared it would take more than the pep talk she'd been rehearsing in her head. *It's cool. You got this. Stay calm.*

Quill approached them, and Skye said a silent prayer of thanks to the God and Goddess for placing him in charge today. The senior Protector's sense of humor created a buffer. Even in the tensest situations, his levity never failed. She hoped Quill was up to the task during their shift because calling Skye and Brack's interactions tense was like calling a hurricane a little wind.

Years of Protector training had honed Skye's self-control, but those skills starred in a disappearing act whenever Brack was nearby. For reasons she couldn't explain, he managed to coax another side of her to bubble up to the surface. Unbalanced. Chaotic. Wild. This long-established pattern hadn't changed between them since they were children. Brack pushed her buttons like no other person on this planet.

But now was not the time to dissect their history; she had greater concerns. If her plan to enlist Brack's help with the Zephyr-Heller situation had any chance of succeeding, calmer heads needed to prevail. Digging deep, she beseeched her Element for assistance. Air and discipline were the keys.

Brack breezed up alongside her, flicking one of her braids. "You look like a five-year-old."

"You're incredibly clever. I really don't know how you manage to be so witty all the time." Her snarky reply popped out automatically. "It must be a gift."

"Relax. I was joking."

"Perhaps, if you actually possessed a sense of humor beyond the musings of a ten-year-old, I might laugh. Your feeble attempts are no joke. In fact, I find them a little sad." *Crap, I couldn't even control my mouth for two seconds.*

Quill tapped his booted foot on the ground. "You two sound like an old Joined couple. Why don't you get a room and burn this shit out already?"

Skye stared at him, appalled. "I think I just threw up in my mouth."

A strange look danced in Brack's dark brown eyes, but he turned away too fast for her to interpret his expression. Skye had no desire to get inside the jackass's head on a good day, let alone when her sister's safety hung in the balance. Keeping Heller and Zephyr away from each other before things got out of hand took precedence over everything else.

Brack would freak out if he saw Zephyr taking up vigil at the mercenary's bedside. When they were kids, he'd appointed himself the leader of her sister's one-boy security team. If anyone looked at Zeph the wrong way, Brack was on them like a cat on a mouse. For years, Skye believed the future Protector and the Guardian of Air were in love. The two laughed off any suggestions of a romantic relationship between them, but Skye always wondered.

She nudged Brack with an elbow. "Hey, listen, I could use your help with something." The words tasted like vinegar in her mouth, but she forced a smile and continued, "It's about Zeph."

"What about her?"

Skye did a quick check on Quill, who was loading his weapon and paying no attention to them. Her voice dropped to a conspiratorial whisper, "She's been spending every free minute with Barrington's henchman, Mr. Heller. The man can't be trusted, but Zeph is completely blind where he's concerned."

"What do you want me to do about it? Zeph's got her mind set on helping this guy, and you know what happens when your sister digs her heels in."

"You really are an idiot." Skye rubbed the back of her neck. "She's into him, you moron."

"No…no, she's not. Zeph would tell me if she had feelings for this guy. She pities him. That's all there is to it, nothing more. You're letting your imagination run away with you."

"You sure about that? Because she hasn't left his bedside since he said her name three days ago." Skye snorted. "Men are clueless…especially you."

Brack glared at her, his nostrils flaring. "You're wrong. I'd know. Zephyr can't hide anything from me. She's way too transparent."

"Well, then, I guess you're even dumber than I thought you were. In fact, she's with him right now. Probably giving him a sponge bath."

His gaze darkened. "I'll kill him."

"Way to go." She clapped him on the back. "That's the interfering jerk I was hoping to provoke. We can't let things go any further between Zephyr and Mr. Personality than they already have. It's disgusting. Even when she isn't talking about Heller, which, by the way, she does all the time, she has this faraway dreamy look in her eyes. It's starting to freak me out."

"Is this just talk as usual, or do you have a plan?"

Skye's cheeks warmed. "I was kind of hoping you could help me come up with some ideas."

Quill's booming voice interrupted their conversation. "If you two are done whispering sweet nothings to each other, Hawk would like us to check out the shields near the gateway again."

She couldn't hide her irritation. "Are you kidding me? No one has found a thing since the initial searches. Does Hawk actually expect us to find something useful after all this time?"

Brack piped up, "It's not our decision to make. Our jobs are to follow our lead Protector's orders, no matter what."

Quill's lip quirked up along with one eyebrow. "Lighten up, dude. It is kind of nuts, but we don't have anything else to go on. Heller's brain is toast. Hawk is desperate. Personally, I think we should be working on restoring the soldier's memory."

"My sentiments exactly," Skye chimed in. "The man is keeping a world of secrets."

"Well, like Brack said, it's not up to us. Hawk is our lead Protector, and what he says goes. So, let's move out. I'll take point. You two, fall in." Quill jogged off at a decent clip.

Brack turned to her. "I'll take care of Heller. Believe me, he'll get the message to stay away from Zephyr, one way or another. And I guarantee I *will* find out what he's hiding." His final words hung in the air.

Yanking Brack onto her bandwagon might've been something she'd live to regret, but what other choice did she have?

****

Brack

"Skye," he mumbled to his empty backyard. "That woman has no idea what she's talking about." Brack stomped onto the deck with a little more gusto than necessary.

It had always been just Brack and his mother. A botanist, Ivy spent her days in the greenhouses and gardens covered in soil. The lavender she'd planted a few years back caught the breeze, and the pungent fragrance wafted toward him. He inhaled deeply, communing with his Element, but Skye's words played in a loop in his head, pushing everything else aside. *She's into him, you moron.*

The holster at his side dug into his hip, dislodging her rhetoric from his thoughts. He unclipped the gun and set it down on the railing. Weapons weren't standard issue for Protectors, but since Barrington's attack, everything in Aether had changed.

He'd scoured the woods for hours seeking non-existent evidence with Skye and Quill. What a waste of time. But orders were orders, and if Brack knew nothing else, he knew the importance of following orders. When care was not taken, and orders were skimmed over instead of followed to the letter, people got hurt and sometimes even killed. He'd learned this painful lesson the hard way before he'd even become a full Protector. Following orders made things simple. Therefore, Brack followed orders…always.

Going to see the soldier would only lead to trouble. He wasn't sure what was making him listen to Skye. After all these years, how did she still manage to rattle him?

It might have been her insanely good looks. As much as she drove him crazy, he had to admit Skye was a knockout. Oh, she may have tried to hide it with that long, dark hair always tied in two tight braids, not a stitch of makeup, and dressed in baggy tactical pants, but any man with eyes could see the Protector was hot—too bad so was her temper.

Sweat clung to his skin, and his throbbing muscles

protested from this morning's pointless search. Brack peeled off his soaked T-shirt and tossed it onto a nearby lounge chair. Next, he toed off his work boots and dirt-stained socks. Leaving them in a messy pile, he stepped off the deck.

The minute his bare feet sank into the soft grass, the world righted itself. The tender blades stretched up, tickling his toes in welcome. Brack smiled for the first time since his worrisome conversation with Skye. Deep, violet Clematis Taiga snaked along the ground, wrapping their long, flowered tendrils around his legs.

Nothing eased his tensions the way being close to the Earth did. Yet, Skye's words fought their way through his Element's restorative power. From the moment he pictured his best friend and the robotic soldier together, Brack had been ready to break one of his own cardinal rules. Hawk's orders were explicit. Even on guard duty, the Protectors were not to speak to Heller unless otherwise ordered to do so.

The Clematis crept its way up Brack's torso, and magic penetrated his senses. But there was no relaxing with the rapid-fire thoughts bouncing around his head. *Who does this Heller guy think he is anyway? He can't just come in here and lure Zephyr away.* The plant life around him grew still, and Brack scrubbed his vine-covered hands across his face.

"I've got to chill out. I can be calm and rational…unlike Skye."

The vegetation safeguarding the backyard swayed in response to his proclamation. Brack's kinship with all things botanical went beyond simple manipulation. He connected with every aspect of a plant's existence: the leaves, the roots, the soil. An ancient oak tapped one of its knobby branches on his shoulder, sending its message loud and clear. *Go. Now. For Zephyr.* The Clematis uncoiled itself, and Brack jumped to his feet. Hopping onto the deck, he grabbed his boots and stuffed his feet in, sans socks. Without a backward glance, he set off at a determined pace toward the Medical Center.

The potent stench of antiseptic assaulted him the minute he walked inside. He held his breath and headed toward the patient rooms with purpose in his step. Two nurses seated at the tall reception desk tossed him some rather odd looks but didn't stop him.

When he reached Heller's door, one of their newest recruits sat in a folding chair, his weapon balanced on his thigh. The kid caught sight of Brack, leaped to his feet, and his gun launched into the air, landing with a clatter.

The poor newbie snagged the gun and sputtered, "Sorry, I wasn't expecting my relief for a few hours. They've been pretty quiet in there—" He gestured with his head toward the open door. "—so, I was sort of…you know…chilling."

Brack cracked his knuckles. "Who's *they*?"

"Oh, uh, Zephyr and Heller. Hawk gave her permission," he added.

"I see." The vein in Brack's neck, which pulsed whenever he got angry, throbbed relentlessly. "Well, I'm not your relief. I'm here to see Heller."

"Um, sorry, but no one is supposed to go in his room except Kai and Zephyr…Hawk's orders."

"No worries. I'll take full responsibility." He tipped his chin in a curt nod, slipped inside, and shut the door with a soft click.

His gaze flew to the soldier asleep in the small hospital bed. He took in the full picture, and a rock dropped into the pit of his stomach. Zephyr sat by Heller's side, head back, eyes closed, their fingers entwined. This time Skye hadn't been exaggerating.

"You've got to be kidding me," Brack blurted out, making no effort to keep his voice down.

Zephyr flew to her feet, her hand covering her heart. "Dear Goddess, you scared the crap out of me." Her eyes narrowed. "What are you doing here?"

"I came to talk to him." Brack pointed to the soldier, his tone laced with venom.

"Why?" Her left eye half closed, and she glared at him suspiciously. "What's your interest in Heller?"

"*You're* my interest in him." He crossed his arms over his chest.

She mimicked his posture. "Oh, really?"

"Knock it off, Zeph. What's going on with you and this robot?" The vein in his neck picked up its pulsing rhythm.

"Ooohh, I get it. You've been chatting with Skye." She stepped into his space. "I'm going to tell you the same thing I told her." Poking a finger into his chest, she emphasized each word with another jab. "Mind…your…own…business."

Brack moved away. "Who are you?" In all the years they'd been friends, Zephyr had never raised a hand to him in anger.

"What the hell is that supposed to mean?"

"It means I don't recognize you at all. Skye warned me, but this—" He shook his head.

Zeph's normally husky voice morphed into a shrill whistle whenever she got pissed. "How about you explain exactly what your problem is with me being here."

"The list is fairly extensive. I'm not sure where to start." Sarcasm tumbled out on impulse, and he didn't care in the slightest. She sneered at him without saying a single word, but he continued to taunt her all the same. "Hmm. Let's see." Tapping his temple, he feigned deep thought before shooting his finger in the air. "Got one. He's a mindless fighting machine sent to destroy Aether and take control of The Elements."

He must have struck a chord because Zephyr's cheeks flushed to a light shade of lavender, and her volume rose several octaves. "Heller is no such thing. He's an innocent pawn in Barrington's scheme. I'm only trying to help him."

"Yeah, well, I'm only trying to help *you*."

"Help me? You're completely full of it. I know I'm only a powerless little Guardian, not a Protector—" She curled her lip. "—but you and Skye taught me well, so I wouldn't need anyone's help. Remember?"

"Of course, I remember, but this is completely different."

"Yeah, how?"

Brack stammered. "Well…because…you're—"

"That's what I thought," she said, victory in her tone. "If it weren't for the Elder's restrictions, we wouldn't even be having this conversation right now because I'd *be* a Protector. In any case, I can take care of myself."

"Zeph, please, listen to me." He ran a hand through his hair. "We don't know anything about this guy. He could be dangerous."

Her cheeks went from lavender straight to bright purple. "None of this is his fault, and I'm warning you for the last time…back off."

Zephyr's emphatic words had barely sunk in when from the corner of his eye, he caught a glimpse of orange and red. The mercenary was alight with flames and headed on a collision course with Brack. He ducked, and Heller missed him by mere inches. Fists balled tight, Brack dove for the flaming soldier.

Zephyr jumped between them, a firm hand on each of their chests. "Calm down, both of you. This is all a big misunderstanding." She pointed to a folding chair on the other side of the small room. "Brack, sit." When she turned back and addressed the soldier, her voice dripped with honey. "Heller—" She stroked his arm, and the flames subsided. "—please, have a seat on the bed. Brack is my best friend. He and I need to come to an understanding, but I'm not in any danger."

The soldier acted like a trained seal, except this time, he performed for Zephyr instead of Barrington. How the hell had this little relationship developed in only a few short days? Brack took a seat on the cold metal chair and glared at the man. If Heller thought he could waltz into Aether and hook up with Zephyr because he'd hijacked Ash's powers, the guy was more out of his mind than anyone realized.

A small breeze picked up in the stagnant air of the hospital room. Zephyr's powers lifted the soldier's blanket, loose tissues skated across the floor, and a half-eaten muffin rolled toward Brack's feet. Even amidst the debris blowing around the room, Heller's attention remained fixed on the Guardian. He and Zeph acted like magnets, drawn to each other by an invisible force. A heavy weight landed square in the center of Brack's chest. *Not good. Not good at all.*

Zephyr stood between the two men, her long hair

hanging in her face. Tossing glances back and forth, she shuffled her feet. "Clearly, the three of us have to talk. But first things first. Heller, meet Bracken Beck. Brack, this is Heller." When her gaze fell on the soldier again, Brack couldn't miss the way her expression softened. "Brack and I grew up together. He's like a brother to me."

"Hello," Heller said, his voice raspy.

Brack tipped his chin. "Hey."

"Well, it's a start." Zephyr gave a weak smile.

Walking over to the bed, she took a seat beside Heller. The minute her ass hit the mattress, a potted Philodendron on the nightstand began to spill over the sides of its container at an exponential rate. The vines crept closer to Heller until they brushed his shoulder.

She turned on Brack. "Seriously? Cut the shit and reel in your powers."

"Sorry," he grumbled. "Instinct." The plant retracted its leaves, settling back in its pot.

Heller's brow knitted, and Zeph moistened her lips, staring into the soldier's eyes before speaking. "I'll explain it later."

Brack got to his feet, heat creeping up his neck. "This is ridiculous. You're acting like a teenager. I'm not going to sit here and watch you ruin your life, not to mention risk Aether in the process, because you've got a lady boner for this guy."

Flames danced in the whites of Heller's eyes, but he remained silent at Zephyr's side.

"That was out of line, and you know it," she said sharply. "I may not have a Protector tattoo on my shoulder, but I've got my own mark of power."

Turning her left hand to face Brack, Zephyr traced a

finger over the raised impression embedded in her palm and glared at him. Marked since birth, she displayed the undeniable symbol, a bold triangle pointing up toward her fingers, bisected by a line with a dot on the end of the left side. Shoving it in his face was her less-than-subtle reminder of the power she wielded as the Guardian of the House of Air.

"This—" She spread the fingers of her marked palm wide. "—means, I kick ass, and—"

Heller seized Zephyr's wrist, examining her mark. "They…b-branded you?"

"No, it's not what you think. When I was a baby—"

Sparks flew from the tips of Heller's fingers. "Who did this to you?"

"Wait a second." Brack flipped. "You think we hurt her? Her own people? That's what this whole peacocking display is about." He belly laughed. "Pretty rich coming from someone who tried to kill us more than once." Taking slow, tentative steps, Brack approached the bed. Seated next to the towering mercenary, his oldest friend appeared vulnerable for the first time in his memory. "Come on, Zeph, let's go," he implored. "This guy is clueless. You're wasting your time here."

"No!" Heller shouted, getting to his feet. Fire spread over his hands. "You stay away from her." The flames surged to his shoulders, dancing up and down the length of his arms.

Brack faced off with the flaming mercenary. "You're the one who'd better stay away from her. This innocent routine you're trying to pull off is a giant crock of shit. I'm sure you remember everything just fine, don't you?"

Heller stared blankly. Brack gave a subtle shake of

his head. *I've got to give this guy credit. He looks like he has no idea what I'm talking about.*

Bear, Elder Protector of Aether, burst through the door, his baritone overtaking the small room, "What in the name of the God and Goddess is going on in here? I heard you shouting all the way down the hall."

Brack's breathing grew ragged as rage oozed from every one of his pores. "Barrington's henchman—" He stabbed a finger in the soldier's direction. "—has been wooing Zephyr. This guy is hiding something, Bear." He snarled at Heller. "You don't have amnesia. Admit it." Brack lunged for the soldier. "How did you get into Aether? What did Barrington—"

Two massive-sized hands came around his chest and lifted him off the ground as if he weighed nothing instead of topping two-thirty. "Enough. What has gotten into you?" Depositing Brack by the door, Bear continued, "Mr. Beck, I have two pieces of advice for you. One, cool off. Two, the next time you enter the Medical Center"—the corners of Bear's eyes crinkled—"I suggest you wear a shirt. This is, after all, a hygienic facility."

"Shirt?" Brack glanced down, and instant heat rose to his cheeks. He'd been in such a rush to confront Heller, he'd forgotten about putting his shirt back on.

Zephyr reached into her front pocket and produced a dollar bill. "Since you look like a male stripper, here's a tip." She tucked the money into the waistband of his jeans and scoffed. "Mind your own business. Now, go home, Brack."

Chapter Three

Heller

Zephyr's angry, shirtless friend stormed out of the room to a symphony of her unabashed laughter. Her head fell back, exposing the long column of her neck, and Heller licked his dry lips. He had never heard the glorious sound before, and a pang of jealousy hit him in the gut. Her laughter should have been his doing, but instead, he'd brought Zephyr nothing but trouble.

The big guy standing by the door bit back a smirk. "Nothing like strong passions to bring a bit of excitement to an otherwise quiet day." His deep timber vibrated through the entire room. This man was an enigma to the tenth power. Built like a pro football player, he was tall, broad shouldered, and wrapped in thickly corded muscles. In sharp contrast, his mannerisms belonged to someone who starred on a kid's TV show.

Zephyr made her way over to the mountain, stretched up on her tiptoes, and planted a kiss on his cheek. "Thanks, Bear. Brack was obviously dropped on his head as an infant."

Bear, the name fit. In fact, Heller couldn't have come up with a better name for the hulk of a man.

Bear canted his head without uttering a single word.

"Fine, he wasn't dropped," Zephyr acquiesced but then whispered under her breath, "His mother probably tossed him out the window."

The man didn't do a particularly good job of suppressing his amusement. "Simply because I have walked on this great Earth for more than four hundred and fifty years does not mean I suffer from hearing loss. Therefore, I must inquire, is that any way for the Guardian of the House of Air to speak?"

Impossible. Heller's mouth dropped open, but he quickly snapped it shut. Four hundred and fifty? *No, no way.* And why was he referring to Zephyr as the Guardian of Air?

Her lips curved into a saucy grin. "Apparently."

Bear's boisterous laugh shook his barrel-sized chest. "You are a cheeky little one." He reached out a beefy fist and gave Zephyr a playful cuff on the chin. "I have always admired that about you. Though, perhaps it would be wise if you demonstrated a modicum of self-restraint on occasion."

"Sorry," she said. "No disrespect intended. I'm just frustrated."

The man's chin dipped, offering the smallest of nods before focusing his attention on Heller. "I am not certain if you remember me, young man. We met briefly, but I am afraid you were not at all well at the time. I am Bear Crane, former lead Protector, and now, an Elder of Aether." Bear extended a hand, and Heller took hold, giving it a firm shake. "I would prefer to move on from Mr. Beck's outburst if you do not mind." The Elder didn't wait for Heller to reply. He merely continued without pause. "I have come on behalf of the Elders to ask you some questions."

Zephyr jumped up and spread her arms out, creating a wall between Heller and Bear. "I don't think that's a good idea right now. He's only been conscious for a few days."

Heller stared at the beautiful woman protecting him, only half hearing her words. Her strength shone through her incredible blue eyes. They were penetrating, and he was certain she could see straight into his soul and free it from its bindings. Had he ever reacted to a woman like this before? Zephyr was special, but his insane attraction to her belonged locked away somewhere deep inside. With his memory destroyed, he had no idea if there was someone out there waiting for him, and acting on pure chemistry with Zephyr would be careless.

Her husky voice hummed, and Heller tuned back into the conversation. "Maybe, you can give the poor man a bit more time to adjust before you interrogate him. And it would be nice if everyone around here remembered Heller killed Charles Barrington, which, by the way, makes him a good guy…a very good guy."

"Thank you for expressing your opinion so enthusiastically, Zephyr." Bear moved with surprising grace for such an enormous person. He stooped, picked up the chair Brack had overturned, and sat. The metal frame creaked in protest against his heavy weight. "You have no need to worry, Mr. Heller. We carry no ill will toward you. In fact, Aether owes you a debt of gratitude for saving us from Dr. Barrington's wrath. The Council of Elders would simply like to gather any information you may have. Please." Bear gestured to the empty chair across from his. "Do you mind?"

"No, sir, of course not." Heller moved toward the seat.

Zephyr took up a position between Bear and him, again blocking his view. "Yeah, well, I mind."

"There is no need for you to be troubled, my young Guardian. You are most welcome to stay and join the discussion if you wish." Although he couldn't see him, he could hear the smile in the old man's voice.

"Fine," she harrumphed, stepping aside to reveal an indeed smiling Bear.

The guard outside Heller's room knocked on the frame of the open door and addressed Bear. "Excuse me, sir, but someone asked me to give this to you," he said, handing the Elder a plastic bag.

"Yes, thank you kindly. You may resume your post," Bear stated, dismissing the guard.

Yup, this Bear guy was definitely in charge.

Examining Heller for a brief moment, Bear thrust the bag toward him. "I have taken the liberty of providing you with garments other than a hospital gown. Recently, I suffered the indignity of donning the infernal, ill-fitting, modesty-stealing—"

"Um, Bear, I think he gets it." Zephyr chuckled.

The plastic crinkled in Heller's hands. "Thank you, sir. I appreciate it."

"Zephyr and I will step into the hallway while you change. Please, let us know when you are ready," Bear instructed.

They closed the door behind them, and Heller dropped onto the bed with a sigh. How could he help these Elders when he couldn't even remember his own name? Reaching into the bag, he removed a neatly folded pair of dark blue scrubs, socks, and slides.

"Nice outfit," he mumbled, but anything was better than trying to keep his ass covered in the hospital gown he'd been wearing.

Yanking the top over his head, Heller struggled to

pull the fabric down and lower his arms. The material gathered around his pecs. He looked down and chuckled. Maybe it was a good thing the hospital room didn't have a mirror. He stuck his hand back into the bag and dug around only to come up empty. Commando was his only option. With a shrug, he tugged on the scrub bottoms. Cinching the drawstring, he peered down. The pants floated above his ankles, and he feared pairing the socks with his new look would only add to his humiliation. He slipped his bare feet into the black rubber sandals, and his toes jutted over the ends. Steeling himself, he opened the door and cleared his throat.

Zephyr was leaning against a wall and nearly toppled over when she caught sight of him. Maybe it was worse than he suspected.

She glared at Bear. "Was this really the best you could do? These clothes are so tight he can barely move." Her voice echoed through the quiet hallway.

Eyeing Heller from head to toe, the Elder stroked a hand over the light scruff covering his chin. "Alas, I had not considered size. Ah, well, nevertheless, your most important parts appear to be covered."

"You're kidding, right?" The fleeting sound of irritation crackled out of Zephyr, but she reeled it in by the time she turned to him. "I'll see to it we get you something more comfortable than just covered."

"Great, thanks. Um, can I possibly…um…get some underwear?" Heller asked, heat climbing up his neck and settling in his cheeks.

"My apologies once again, young man. It never occurred to me to provide undergarments, as I do not believe in restraining one's—"

"Bear!" Zephyr shouted. "I'm begging you to stop

before you say something which may melt my ears."

Heller suppressed a laugh. This woman's spirit and insane sex appeal posed a dangerous and irresistible combination for a soldier determined to keep his distance.

The Elder flicked a dismissive wrist in Zephyr's direction. "Very well then, let us proceed." He retook the chair he'd previously occupied and brought it over to a small table in the corner of the room.

Zephyr laced her fingers with Heller's and led him to sit across from Bear at the table.

"I have come to officially welcome you to Aether, Mr. Heller. I speak on behalf of the entire Council of Elders when I say we are very pleased to have you on our side. You are on our side, are you not?"

Heller cleared his throat. "Yes, sir."

"Good to hear. But I would appreciate it if you could tell me *specifically* what happened to you, Mr. Heller." The Elder stared him down like a top-notch litigator.

Heller rubbed his temples, fighting to find his memories. "I don't remember much. It was like walking in my sleep. Barrington's voice constantly droned in my head. I don't blame you for doubting me, especially considering how I ended up here. But in my heart, I feel like I'm a good man." He paused for a long minute before starting up again. "And if I wasn't, I want to be now. I don't know why, but I'm drawn to this place."

Zephyr squeezed his hand under the table, and the feel of her soft skin against his own deflated the tension in his muscles. Her touch fortified him with courage, and he continued, "I'm afraid the few memories I've managed to unbury are merely flashes. And…as far as my physical condition…well, I don't…I can't explain—

" He sagged into the chair, and his free hand hit the table with a thud. A flicker of blue sparked from his fingers, and it took everything inside him not to plunge his hands into the silver pitcher sitting on the table.

The sparks morphed from blue to purple until they burned a deep crimson. Visions of Zephyr's beautiful skin burning sent terror streaking through Heller. He wrenched his hand back, but she kept their fingers laced in an unrelenting grip. Was this girl super strong, or did Barrington's drugs screw him up more than he realized? Struggling against her firm hold, he tugged harder.

Her sexy voice rushed out in a husky whisper, "Stop fighting me. I'm perfectly fine." Her words hummed, low and deep. "It only feels warm…really warm."

The flush of her cheeks *warmed* him, and in all the right places, but at the worst possible time. He heaved a sigh of relief to be discreetly hidden from view. The Elder wouldn't think much of Heller if he knew he lusted after Zephyr.

****

Zephyr

Fire blazed bright orange, ebbing and flowing along Heller's muscular forearms, but Zephyr refused to relinquish her hold on his hand. The flames heated her flesh, but her skin did not scorch or blister. She didn't know what her immunity to Heller's power meant, if, in fact, it meant anything at all. What she did know was it felt right when they touched…very, very right.

Bear's sage eyes lingered on the fireworks show creeping toward Heller's shoulders. The soldier's anxious gaze raked over the Elder's lined face, and Bear studied the stranger with equal measure. Heller stiffened, and his Fire climbed higher. A hint of panic glistened in his blue eyes, and his hand twitched in her grip. Zeph worried he might drop to the ground at any moment and begin rolling around to smother the flames.

She understood better than anyone what it felt like to be overwhelmed by the powers you'd been gifted. The pressures of growing up a Guardian had been intense, and as a child, Zephyr's fascination with becoming a Protector only added to the stress. As much as she loved her role in The House of Air, she yearned to become the first Guardian-Protector in Aether's history. It never made sense to Zephyr why the Elders refused to even entertain the idea. Each time she'd presented her case, they'd shot her down. Talk about being stuck in the past. The Elders gave a whole new meaning to the phrase. Maybe if she helped uncover Heller's hidden memories, the Elders would finally be able to see her in a new light, the way she saw herself, as more than a typical Guardian.

She clamped down on Heller's hand, hoping to restore his confidence, but instead, a tug of war raged under the table. Apparently, he wasn't very reassured. His face reddened in the battle to free himself from her clutches, and Zephyr let out a quiet chuckle. This man had no idea the tenacity and power Guardians were endowed with, but if he didn't stop fighting her, he would find out soon enough.

In an extra demonstration of her strength, Zephyr compressed their fingers together. Heller's eyes widened, and a smirk she couldn't hold back broke free. "Chill."

His hand relaxed, and his Fire receded, disappearing with a whoosh. He let out a breath and tossed Zephyr a small nod-smile combo. She found the effortlessly sexy move way too appealing, especially under the Elder's current scrutiny. Bear possessed many gifts and a keen sense of observation. The connection between Zephyr and Heller emitted its own current of electricity the Elder wouldn't easily miss.

Bear's voice broke through their hushed conversation. "If you two are quite finished, perhaps we may proceed with the matter at hand."

Zephyr swallowed the nervous lump in her throat. "No disrespect, Bear, but I wish you'd keep in mind how shocking all of this must be to an ordinary human." She leaned down to Heller and mumbled a faint "Sorry" before persisting with the Elder. "Um, maybe you can take it easy on him?" Pausing, she conjured up her best pleading look. "He's been handling things pretty well and getting stronger every day. Kai believes his memories will return in time."

"I am afraid time is a luxury we have not been afforded. I apologize for my abruptness, Mr. Heller, but time is of the essence if we want to prevent Doctor Barrington's final threats from coming to fruition. Aether plays but a small role on this Earth. We are merely Guardians of the Elements, striving to maintain balance on the planet. May I ask, what is it you do remember?"

Sparks ignited from Heller's fingers, but this time, he quashed the power before the blue glow developed into full-fledged flames. "I'll give it a shot, but mostly all I get is a massive headache."

He rested his elbows on the table and brought his fingertips to his temples. His shoulders shook, and Zephyr couldn't miss how his grimace distorted his perfect lips. A clock on the back wall ticked out a loud, steady rhythm while they waited in silence for the pensive soldier.

Zephyr stuck her face in his line of vision; her brow wrinkled. "Are you okay?"

Beads of sweat dotted Heller's forehead. He offered her a small, weak smile. "I'm fine. I'm not going to let a bit of pain stop me from trying to remember."

"Please, enough of this." Locking eyes with Bear, the Guardian in Zephyr took over. "Can't you see he's in pain, and—"

Heller stroked the back of her hand. "No, I want to help. I'll be all right." His gaze shot back to the Elder. "I remember two men came to my room. They…they—" He winced. "—killed the kids stationed outside my door. Afterward, I remember feeling…anger, a whole lot of anger. So, I, um, killed the mercenaries and took their guns. The rest of the memories come in bits and pieces." Heller's chiseled jaw clenched. "But I'll never forget the, um, compulsion, yes, that's what it was, a compulsion, to find and stop Barrington. I'm sorry I can't explain in more detail." His chin fell. "I truly wish I could help you."

"How did you find us at the chapel?" Zephyr's voice dropped to a whisper.

"Followed the smoke and noise. When Barrington shot that woman—" Heller squinted, shaking his head. "—No. Cassy. Zeph told me her name is Cassy. Unarmed. She jumped in front of Brooke, her granddaughter, right—" He threw a glance toward Zephyr for confirmation. "—and when she hit the ground…I…I saw red. The last thing I remember is Zephyr talking to me." He gifted her with an intimate gaze she hoped the Elder didn't catch.

"Good man." Bear winked at Heller. "I regret I did

not dispatch Doctor Barrington when I had the opportunity. Though we should all remember the immortal words of Isaac Asimov, *Violence is the last refuge of the incompetent.*"

Where did he come up with these esoteric quotes? Did he have mountains of books lining his walls filled with famous sayings? Maybe if Zephyr made it to Bear's age, she'd be quoting weird crap too.

"Well, Mr. Heller, if there is nothing else you can tell us at the moment, I shall take my leave." Bear stood.

Zephyr scrambled to her feet. "Please, wait. I've been thinking…living in the Medical Center is no place to recover properly. I'm sure he'll be released soon. He can stay…um, he's welcome to stay in the East Tower with me. I…I…have plenty of room."

"I am afraid you are getting ahead of yourself, my young Guardian." Bear's lip quirked up, and Zephyr knew the Elder well enough to recognize his amusement. The oversized man clasped his hands. "Kai will determine the needs of our guest during his recovery, not you."

"Excuse me, sir, but you said…*guest.* Heller isn't a guest. He's an Aetherian now. You can't send him out into the human world. He doesn't even understand what's happening to him." Acid churned in Zephyr's belly, burning along with the thought of never seeing Heller again.

"Please, take a breath, Zephyr. No decisions have been made concerning Mr. Heller's status in Aether. The Council merely wishes to stay apprised of all new and pertinent information regarding Dr. Barrington." Bear paused in the doorway and turned back to the soldier. "Mr. Heller, as a *friend* of Aether, we expect you to report any breakthroughs you experience. Dr. Barrington's work must cease and desist immediately."

Dropping her hand, Heller rose and tipped the Elder a small salute. "Aye, sir."

"He's got it, Bear." Zephyr scowled, moving to Heller's side.

"Very well. Zephyr, it appears to be a lovely day for a walk. Perhaps you should get some fresh air with Mr. Heller."

As soon as the Elder was out the door, Zephyr rushed around the room and began opening drawers in the small dresser he'd been supplied with. "Is there anything else in here you can wear?"

"Hey, slow down. Where's the fire?" Heller asked, walking up beside her.

As soon as the words left his mouth, she stopped and stared up at him, dumbfounded.

He chuckled. "Thought that might get you."

"I had no idea you were funny," she said, nudging him with her shoulder.

"Yeah, well, that makes two of us."

Heller couldn't mask his pain with the sarcastic comment. Zephyr read it in his wistful eyes. She thought about what it would be like to have no memory of her life and simply couldn't wrap her head around the idea. Her heart broke for Heller and for everything he was going through.

"Well, if you weren't funny before, you sure are now." Zephyr glanced over at his too-small scrubs and smiled. She looped her arm through his and nodded toward the door. "Actually, you look perfect exactly as you are. What do you say we take that walk now? I'm looking forward to showing you around Aether."

"Sounds nice. Lead the way." He shot her a smile that she wanted to patent.

****

Heller

As they walked, he gazed out into the forest, which expanded beyond the village in every direction. Laden with lush canopies of green, the timbers filled the empty spaces between the mountains peeking out in the distance. The blue sky shone brightly, giving it the appearance of having been painted on a canvas rather than existing in nature. A variety of bird calls created a symphony of natural sounds, and a light breeze blew through the tall trees. Heller lifted his face to the late spring sun, enjoying its warmth. He drew in a slow, deep breath. When was the last time he breathed in fresh, clean air?

This world was a cascade of colors and sensations. And although he couldn't remember his name or where he came from, Heller knew without a solitary doubt this was the most wondrous place he'd ever been in his entire life. He felt a strong connection to this new magical world and especially to Zephyr. What was it about this place? And, more importantly, what was it about this woman?

As they walked away from the Medical Center, a smooth cobblestone pathway opened onto a town square. In the center, a giant mosaic compass directed visitors toward four stone towers at each of its points. They were timeworn, identical, four-story structures, and these mini castles appeared to guard the village's heart. Heller suspected Aether, Zephyr had called it, had been here for a long, long, long time.

"Would you like to sit?" she asked.

"Sure."

He followed the wiggle of her hips as she made her way over to an old stone bench in front of one of the towers. Zephyr sat but jumped up the second her butt touched the surface.

"Ow, that's hot. I wasn't thinking," she moaned, rubbing her spectacular backside, peeking out from beneath a pair of tight-fitting shorts.

Stepping back, he pulled his shirt over his head, and Zephyr's gaze fixed on his abs. The fitted hospital gear left impressions on his skin. The way she was staring, he must've looked like a freak. Back in the day, he had a six-pack, but maybe he'd gone soft.

Heller spread the scrub top out over the heated stone. "Here, sit on this."

Zephyr lowered herself onto the square of fabric with care, protecting her backside. She pulled her feet up onto the bench and hugged her knees to her chest. "Thanks. You're so sweet. I'm not used to this kind of chivalry."

"Seriously? I would think the men around here would fall at your feet."

She leaned back and laughed, her long dark hair falling in a curtain around her slim shoulders. "Yeah, right. I'm every man's dream girl."

His gaze lingered on her gorgeous legs. Zephyr was definitely somebody's dream girl. Too bad he couldn't be anybody's dream guy; he was a complete blank as a person.

"Are you just going to hover, or are you going to join me?" She inclined her head toward the vacant space beside her.

"I'm sorry. I didn't mean to gawk…you're…you're

just so beautiful."

A rosy glow spread over her cheeks and down her neck. "You're not so bad yourself."

Taking the empty seat, he offered her a weak smile. "Thanks but looks don't mean much when you're the poster boy for amnesia." He picked up her hand and turned it over. "You're special, and I'm a lost soul." He traced the rough mark embedded in her flesh. "This means you're the Guardian of The House of Air. You're strong. You can make wind and move things with your mind."

"Yes, that's right. And you can make Fire."

"How?" He raked his fingers through his hair. "Please, I don't understand. Why can't I remember? I know how to talk and how to walk, but I can't remember my own name. It's like…I've been erased." He clenched his fists at his sides.

"I know it's hard, but you have to be patient. Kai and Brooke said it was going to take time to recover all your memories, especially the ones Dr. Barrington repressed the most. You're strong. I know you can do this. Have faith. You're an Aetherian now."

Chapter Four

Skye

Skye's phone vibrated, and she tugged it from the side pocket of her cargo pants. After an exhausting shift patrolling the forest, she was in no mood to talk to anyone. She swiped her finger across the slick screen and braced for another order from Quill.

Zephyr *—Meet me in the Atrium. I left the door open for you.—*

"This can't be good," Skye groaned.

Dragging her feet like a petulant child, she headed down the path toward home. If her sister was summoning her for a talk at the top of the East Tower, no doubt something major was about to go down. Skye didn't need her twin bond to figure out the broody soldier was somehow involved.

When the Guardian of Air set her sights on something, there was no stopping her, and it was obvious saving the soldier had become her sister's current mission. Zeph could pretend the guy was a guest of Aether, but Skye knew the truth. He was an invader, an interloper, a stalker, and Zephyr was the one who needed saving whether she knew it or not. Soliciting Brack's help had turned out to be her dumbest idea yet. The jackass only managed to make things a thousand times worse, alienating Zeph and pushing her straight into the soldier's arms.

Skye fought the urge to run in the opposite direction because Protectors didn't run from conflict. They ran toward it. She steeled herself and pushed the door to the East Tower open. It creaked on its weathered hinges, and her powers kicked up a slight breeze.

She was being ridiculous. Skye and Zephyr were more than sisters. They were more than twins. They were connected. No way Heller would ever come between them. Running her fingers over the cool stone walls, she inched her way up the tightly wound spiral staircase.

She didn't recognize this apprehensive version of herself. Skye Anani did not get nervous or freak out. And she most certainly did not avoid her own sister. If she remained calm, rational, and explained things the way she saw them, then Zephyr would have to listen. Skye reached the top of the stairs and slipped through the door which had been propped open by a large rock.

"Hi. Thanks for coming." Zephyr's raspy voice floated on a current of Air. "I know your shift just ended, and I wanted to catch you before you got into doing something else."

"What's up?"

Her sister ignored her question and hopped up onto one of the wide window ledges. She gazed down at the Village below, and her tone went dreamy. "Remember the first time I snuck you up here?"

"How could I forget?" Skye wondered where this was going, but she couldn't help smiling at the memory.

"Indra nearly killed us both."

Zephyr's mentor, the previous Guardian of the House of Air, could be a bit rigid, and the twins took pride in pushing her buttons.

Skye smirked. "Yeah, with lectures about how only full-fledged Guardians were permitted to enter the Atrium with a guest. Blah, blah, blah."

They burst into a fit of giggles, like the ones they used to get in trouble for as little girls. It was the kind of laughter that brought tears and belly pain. Skye couldn't remember the last time she'd let loose, and it felt damn good. Tamping down any remaining apprehension, Skye moved toward the center of the Atrium.

"From the very first time I came up here, I was mesmerized by the power of the Vessel." Skye stopped in front of the pedestal. "I doubt I'll ever stop being a bit in awe…and not just of the Vessel." She met her sister's gaze. "Talk to me, Zeph. Why did you ask me to come up here?"

Tears filled Zephyr's voice. "I thought it would remind you that we're a team. You've always trusted me and my instincts." She jumped down and came up beside Skye. "As your sister…your twin…I'm begging you to believe in me, even if you can't believe in Heller." Zephyr let out a long, slow breath before adding, "Because the Elders have agreed to allow him to move into the tower with us, and I'm hoping you're not going to make things difficult."

Skye brushed her fingers across the ancient stone Vessel. Symbols representing the four Elements marked the basin with faded etchings. The vortex of Air housed within its confines danced and swirled, rising and falling in gusts. Skye sighed. Nothing would have made her happier than to embrace the soldier and become one big sit-com family, but she lived in the real world. Zephyr, on the other hand, had been sucked into life in a bubble ever since Heller appeared. This situation was a disaster in the making.

****

Brack

Music blared from the sound system, warring with the drone of the Tech Center's computers. Cadence worked on three devices at once, his fingers flying across the keys. Dressed in his typical uniform of a classic rock band Tee and jeans, Brack's best friend fit the mold of a college student in a dive bar rather than a computer genius.

"Yo!" he shouted and pointed to the speakers vibrating in the ceiling.

Cadence clicked something on his phone, and the volume lowered.

"Anything?" Brack asked, knowing Cadence understood what he was referring to without having to specify.

"I'm working on it. Barrington warned us he had another subject at one of his laboratories ready to go, so locating the lab is the Elders' main concern right now. The clock is ticking. If I recall correctly, Bear's exact words were—*find it yesterday*."

"He's one hundred percent right. The last thing we need is another Heller showing up. We'd better figure out something because we're screwed if they come for us again."

"I synced our computer system with the laptop Hawk lifted from Barrington's house." Cadence clicked a few keys, and a map appeared, revealing several highlighted areas. "I'm searching a broad quadrant in the northeast for possible locations."

"What's next?"

"It's a waiting game. I'm hoping to get a hit soon,

but I'll expand the search if nothing turns up." Cadence avoided Brack's gaze. "So, I've been meaning to tell you something. Don't freak out, but Zeph came to see me the other day. She begged me to try to find information on Heller, anything at all. I opened a couple of backdoors into the government's system, and I started digging through some military files."

Brack got to his feet. "You shouldn't be doing that. You need to concentrate on finding the lab."

"Take it easy." Cadence raised his hands in surrender. "I'm running multiple searches as we speak. If anything matches, I'll get a notification. Meanwhile, what's the big deal in helping Zephyr? Aren't you the least bit curious about this guy?"

Brack paced the large room. "Maybe, but I'm more concerned about Zeph getting hurt. And you need to keep your priorities straight."

"My priorities are fine. It's not like I can ride up and down the entire east coast checking every nook and cranny. There's nothing else for me to search right now. Besides, maybe finding out about Heller will help find the lab."

"I don't agree. You need to stick to the Elders' plan."

"You know, I'm more worried about you than I am about Zeph. You need to lighten up."

Brack sat in a vacant chair and crossed one knee over the other. "My instincts tell me this is a very bad idea."

Cadence shrugged. "Well, *my instincts* are telling me to help Zephyr. She is the Guardian of Air and one of our best friends."

"I think her judgment may be a bit skewed right

now. She's obsessed with Heller."

"You know," Cadence teased. "You sound like a jealous boyfriend."

"Jealous boyfriend? You know better than anyone it's not like that between Zeph and me. I love her, but we're friends, nothing more."

"I always suspected one day you two would wake up and realize you were in love." Cadence paused and shot him an assessing look. "Are you sure your feelings haven't changed?"

"Of course not."

"Then why haven't you gone out with anyone? I mean…when's the last time you even got laid?"

"Excuse me, how about you mind your own fucking business?"

"We've been best friends since we could crawl. That makes it my business. Admit it, you've taken yourself out of the game because you have your eye on someone. If it's not Zeph, then who is she? Spill."

"You don't know what you're talking about. There is no *she*." Brack tugged at the collar of his T-shirt.

"You've always been a bad liar. I'll figure it out. I'm smart like that." He gave him a knowing smirk.

"Knock yourself out, dude." Brack gestured toward the monitors in front of them. "In the meantime, how about telling me what you found out about Heller?"

"Not…one…damn…thing."

****

Skye

Skye poked her head into the computer lab. Brack and Cadence were huddled over a bunch of screens. Brack spun around in his wheelie chair and produced a wide grin, perfect white teeth on full display.

Unexpected warmth rushed through her body. Was she having a brain bleed? The guy was a total a-hole. Who cared if he looked like a sex god when he smiled? Skye buried her bizarre reaction to her lifelong frenemy and tipped her chin toward Cadence instead.

“Hey, how’s it going?” she managed.

“It’s going.” Cadence’s shaggy brown hair flopped down over his forehead, and he brushed it back.

“Good one, Dad,” Brack teased.

Skye let out an indelicate snort and covered it with a cough. The guys acted as if they didn’t notice her graceless flub. It had been years since she’d reached “one of the guys” status. Sometimes it came in handy. And sometimes, Skye wished they’d remember she was definitely *not* one of the guys.

“Can I talk to you outside for a sec, Brack?”

His dark eyes narrowed. “Um, sure, I guess.”

“Go ahead,” Cadence said. “I’ve got this.”

“K, text me if you find anything, and I’ll come right back.” Brack held the door for Skye and gestured for her to go ahead.

Brack and chivalry didn’t travel in the same circles. This was no time for his personality disorder to go into overdrive; she had a sister to save. Whether Zephyr wanted to be saved was an entirely separate issue. The point was Skye needed a plan of attack regarding Zephyr’s latest bombshell, and she wasn’t about to let Brack’s weird mood get in her way. The only reason she came to enlist his help was because she needed backup, pronto. First and foremost, how was she—correction—how were *they* going to get Heller out of the tower and, more importantly, extract him from her sister’s life?

Skye headed straight for the exit and didn’t stop.

The sound of Brack on her heels quickened her pace, and she didn't slow until they reached a familiar bench on the edge of the forest. Hidden by heavy brush, it had been carved from a large fallen timber, a common practice in the village to give new life to that which, in the typical human world, would be discarded.

Brack sat and stretched out his long, muscular legs. Keeping his keen gaze focused on her, he asked, "What's going on?"

Skye plopped down beside him, let out a heavy breath, and with it, the words spewed out in a rush. "He's moving into the tower. We have to do something. This is out of hand. I don't know what to do." She sprang to her feet. "He's going to take my sister away, and there's nothing I can do about it. He's corrupted her." Panic swelled in her gut, and her power took control. A huge gust of Air blew her braids back and sent leaves and debris flying everywhere.

Two strong hands reached through the swirling vortex Skye had created and grabbed her by the shoulders. "I'm sorry," Brack's rough voice scratched out.

Her expression went slack. "Sorry? What are *you* sorry for?"

"This," he said, and then his lips were on hers.

Bracken Beck was kissing her, truly kissing her, like no joke kissing. Skye couldn't think. She couldn't breathe. She couldn't move. She could only kiss him back. The most infuriating guy she had ever known was kissing her, and man, was it amazing. Skye melted into the sensation. Brack's lips were warm and soft, nothing like she expected. Not that she ever imagined kissing her sister's best friend because that would've been an insane notion. Yet, there was no doubt about it, Bracken Beck was kissing the lips right off her face.

Overcome, Skye jumped away from the heat of Brack's body. She balled up her fist and without thinking, drove it full force into his stomach. A loud *oof* escaped his lips, and he bent at the waist.

"Whad ya do that for?" He groaned and then straightened back up to his full height.

"You surprised me." She ran her fingers over her parted lips.

"And you thought slugging me was the right move?" He ran a hand over his sexy scruff.

"Well… no…but I don't like to be caught off guard," Skye admitted. "I prefer to be in charge."

"So I've noticed." Brack smiled broadly, revealing those dazzling white teeth of his.

"Why did you kiss me?" Her chest tightened.

"I don't really know. You were rambling and getting hysterical. Seemed like the only way to shut you up." He shrugged. "Felt like the right thing to do at the time. But I guess—"

Skye stepped into his space, bringing them chest to chest. "It wasn't a bad idea."

Brack's eyes went midnight dark the moment before she pressed her lips to his. There was no taking control with this man. It was a battle of the Protectors. His fingers deftly snapped the elastic bands holding each of her braids, never taking his lips off hers. Skye was lost, dizzy with heat, desire, and sensation. Brack's hands tunneled through the tightly woven strands of her hair, releasing it.

Fisting a handful of his T-shirt, she tugged him closer. Her tongue sought out his, and the duel began.

She had no idea how long they'd been wrapped up in each other when Brack leaned back on his heels, breathless.

"Holy crap," he managed.

"Understatement of the year," she huffed back.

"Who knew?" Brack brushed his thumb over her swollen lower lip.

Skye's entire body stiffened. "No one better know. The other Protectors would never treat me the same way if they found out." She glared.

"Of course, no one is going to find out. We'd never hear the end of it. But what I meant was, who knew it could be like this between us." Brack lowered himself onto the bench again, elbows on his knees.

"Don't get any bright ideas. This—" She gestured between them. "—whatever *this* is…is a one and done."

"Absolutely," he said, pressing his lips together in a slight grimace.

"Fine, so let's consider this little matter resolved and get back to what's important. Are you going to help me get Heller out of the tower or what?" Skye stood over him, hands on her hips. Brack looked up, his gaze zeroing in on her boobs. She waved a hand in front of his face. "Hello? Earth to Brack. Did you hear me?"

He smiled lasciviously. "Oh, you've definitely got my attention."

Men. Skye rolled her eyes. *I think I may have unleashed a monster.*

Chapter Five

The Soldier

He flicked a finger against his earpiece, and the busted piece of crap didn't so much as crackle. Tossing it in the dirt, he smashed it with his fist for good measure. Belly to the ground, he inched closer, and another missile sailed overhead.

Adjusting his combat helmet, he called to his men, "Take cover!"

He flattened his body against the hot, dry desert floor and braced for impact. A trio of back-to-back explosions ripped through the settlement behind the hill where he'd taken position. Heart thundering, he strained to listen for any signs of his team.

Out of options, he didn't care if he had to eliminate every target standing in his way. His guys needed extraction, pronto. The team's safety was priority number one and the responsibility of his command. Heat radiated straight through his tactical vest, and sweat soaked his uniform. He crawled toward the row of shacks. When the recognizable sound of a noisy muffler headed his way, he stopped in his tracks. A white minibus, its windows covered in black paint, bounded over the compacted rocks and dirt forming a makeshift road. Loud shouts in Pashto penetrated the turmoil.

A faint voice rose from the abandoned mud hut

they'd been using as a base. "Cap—"

There was no time to respond. The van's doors flew open. Several masked men jumped out and made a beeline for the hills. They didn't get more than a few meters when their primitive car bomb rocked the surrounding area. The blast threw him backward. He flew into a massive boulder, and then tumbled a few times before coming to land in a heap. Giant squalls of sand enveloped him and obscured his vision with thick caustic clouds. Ears ringing, head spinning, he stayed down until the worst of it cleared. He sat up, squinting through the haze.

"Can anyone hear me?" he hacked out. "TJ? Moose? Zeke? Respond!"

Securing a bandana across his mouth and nose, he made his way through the rubble. As he edged closer, several windowless, clay buildings came into view. The one on the northern slope, the one which had housed his team, had been reduced to a gaping crater. Acid churned his gut. They got out. Of course, they did. He removed his helmet and placed it in his lap. Sitting back on his heels, he tugged off the bandana and wiped his brow. His gaze fell, and he read the name, etched in thick black marker on the back of his helmet. Hellfire.

****

Heller

He woke to the sound of his own shouts. Sweat clung to his skin and soaked his T-shirt. Where was he? Chest heaving, he propped himself up. Moonlight shone through a single window, and he did a quick scan of his surroundings. *Bedroom. Four points of entry. Two doors. Two windows.*

Door "A" swung open, and a beautiful woman raced

to his side. *Zephyr.* It all came back in a rush. *East Tower. Safe. Barrington—dead.*

"What's going on?" The husky timbre of Zephyr's voice was sexy as hell, and it sounded even more so in the middle of the night. Dressed in an oversized T-shirt that skimmed the tops of her luscious thighs, she gingerly lowered herself onto the edge of the mattress beside him.

Running his fingers through his damp hair, he met her gaze. "I had another dream…a bad one."

"Do you remember anything this time?" she asked, all concern and no judgment.

Zephyr's sister barreled into the room, Glock in hand. "What's the situation?" she asked, her weapon sweeping the room.

"For Goddess' sake, Skye," Zephyr scoffed. "Put your gun away. There *is* no situation. Heller had a nightmare. Go back to bed."

Skye tucked the weapon into the waistband of her snug-fitting yoga pants. "Sorry. It's a Protector reaction."

Heller nodded. He may not have known who he was, but he understood instincts, and his screamed danger. This dream was the most revealing he'd had since withdrawing from Barrington's drugs. An actual piece of his past. The information had to mean something. Heller coughed, clearing his lungs of imaginary smoke. His ears still buzzed with the sounds of war. At least he didn't set the bedsheets on fire this time.

Zephyr scooted closer, exposing more of her gorgeous legs. Stroking a gentle hand down his stubbled cheek, she lingered. Heller rested his hand over hers, holding it in place, and nuzzled into the warmth of her touch. He inhaled a long, slow, deep breath. Zephyr's presence soothed his frayed nerves like a salve to a wound. Reluctantly, he released her. As amazing as it was to have her hands on him, he couldn't allow her to touch him so intimately. The temptation was far too great. All efforts at keeping his distance fell away when Zephyr's hands slid down to his neck, kneading the knots of tension. This girl was going to kill him.

Skye cleared her throat in an exaggerated fashion. "Zeph, can I talk to you in private for a moment?"

The Protector was not a subtle woman, and Heller fought the urge to chuckle. He was pretty sure Skye didn't have much of a sense of humor where he was concerned. If Zephyr didn't kill him with her sweet, alluring sex appeal, then surely Skye would shoot him in his sleep.

Zephyr's hands stilled on his shoulders. "Can't it wait? Heller needs—"

"I'm fine," he said. "Go talk."

Zephyr's brows drew together. "You sure?"

"Are you kidding?" Skye stood by the open door, tapping her foot. "We're going into the hallway, not to Timbuktu."

Heller smiled. Skye was growing on him, and he was pretty sure he was growing on her, too. Since he'd moved into the tower, she'd been treating him with a bit less disdain. Oh, he knew she still couldn't stand the sight of him, but occasionally, Heller caught her watching him with a combination of fascination and amusement.

"I promise I'm fine."

"All right, but I'm coming back to check on you," Zephyr insisted as she headed toward the door.

It didn't take more than a few minutes before their

elevated voices barged in from the hallway. Hearing Zephyr fight with her sister kicked Heller straight in the gut. This was all his fault. She kept putting herself between anyone who dared challenge his continued presence in Aether. Guardians, Heller was beginning to learn, were exceedingly strong, both physically and mentally. In Zephyr's case, stubbornness featured as a dominant trait, and he had to admit he found her equal parts infuriating and adorable. Perhaps the time had come for Heller to start protecting the beautiful Guardian instead of the other way around.

Zephyr burst back into the room. Her cheeks flamed with fury, and her eyes darted about. "Skye has got a brass set—"

"Please, I can't stand being the cause of this strife. You guys are twins. That's a special bond."

"Yeah, well, it's not all it's cracked up to be." She let out a heavy breath. "I don't want to talk about my sister. I want to hear about your dream."

Heller nodded and took a seat in one of the cushy armchairs. "You're right. I should talk about it before it fades from my memory."

Sliding into the companion seat, Zephyr gifted him an affectionate smile and another great view of her bare legs. "Take your time. Lean back and close your eyes. Let the memories come to you. Don't force it."

He closed his eyes and winced as the sounds of imaginary gunfire filled his head. His voice grew distant even to his own ears, "In my dream, I was a Marine with a special forces team. My guys were surrounded. Don't know where. It was hot…like can't catch your breath hot—" His words dried up.

"It's all right. You're doing great. Can you tell me

more?"

"The team…they…there was a bomb. I can't be sure, but I think they all went down." Heller's hands and voice both shook. "I'm not even sure if it really happened." Fact or fiction, the nightmare felt real, and nothing else mattered to him. He'd watched his friends die, and there wasn't a damn thing he could do to stop it, then or now.

"Dear Goddess." Zephyr gasped. "I'm sorry, Heller. I can't imagine reliving such an awful moment."

"There was something else I saw in my dream. I had a combat helmet, and it had a nickname penned on the back. *Hellfire*."

A wide grin spread across her pretty face. "This is huge," she cried, her eyes alight. "It feels like a real breakthrough. Do you think it's connected to the name Heller?"

"I can't be sure of anything. My mind is a jumbled mess."

"It will all make sense in time." Zephyr surprised him with a kiss on the cheek. "Why don't you go take a shower and clear your head? I'll make you a little midnight snack."

"Thanks, sounds good."

Zephyr walked out the door with a glance over her shoulder as if she didn't trust he was truly all right. Her sweetness and concern couldn't push away his feelings of frustration and anger. There had to be more to these troubling dreams. If only there was a way to dig into his brain, he could find the answers he craved.

****

Zephyr

Zephyr plucked a bright red strawberry from the

basket on her kitchen counter and dipped it into a bowl of melted dark chocolate. Preparing treats in the middle of the night was nothing new for her. Insomnia had plagued her since her teens, and cooking cleared her mind. Lining up the confections on a tray, she pondered the power of her favorite food. Using an aphrodisiac felt like a desperate move, but Zephyr's experience in the art of seduction amounted to a measly bit of harmless flirting. Her limited repertoire had been gleaned from movies, magazines, and romance novels and served no practical purpose in the real world. After Heller moved into the tower, she figured he'd make a move—but nope, nothing, nada, zip.

Maybe she was reading the signs all wrong? His eyes followed her when she crossed a room. Attraction or caution? His body tensed with a hardness when she was near. Arousal or revulsion? Zephyr nibbled her lower lip, her determination plummeting. This new and unfamiliar territory rattled her confidence, throwing the Guardian into a tailspin.

She shook her head at her own brashness. Trying to seduce a man with chocolate was a dumb idea. Zephyr wasn't sure what she'd been thinking. She fiddled with the loaded tray of berries and let out a heavy sigh. Perhaps she'd simply sneak in and leave the treat for him to find when he got out of the shower.

Heller's bedroom door stood ajar, and Zephyr put an ear to the crack listening for any signs of movement. The sounds of water rushing through the tower's old pipes echoed back instead, so she pushed her way inside. Heller's scent permeated the guest room, like cinnamon rolls baking in the oven. The delicious fragrance seeped into Zephyr's nose, setting off a barrage of inappropriate snapshots.

She attempted to block visions of him naked, covered in soapy water, behind the bathroom door, but the glorious pictures could not be quashed. His strong hands ran down slick bubble-covered skin, rippling with taut muscles. Her knees buckled, and she caught her balance on the bed frame. Shaking off the near disaster, she slipped the chocolate-covered berries onto a small table. *Now, for a slick exit.*

The water cut off, immobilizing her. *I should leave.* The glass shower door rattled. *I should really leave.* Drawers opened and closed inside the bathroom. *I should most definitely leave.* Zephyr didn't leave. A power she had never encountered before held her in place. Her Element took command, surging through her veins, and a steady breeze kicked up inside the room.

Heller emerged from the bathroom and stood framed by the doorway, wearing only a towel wrapped low around his trim waist. Clouds of steam surrounded him, and an ethereal glow illuminated his image from behind. It was as though the gates of Arcadia had opened and deposited a god right in front of Zephyr's eyes. The man's muscles had muscles. Every inch of exposed flesh glistened with a fine sheen of water, highlighting each ridge and ripple. His military haircut had grown out since his arrival in Aether, and his blond hair was slicked back, accentuating his chiseled jaw. Her mouth went desert dry, and she swept her tongue over her parched lips.

Heller's eyes went wide, and he appeared as paralyzed as she felt. Was this one of those moments she'd been misinterpreting? She couldn't tell if he was horrified by her intrusion or if he welcomed her scantily clad presence. Regardless, her feet remained rooted to the spot. Doubt niggled deeper inside her the longer he stood immobilized. She wrapped her arms over her chest, inadvertently exposing more of her breasts. Heller zeroed in on her cleavage, and in her head, Zephyr did a fist pump. She may not have been wise in the ways of men and relationships, but even she was smart enough to recognize an obvious ogle.

"Hi," her voice scratched out. She picked up the tray and thrust it toward him. "Chocolate-covered strawberry?"

Heller's gaze traveled from her body to the treats and back again. "Thank you," he said softly.

She plucked a berry from the tray and held it to his lips. "They're good. Try one."

He stiffened and took two steps back. "Um, maybe in a little while."

Her cheeks flamed, but she forced herself to ask the burning question tormenting her existence. "Am I doing something wrong?"

"I…I don't know what you mean."

"Really? You're going to play it like that and make me feel crazy?"

Heller relieved her of the tray and placed it on the table. "No. You're definitely not crazy." He picked up both of her hands in his, gave them a small squeeze, and then dropped them. "You're incredibly beautiful, Zephyr. And if you think for one minute I don't want to be with you, then you *really* are crazy. Things are just so—"

"Complicated," she finished for him.

"Kind of an understatement, huh?"

"You think?" She smirked, but her next words came out on a shaky breath. "It doesn't explain why every time

I get close, you move away from me like I'm the one who's on fire." Emotion clogged her throat. "It's better if you're honest with me. I'll…I'll understand."

"You're the most gorgeous woman I have ever seen."

"Says the man who can't remember his own name."

A smile spread across Heller's handsome face. "Touché." But then something in his intense blue gaze shifted. *Heat?* He stroked a gentle finger down her cheek. "I don't need my memories to see what's right in front of me. You're—"

"I'm what?" Her voice rasped out. The Guardian had never been a provocateur, but this man stirred up something hidden inside her. She pulled her shoulders back, and the tops of her breasts peeked out from beneath the V-neck of her sleep shirt.

"Now who's playing dumb? You know you're stunning. And it's not only how beautiful you are. Look what you've done for me…a complete stranger."

"So, what's the problem? You like me, and I like you."

"Believe me, I wish it were that simple—" He dragged his fingers through his damp hair. "—but…I don't know who, *or what*, I am. What if your sister is right? What if I'm dangerous? What if I have a family somewhere?" His gaze fell.

"First of all, there is no way you'd ever hurt me. Second of all, that's your past. Aether is your future. Even if you have someone out there—" She rested a hand on his muscular forearm. "—they most likely think you're dead. I know how harsh that sounds, and I'm really sorry, but this is the reality of your situation. The only way to keep our world, *your* new world, safe is for you to stay dead. You have no choice. You're one of us now, and you are duty-bound to protect Aether and the Earth."

"What about my duty to my previous life? The military unit I've been dreaming about. I have to find out who I was, or I'll never have any peace." He placed his hand over hers. "And neither will you."

The walls Heller had erected were as thick as the stone caves built into Aether's forest and as high as the mountains towering beyond its borders. She sandwiched his hand between her own, brought her lips mere inches from his mouth, and whispered, "I'm more of a live-in-the-moment kind of girl." Brazen, flirtatious, provocative, where was this side of Zephyr coming from?

She brushed her lips against his. This moment was the one she'd fantasized about since she first laid eyes on him, and holding back wasn't an option. Zephyr slid her tongue over his full bottom lip. The man tasted like heaven, cinnamon with a touch of sugar. He moaned softly and tugged her against him, deepening the kiss. Fire powered body heat seeped into her flesh, sending warmth racing to long-neglected parts of her anatomy. The world melted away in a haze of desire. She wanted more, much more. Her hand crept toward the knotted towel at his waist, her fingertips brushing the soft terry cloth.

"You said nothing was going on between you two." Her sister's pained voice broke through the moment of bliss.

They jumped apart.

Zephyr gasped for breath. "Skye—"

Skye put her hand up, casting a lethal glare Zephyr's

way. “I can’t believe you lied to me. My twin…my other half.” Her cheeks flushed bright red, and she charged out of the room, slamming the door behind her.

Chapter Six

Brack

"The guy was wearing a towel and nothing else. And don't get me started on the kiss. His tongue was down her throat…like all the way down. It was revolting." Skye's whole body shuddered.

Brack rolled his eyes. "Why do I get the impression you're exaggerating?"

"Because you're a jerk who never believes a word I say. My honor as a Protector." Skye covered her heart. "I'm not blowing this out of proportion. I wish I were."

"It was only a kiss. We both know a kiss doesn't mean anything, right?" The lie tasted like acid on his tongue.

Whatever was happening with Skye unequivocally meant something, but downplaying his growing attraction had worked pretty well thus far, and Brack saw no reason to upset the status quo. *Act casual* had become his new motto, even if the sexual tension building between them thrummed with its own pulse.

A pale blush flooded her cheeks. "Yeah…of course, but there are kisses, and then there are *kisses.* Zeph and the soldier were definitely in the latter of the two camps."

Brack camouflaged a chuckle behind a cough, and Skye's eyes went stormy. Instinct told him to duck from the fist about to fly in his direction, but he stayed upright and conceded instead. “Sorry, I know it’s not funny.”

“Damn straight.” She crossed her arms over her chest, and the swells of her sexy, pert breasts spilled over the top of her tank.

Being near the girl was like being near a volcano, and she had absolutely no idea. His urges regarding Skye vacillated between extremes. He either fought the compulsion to throw her through a wall or to fuck her against one. This unfamiliar rock and roll between them was wearing him down. He glided forward, placed a gentle hand on her wrist, and unfolded her arms. Skye’s eyelids shuttered down for the briefest of seconds, and he watched goosebumps prickle across her flesh.

Brack repressed a smile and asked, “I couldn't help wondering which category you thought our kiss fell into?”

She shuffled backward a couple of steps, and he shadowed her movements. Her lips parted, and she swept her tongue across the deep red bows.

He took her by the hips and dropped his voice several octaves. “So was ours a kiss or a *kiss*?”

Her breathing quickened, and she froze in place. “Um—”

“Don’t bother answering because I already know it was the hot kind. The steamy, we can out kiss those two amateurs any day of the week, kind. No need to deny it.” He may not have been of The House of Fire, but even he knew messing with fire was a dangerous prospect…and messing with Skye was definitely messing with fire.

“I, uh, I—”

Rendering the sharpshooter speechless felt like a victory, but he pressed on without mercy. “Since you seem to be at a loss for words, why don't we test the theory?" Brack didn't wait for Skye to answer. He gave her a gentle tug, bringing her snuggly against him. When she leaned into his touch, he let loose.

He couldn't get enough of her taste, clover honey with a hint of spice. Brack forced himself to slow down before he got carried away. What was it about this girl that made him go from rational to bat-shit crazy in two seconds flat? Taking one of her braids in each of his hands, he smoothed his fingers over the silky, woven strands before giving them an erotic tug. Skye let out a soft moan, and satisfaction ripped through Brack. His hands fell to her hips, and a perfect set of breasts flattened against his chest. When her pliant form melted into his hardening body, the sensation was enough to drive him over the edge.

The powerful shift taking place between them made him question everything he'd known about Skye. She was snarky and strong, but now he was beginning to see beneath the surface. Layered under all that bravado, she was tender and gentle.

Her pelvis bucked against him and knocked the words *tender* and *gentle* right out of his head. On sheer instinct, he deepened the kiss. The press of her heated body against his brought blood rushing straight to his dick. She felt so damned good. Her hands slid up his chest, and his mind went to mush.

Her fingers stilled, and he barely noticed until she stiffened. But before he could process what was happening, she shoved him away hard. He teetered on his feet but caught himself on a nearby tree limb. An icy breeze washed over him.

"What the hell?" Brack's question rushed out in a

rough, breathy whisper.

“Well, it’s your own fault for kissing me *again.*” Skye ran a finger over her swollen lips. “Why do you keep doing that?”

“I…well…you…we—”

“I’m waiting.” Her foot tapped an impatient rhythm on the ground, and a tiny cloud of dirt swirled around her legs.

“I—” His shoulders slumped in defeat. “—have absolutely no idea.”

What he said wasn’t entirely true; he had a pretty good idea why he kept kissing her. Brack never wanted to stop kissing Skye, ever. Since the first time their lips touched, his dreams had been consumed by the beautiful Protector, and they had nothing to do with their common duty to Aether. It was about veiled lust and secret passion. It was about need and desire. There was no reason to pretend there was more to it. They couldn’t possibly be developing a connection, could they? Uncertainty plagued him with one exception; he wanted her in the most painful way.

“I guess I believe you,” she said skeptically.

He kicked a small rock on the ground, not meeting her gaze. “Um, how come you kissed me back?”

“Same as you.” She shrugged. “I’m not really sure, but we’d better cut it out.”

“I’ve been giving the subject quite a lot of thought lately, and it’s not like anyone is going to find out. So I really don’t see why we can’t have some fun together.”

“Because you’re a guy, and all guys think with their dicks.” Skye slid another couple of paces backward and wrapped her arms around her middle. “It’s like there’s a short circuit in your brains or something.”

Stray hairs escaped from her normally perfect braids, and she looked disheveled in the sexiest way possible. Whisker burns marred her cheeks. Her lips, plump and red, gave the appearance of having been thoroughly kissed. Brack had done that to Skye, left his mark.

"Sex isn't the only thing we think about. It's definitely among the top three—along with eating, sleeping—" Brack eliminated any remaining space between their bodies, his voice going husky. "—and with you, I think there is a fourth—fighting."

His gaze met hers, and her blue eyes flamed with heat.

"I enjoy mixing it up…with you." Brack brought his lips to her neck and pressed soft kisses along the slim column. "I dare you to tell me you don't feel whatever this is between us."

Her fingers tunneled into his hair, and she whimpered, "What are you doing to me?"

"Trying to get you to stop thinking and go with this. Whatever *this* is—" He pulled back a fraction and gestured between their bodies. "—I don't think we should ignore our mutual attraction."

Skye's fingers slid from his hair, and she strode backward until her ass bumped a giant oak. "I one hundred percent disagree. We don't even like each other. Besides, we keep preaching to Zeph about staying away from Heller, a man filled with secrets, and you want me to lie to my sister, your best friend, and everyone else in our lives with this little game. Let me think about it." Tapping a finger to her temple, she feigned deep contemplation. "Yeah, well, no. I'm done with this. You may as well give up on anything ever happening between us again. So, can we please get back to the only thing that matters right now, Zephyr and Heller?" Her hands moved to her slender hips. "Are you going to help me or what?"

Brack nodded, unable to keep the amusement out of his voice. "Of course, I'm going to help you. But I'm on duty at PH in twenty. Let's head back, and you can tell me all about your plan."

He picked up Skye's hand, and there it was again, an electric current buzzing between them. Brushing the back of her knuckles with his thumb, he took pleasure in the feel of her soft skin. Skye shoved his hand away with a loud smack. Man, he'd like to give that sexy ass of hers a spanking she'd never forget for pushing him away. Good thing Protectors couldn't read minds the way Ashlyn could read Hawk's. Skye would shoot him in the balls if she had any inkling of all the pervy shit running through his brain.

They walked together in a comfortable silence, leaves and sticks crunching beneath their feet. Once they reached the Village Square, the sounds of forest echoed in the distance and were replaced by the loud clomping of their boots on the ancient cobblestone. It had taken the entire walk for his libido to settle, but he was in complete control now. As long as Skye didn't do anything overtly sexy, he'd be all right…most likely.

Her unsteady voice broke the silence, "I had a crazy idea."

"And this is new, how?" Being sarcastic worked wonders as a defense mechanism. It was way more acceptable than his true desire, which involved stripping her naked and taking her over the nearest downed tree.

She curled her lip into a mini sneer. "Cute. Seriously

though, what if we try some good old-fashioned reverse psychology?"

"You lost me."

"Do you know that old saying, *you get more flies with honey than vinegar*?"

"Yeah, so?"

"We've been going about this all wrong. We need to make friends with this guy to figure out what he's hiding."

"You have my attention."

"Well, I was thinking—"

"Not that again." He chuckled.

"Do we need to have another chat about your maturity level?"

"Nah, I'm good. Please proceed."

She rolled her eyes. "Anyway, as I was saying. If we can find the lab, then I bet we can force one of Barrington's scientists to change Heller back into an ordinary human."

"Interesting theory. Only…what if he really doesn't know anything? Or…what if he can't be changed back? Then what?" Brack dropped a hand to Skye's shoulder, halting her movement. He met the concerned look in her blue eyes and softened his tone. "You also need to deal with the real possibility that it won't matter to Zephyr if the guy is an Aetherian or not."

"If he's not an Aetherian anymore, Zephyr won't be into him, and we can send him packing. You'll see."

"I'm not sure you're very objective where Heller is concerned."

"Whatever." She flicked a dismissive wrist in his direction. "I'll go talk to Zeph and work our crap out. I think you and Cadence should take him to the pub for a beer or something. You know, olive branch and all that shit."

"I'll think about it. Let me know how it goes with Zeph."

Skye nodded. "I will."

A strong wind followed Skye as she stalked past, bumping him with her hip on the way. Brack's gaze zeroed in on her shimmy. The woman had a way of making determined look sexy as hell.

****

Skye

"What do you say?" Skye popped out her best booboo lip and batted her lashes. "Truce?"

"You're impossible. You know that, right?" Zephyr dropped onto the couch.

"It's part of my charm." Skye joined her, scooching in close. "Haven't you figured that out yet?"

"Nope. Twenty-five years, plus seven months in the womb together, and I still haven't deciphered the enigma known as Skye Anani."

"Fair enough." Skye laughed. "But you're not exactly a *breeze* yourself, Ms. Guardian of Air." She paused and then rested her head on her sister's shoulder. "Can we please talk about it?"

"I suppose we should," Zephyr whispered.

Skye sat up. "Where's Heller?"

"He's taking a walk. Sometimes it helps him clear his head. Why?"

"Because I know you don't like to leave him alone, and I had a great idea. How about we go for some target practice? We can chat at the range."

"Brilliant!" Zephyr jumped to her feet and raced toward the door. "I'll get my crossbow."

“Cool.” She smirked, delighted that she still knew the way to her sister’s heart.

The practice range their father built for them was less than a half mile from home. Since Barrington’s attack, Skye had taken to wearing a sidearm on each hip. She grabbed several extra clips and stuffed them into her pockets. The Protector in her wasn’t taking any chances with Zephyr’s safety.

Bursting back into the room, bow in hand, Zephyr swung the graceful weapon over her shoulder and scooped up a quiver of bolts propped against the wall. “Ready—” Her sister met her gaze and then froze wide-eyed. “Hey, wait a sec.” She grabbed hold of Skye’s chin and turned her head gently from side to side. “What happened to your face? You look like you have road rash.”

“I, uh, was sparring with Brack, and he, um, got my face.” Heat rushed to her cheeks. She figured Zephyr would’ve been too preoccupied to notice a little thing like a bit of whisker burn.

“Do I need to talk to him about taking it easy on you? It’s one thing to train hard, but he shouldn’t be leaving marks on you.”

Oh, Brack had left his mark all right, no question there. Skye suppressed a laugh, keeping her poker face intact. “Thanks, I appreciate the support, but I gave it to Bracken Beck equally as hard.” She wasn’t ready to share what was happening between her and Brack with Zephyr right now. Not that she understood what the hell was happening herself.

The two sisters strolled at a lazy pace beneath the forest’s lush canopy. As was their norm, their footsteps fell in sync, but their lack of easy conversation felt foreign. The recent distance between them gnawed at Skye, and her stomach twisted in knots. With each step she took, more questions wafted around her head. What if Zephyr chose Heller over her, or worse yet, what if she chose him over Aether?

When they reached the range, Skye held her sister back with one hand. Zephyr let out an indelicate grunt but stopped with little more than an eye roll for a reply. Skye moved forward and swept the area with a single weapon in her sights. There were a lot of frazzled nerves among the people, and the last thing Aether needed was a stray arrow or bullet to scare the crap out of someone. "All clear," she shouted to her sister, who had slipped away and was already setting up the targets.

Zephyr stood several feet back. Wrists bent, palms out, she waved her arms in a circular motion, adjusting the straw-filled forms. After all these years, the display of the Guardian's telekinetic Air power still dazzled, likely because Zeph rarely relied on it. The control she reigned over their Element never ceased to amaze Skye. All Guardians were born with an extrasensory gift, but to Skye, no one rivaled her twin.

They busied themselves checking their equipment. Zephyr fiddled with her crossbow and examined each of the bolts in her quiver with an investigative eye. Skye pulled several clips from the pockets of her TAC pants and placed them on the tall boulder they used for such purposes.

Her sister settled one hand under the foregrip of her crossbow, slid a bolt into the flight groove, and drew back until the mechanism clicked into place. Zephyr's head cocked at a slight angle, and she shifted her feet, adopting the stance Skye would recognize anywhere.

The Guardian's gaze narrowed in on the bullseye.

A Glock in each hand, Skye stood mesmerized. Her sister's unique brand of magic, symbiotically fused with pure skill, warranted one's undivided attention. Skye was known to be the best sharpshooter in Aether, but her powers could never match that of a Guardian, especially Zephyr.

A loud snap was followed by the signature sound of her sister's bolt whooshing through the air and striking the target. Barely pausing for a breath, Zeph reloaded and took aim once again. Her arrow spiraled toward the bullseye, but its intended target was suddenly eclipsed by a large figure. Heller stood blank faced, the bolt now embedded in the flesh of his muscular bicep.

Zephyr screamed and dropped her crossbow. She raced toward him, her cries echoing through the forest. "Dear Goddess! I didn't see you. I'm so sorry."

The way he casually glanced down at the arrow sticking out of his arm, it was if Heller had suddenly woken from a sound sleep. A chill ran down Skye's back. The old Heller, the robotic mercenary, was back.

"I saw him," he said flatly.

"What? You saw who?" Zephyr asked gently.

"Barrington."

"Uh, I'm afraid that's not possible. You killed him," Skye reminded.

The soldier's expression remained blank. "Not here. The desert."

"You're not making any sense," Zephyr replied. "How about you take a seat?" She took him by his good arm and guided him to a nearby tree stump.

His knees hit the edge, and he mechanically sat, but when he glanced up, his eyes lit with recognition.

"Zephyr," he said, getting back on his feet and stepping away in one swift motion. His voice barely rose above a whisper, "Charles Barrington killed my men…all of them…and he made me this." Fire burst from the tips of his fingers.

"I know." Zeph approached him, arms raised in surrender. "But it's going to be okay." She picked up one of his flaming hands.

"No!" He jerked out of Zeph's hold. "You'll get hurt. I have to leave."

Skye watched on, a silent observer, the weapons in her hands growing suddenly heavy. What the hell was this guy talking about?

Zephyr tore a strip of fabric off the bottom of her T-shirt and wrapped it gingerly around the bolt sticking out of Heller's arm. "You're not going anywhere except to the Medical Center. Kai needs to remove that arrow." She tied a knot at the end and lowered his wounded arm to his side. "You have to let me help you."

His gaze fell to the impaled bolt. He stared at it for a moment and then seemed to contemplate the trail of blood dripping down between his fingers. "Yes. Take it out. Then I'll go," he said, sounding like one of those computer-generated voices.

Agreed, you definitely need to go. Skye stuffed the ammo she'd lined up for target practice into her pockets and then scooped up Zephyr's crossbow and quiver, all without saying a single word.

Chapter Seven

Heller

The extent of Zephyr's support rattled Heller for numerous reasons. Her defense of him was unconditional, and he hadn't done a thing to deserve that kind of loyalty. There was also no way he could ever repay her kindness, and of course, there was the meaning behind her actions. He knew Zephyr was attracted to him, but was there more to it? Did she see a future with him? How could he have a future with anyone when all he owned in the world were his spotty, questionable memories?

Rolling his shoulder, he tested his injured arm. Aetherian regenerative powers were a marvel. It had only been a few days, and the wound was nearly healed. Poor Zephyr was still beating herself up even though the incident had been entirely his fault.

On the day he'd been shot, he was taking a walk when he heard voices rising in the distance. He followed the sound, but then the trees, the sky peeking through, and the ground beneath his feet all morphed before his eyes. Aether's forest, alive in its vivid shades of green, faded away and was replaced by an arid, dank, scorching desert.

Heller should have been concerned about losing touch with reality, but he was too worried about Zephyr getting hurt to focus on the implications of his mania. His desire for the beautiful Guardian hadn't lessened with his growing insanity. In fact, he was more drawn to her every day, but nothing good could come from his falling for someone he couldn't have. Zephyr was a Guardian, and Heller was a lost soul who didn't even know his real name. He cracked his knuckles one at a time, his body wrought with tension.

Skye's empty hammock blowing in the light breeze caught his eye. Kai had suggested meditation as a tool for Heller to get a handle on his visions. He couldn't think of a better place to give the doctor's theory a go. After all, hammocks were synonymous with relaxation, weren't they? The striped canvas swayed, inviting him closer. It looked nice…nice and relaxing.

Steadying it with one hand, he climbed atop, but the infernal contraption took off in a full pendulum swing. It seemed fitting the hammock belonged to Zephyr's sister. After all, Skye had been trying to dump him on his ass since they'd met. He gripped the sides, centered his weight, and the hammock settled into a smooth rhythm. Sinking into the sensation, he closed his eyes.

"Don't think, just breathe," he murmured. "One breath in." He paused. "One breath out."

Regardless of his efforts, the familiar pull of a vision tugged at him, and he fought against its traction. He opened his eyes, but the back of the tower and the woods around it were fading into a hazy image. Bright light sharpened the corners of his vision, and he focused on the picture emerging in Aether's stead.

Somehow, he was in both places at once, grounded in Aether but suspended in his memory of the desert. His corporal form rested in the hammock, but a phantom version of himself got to his feet…

****

Dark, jagged peaks stood ominously in the background of a landscape dominated by sand. A thick layer of gray smoke saturated the air, and the taste of ash filled the soldier's mouth. Not even a cold beer could wash away the flavor lingering on his tongue.

Ears ringing, vision wavering, he locked his knees. He had to find his men. Dirt and sand caked his sweat-dampened skin, but he stumbled over to where the hut the team had been using as its base should have been. In place of the dilapidated shed, a gaping hole, edged by scorch marks, consumed the space. There were no signs of life; there were no signs of anything but a black abyss.

"I've been waiting for you," an out-of-place, aristocratic voice called from behind him.

He spun on his heels, weapon at the ready. The voice was attached to a man dressed in an expensive suit and shiny black shoes. His salt and pepper hair was professionally styled. He telegraphed power and wealth even surrounded by the harsh desert. For a moment, the soldier thought the blast had messed with his head until the newcomer spoke again.

"And I do not like to be kept waiting," the stranger stated as if he had every right to do so. Cold merciless eyes transformed the man's otherwise handsome face.

The soldier raised his gun and fixed the sight on the nutjob dressed for a business meeting.

"Oh, I wouldn't do that if I were you." The man nodded, and two armed mercenaries dragged his first lieutenant out from behind an armored vehicle.

"Cap," TJ managed to croak out as he struggled against his subduers.

One of the guys sported a bloody lip, and he was proud his best friend had clearly gotten a few licks in. As kids, TJ had been a head taller and broader than any of the other boys. And after boot camp, he'd been transformed into a massive wall of muscle who could move on silent feet. He wasn't sure who the hell these men were, but they must have been damn good if they got TJ since he was nearly unstoppable.

"I'm so sorry. They caught us off guard." Blood trickled out of the corner of TJ's mouth. One eye was swollen shut, and angry, red abrasions marred his opposite cheek.

He clenched his fists to keep from exploding and addressed his best friend, ignoring the strange man and his armed guards. "Who is this asshole, and where the hell did he come from?"

"My name is Dr. Charles Barrington III, but you may call me Dr. Barrington."

"If you don't let him go and return the rest of my team"—the soldier cinched his grip on his sidearm—"I'm going to be calling a mortician...for you."

"I'm not sure you've grasped the way things are going to work henceforth, Captain." Barrington nodded again, and four more heavily armed guns for hire stepped out. "Now, drop the weapon, and everything will go much more smoothly for everyone involved."

"Fuck you." He spat on the guy's fancy shoes.

The man looked down, ignored the wad of saliva, and smiled, a creepy, pod-person kind of smile. "You are even more impressive in person, Captain. But I'm afraid we are failing to communicate." Barrington nodded once more, and one of the mercenaries jammed the butt of his gun into TJ's gut. His friend fell to his knees.

Doubled over on the ground, TJ tried to catch his breath, but the mercenary clocked him over the head, and he crumbled into an unconscious heap.

"Enough. Enough!" The soldier tossed his gun in the sand and kicked it toward Barrington.

"Once again, you seem unclear as to who is in charge. Please, allow me to reinforce my point." Barrington walked up to one of the men hovering over TJ and whispered to him.

The mercenary retrieved a pistol from his holster, and before the soldier had time to blink, the guy shot TJ point blank in the head. He lunged for Barrington, but two huge men seized him under the arms, preventing the doctor's imminent strangulation.

Every muscle in his body strained against the confines of his skin, and his pulse pounded in his ears. His oldest and closest friend was dead at the hands of a certifiable maniac. But vengeance would have to wait. He took a cleansing breath to keep himself in check and focused on his training. If there was any chance of saving the rest of his team, he needed to tread carefully. "Listen, Mr.—"

"Doctor," the man shot back with a pointed stare.

"Yes, of course. My apologies, Doctor. What is it exactly that you want from me and my men?"

"All in due time, my good Captain." The doctor tossed a glance over his shoulder and tapped an impatient spit-covered shoe on the ground. "Come on already, Thomas," he called toward a set of massive black SUVs lined up along the makeshift road. "This is ludicrous."

A young man emerged from behind one of the armored vehicles, his approach tentative. He didn't move like the other mercenaries, nor was he dressed like them. Wire-rimmed glasses rested on the bridge of his straight nose, and a baggy pair of khakis hung off his scrawny frame. He looked more like a college kid than a killer for hire. Junior's hands shook with a slight tremor, and his gaze oozed remorse.

"Get on with it," Barrington ordered, his tone brusque.

The kid gave a tight nod in reply and lifted a syringe clutched in his jittery grip. The soldier could've sworn he saw the guy mouth the word sorry *before he jammed the needle into his neck. The liquid burned, scorching his veins as it traveled through his system. His knees buckled, and he dropped to the ground. The helmet he'd been wearing rolled away, stopping at Barrington's feet.*

The doctor picked it up, turning it over in his hands. "Hellfire, like the missile," he said, with a smug air. "So, you enjoy a good nickname, do you? I think we can accommodate that tradition. Henceforth, you will be known as Mr. Heller, the original super soldier."

"What in the ever-living fuck are you talking about?" Anger rose in his gut.

"You have been selected to be the very first recipient of a formula I've created to build an army of elementally enhanced soldiers. It is unfortunate that your entire regiment had to perish for my plan to come to fruition. But that's the thing about special ops teams, no one will miss you because your own government won't acknowledge your existence."

"Why?" the soldier slurred. The drug they'd given him made his tongue feel too big for his mouth.

"Because...you, young man, are the perfect specimen. I've studied you. Extreme intelligence.

Unparalleled physical prowess. Trust me, Mr. Heller shall be one of a kind. A super soldier, programmed to accommodate the highest bidder."

"Psycho—" he managed to croak before his vision went dark.

****

Opening his eyes to the bright sunlight, the Earth spun in nauseating circles. The soldier hadn't felt anything this real since he began having dreams and visions of his past. Before this latest episode, he questioned their veracity, never quite sure if they were confabulations or actual memories. But after today, he knew in his gut these were true experiences from his life, the real deal. He was a soldier, a marine, and Charles Barrington had killed his entire team, including his best friend.

White-hot fury ignited from the center of his chest, and Fire crackled beneath the surface of his skin. He couldn't stop his Element's rage on behalf of his friends. Barrington had ordered their murders. Flames engulfed his entire body, and Skye's hammock went up in a flash of red and orange. The ropes suspending him disintegrated, and he dropped to the ground with a heavy thud. Jumping to his feet, he stomped the burning fabric, smothering the flames. He gathered the singed remnants, and bits of the charred material stained his hands black.

He let out a heavy breath. "Way to win friends. Set their stuff on fire." Turning, he headed back toward the tower, shedding pieces of the hammock in a winding trail with every step.

****

Zephyr

The sun dipped low in the sky, flooding the area

behind the tower with warm color. Zephyr flipped the burgers she was grilling and tossed a bunch of veggies onto the hot grates. The fragrant steam hit her nose, and her stomach rumbled in reply.

"Hey, Heller, grab the buns, will ya?" Skye called to the gorgeous man filling the doorframe.

Crossing his arm over his broad chest, he glared at her sister. "My name isn't Heller," he repeated for the tenth time.

"So, you've been saying all day, but what is it you'd like us to call you since you can't tell us your *real* name?"

"Knock it off," Zephyr said between gritted teeth.

Skye rolled her eyes and offered no apology.

"Ignore her." Zephyr smiled at him. "She's still a little pissed off about the hammock. Which I offered to pay for," she added the last bit in the sing-song voice Skye hated.

"I don't care about the stupid hammock. I just don't think we should put so much emphasis on another episode of *Heller-vision*."

"That's enough, Skye! You're being a total bitch. If the man doesn't want to be called by a name concocted by that psychopath, then I think *you* need to respect his wishes."

"Fine then. What would you like us to call you?" Skye's hands landed on her hips, and her gaze narrowed. "And don't even think about saying *sir*."

He laughed, a real, honest-to-goodness belly laugh, and Zephyr knew everything would be all right between her sister and the man she was falling for…eventually.

****

Heller, or Cap as they had decided to call him, had

been distant since his latest episode. He'd had the strangest look in his eyes, and Zephyr had no idea what to make of it. Her mind had been a restless jumble from the moment they'd said good night. She tossed and turned, her legs tangling in the covers. Sitting up, she huffed out a frustrated breath and removed the twisted bedding like an animal freeing itself from a snare. She slipped off the bed onto the cool slate floor. The tower was silent at the late hour, and she didn't bother getting dressed.

The sanctity of the Atrium called to her inner Guardian, and she climbed the tower's winding stone steps. An ever-present breeze swirled around the passageway. It blew up her nightshirt, which barely covered her butt, and a cascade of goosebumps prickled along her bare flesh. She was being childish; there was nothing to worry about. The Air would guide her, as it always had and always would.

With a touch of her Guardian mark, the chamber's ancient door clicked open. Zephyr approached the basin in the center of the Atrium. The Vessel sat on its pedestal, the vortex within its confines churning, rising, and falling in great gusts. She stroked the timeworn symbols etched in the stone as she had done a thousand times before.

Only this time, her left palm heated beneath the rough surface, but it was a purple spark that sent her jumping back. She flipped her hand over and examined her Guardian mark. It blazed bright orange, and tiny red flames danced along the edges. Like Cap's touch, it didn't burn, but warmth crept up her arm, spreading across her right shoulder blade, tingling with a more intense heat. Her fingers flew to the exact spot the

Protectors wore their tattoos.

The Air whispered all around her. *Save Aether. Your destiny still awaits.* Then the words drifted off on a current, escaping out the Atrium's enormous cutout windows. Stormy clouds began to gather inside the Vessel and formed an image that left the Guardian stunned. The emblem she longed to have permanently marked on her skin, the Protector's symbol, danced around in the cumulus clouds. She watched it until it dissipated, leaving her to wonder if she had imagined the whole thing.

As she contemplated the possibility of her impending madness, she gazed down on the world beneath the tower. A light flickered, catching her eye. The movement which followed was so subtle Zephyr almost missed it. She peered down and spotted someone skulking in the dim glow of the moonlight. It was Cap, crouched low, a sizable duffel at his feet. With his back pressed against the deck's railing, he was frozen in place. He stood there for a long time, and she wondered what was going through his mind. It really didn't matter; all that mattered was he was leaving.

A wave of shock ripped through Zephyr, but she quickly recovered and darted for the stairs. She knew he wanted to leave, to figure out his history, but it had never occurred to her that he would sneak off in the middle of the night. The thud of the heavy door slamming, and the sound of her own breathing, echoed around the stone walls. By the time she reached the bottom landing, something inside her had percolated, stirring and simmering until it nearly bubbled over.

Skye had packed a couple of bug-out bags for emergencies, and Zephyr grabbed one from the closet.

She slung it over her shoulder along with her crossbow and quiver. A hoodie hung from a hook by the back door, and she tied it around her waist while slipping her feet into a pair of flip-flops. She opened the door a fraction of an inch at a time. No way she wanted Skye involved in this. If it were up to her sister, the soldier would be out of their lives forever.

Zephyr didn't call out to him. He was gone, but she had no trouble following his trail through the woods. She emerged from between the trees, coming out by Aether's parking area and storage sheds. The secluded location of the village made travel in and out complicated; Cap needed a ride.

The clank of metal hitting concrete drew her attention to the garage painted dark blue, Quill's private space. Zephyr crept closer and peered in a side window. Cap's broad back faced her as he searched a pegboard filled with keys. Quill loved anything with an engine but especially motorcycles. His collection was impressive. The soldier stepped back, admiring a beautiful bike set on an elevated platform. He ran his hands over the restored leather seat.

She stepped inside, a strong breeze following close behind. "That's from the 1960s. All the cool movie stars rode bikes exactly like this one. It's a classic."

Cap spun around. "Zephyr? What are you doing here?"

"Funny, I was about to ask you the same thing?"

He had the good sense to look guilty. "I had another dream. Something—"

"So, you sneak off without even saying goodbye?" Tears stung her eyes, but she held them at bay.

"I'm so sorry," he said, his voice tender. "I thought

it would be easier this way."

"For me or for you?"

"For both of us." He reached out and stroked her cheek. "I didn't know how to say goodbye to you."

"Then don't. Take me with you." Zephyr stepped back. She brought her palms together and spun one hand over the other until a tiny twister formed in her open grip. "Don't forget, I'm a Guardian." She clapped her hands with a loud smack, and the swirling Air vanished without a trace.

"I could never forget what and who you are. That's why, if you got hurt, I'd never forgive myself. You're too important."

"Yeah, well—" She advanced until only inches separated their bodies. "—you're important to me."

"Zephyr," he said on a sigh. "Please, don't make this harder than it already is."

"Why not? You deserve it for running away. Besides, there's something else you're forgetting."

His brows furrowed. "What's that?"

She poked a finger into his massive bicep where her arrow had struck him. "I can shoot."

He laughed. "Yes, you certainly can."

"I'm just going to follow you if you try to leave me behind."

Cap let out an exasperated breath. "Fine." His gaze traveled up and down her bare legs. "But can you please put some clothes on? And real shoes?"

Warmth flooded her cheeks. "That was my plan, but I wanted to catch you before you did something crazy…like leave without me." She picked up her bag and tugged out a pair of jeans.

Cap fiddled with one of the bikes, but Zephyr caught

him checking out her reflection in one of the darkened windows. *Score.* She took care to add a little extra shimmy as she wiggled her way into the snug-fitting denim. After the show, she shoved on a pair of running shoes and stuffed her flip-flops into the bag.

"Ready," she said, slinging the load over one shoulder.

"Maybe we should take a car instead of a motorcycle. You'll be safer."

"Yeah, but it wouldn't be nearly as much fun." She grabbed a single key dangling off the pegboard and walked toward the motorcycle displayed on the platform. "Come on, let's get out of here before the sun comes up."

"I'd love to, but we can't steal this bike. What if something happens to it? This has got to be worth a boatload."

She rolled her eyes. "Fine, we'll take one of the community jeeps." Returning the key to the hook, she nodded toward the door of the oversized garage.

"I'm not sure we should be stealing from Aether. I've been second-guessing myself from the minute I walked in here. Everyone has been great to me. Maybe we can make it on foot?"

"First of all, we're not stealing. We're borrowing. There's a huge difference. And second of all, yes, we can."

"Who do all these bikes belong to anyway?" Cap gestured around the expansive garage.

"Quill."

"Are you kidding? He already hates me because I shot him. I tried to explain that I was under the influence of Barrington's drugs at the time, but he wouldn't listen. He just ripped off his shirt and showed me his scar for the tenth time."

"Yeah, well, Quill is Quill," she said, holding in a laugh. "He's one of a kind. Most of us don't take him too seriously, and you shouldn't either."

"Maybe, but I doubt stealing one of his classic motorcycles will win me any points with the guy. And I'm not sure taking one of the community cars is any better. I think we should walk."

"And I think you're nuts. It's miles and miles of forest before you even reach a remote road. Trust me, we need a vehicle."

"Quill is just so…angry. I don't want to piss him off more than I already have."

"The community cars belong to everyone. I'm borrowing it, not you." She took him by the arm and led him out the back door. She snatched keys from the gray metal cabinet set at the top of the large parking area. "Quill and Coal just did some work on this jeep. I bet it goes fast." She jangled the keys and waited a beat. "I'll let you drive."

Smiling, he plucked the keys from her hand and loaded their stuff into the back. They slipped into the plush leather seats, and Cap adjusted the mirrors. When he was satisfied, he pushed the button to start the engine, and they coasted out of the lot, gravel crunching under the tires. Zephyr had no clue where they were headed or why, but she didn't care. Cap needed her. This had to be the destiny her Element was talking about because she had never been so sure of anything, or anyone, in her entire life.

Chapter Eight

Skye

The coffee maker sat idle, no fragrant aroma, no warm steamy brew, no caffeine. “That’s weird,” Skye mumbled to the empty kitchen.

She lowered her favorite mug onto the table with a clank. Her sister was *always* the first one awake in the mornings. She *always* made the coffee, and she *always* teased Skye about it. Recently, Zephyr had taken to ordering specialty blends she’d read about online. Mongo’s was her newest discovery from Long Island, New York, and Skye was looking forward to checking it out. The roastery had amazing reviews, and they’d waited weeks for the coffee to arrive.

“Hey, what happened to the coffee that was going to change my life?” Skye called into the living room. She paused for a couple of beats and got nothing but crickets in reply. “Great. Guess Zeph and Captain Tension left early.”

She scanned the counter for one of her sister’s annoyingly cute notes. *No note.* Tugging her phone from her pocket, she glanced at the screen. *Eight twenty-five.* She swiped a finger across the slick surface. *No texts. No voicemails.* It wasn’t like Zephyr to leave without a word, but her sister took her cues from the soldier these days. Ever since he torched her hammock yesterday, he was acting even stranger than usual.

Skye had no time to figure out the inner workings of The Guardian and The Captain. Her shift began in less than an hour. Too bad she wouldn't be able to take advantage of the rare opportunity to have the tower to herself. Lately, everywhere she turned Zephyr and Cap were together; lounging, cooking, whispering. The solitude would've been a nice change of pace from the flirt fest.

There was no need to make her own coffee at home when the café was steps across the Village Square. She stuffed her feet into her boots, strapped on her holster, and walked straight out the door. Summer heat blasted her in the face. It radiated off the ancient stone pathway, and she hurried into the café. As soon as she stepped over the threshold and the cool air conditioning hit her overheated skin, she stopped in the doorway.

"Hey, Skye," a deep voice rumbled behind her. "You planning on going all the way in?"

Brack. Her nipples puckered, but it wasn't from the AC. She crossed her arms over her chest and turned to face him. "Yes," she said, deadpan.

"Not feeling very playful this morning?" he asked.

Oh, she was feeling playful all right. If he only knew how much she wanted to play with him. Skye had entertained every naughty fantasy in her repertoire where Brack was concerned. *Restraint mode, please.*

"My shift starts soon. And Zeph didn't make any coffee this morning, and I'm cranky without my caffeine."

Brack lifted one of her braids and rubbed the ends between his fingers. "You're chronically cranky." He winked. "It's one of your finest qualities."

“Thanks,” she said, adding a sneer for good measure.

“No prob. You can always count on me to keep it *realsie*.”

It was too early to deal with Brack’s missing link of a sense of humor. Good thing the man was hot as sin, or he might never get laid. Her stomach tightened. Why did the idea of Brack with another woman make her blood boil? It wasn’t like they were together or anything.

She was about to place her order when he stepped around her. Elbows on the counter, he leaned in to speak to the pretty young girl working up front. “Hi, Daisy. Can we please get two egg sandwiches, two coffees, one black, and one with milk and two sugars? Oh, and can you make that to go?”

“Sure, Brack.” Daisy smiled, her cheeks flushing bright pink.

Skye waited for her to go into the back before she poked Brack in the ribs. “You’d better watch it. That girl has a massive crush on you.”

“No, no, she doesn’t. She’s friends with my little cousin.” He shook his head. “Seriously, your mind.”

“Clueless much? Believe me, I know a crush when I see one, and that girl has it bad for you.”

“She’s seventeen, Skye.” He brushed a single finger down the length of her arm. “I like women, not girls.”

She shivered. “I, um—”

Daisy placed their order on the counter. “Here you go. Have a great day.”

“Thanks, you, too.” Brack grabbed the bag and turned back to Skye, who was standing with her mouth agape. “You coming?”

“Yeah. Uh, bye, Daisy.”

"Bye." Daisy tossed her blonde hair and gave a little wave.

Brack pulled out her coffee, flipped the top, and handed it to her. He knew how she liked her coffee, and here she was thinking the man was a clueless wonder. Okay, so he was familiar with her beverage preference, but that was a matter of repetition not some sign from the God and Goddess. Yet, she couldn't help asking herself, what else did Bracken Beck know about her?

She didn't meet his gaze. "Thanks." The word came out as a soft whisper.

He unwrapped her sandwich, tucked the paper around the edges, and held it out.

"Thanks," she murmured once again. Reaching for the sandwich, their fingers brushed ever so slightly. But Skye felt it everywhere all at once.

One of his brows cocked in its uniquely Brack way, and damn if the guy didn't look sexy as hell. He had a perpetual inch of scruff, and she knew from personal experience how amazing it felt when he ravaged her mouth. She also remembered his natural minty taste, the lure of the memory impossibly strong.

"Since when are you a woman of such few words?" he asked, interrupting her salacious thoughts.

"I, uh, told you, I'm tired."

"Yeah, sure, whatever you say." Brack took a massive bite of his sandwich, and half of it disappeared. "You gonna eat yours?" he asked around the mouthful.

She nodded and took a small nibble. They walked side by side toward PH, but she was on autopilot. Why was she being so weird? This was Brack. So, what if they shared strong feelings of lust for one another. It was their mutual love and devotion for her sister that truly connected them. This passion between them was fleeting because no matter how he denied his feelings, Skye knew Brack was secretly in love with Zephyr, and he always would be.

"You're kind of freaking me out with this silent treatment thing. Did I do something wrong?" His gaze fell to their feet which were moving in sync over the cobblestones. "Are you mad about our kiss the other day?"

"No, don't be ridiculous. Why would I be mad? It didn't mean anything, right?" She kept her tone clipped.

"Uh, yeah, of course not." A ruddy flush colored his cheeks.

Skye's curiosity sparked. *No, you're not going there. Subject change, please.* "Hey, did Zephyr happen to mention if she and Heller—"

"I thought we were calling him Cap now?"

"Oh, whatever, *Cap*. It's insane. Next week, the guy will have a new name. I wanted to come up with something more permanent, but Zeph wouldn't hear of it."

A broad smile broke out across his face. "I can't imagine why."

"Anyway." She rolled her eyes. "When I got up this morning, they were both gone and there was no coffee." She held up the takeout cup from the café and then took a sip.

He opened the door for her. "I'm sure they just wanted some alone time."

"Probably," she acquiesced.

"I'm on with Coal and Quill, so I'd better go." Brack gave her a playful nudge. "Don't worry, she's fine. I'll see you later."

As he walked down the hall, she wasn't thinking about her sister anymore. Instead, her mind went straight to his tight ass, clad in worn denim, and how much she wanted to grab the firm globes. *There's something wrong with me…very wrong.*

****

Brack

The warm spray of the shower seeped into Brack's aching muscles. He'd ended up working a double, and his body was in clear protest of his overexertion. Cadence had called at least a dozen times trying to get him to go to the pub tonight, but Brack was beat. All he wanted was a date with his pillow.

He stepped out of the shower, the bathroom thick with steam. Grabbing a towel, he dried off and then hung it back on the rack. His mother was away for the weekend, so there was no need to cover up. Instead, he padded to the kitchen for a drink of water. Bright moonlight flooded the room, and he didn't bother turning on any lights. He filled a glass and drank in greedy gulps.

Water trickled down his chest and when he turned to snag a kitchen towel, he caught a flash go by the sliding glass doors. Who the hell would be sneaking around out there? He'd left his sidearm on his dresser, and his fingers itched for it in his grip. Great, he was buck ass naked armed only with a kitchen towel. Since Barrington's men found their way around Aether's magical borders, the Protectors were all on high alert, including Brack.

He pulled a long knife from the block on the kitchen counter and edged his way to the glass sliders. No one in the village ever locked their doors, and it glided silently across the track. He inched out, and the tall fountain grass planted beside the deck rustled. Sliding his feet across the wooden planks, he worked his way toward the swaying foliage. Using his powers, he called to the fronds, and they wrapped themselves around the peeping tom's limbs. Knife out, Brack reached down and yanked the culprit up by the back of the neck.

"Hey, let me go," said a familiar voice.

"Skye?" His brain couldn't process what was happening. "What in the hell are you doing?" Brack lowered the knife and the blades of grass loosened.

"I, uh, just…just wanted to talk to you. Zephyr never came home."

"You scared the crap out of me." He let out a heavy sigh. "Come inside. I'll call her from my phone. She's probably just messing with you."

Skye's gaze dropped, and she jumped back like he was on fire. "Dear Goddess! Why are you naked?" she shrieked.

For a split second, he was puzzled but then he looked down. He was completely in the buff, not so much as a pair of underwear or socks. The dish towel was still in his hands, and he draped it over his dick, nearly slicing himself with the knife. There was shock in Skye's eyes, but there was something else lingering there along with it.

"Why are *you* snooping around?" He spread the towel wide, making sure his junk was covered. "You could've just called?"

"I did call, but it went straight to voicemail."

"Damn. I turned my phone off because Cadence wouldn't stop harassing me about going to the pub."

"Okay, but you didn't answer my question." Skye's heated gaze traveled the length of his body, stopping on the small scrap of terrycloth. “Why are you naked?”

“My mom is away for the weekend.” His cheeks blazed. “I wasn’t exactly expecting company at this hour. Can’t a man get a drink of water in his own house?”

“Of course, you can. I’m sorry.” She averted her eyes. “But since I am here, would you mind putting some clothes on? This is important. I think something’s happened to Zeph.”

“Uh, yea. I’ll be right back. Wait here.”

Backing away, he stumbled, and when he reached the door, he turned and covered his bare ass. Once safely inside, and away from prying eyes, he slid the knife back into the block on the counter and headed into his bedroom. Swiping a pair of basketball shorts off the floor, he slipped them on commando and hurried back outside.

Skye was pacing the length of the deck when he returned. He stood in the open doorway and waved her inside. Her blue gaze swept over his bare chest and stopped on his shorts.

With her eyes on him, Brack still felt naked. It had him rethinking the whole no underwear decision.

“So,” he said, dropping onto the couch. “What’s this all about?”

“I told you this morning in the café that Zephyr was gone when I got up.” Skye took a seat beside him, her exposed thigh pressing against his leg. “And she never came home today. I’m worried, Brack. What if Heller did something to her?”

“She didn’t come home at all.” Brack grew still. “Are you sure?”

Tears welled in Skye’s eyes but didn’t fall. “Her bed was unmade. No coffee this morning. And one of the bug-out bags I put together is gone."

Zephyr's meticulous nature was a constant source of amusement for her friends. She never left her bed unmade or dishes in the sink. Laundry was folded and promptly put away. Zeph often teased Skye about being a slob. He'd heard them bicker on the subject a million times.

"You've texted and called, and she hasn't responded?" he asked.

Skye nodded, and a single tear slid down her cheek. "Do you think he did something to her?"

With the tip of his finger, Brack wiped away the droplet of moisture and gave her a reassuring smile. "Of course not. You can tell by the way he looks at her that he'd never hurt her."

"You'd better be right, or I'm going to hunt him to the ends of the earth and make him pay."

"Take it easy, tiger. Why don't I see if she answers my call? Let me grab my phone from the bedroom."

He got up, and Skye followed. The idea of her in his bedroom did unexpected things to his body. His dick hardened, tenting his shorts. Surreptitiously, he reached down and adjusted his stance. *Stay focused.* Grabbing his phone, he found Zephyr's contact and hit send. The call went straight to voicemail, and his stomach lurched, diverting his sexual thoughts.

Skye plopped onto his bed. "See."

Brack tossed the phone and scooted next to her. "I get it." He wrapped an arm around her shoulders and tugged her close. "But there's nothing we can do in the middle of the night. We'll start searching at daylight."

She sniffled. "Fine."

"I'll grab a pair of shoes and walk you home."

Skye looked up with tear-filled eyes. “Could I, uh, maybe stay here? I don’t want to be alone.”

“I guess so,” he said, hoping to sound cool, but a hallelujah chorus broke out in his head.

Every fantasy he’d stored in his playbook came to the foreground of his mind: Skye in his house, Skye in his bed, Skye barely dressed. Did that make him a Class A prick? The moment he tried to convince himself this was a bad idea, she crossed one long, lean leg over the other.

“I can sleep on the couch.” Her voice was soft.

“Don’t be ridiculous. You’ll sleep in my bed, and I’ll sleep in the other room.” Brack pulled back the corner of the blanket. “Come on, scoot in. You must be exhausted.”

Skye kicked off her sneakers, and for the first time, he noticed what she was wearing, or rather, not wearing. A skimpy pair of sleep shorts exposed most of her legs, and a sheer tank top revealed the outline of her brown nipples. Her long, dark hair hung loose around her shoulders. Brack licked his lips. She had no idea how gorgeous she was.

“Will you stay with me until I fall asleep?”

“Sure.” He walked around the bed and stretched out next to her. It was going to be a long night. The woman who dominated his dreams was half naked in his bed. He resisted the urge to pull her close and prayed staying above the covers would act as a barrier.

Skye sat up. “Are you going to sit here and watch me sleep?” He nodded, and she rolled her eyes. “You can get under the covers with me. I won’t bite,” she said, a hint of challenge in her voice.

Brack’s body heated. She was tempting the beast

he'd been keeping leashed. The building sexual tension between them was near boiling over. He slipped beneath the cool sheets but hovered near the edge of the bed. Warmth radiated off her in waves, and he fisted his hands to keep from reaching for her.

Her ass thrust back against him, and he stiffened, everywhere. "Um, Skye," he managed.

"Yes," she said, her sweet voice gone raspy.

"What are you doing?"

"Getting comfortable." She rocked against his hardness, and his eyes rolled into the back of his head from the pleasure.

"You're playing with fire, sweetheart."

"Maybe I like fire." She turned to face him, leaned in, and nibbled on his earlobe. "And don't call me sweetheart." Her warm, soft lips kissed a path along his clavicle. "I'm tired of fighting whatever this is between us. Aren't you?"

"You're upset and worried about Zephyr. Are you sure this is what you really want? I mean…me, you *really* want me?" he asked.

"Yes, yes, I do." She gripped his shoulders. "This isn't about my sister, and I'm not asking you to get Joined or anything. It's just…well…I think we need to burn out whatever this is between us so we can get back to the way things used to be."

"And that's it? You sure?" He ran his fingers through the soft strands of her hair. "I wouldn't want you to regret being with me."

"I'm more than sure." Skye slipped her hand down the front of his shorts and wrapped her fingers around his hardness. "I can already tell I'm not going to regret a thing." She smiled a sexy, lascivious smile. "I want you,

Brack. Twenty-five years is more than enough foreplay."

He didn't bother reminding her there would be no going back if they had sex. One time was never going to be enough to burn this out. In fact, he wondered if a lifetime would be enough. But Brack didn't speak. Instead, he took Skye's mouth in a searing kiss. Her sweet and spicy taste was becoming an addiction.

She pulled back, and he feared she'd changed her mind. But Skye tucked her fingers beneath the hem of her top and yanked it over her head. It landed on the bedside lamp, and the room dimmed. Laughing, she threw it onto the floor and turned off the light with a click.

Moonlight shone through the window and cast a soft glow over her tanned skin. Skye's nipples hardened to fine points, and Brack grew hungry for his first taste of her. He leaned down and licked a circle around one bud and then the other. The moan which escaped his lips coincided with her gasp of pleasure.

"Mmm," he rumbled against her soft flesh. "I knew you'd taste amazing, but the real thing is way better than my fantasies."

She spoke in a breathy whisper, "You had a fantasy…about me?"

He laughed. "One? Try a thousand and one."

"Is it confession time? Because I may have had one, two tops, fantasies about you."

"Is that so?" Brack nuzzled her breasts. "Perhaps, you'd like to share one with me right now." Propping himself on an elbow, he gazed down at her. "Wait a sec. You're not going to hit me again, are you?"

Skye laughed, and the sound was like music, rich and melodic. Brack knew he would never tire of hearing it spill from her lips. He lowered his mouth to hers, and her chuckles morphed into sweet little moans. She threaded her fingers through his hair, a bit of bite in her grip. Now, it was his turn to moan.

Brack shifted her minuscule shorts to one side and brushed his thumb over her heat. Her hips came off the bed, and he took it as an invitation for more. Grabbing hold of her waistband, he tugged until the flimsy material slid down her long legs. He tossed them aside and placed slow, wet kisses from her ankle all the way to her core.

A sharp pull on his hair had him looking up to meet Skye's lustful gaze. "As much as I love what you're doing—" She took a long, slow breath. "—I need to see you, all of you."

Her tongue swept over her bottom lip, and he kicked his shorts off in one move. She laughed, a deep throaty sound.

"This is all of me," he said, momentarily self-conscious.

"Your hotness is not overrated." Skye's fingertips grazed his abs, and he tightened on reflex. "It's like you've been sculpted or something," she mused.

He placed one palm on each of her ass cheeks and eased her toward him. "And you are beautiful."

Skye reached between them and took his hard cock in hand. "Please, Brack, don't make me wait anymore. I want you."

"Are you sure you're ready for me, sweetheart?"

"I'm definitely ready." She panted. "And don't call me sweetheart."

Brack poised himself at her entrance, and Skye wrapped her legs around him, taking several inches of his length inside her tight heat. Her head fell back, and her lips parted. She looked like a goddess. He paused, giving her time to adjust to his size. Aetherian men were known for being well endowed, and Brack feared hurting her. No matter how tough Skye appeared to be, he knew she was more tender than she let on.

"Move, now." Her words were barely audible.

It was quintessential Skye. Brack smiled and did as the Protector instructed, plunging his cock deep.

"Ooh," she murmured.

He drove into her, and she bucked her hips, meeting his every thrust. She was even more amazing than he'd dreamed. He leaned down and took her mouth. The taste of warm honey coated his tongue. Skye's fingernails raked his back, encouraging him to move faster. Brack reached between their entwined bodies and rubbed a finger over her sensitive bud. She cried out, coming apart around him and setting off his own climax.

Skye whispered his name over and over, holding him tight. He had never heard anything more beautiful.

"That was amazing, sweetheart." Brack stroked her hair and held her close.

"I agree." She clung to him, his cock still fully seated inside her. "But don't call me sweetheart."

Chapter Nine

Zephyr

Zephyr guided Cap through the dense forest, directing him on a meandering path to avoid the Protector's overnight patrols. He brought the jeep to a full stop in front of a magnificent arbor that stood fifteen feet tall. The greenery was covered with hundreds of flowers bordering the framework, and fireflies clung to the foliage, twinkling like tiny lights.

It had been a long while since Zephyr had driven through Aether's main gateway, and she'd almost forgotten how free she felt whenever she approached the threshold. The Elders did not rule the outside world. Beyond the borders of her home, no one told Zephyr who or what she was. Her life and her dreams belonged only to her.

"This is incredible." Cap's wide-eyed gaze fixed on the archway. "I don't remember being here." He shook his head, frustration written all over his handsome face. "It's a complete blank."

"Maybe, you came in another way. We still don't know what Barrington did to breach our magical shields, and we may never know. What's the difference at this point?" she asked.

"It's important to me. I can't allow history to repeat itself. The sanctity of Aether has to be protected."

“I agree, but it’s not only up to you. We’re a community, a family. We work together.” She shot him a sly wink. “Besides, I have skills that might come in pretty handy. We’ll figure it out. I’m quite resourceful.”

“I have no doubt as to your resourcefulness.” His lips pulled back into a sexy grin, which looked hot on the typically serious soldier.

“Good, because doubting me would be a big mistake.” She gave him a playful nudge with her elbow. “Do you plan on parking here, or are we leaving Aether before someone finds us?”

Cap tipped his hand in a small salute. “Aye, ma’am, let’s roll.” He threw the car into gear and passed beneath the arbor.

“Drive between the trees on your right.” She pointed through her open window. “It’s the most direct route out of the woods.”

“Will do.”

Darkness overwhelmed the forest, the glow of the moon barely visible through the thick canopy. Cap drove with the skill of an off-road racer, and Zephyr gripped the edges of her seat to keep from shifting from side to side. Miles upon miles of trees grew in clusters until, finally, they broke through the thicket onto a dirt road.

Cap pulled over, shifted the jeep into park, and turned in his seat to face her. “Are you absolutely sure you want to come with me? It’s not too late to go back.”

She rolled her eyes. “Get over it. We’re in this together.”

“It might be dangerous.”

Zephyr reached into the backseat, grabbed her crossbow, and held it aloft before securing it again. “I’m dangerous.”

"Stubborn woman," he grumbled.

She batted her lashes in a mock gesture. "Who, me?"

He didn't say anything, but she couldn't miss the smirk he was attempting to hide behind a scowl.

"Seriously, everything is going to be fine," Zephyr reassured, her hand falling naturally to cover his own. A zing ran from her palm straight between her legs, and she pulled back, tamping down the moan she craved to set free. Instead, she folded her hands in her lap. "Why don't you start by telling me where we're headed?"

"I'm not one hundred percent sure." His wide shoulders sagged. "Florida, Pensacola, maybe?"

"Ooo-kay. That sounds kind of vague. Do you have a bit more to go on?"

"I was hoping something might look familiar once I get closer. In my dream, I saw a bar, or maybe it was a restaurant. I only caught part of the name on the sign."

"What did you see?"

"The sign said, *The,* and then only the letters P-O-R were visible." He ran his hands through his hair. "The rest of the sign was blocked by a huge truck. It had an orange that was sailing a boat painted on the side. Florida feels…right. I can't explain it."

"You don't have to. You're an Aetherian now. Sometimes we just know stuff. Your powers come from Ashlyn, and she's a Guardian with very special gifts. Trust your instincts."

"Well, my instincts are telling me I've lost what's left of my mind. What are yours telling you?" he asked.

She tossed a glance over her shoulder toward home. "That you'd better start driving if you don't want to be dragged back to Aether."

"Right." His gaze followed hers toward the

darkened forest and lingered for a moment before he hit the gas.

All the windows were down, and Zephyr stretched her arms out to catch the breeze. The Air moved all around her, and she took control with a wave of her hands, swirling the currents in spirals. Her hair blew back, and she got lost in the power of her Element. The Vessel of Air said her destiny awaited. She'd seen the Protector's symbol. What now? Could she be the first Guardian-Protector in the history of Aether, or was she destined for trouble? Her mind wandered with the endless possibilities.

"Ahem." Cap cleared his throat. "You still with me?"

"Sorry." Her cheeks heated. "I was thinking about the future. And how, when all of this is over, the Elders are either going to blow their corks or finally let me train to be a Protector."

"Why won't they let you be a Protector? Your sister is one, right?"

"Yeah, uh, it's a Guardian thing. The Elders don't think I can handle both."

"That can't be true," he said on a chuckle. "There has to be another reason. Haven't they seen you shoot?"

"Yes." She laughed, but the sound was strained. "They've seen me shoot. It's just that…well…it's never been done before. The Elders don't know what to make of me. When you're several hundred years old, it's hard to handle any kind of significant change. The concept of a Guardian who is also a Protector appears to be beyond their scope of acceptance."

"Then I guess we'll have to expand their line of thinking." He reached across the console and tucked a loose strand of her hair behind her ear. The gesture was simple, gentle, but it made her entire body tremble with need. "I have faith in you." His deep voice washed over her. "If you want something, I know you'll make it happen."

As his words sank in, she nearly melted. This man got her like no one else ever had, not even Skye or Brack. Her sister and her best friend supported her, but she wasn't sure they fully understood the depths of her passion. Zephyr was born with a mark which made her unique and special even when she didn't want to be. Being a Guardian came with many privileges, but it also came with duties and obligations.

"Thanks for saying that, and *I* know we're going to figure out who you are and where you came from."

Zephyr wasn't sure what they were going to discover on their quest for answers. Her heart ached at the thought of losing him in the end, but as an Aetherian, she'd been taught to face challenges head on. Cap needed peace of mind, and Zephyr wouldn't let him down no matter what it may cost either of them.

****

Cap

Zephyr's head lolled to one side, and tiny puffs of air escaped her slightly parted lips. The long strands of her hair fell in dark, shiny waves, draping over one shoulder. Man, she was beautiful. Even in her exhausted, rumpled state, she took his breath away. It was time Cap got Zephyr to bed, even if it wasn't in the way he longed for.

Bright neon-yellow letters flashed from a huge sign which was likely visible from space. Cap pulled into the half-filled lot and parked by the entrance. The place was simply called, *The Motor Inn.* He stared at the wad of bills Zephyr had shoved into the cupholder earlier. Apparently, the Aetherians were pretty good at squirreling away money and other valuables. Borrowing money was a line he didn't care to cross, but what choice did he have? He owned nothing, not the clothes on his back—not even his own memories.

Zephyr looked too peaceful to disturb, so Cap plucked a few bills from the stash and silently closed the door. After scanning the wide lot for any signs of danger, he headed into the motel office. Anxious to get back to Zephyr, he hurried the gray-haired clerk along. Cap grabbed his newly acquired keycard and shoved it into his pocket. When he got back to the jeep, he was relieved to find Zeph passed out in the exact same position he'd left her in. Sliding in behind the steering wheel, he drove around the building, getting as close to their room as possible. He backed it into a space, leaving a wide berth on both sides.

Cap reached out and brushed Zephyr's hair away from her face, revealing high cheekbones and deep red lips that called out to be kissed. He couldn't resist running his fingers through the soft strands of her hair. He leaned in and whispered her name. A light wind, carrying her intoxicating fragrance, stirred, but she didn't budge. He pressed a soft kiss to her temple and lingered longer than was appropriate.

"Zephyr, come on, honey, wake up so you can go to bed."

"That makes no sense," she mumbled without opening her eyes.

He chuckled. "Well, appease me and pretend that it does."

Hazy blue eyes blinked up at him. “Where are we?”

“A motel. I thought maybe we could get something to eat besides junk food, shower, and catch a little shuteye. What do you say?”

She tipped her head from side to side, cracking her neck. “I say, it sounds like heaven.”

“Good because I borrowed some of your money and got us a room.” His hands tightened on the steering wheel. “I promise, I’ll pay you back.”

“Not that again.” She clicked her tongue against the roof of her mouth. “Chill. You have to trust me when I say money is not an issue. I’m happy to take care of it.”

“I’d like to take care of *you* for a change.” He kept his tone smooth, but his mind went straight to sex. Taking special care of every one of Zephyr’s needs was his number one fantasy. He quickly squelched the thought and took the keycard out of his pocket. “This will have to do for now. Our room is across the way. I’ll get the bags.”

He turned to open the door when something hard jabbed him in the back. Damn, he’d almost forgotten. Dropping a hand on Zephyr’s arm, he stopped her from getting out of the car.

Her brows knitted in confusion. “What’s up?”

“Um, there’s something I need to tell you, and I don’t think you’re going to like it.” A grenade sized lump formed in his throat, and he produced a Glock secured in the waistband of his jeans. He’d tucked it away last night as a precaution. “I kind of borrowed this from your sister’s collection.”

Zephyr’s eyes went wide. “Wow, you really have a death wish, don’t you?” She shook her head, and a laugh bubbled up. “Skye gives all of her weapons names. It’s a secret, of course, but I know everything there is to know about my sister."

"You're joking?"

"Nope, afraid not. I'm not sure which one you *kidnapped*. Gertrude? Giselle?" She patted his hand. "Anyway, good luck with that. I'm sure she'll be totally cool with it."

He shoved the gun back into his waistband and pulled his T-shirt down to conceal it. "She's going to kick my ass, isn't she?"

Zephyr squeaked out a simple "yup" between snickers. "But I get why you did it. Brack always says *you never know what might be lurking in the shadows*. I'll get my crossbow, and this way we'll both be covered."

He tried not to let it bother him how often Zephyr quoted Brack. She insisted the two were childhood friends who were more like siblings than anything else, and he had no reason to doubt her. Besides, Cap was a man with no memory, no history, no identity, and didn't have any right to his jealousy. But in any case, he sure as hell wished Brack was a little less quotable.

Zephyr came up alongside him, her crossbow and quiver hanging over one shoulder. She reached for her bag. "I can carry my own stuff, thanks."

"Of course you can, but I've already got it. Come on, follow me."

He led her to the room marked seventeen, tapped the keycard to the pad, and the lock clicked open. Zephyr stepped around him, and Cap wrapped an arm around her waist, holding her in place. "Wait, I want to check the room first."

Brows furrowed, she scoped the area. "Check for

what?"

"Threats," he said, guiding her to stand against the wall. "Give me a second. I'll be right back."

He withdrew the Glock. Skye's weapon was in excellent condition. Somehow, he remembered handling one like it before, but the details remained fuzzy. Cap released the magazine, rechecking it for the third time, and stepped over the threshold. Now that Zephyr was with him, he couldn't afford to let anything go wrong. Her safety was too important to Aether and even more important to him. He did a quick sweep of the room, closet, and bathroom before replacing the gun at his back. Grabbing their bags, he ushered her inside.

The room smelled of pine-scented disinfectant. At least it was clean if not a bit threadbare. Cap set their bags down atop the chipped, faux wood dresser. Zephyr placed her crossbow on one of the two double beds decked out in a gaudy floral pattern and plopped down on its mate.

"I'm dying for a shower," she said, inclining her head toward the bathroom. "Do you mind?"

"Of course not. Ladies first."

"Thanks." She grabbed her backpack and slipped into the bathroom.

The water cut off, and a few minutes later, Zephyr walked out surrounded by a cloud of steam. She had on a similar T-shirt to the one she'd been wearing, but this one was a pale blue, and the outline of her dark nipples peeked through the sheer fabric. The hem stopped mid-thigh, showing off her bare legs, and Cap's gaze followed the line. Running his tongue over his bottom lip, he contained a groan. This woman was bound to kill him with her understated sex appeal.

"Your turn," she said, toweling off her long hair.

The simple task shouldn't have been a turn-on, but everything Zephyr did turned him on. "Thanks," was the only word he could manage.

He took hold of his duffle and entered the compact bathroom. Her intoxicating scent wafted among the lingering fog, and he held his breath to keep from bursting into the other room and throwing her on the bed. Instead, he tossed his bag in the corner and stuffed the Glock inside. Peeling off his clothes, he dropped them in a pile and made quick work of showering.

When he was finished, he slipped on his underwear, a pair of sweats, and a soft gray T-shirt. Normally, he slept only in his boxer briefs but out of deference to Zephyr, he added an extra layer between her and his overzealous dick.

A picture of the beautiful Guardian sprawled out on the bed waiting for him popped into his head, and Fire crackled under his skin. It was going to be a long night if he didn't get a grip. Inhaling deeply, he took a few cleansing breaths and forced the image away, but the moment he stepped over the threshold, it was clear his efforts had been an exercise in futility.

Zephyr had pulled back the covers, and her bare legs were stretched out across the crisp white sheets. The flimsy T-shirt she wore bunched up around the top of her thighs, and its deep V-neck revealed just enough cleavage to make him salivate. He swallowed hard and busied himself with his bag. Staying away from Zephyr was becoming more difficult by the minute. He longed to pull her close. He longed to taste her on his tongue. He longed to slip inside her heat.

"Cap?"

The sound of his name snapped him out of his lustful haze. "Huh?"

"Is something wrong? I've been calling your name, but you've just been staring into space."

"Sorry, a lot on my mind. You hungry? I saw a couple of take-out menus in the drawer. How about some pizza?"

"Only if it's pepperoni."

"Is there any other kind?"

Zephyr smiled. "None worth eating."

He nodded, fished out the menus, and twenty minutes later, they were munching on slices of cheesy goodness topped with a layer of spicy pepperoni. Zephyr sat cross-legged, her T-shirt tucked tight over her knees, while he sat with his feet firmly planted on the floor. They shared the top of the box like a giant plate and used tissues from the bathroom in place of napkins.

Watching Zephyr was fascinating to Cap. She tore the crust off her pizza, ate it first, and then finished off the rest of the slice.

"What?" she asked, chewing around a bite.

"Nothing." He smirked. "I like the fact that you have your own unique way of doing things."

"Is that a nice way of calling me weird?"

"There are a lot of words that come to mind when I think of you, but weird is definitely not one of them." His gaze moved over her body and stopped on her face.

A flush rose to her cheeks. "What kind of words?" she asked, her voice tentative and soft.

He was tempting the devil, but how long could he resist the pull of attraction he felt toward Zephyr? "Kind, smart, caring—"

She got to her feet, moved the pizza box to the other

bed, and came to stand in front of him. "Really? Is that the best you've got?"

"Zephyr," he warned. "There is still so much we don't know about me. Nothing has changed. I don't want you to get hurt."

"You won't hurt me because I understand the risk I'm taking, and I want to be with you anyway. Don't you want me?" Uncertainty laced her tone.

Running his hands down both of her arms, he gazed into her blue eyes. "More than anything. But…I need to protect you, even if it's from me."

"I'm sick of being protected. I'm *over* protected." Zephyr stepped between his legs, leaned in, and brought her lips to his in a wanton kiss.

They were soft and full, and his body reacted in an instant, his cock turning to stone. Fire sparked from the tips of his fingers, and he pulled back. "Please, Zephyr, my Fire, I can't control it."

"Good. Don't."

She kissed him again, her tongue licking at the seam of his lips until he opened for her. Cap moaned and gave in to the sensations bombarding him. He drank her in, savoring her sweet taste. Zephyr attempted to straddle his lap, and he held her at bay, taking her by the wrists. If she touched him, he feared he'd explode on contact. He didn't know much about his past, but surely, he had more finesse than this. Her next attempt was more brazen, and his hands flew to her ass in response. His palms met smooth, warm skin.

"You…you're…not wearing any underwear?" He said it like it was a question even though he had one of her gorgeous butt cheeks in each of his hands.

"Whadya' know." A lascivious smile spread across

her face.

Nuzzling Zephyr's neck, he spoke in a hushed whisper, "This is a very bad idea."

"You're saying no, but your eyes are saying yes." She reached between them, and he blocked her hand.

As much as he wanted her in every conceivable way, Cap needed to keep himself in check. Her well-kissed lips parted, and she ran her tongue over the deep red bows. He lifted Zephyr under the arms and gently flipped her onto the bed. Her breath whooshed out in surprise.

"Hey, why did you do that? I want to touch you." She pouted.

"I told you. I want to take care of *you*, and I meant it." He lifted the hem of her nightshirt and pulled it over her head. She was gloriously naked, all her luscious curves on full display. "You are incredibly beautiful." Reaching down, he brushed her hair back over her shoulders, exposing her full, pert breasts. Her dark brown nipples peaked, and he leaned down, taking one in his mouth. "Mmm," he murmured against her skin.

"I…I…dear Goddess." She arched her back.

"You like that?"

"Y…yes," she moaned.

A wide grin spread across his face right before he took the other nipple into his mouth. She was writhing by the time he looked up. "How about that? Do you like that?" he said as he continued to torment her.

"You know I do, now stop teasing me, or you're going to regret it."

"I'm not teasing you. I'm building the anticipation." He licked his lips, and her body quivered. Running a hand along the inside of her thigh, he stroked a finger through her moist heat and then brought it to his lips. "I knew you'd be sweet." He sucked it into his mouth, savoring her taste.

"Cap, please, I need you," she begged.

"Not tonight, honey. Tonight is about you."

He kissed his way down her body, tasting every inch of her skin. When he reached her core, he slipped two fingers inside her tight channel. He stroked them in and out, slow at first and then picking up speed. Her hips rose and fell with his motions, and he flicked his tongue against her sensitive bud. Zephyr's hand tunneled into his hair, bringing him closer as she thrust up hard against his mouth. She exploded in a wave, pulsating around his fingers, and he whispered words of admiration. "You're amazing. So beautiful. So sexy."

When she caught her breath, she propped herself up on an elbow and gazed at him. "Your turn." She reached for the waistband of his sweats.

He took hold of her wrist, halting her progress. "Next time." Placing a gentle kiss on her lips, he tugged her to him. "Let's get some sleep."

She wiggled in his grip. "But—"

"No buts." He wrapped his arm around her waist and brought her back to his chest, being sure to keep his erection far from her. "Sleep now, argue later."

Zephyr yawned. "You don't know what you're missing."

"Believe me, I do." He sighed into her hair.

Cap promised himself he wouldn't hurt Zephyr, and he was doing his best to keep that promise even if it killed him.

Chapter Ten

Skye

The morning's first rays of sunlight spilled through the shade-free window, filling the room with warm color. A long, muscular leg, covered in a light dusting of dark hair, curled around Skye's hip, and a matching arm spooned her close. Body heat seeped into her skin. Holy crap, she'd slept with Brack last night, and if the massive erection pressed into her back was any indication, she'd be doing it again very soon.

Brack nuzzled her neck and inhaled audibly. "Mmm, you smell like my mom's garden." He took another deep breath, and warm air fanned her hair. "It's lavender, that's it. You smell like lavender." His tone grew seductive. "Yummy, good enough to eat."

Tingles traveled straight to her core along with his suggestive inflection. Skye turned around in his arms, and a light breeze kicked up in the room. She didn't speak for fear she would say something to ruin the moment. Instead, she looped her arms around his neck and kissed him.

When they emerged into the real world from their lust-fueled frenzy, Skye's euphoric buzz lingered. It was no surprise how hot things had been between them. Their recent days had been spent with nothing but sexual tension. The two had turned flirting into its own form of foreplay.

With his nude body on full display, Brack sauntered around the bedroom whistling a tune Skye didn't recognize. She watched him from her perch beneath the covers as if she had done it a thousand times. His light-brown, sun-kissed skin rippled over his muscled abs. When he turned to her and winked, his espresso-colored eyes sparkling, her mouth went desert dry. She swallowed what felt like a wad of cotton. His face, his voice, his touch had hijacked her every thought. All right, the man was good looking, but she needed to stop fixating on him.

"Come on, it's past six. You were the one yelling at me a few minutes ago," he said, yanking her from her moment of obsessive panic. "Do you want to take a shower?"

Tugging the sheet up to her chin, she hid her flushed cheeks. "It's not going to lead to another round of sex, is it?" she asked.

Brack laughed. "We'll take turns." He raised his hands in surrender. "I promise I'll keep my distance."

Skye let the covers fall to her waist and got out of bed. "Great, I'll go first." She brushed her breasts against his chest on her way to the bathroom and was sure to add a little extra wiggle to her walk.

She could feel Brack's eyes on her bare skin as his footsteps fell in behind her. Skye strode into the shower and adjusted the temperature until the water was barely hot. There was enough heat radiating off her body simply by being in such a confined space with the man. She tried not to think about how amazing last night had been and focused on the mundane motions of washing up and getting ready.

Brack avoided eye contact before he escaped to the kitchen; he must've been fighting the same urges she had. A moment of weakness had hit her when he'd climbed into the shower still filled with clouds of steam. The image of him wet and soapy had elicited new levels of self-control in Skye. She squeezed her thighs together and shook the idea loose from her brain. This was getting ridiculous. It was like being a teenager all over again.

She inhaled a steadying breath and then walked into the kitchen. "Ready when you are."

"Great, let's head back to the tower and see if we can find anything," he said, handing her a travel mug.

Skye knew it would be filled with coffee prepared exactly the way she liked it, and her stomach did a flip. What was going on here? This little domestic scene felt way too natural. She brought the cup to her lips and took a small sip. *Yup, milk and two sugars just the way I like it.*

"What's wrong? Too much milk? Not enough sugar?"

"Um, no, it's perfect. Thanks." She headed for the door. "We'd better go."

They walked to the East Tower in silence. Every once in a while, Brack's knuckles grazed against her hand, and an uncontrollable zing shot through her body. He was whistling that stupid tune again, and she wavered between wanting to smack him and wanting to hum along. Brack twined their fingers together, catching her off guard.

Skye ripped her hand away. "What do you think you're doing?"

"Relax, no one is around this early on a weekend."

The guy couldn't leave well enough alone. He had

to use the one word sure enough to set any rational woman off on a tirade. She stopped and crossed her arms over her chest.

"You should know by now it's a very bad idea to tell a woman to *relax.*" She narrowed her gaze. "Especially if that woman happens to be a Protector…you're lucky I'm not packing."

Brack's gaze fell to his feet. "Sorry, I, um…I like touching you."

In truth, she liked him touching her too, way more than she was willing to admit. "There are a lot of prying eyes around here."

"It won't happen again." He elbowed her playfully. "Still friends?"

Is that what they were, friends? "I'm not your friend," she shot back.

"I don't know about that. I'd say you were pretty friendly last night." Brack waggled his brows. "And this morning."

"Don't be an ass."

"That's part of my charm, sweetheart."

Skye's cheeks heated. "I'm pretty sure I've told you repeatedly not to call me sweetheart."

"You know you secretly like it." He winked.

"Yeah…no, I really don't." She sneered.

Brack shrugged and started walking again.

Skye reached the East Tower's main entry, but fear kept her frozen in place. Hand shaking, she reached for the latch and prayed that when she opened the door, Zephyr and the soldier would be snuggled up, hogging the couch. The idea of her sister out in the world with only a crossbow and a guy who didn't even know his own name terrified her. But one thing scared her more, what if Zeph didn't go willingly?

A large hand came down to rest on her shoulder, and Brack's voice whispered in her ear, "We're on this. Take a deep breath, and let's go look for clues."

She glanced over her shoulder and rolled her eyes. "Whatever you say, Mr. Holmes."

"Wait, does that make you Dr. Watson? Because that could work for some real role-playing possibilities," he retorted with a sexy smirk.

They laughed in unison. As much as it pained her, she couldn't resist his idiotic sense of humor or his charm. Brack made her laugh, even if he was more irritating than anyone she knew. And his comedic diversion worked to defuse her anxiety. She clicked the latch down and pushed. The door creaked open, and Brack gave Skye a tiny shove from behind.

"Stop being a baby, and go on in. I've got your six."

Skye gave him one of her patented dirty looks and stepped inside. It was quiet, too quiet. She cleared her throat and called out, "Zeph? Are you here?"

They waited a beat and got nothing but crickets. Brack hovered close, his warm breath on her neck. When she didn't move, he nudged her forward until she was standing in their empty living room. Beads of sweat glistened on her forehead. Skye didn't need to search the entire tower; she knew her sister and the soldier were gone. There was an empty space where her other half should have been, and she felt it in her heart.

"Zephyr? Cap? You guys around?" Brack called out.

She punched him in the arm. "I tried that already, genius."

"I thought maybe they didn't hear that sweet, sexy,

little voice of yours."

"Are you trying to lose a testicle?" Skye clenched a fist and brought it to his nose.

"Aw, come on, you like my testicles right where they are."

"Your testicles are of no consequence to me. Can we please just search and see if there is something here that can help us find my sister?"

"Anything for you, sweetheart." Brack smiled, and though she wanted to clock him, that smile still did naughty things to her insides. "I'll check Cap's room, and then I'll come find you," he said.

Brack sauntered off, leaving her standing alone in the empty room. Skye headed straight for Zephyr's suite. Just as she'd left it yesterday, her sister's bed was a tangle of sheets and blankets. The Guardian in Zephyr demanded order in all things, and her room was normally immaculate. Skye looked around, and everything, apart from the bed, was in perfect order. There were no signs of a struggle. A heavy sigh slipped out.

Their office was the next logical place to search. She and her sister each had a designated area in their shared workspace. Skye's side was sleek and clutterless, the perfect place to concentrate. She kept her prized gun collection in a locked display case and spent hours cleaning and caring for each weapon. The glass door stood ajar, and Skye zeroed in on the empty space where Gigi, her favorite Glock, belonged. She checked her ammo stores, and several boxes were also gone.

Brack's deep voice jolted her. "I was worried. I couldn't find you anywhere."

"Well, it seems you've found me now." She turned to face him, a rock in the pit of her stomach. "One of my

Glocks is missing and a decent amount of ammo."

"Shit, I didn't think he'd have the nerve to steal from you. Gotta give the guy credit. He's got a brass set."

"Don't joke around. What if he took the gun to force Zephyr to leave Aether or to hurt her? I'm scared, Brack."

He glided forward until he was standing inches from her and wrapped his arms around her, pulling her close. "Don't be scared. I don't think he took her."

"How can you be so sure?"

"Because I've seen the way Cap looks at Zephyr. No man who looks at a woman like that wants to do anything but take her to bed. Trust me, I understand the feeling."

Heat rose to her cheeks. "Well, um, good for you. I'm not as easily convinced. Let's go see if Cadence can help. He's the most logical person we know. I'm sure he'll figure something out."

"I sure hope you're right. Because if anyone else realizes Zephyr is gone, the shit is going to hit the fan."

****

Brack

Brack and Skye made their way through the woods, the air thick with early summer heat. He tried to fix his gaze anywhere but on Skye's ass as she moved ahead of him, yet the sway of her hips acted as a magnet. All he could think about was how he'd palmed that gorgeous ass only a few hours ago and how much he longed to sink into her tight heat until she moaned her pleasure over and over again.

Before they'd left the tower, Skye had changed her clothes and tied her hair back in her usual braids. The just fucked look she'd worn since last night had faded to a light glow, and he had to admit he was disappointed.

He'd much rather take her back to his bed and remind her how hot things were between them instead of searching for someone who didn't want to be found. Zephyr and the soldier probably needed some alone time, and Skye was in an uproar over nothing. One thing was for sure, Cadence was going to kick their butts for waking him this early on a rare day off. Hawk had him working overtime searching for the lab.

"He's probably still sleeping," Brack said.

"Not for long." Skye smiled.

A few years back, Cadence built a one-bedroom cabin in an isolated section on the north side of the forest. He'd supplied the beer and barbeque, and their friends supplied the labor. It was fun, and everyone loved hanging out there because they could make as much noise as they wanted. Cadence's place was nothing fancy, apart from his computers, but it was cozy and comfortable.

Skye waltzed up to the door and knocked hard using the butt of her gun. It was yet another Glock. Brack knew she had names for all her weapons, but he feigned unawareness. She didn't seem to realize how much time he'd inadvertently spent studying her and her habits. He hadn't realized it himself until he found himself fixing her coffee every day and ordering her preferred food choices.

Five minutes later, his best friend opened the door. Shaggy hair sticking out in a million directions, he rubbed his bloodshot eyes. "What the hell, you guys? It's the butt crack of dawn, and I've barely slept in a week." Cadence opened the door wider but didn't invite them in.

"Sorry, buddy, but it's kind of an emergency." Brack canted his head in Skye's direction.

She stepped around both men and straight into his cabin. “Zephyr is missing,” she said over her shoulder. They followed her inside, and Cade closed the door, the look of irritation on his face fading with Skye’s declaration.

Taking a seat on the couch, she placed her weapon on the coffee table and sank back into the cushions. “I think the soldier took her at gunpoint.”

“Wait a sec,” Brack said. “We have no proof of that.”

“Oh yeah, then tell me why the good Captain kidnapped Gigi?”

“Um, who’s Gigi?” Cadence asked.

Brack glanced over at Skye and then turned to his buddy, doing his best to keep a straight face. “It’s one of her Glocks.”

Cade’s eyes bugged out. “It…it has a name?”

The poor guy was either in awe of Skye or terrified of her; Brack wasn’t sure.

“Oh, shut up.” A deep rose color flooded her cheeks. “That’s not the point. The point is, he took my gun and a slew of ammo. If they were running off for a little sexcapade rendezvous, then why would he need a weapon?” Skye asked, fire in her eyes.

“To protect your sister?” Cadence said it like a question, even though it was a statement.

“If he didn’t take her away from her home in the middle of the night, then she wouldn’t need protection, now, would she?” Skye’s complexion went from rosy to purple.

“Chill.” Cadence’s hands came up in surrender. “I’m on your side, remember? I’m only trying to run through some scenarios.”

"Sorry." Elbows propped on her knees, Skye's head fell into her hands. "I'm really worried, you guys. We have to find her."

"We will." Brack sat next to her and wrapped an arm around her shoulders.

"Have you tried tracking her phone?" Cadence asked.

"Huh? How the hell would I do that?"

"Have I taught you people nothing over the years?" Cadence let out a heavy breath and stuck out his hand. "Give me your phone."

Skye handed it over. Cadence swiped left and right, tapping here and there. In less than five minutes, they were huddled together, watching the icon representing Zephyr's phone flash on the screen.

"It looks like Zephyr and the Captain are somewhere near the Georgia border," Cadence said.

Brack ran a hand over his scruff. "That's odd. I wonder what they'd be looking for down south."

"I figured they'd be searching for the lab. Barrington made us believe it was in the northeast." Skye's nose scrunched up in the cutest way. "This doesn't make any sense."

"Sure it does," Cade insisted. "Cap is trying to find out who he is. I don't think the guy gives two shits about how Barrington made him. His first order of business is to discover his true identity." His friend's logic made perfect sense to Brack, but Skye was much tougher to crack.

"Dear Goddess, he's not a superhero." Skye got to her feet. "He's a kidnapper."

"Cap did *not* kidnap Zephyr," Brack insisted.

"Yeah...well, he took Gigi." She dropped back

down onto the couch with a harrumph.

"Sweetheart, I'm not sure your Glock going missing counts as a kidnapping," Brack said.

She shot him a death glare and spoke through gritted teeth. "I have asked you repeatedly not to call me sweetheart."

Cadence stood stock still for a split second, and then his gaze swung back and forth between Skye and Brack. After a moment, his eyes lit up with recognition. Guess he finally caught onto the change in dynamics between them. But no matter what his best friend thought, Brack was certain he had no clue about the incredible sex Brack had shared with Skye.

"Sorry, I didn't mean anything by it. I only want to help." Brack was learning it was easier to apologize than to fight with her.

Skye let out a heavy breath. "I appreciate it, and I'm sorry for being so cranky." She gave him the side-eye. "I didn't get much sleep last night."

Frowning, Cadence glared at the pair of them. "What the hell is going on with you two?"

Now that was a million-dollar question to which Brack didn't have the first clue how to answer.

Chapter Eleven

Cap

The sound of Zephyr's even breathing was a balm to Cap's nerves. The beautiful Guardian deserved to rest after he'd whisked her away under cover of darkness. He prayed he could keep her safe on his quest for self-discovery because he'd come to need her like a drug. Reaching out, he stroked his fingers through the silky strands of her long, dark hair. Zephyr had to be the most gorgeous woman on Earth. Watching her face as she came apart around his fingers and against his tongue was his favorite new memory. He was keeping a mental list, and they all included the beautiful woman curled up in his arms. Once he confirmed what he already knew in his heart, that he was unattached, Cap would take Zephyr and make her his own forever.

Sleep called to him. Cap's eyelids grew heavy until they fluttered closed, and he tumbled headfirst into a dream…

****

Turning off Pensacola Beach Boulevard, his pickup bumped into the lot of The Porthole. The cobalt blue building stood out against the pale, cloudy backdrop. Its massive signage, the one where the O's had all been replaced with oversized portholes, could be seen for miles. Located on the marina, the place boasted an enormous deck that wrapped around the entire structure. Tables outfitted with matching striped umbrellas were strategically placed every few yards. The bar was home to fishermen, surfers, and friends and was more of a local hangout where not many tourists ventured.

A few boats were moored to the dock and bobbed in the light current. He braced his hands on the smooth wooden railing and looked out onto the water. The breeze carried a fine mist, and he took a long, slow breath, drinking in the smell of home. He and TJ were leaving for a nine-month deployment to Afghanistan in a few days, and he would miss this place like crazy.

****

Cap woke with a start, sitting bolt upright in bed. Zephyr followed suit and wrapped a comforting arm around his shoulder. Morning sunlight peeked around the edges of the blinds, and he read the concern written all over her pretty face.

"Bad dream?" she asked, her husky voice gone soft.

"Actually, no." He chuckled. "It was just a weird little snippet, but I saw that same bar again. *This time*, I got the name. It's called The Porthole. I'm pretty sure I lived above the restaurant with my buddy, TJ."

"That's amazing. Was it in Florida?"

"Yes, Pensacola. There's a marine base located there. It has to be the place. I feel it in my gut."

"Well, in that case—" She tossed her legs over the side of the bed. "—let's get out of here and back on the road. We need answers."

"Slow down there."

"Why? No time like the present."

"I was hoping maybe you could call Cadence and have him do another search before I drag you into the unknown."

Her cheeks glowed with a soft pink tinge. "Uh, yeah, about that…I kind of didn't tell anyone I left."

"Please, tell me you're kidding. You didn't even send Skye a text?" He mentally ticked off all the reasons this could be a very bad thing.

Zephyr winced. "Afraid not."

He reached over, grabbed her phone off the nightstand, and handed it to her. "You need to call your sister right now. I'm sure she's worried sick, and we don't need to give her another reason to hate me."

"Skye doesn't hate you. She just—"

"Do me a favor." He smiled. "Please, don't finish that sentence. I may not have all my memories, but I can definitely tell when someone doesn't like me."

"Try not to take it personally. She's…slow to warm up. You'll see. She'll come around."

"I'm pretty sure stealing one of her guns, not to mention her sister, in the middle of the night isn't exactly the best way to endear myself to her."

Zephyr laughed. "You're probably right, but it's too late now."

His shoulders dropped. "Grrreat." Cap gestured to the phone in her hand. "Go on, make the call."

She switched the phone on, and the second it connected, the thing started flashing and beeping with a million texts and missed calls. Zeph swallowed hard. "Um, I think I may be in trouble." A heavy, defeated sigh slipped out. "They're going to kill me."

"I think it's *me* they're going to want to kill, but you may as well get it over with."

"This should be fun…not." She scrolled through her contacts, bit her lip, and hit send.

Cap whispered, "Don't worry, I've got your back, always."

****

Zephyr

Skye answered on the first ring. "Zeph? Are you okay?"

"I'm fine, Skye. Chill."

"Are you serious?" Her sister's voice was thick with tension. "You disappear without a trace, and you expect me to chill." Skye's volume ratcheted up. "We…I…I've been out of my mind!" It wasn't hard to picture her sister's face beet red, lips tight.

"I'm sorry." Zephyr grimaced. "Things happened fast, and I didn't have a chance to fill you in on the situation."

"You turned your phone off, Zeph. Have you ever heard of this thing we call texting or, oh, I don't know, a phone call?"

She deflated. "I *really* am sorry. It's just that—"

"I thought he kidnapped you at gunpoint. We've been scared shitless searching for you."

"We?"

"Yes, *we*. Me and Brack…and Cadence."

"You told them?"

"Of course, I told them. What did you expect me to do? You've been gone for more than twenty-four hours without a word."

Brack's voice came over the line. "What the fuck, Zeph. How could you leave and not tell a soul?"

Guilt twisted her stomach in knots. She didn't mean to panic them; she only wanted to help Cap.

"I don't know what else to say except that I'm truly sorry." Zephyr stood and began pacing around the small room. "It wasn't my intention to run off. It…just…sort of happened."

"Fine," Skye huffed out. "So do you mind telling us what the hell you're doing in Georgia?"

"I'm helping Cap. Hey, wait a sec, how did you know we're in Georgia?"

"Duh, Cadence tracked your phone." The frustration in Skye's voice cut straight across the phone line.

"Please, you have to try to understand. Cap can't move forward until he knows who he was before Barrington changed him, and neither can I. This is important to me…to all of Aether."

Although she couldn't see her sister's expression, Zephyr knew without a doubt that Skye's eyes were rolling into the back of her head. "Give me a small break, will you? There are important things happening here too."

"What could be more important than Cap discovering the truth?"

"Finding Barrington's secret lab. Your home. Your people. Your family."

Zephyr fell silent.

"You need to get back here. The shit is going to hit the fan when they realize you left on a wild goose chase with the soldier," Brack said.

"I'm sorry, guys, but I need to see this through. I promise we'll be back as soon as we figure out who Cap is."

"And what if the good Captain finds a wife and six kids waiting for him? What then?" Skye was unrelenting.

"We'll deal with whatever comes our way. I've gotta go. We're heading down to Pensacola. Cap had another dream, and we have a real lead this time. I'll leave my phone on, and I'll keep you posted."

"Zephyr, this isn't your problem. Please, come home." Skye rarely pleaded for anything.

"I will. As soon as we figure this out. I love you, sis. Stay safe, and don't do anything stupid." Zephyr didn't give Skye a chance to respond; she simply ended the call.

****

Cap

He let out an audible breath. "That went well."

Zephyr shimmied into a pair of jean shorts and zipped them closed. "It went as well as I expected."

Cap's gaze raked over the sexy curves of her gorgeous body, tying his tongue in knots. "Yeah, uh—" He swallowed hard and found his words. "You almost ready to go? The sooner I get you back to Aether, the better chance I have of Skye only maiming me instead of killing me."

She laughed. "I left of my own volition. Skye is my sister, not my keeper. She's not going to be maiming or killing either one of us. I'm an adult, and I don't report my every move to Skye or anyone else."

"I'm not sure the Elders would agree with you. You're a Guardian, Zephyr. You have responsibilities. Maybe you should go back." His heart sank a little even as he said the words.

"There's no way I'm leaving you on your own. We're in this together." She slung her bag over one shoulder and her crossbow and quiver over the other. "Let's get out of here." Power radiated off the Guardian of Air, and a light breeze swept through the room.

Cap checked the Glock at his back, then scooped up his bag and followed Zephyr out the door. She'd told him, and he kind of liked it.

Four and a half hours later, he pulled the jeep into the entrance of The Porthole. It was eerily like his dream. Fire sparked at the tips of his fingers.

Zephyr placed a hand on his arm, and the sparks vanished. "Everything will be fine."

"Yeah, of course." He parked at the far end of the lot and ignored his churning gut.

"*We've* got this," Zephyr said, her fingers on the door handle.

Cap stopped her with a gentle touch to the shoulder. "Wait, please, I need you to stay behind me. We didn't exactly get a chance to ask Cadence to check this place out, and I'm not sure what sort of situation we're walking into."

She sagged in the leather seat. "I'm sorry. It's my fault. They were so upset with me I completely forgot. I can call them back."

"No, I think we should let them settle down a bit." He laced his fingers with hers.

Zephyr leaned closer, bringing her mouth an inch from his. "Together?" She kissed him hard on the lips.

Heat shot through his body. "Together," he managed to repeat, suppressing a moan. Locking the car, he came around to Zephyr's side. "Now remember what I said and stay behind me." He'd made her leave her crossbow in the jeep for fear it would draw too much attention, and he could tell Zeph was twitching for it.

"I heard you the first fifty times you said it." Her hands rested on her hips. "And I'd like to remind you, my crossbow is not the only weapon in my arsenal. I'm a Guardian." She winked and flashed the mark embedded in her palm.

"I know," he whispered, tracing a finger down her

cheek. "But the thought of anything happening to you—"

"Um, it's a bar, not a battlefield. Get over yourself."

"Got it." He chuckled, picked up her hand, and headed inside.

It was late for lunch and a bit too early for dinner. A few scattered patrons were seated outside on the deck, but the bar inside was empty. The Glock at his back was within easy reach, and he tucked Zephyr in behind him. He was scanning the room when a door behind the bar opened. A thirty-something-year-old guy with broad shoulders covered in elaborate tattoos entered. He greeted them with a warm smile, and then the man's eyes lit with recognition. Cap's body went rigid.

"Well, as I live and breathe, if it ain't my old friend come back from overseas," the barman said, stepping closer.

Cap looked over both shoulders and confirmed the guy was talking to him. "You know me?"

"Very funny, Drake. We've been friends for years. You and TJ have lived above my bar for the last three."

"Drake? Did you call me Drake?"

"That's your name, ain't it?"

Zephyr stepped out from behind him and extended her hand. "Hi there. I'm Zephyr, a friend of…Drake's."

The stranger took her small hand in his much larger one. "Brady, and I'm sure glad to meet ya."

A wave of dizziness hit Cap, and he grabbed the edge of the bar.

Zeph rushed to his side and wrapped an arm around his shoulders. "I've got you." She guided him to a barstool.

He took a seat and kept Zephyr close. "Hey, Brady,

you mind if I ask you a dumb question?" Cap asked.

"Shoot."

"Is Drake my first name or my last?"

"What happened, pal?" Brady's brows furrowed, and his voice filled with concern. "You get whacked on the head over there in the war?"

Cap shook his head. "Not exactly."

The big man placed a hand on Cap's forearm. "Your name is Aidan, Captain Aidan Drake."

Chapter Twelve

Skye

Tap…tap…tap. Skye groaned. "Knock it off, Brack. We've hardly slept."

"Not me. Door," he mumbled.

Skye shot out of bed. "Dear Goddess! Get dressed and get in the kitchen ASAP."

Brack propped himself up on the headboard, and the covers slid down to his waist. His gaze scanned her nude form, and he ran his fingers through his sex-mussed hair. Every muscle in his six-pack rippled. Skye's body ignited, and she moistened her lips with the tip of her tongue before mentally slapping herself. After another sex marathon with Brack, how was it all she could think about was climbing on top of him yet again? She had no idea what time it was, and someone was knocking on the door. Skye needed a shrink.

"Why don't you tell whoever it is to go away, and then you can come back to bed." Brack waggled his brows like a pubescent teen, yet somehow, she still found it charming.

Skye rolled her eyes. "I can't. What if it's for Zephyr?"

He stretched, dropping the blanket a bit lower. "Then you can definitely tell them to fuck off."

"Please," she said, rummaging through their pile of

discarded clothing.

"Fine." He got out of bed, not bothering to hide his erection. "Whatever. I'll go make some coffee."

"Thank you," she said, trying to look away but failing miserably.

"My pleasure." Laughing, Brack strolled into the bathroom, giving her an amazing backside view.

Skye forced her libido into submission and plucked her black bike shorts and a T-shirt from the mound of clothing on the floor. She tugged them on, every move generating a tremor of muscle aches. Their sexcapades had Skye in touch with her body in novel and erotic ways. Finger combing her wild hair, she paused in the doorway. *Act natural.* She took a slow, deep breath and let it out before opening the door.

The Guardian of Water wore a bright smile that instantly faded when she took in Skye's appearance. "Hi, I'm sorry," Brooke said, eyeing her up and down. "Were you sleeping?" Brooke glanced down at the phone in her hand. "It's after ten."

"No, of course not. I was…um…doing stuff." *Smooth, Skye.* She covered with a fake smile. "Zephyr isn't home right now. I can tell her you stopped by."

Brooke gave Skye the same fake smile in return and stepped around the partially open door. "Then I need to speak to *you*."

"O…okay, sure."

"This is important, Skye, or I wouldn't barge in." Brooke headed for the kitchen. "How about some coffee? Cause it's way too early for anything stronger."

"Hey, hold on a sec—"

But she couldn't stop Brooke, and she walked straight into the kitchen. Skye followed, nearly slamming into a shirtless Brack, who in turn held the stunned Guardian by her shoulders.

Brooke stumbled out of his grasp. "Oh, dear Goddess, I'm so sorry…I…uh…had no idea."

"Wait. Come back. It's not what you think." Skye caught her by the arm. "Seriously, he was—"

Brack lifted his chin, gesturing to the sliding glass doors. "I was doing some work out back, and it's hot as hell."

"Yes, that's right, the *thing*, outside." Skye gritted her teeth. "Why don't you go finish taking care of *that*…while I talk to Brooke."

"Whatever you say, sweetheart. See ya, Brooke." He turned, and Skye noticed he was not only shirtless but barefoot as well.

"Be careful you don't hurt yourself," Brooke added, a smirk tugging at the corners of her mouth.

"Skye, I'll be taking care of that *thing*. When you two are finished chatting, hows about we finish our little chat." His wink was subtle, but she caught it as the door closed behind him.

Brooke took a seat at the table. "Nice try."

"What?" Skye feigned innocence.

"Give me some credit, will you? I may be new to Aether, but I'm not new to the world."

Skye poured two mugs of coffee and joined her friend. "You're not going to tell anyone, are you?" she asked, sliding one of the cups toward Brooke.

"Of course, not. Whatever is between you and Brack is private." The beautiful Guardian lowered her elbows onto the table and rested her chin in her hands. "But if you don't mind me saying, he is mighty fine. In fact, seeing him shirtless only enhanced my opinion."

Skye couldn't hold back a laugh. "He does look amazing, but I'm still trying to figure out why the idiot didn't put a shirt on."

A broad smile stretched across her friend's face. "Maybe because someone took his?"

Dropping her gaze, Skye realized her mistake. She was wearing Brack's shirt, the one with his number for basketball on the front and the name Beck printed on the back. She'd been anxious to get to the door and hadn't given much regard to what she was grabbing from their pile of discards.

"Great. If I know Brack, he's loving every minute of this situation." Skye sighed.

"And as much as I'm enjoying this little show, I need to talk to you about something serious."

"What's up?"

"I had a vision," Brooke blurted out on a forceful breath. "A vision about your sister."

"Zephyr?"

"Do you have another sister I'm not aware of?"

"Of course not. You just caught me off guard." Skye twisted a loose strand of hair around her index finger, tight enough to make a tourniquet. "Anyway, like I said before, Zeph's not here."

"What's going on, Skye? You're acting a little nuts, and I know it's not only about Brack."

"What do you mean?" She wiped her palms down Brack's oversized T-shirt.

"Cut the crap, Skye. You have to listen to me. Zephyr is either in trouble or about to make some."

"She's out for the day with Cap. She'll be back later."

Brooke gave her head a little shake. "I'm the

Guardian of Water, and you know damn well about my visions. I saw your sister with *a dragon*, and I have no idea what it means. Please, you have to tell me the truth. Is Zephyr in some kind of trouble?"

Skye's body sagged into the chair, and she nodded. "Well, I don't know anything about dragons, but Zeph left home in the middle of the night. She claims she went on a trip with the soldier of her own free will, but one of my guns is missing. I'm praying to the God and Goddess it's the truth, or else the good Captain is a dead man."

"You can't take my vision lightly. I could feel the danger surrounding Zephyr, and that's why I came to her first. Normally, I would've gone straight to Quill, but he's out of range today. We need to tell Hawk." Brooke rose to her feet. "I'll come with you."

"How about we give Zephyr some privacy and the benefit of the doubt?"

"What about my vision?"

"I'll call her, warn her to watch her back. Please, one more day. That's all I'm asking. It's not like there are real dragons flying around out there." Skye gazed imploringly at her friend.

"Fine." Brooked huffed. "But, for the record, I don't like keeping secrets from Quill, and I pretty much suck at it. You have until tomorrow. If you don't tell Hawk or Quill that your sister is AWOL then I will, K?"

"Yeah, definitely," Skye said, knowing full well she'd never betray her sister by telling the Protectors.

"Why don't I believe you?"

Skye tossed her a cheeky grin. "Because you're a wise woman."

****

Brack

Brack peered through the glass, checking to make sure Brooke was gone. When the coast was clear, he went inside. Skye was sitting at the kitchen table, looking grim. His sneakers, socks, and underwear sat on the floor beside an empty chair. He sat, shoved his feet into his shoes, and stuffed the rest into his pockets.

"I thought she'd never leave. What did she want?" he asked.

"To warn me about a vision she had."

"What sort of vision?"

"She saw Zephyr with a dragon, and she was in some kind of trouble."

"You serious? A dragon?"

"Never been more serious in my life. Brooke expects me to tell Quill or Hawk about Zephyr and Cap leaving Aether. She thinks her vision is related, and she's afraid for Zeph. What am I going to do?"

"Maybe she's right, and we should tell Hawk about those guys taking off." Brack rose, filled a mug with coffee, and came back to the table, sitting across from Skye. "Zephyr isn't exactly seeing things clearly right now. The soldier's grip on her is pretty tight, and I'm a little worried. Aren't you?"

"Of course, I'm worried, but ratting my sister out to our lead Protector probably isn't the best way to help her."

"How about we go talk to Hawk? You know, get a feel for his mood."

"And say what? If you just had sex with your Adara, can we chat?" Skye got up and poured the contents of her mug down the drain. "Do you have any reason to go see Hawk?"

"Well, no, I guess not, but we have to do something.

Zephyr needs help whether she realizes it or not."

"Let's not do anything rash. Like I asked Brooke, how about we give Zeph a drop more time? Maybe she'll get off this *save the guy kick* of hers and come home."

"Fine, I'll keep it under wraps…for now. We can call Zeph together and tell her about Brooke's vision. First, I'm heading back to my place to shower and get a shirt." He fixed his gaze on her chest, where his number was emblazoned over her heart and smirked. "It seems someone kidnapped mine." Brack stood and placed a kiss on the top of her head. "It looks way better on you, sweetheart." He slipped out the back door, but he could hear her shouting her displeasure with his new favorite term of endearment for his little badass.

The air outside was stagnant and thick with humidity. Brack cut through the woods to his house, staying under the forest's shady canopy. He expected his mom back late yesterday, and he wondered if she had any inkling of where he'd spent the night. No doubt, the thought of him and Skye in bed together never crossed her mind.

Brack stepped onto the back deck and entered the house through the sliding glass door they preferred to use. "Mom? I'm home," he shouted.

Nothing but the soft creaks of their old house answered his calls. He headed toward her bedroom. Poking his head inside the open door, he called out again, more softly this time, "Mom? You in here?"

No light leaked in from the darkened room or its adjoining bath. Brack pulled his phone from his pocket and checked his messages. Not a word from his mom since before the weekend. It was odd for her to be out of touch for more than a day. If he hadn't been so busy worrying about Zephyr, not to mention having nonstop sex with Skye, he'd have realized it. He shot off a text to her and shoved his phone back into his pocket.

Ivy Beck could most assuredly take care of herself, and at the moment, Brack had more immediate issues to handle. He had to figure out what to do about Zephyr. Trusting his best friend came easily but the soldier not so much. Brack hadn't stopped worrying about Brooke's vision and the danger Zeph might be in. A moment to breathe and regroup was all he needed to clear his head.

Reluctant to wash away Skye's lavender scent from his skin, Brack forced himself into the shower. She was worried about their loss of privacy now that Brooke had uncovered their secret relationship, but Brack worried he was losing himself. Things with Skye were changing him. Before he slept with her, he wouldn't have hesitated to contact Hawk the moment Zephyr disappeared with the soldier. The Guardian's safety had to be put first, and if Skye was angry with him, he had plenty of ways to make it up to her.

Mindlessly dressing, he hatched a bogus excuse to gauge their lead Protector's mood. He dawdled around the house before forcing himself out the door. Brack walked in the silence which only comes from solitude, playing the scenario over in his head. He arrived at the South Tower, and a wave of unease made his stomach rumble. Skye was going to kick his ass—or worse—she'd refuse to have sex with him ever again. *Do it for Zephyr.*

He stood a few feet from the door and smiled at Hawk's newest addition to the South Tower. One of four ancient structures, the House of Fire dated back to the origins of Aether. Each tower had been modernized over the years, but no one had ever added a doorbell of any kind until now. Other than the Protector's weapons storage unit, doors were kept unlocked in the village. Aether was a knock-and-enter kind of place.

Brack let out a quiet snicker. This was Hawk's first line of defense. Hanging juxtaposed to the tower's original wooden door, a video doorbell had been mounted. Brack recalled their lead Protector's recent announcement to everyone on duty. "*My honeymoon is still in full swing, and I need to go home to take care of my Adara for a few hours. Don't bother me unless it's a true emergency.*"

He reached out to ring the bell but hesitated, his finger hovering over the button. "Maybe this is a bad idea," he whispered to no one.

"What do you want, Beck?" Hawk's gruff, disembodied voice came over the speaker.

"Uh, oh, uh," he fumbled, forgetting his entire plan.

The door swung open, and Ashlyn smiled up at him. "Hey, Brack, don't mind my Kanti. He has no manners." Her mane of red hair was more wild than usual. "Would you like to come in?"

"Yeah, uh, no thanks, Ash, I…never mind." Brack spun on his heels and headed toward the cobblestone path.

"Where are you going?" boomed a loud voice from behind him.

Brack stopped and closed his eyes for a second before turning around. "Oh, hey there, Hawk. I didn't mean to disturb you or anything."

"Too late." The big man pulled his broad shoulders back. "What can I do for you?"

"It's not important. We can talk another time."

"If it's not important, why are you at my door?"

His phone vibrated in his pocket, and he yanked it out. Brack swiped his finger across the screen. "Hi, Mom, hang on a sec."

He hit the mute button and smiled at Hawk. "Sorry, Ivy is away, and she needs me. I'll catch you later. Thanks a lot, Hawk. Good talk."

Brack jogged off and unmuted the call. "Hi, Mom, sorry about—"

"This isn't your mother." An unfamiliar male voice came over the line. "I'm a…a friend of hers. Ivy is in trouble, and she needs your help. She begged me not to call you, but there's no one else I can trust."

"Who the hell is this, and how did you get my mother's phone?" Brack demanded.

"My name is Tyler, Tyler Ward, and like I said, I'm a…a friend. Please, I can't do this alone. Ivy's life depends on you, Brack. She's locked in Barrington's lab. You have to help me save her."

"Barrington? How is that possible? Who are you really? I want to speak to my mother now!"

Loud rustling came over the phone line, and then Tyler was back. "Someone's coming," the stranger whispered. "I'll call you back."

"Wait a sec—" The call dropped, and Brack's home screen glowed in his hand.

Chapter Thirteen

Zephyr

She rolled over and reached for Aidan, but his side of the bed was cold. With no sleep, the man had to be running on fumes. The former captain had interrogated poor Brady for hours. Well past midnight, Aidan finally acquiesced and returned to his apartment but spent the entire night searching the place with a fine-toothed comb. Exhausted, Zephyr had crawled into bed around two in the morning.

Yesterday had been overwhelming, and she was only on the sidelines. Aidan discovering his true identity brought up as many questions as it had answered. He was still lost, and she didn't know how to help him. Zephyr slipped out of bed and stretched her aching muscles. Her back cracked with a loud snap, and she let out a quiet moan.

"Good morning," Aidan said, his voice deep and sexy.

Her hand flew to her chest, and she spun on her heels to face him. "Hi, I, uh, didn't hear you come in."

"My marine stealth moves are coming back." He smiled, and it lit up his handsome face.

His excitement was contagious, and her return grin was automatic.

"Is there any chance this marine can supply coffee

for his sleep-deprived guest?"

"Yes, ma'am." He stood up straight and saluted. "Of course I can." Aidan winked. "In fact, I have a few surprises I think you're going to like."

"Surprises? Sounds intriguing."

Her stomach fluttered at the thought of the kind of surprises he had in mind, but then it gave a loud rumble, reminding her she hadn't eaten anything since last night. Heat flooded her cheeks, and if the well-mannered marine noticed, he didn't mention it.

Aidan gestured toward the bathroom. "I found some new toothbrushes under the sink, and I left you one on the counter. The towels hanging up are fresh. Brady said he has someone come in and clean the place every couple of weeks."

"Great. I could use a shower, but then I'm at your mercy."

"As much as I like the sound of you being at my mercy, I think I'd better feed you some breakfast first."

"I, uh, I didn't mean it like that." Zephyr's cheeks were on fire, and a small breeze kicked in the room. This man made her lose control, and she still wasn't sure if that was a good thing or a bad one.

"I know," he said with a smirk. "Whenever you're ready, I'll be in the kitchen."

The minute Aidan walked out of the room, the Air settled around her. Zephyr hurried, showering and dressing in record time. The smell of coffee and bacon frying wafted through the air and drew her straight to the kitchen. She sat on one of the barstools on the opposite side of the island.

"Where did all this food come from? Last night we ordered pizza because you didn't even have a bottle of ketchup."

"Brady dropped off some essentials early this morning."

"He's such a nice guy and a real friend. Have you had any more breakthroughs where he's concerned?"

Aidan stopped stirring the large bowl in front of him. "Not much. Everything feels so…familiar, but there are missing pieces. Whole chunks of my memory are gone. What if I never remember?"

She walked around the counter and wrapped her arms around his waist. "Give it some time. Your memories will come back. Think about how much progress you've made just being here for one day."

He kissed the top of her head. "True. Brady was extremely helpful. The guy knows me better than I know myself."

Zephyr looked up into his blue eyes. "The person you are right now is the only person I care about."

"I wish it were that simple for me." His breath whooshed out and ended with a sigh. "There is still so much I don't know. Brady said I was evasive when it came to questions about my personal life and, specifically, my childhood. From one of my dreams, I'm certain TJ and I were in foster care together, but Brady couldn't confirm my theory. It's funny."

"What's funny?" she asked.

"Brady knows stuff like my favorite beer, how I like my burgers, and where I hang out, but nothing personal. Not—one—single thing. It's no wonder Barrington took me. I was an invisible man."

"We'll unravel your past, but you have to, um…stay calm." She tipped her chin toward his hands.

Bright orange flames glowed from his fingers, and

the bowl in his hands transformed into molten plastic lava. He jumped up and shouted, “Shit!”

She relieved him of the melted bowl and dumped it into the trash. Toxic-smelling fumes billowed up, and Zephyr poured some water into the can, dousing the entire mess. Satisfied they wouldn’t be asphyxiated, she approached Aidan. His back was hunched, and she began rubbing small circles across the broad surface. He turned around and took her in his arms.

“I’m sorry,” he said.

“Stop,” she whispered against his chest. “You don’t need your life sorted out in twenty-four hours. You have a name and, in my opinion, a very appropriate one at that.”

“What are you talking about?”

“Both of your names are elementally based.”

“Is that significant?”

“Duh. You haven’t noticed that Aetherians name their children after elemental characteristics…always?”

He shrugged. “Guess I never gave it much thought.”

“Our people believe it’s essential to our connection to the Elements. We had to study tons of this useless crap growing up. The name Aidan means *little fires,* and Drake means *dragon.* You see—” Zephyr pulled back a drop, rose up on her tiptoes, and pressed her lips to his. “—it was meant to be. You’re Aetherian through and through.”

****

Captain Aidan Drake, US Marine

It was time to thoroughly scrub Mr. Heller away until only Aidan Drake remained. A United States Marine enhanced with Aetherian blood would be the one to bring Barrington’s legacy to its knees. Aidan’s hands tightened into fists, his knuckles going white. No more experiments. No more pain. No more stolen lives.

Zephyr acted as if the details of his life didn't matter, but Aidan's very existence depended upon the truth and nothing more. Only the truth could set him free of the burdens carried by his lost memories. There was no way to move forward without looking to his past. Who was Aidan Drake, and what horrific deeds had he done as Mr. Heller, Dr. Barrington's creation? The unanswered questions sent his stomach churning in nauseating loops.

Brady insisted Aidan Drake and TJ Smith were good men, hardworking and loyal. According to the bartender, the soldiers were the best of the best, but in Aidan's current state of mind, he was having a hard time believing the guy. In fact, he was having a hard time believing in anything apart from Zephyr. Aidan believed in her like no one and nothing else.

The defiant, dark-haired beauty fed his soul the way oxygen feeds a fire. She was the perfect blend of brains, strength, and kindness. He was drawn to her, his body igniting with desire whenever she was near. Zephyr was becoming impossible to resist. Perhaps it was the Guardian blood pulsing through his veins, but he didn't care; he wanted her more than all his lost memories combined.

"Would you like a glass of wine?" she asked, interrupting his thoughts.

"Sure, that sounds great. But I didn't know I had any wine." Aidan chuckled.

"You didn't." She gestured to a couple of bottles on the table, one half empty. "Brady gave me some. He told me you were a big fan of this particular red." She poured the crimson liquid into a goblet and handed it to him.

"What should we drink to?" Zephyr smiled and lifted her glass.

"To answers," he said on impulse.

Her lips pressed into a tight line. "How about we drink to the future?" Her confident, husky voice transformed into a soft, timid whisper.

Man, he was an asshole of the first order. Zephyr deserved better than he could offer her now or maybe ever. She was looking to the future, and Aidan was still trying to unravel the past.

His gaze fell to his feet. "I'm sorry, Zeph, I'm frustrated with myself. My attitude has nothing to do with you. Honest."

"I get it. I do, but you're not helping yourself this way. I was thinking…well…maybe we should head home."

"Home?"

"Yeah, home, to Aether."

"I'm not sure Aether is my home. What if—"

"You're not still on this kick about having a life away from Aether, are you? You know that's not possible, right?"

"I'm sorry, Zephyr, but I don't know anything right now."

Her hands flew to her luscious hips. "Really! You're still not sure about *anything*, including *me*?"

Aidan snaked an arm around her waist and pulled her close. "Wrong. The way I feel when I'm with you…the way I feel *about you*…well, it's the only thing I have total faith in."

Zephyr returned his embrace, and her phone buzzed against his leg. She slipped out of his hold, tugged it from her pocket, and glanced down.

"It's Skye." She moaned. "I'd better answer it, or she'll go ballistic."

Skye's voice was uncharacteristically frantic. "Zeph, thank the Goddess. Brack needs your help."

"Brack?" Her brows scrunched.

"Yes, Brack, your best friend since forever. You remember him, don't you?"

Zephyr closed her eyes and took a deep breath. "Skye, can you please curb the hostility and tell us what's going on?"

"Us? Is Heller listening?" Skye sounded appalled.

Aidan tensed. Zephyr's sister truly hated his guts.

"His *name* is Captain Aidan Drake. And to answer your question, of course, he's listening."

"Well, that's just dandy." Sarcasm oozed from Skye straight over the phone line. "I'm super happy your boyfriend discovered his secret identity, but this is an emergency. Ivy has been kidnapped by Barrington's people."

"W…what? How?" The color drained from Zephyr's face, and she clutched at Aidan's shoulder.

"Forget the details right now. I don't have time to explain. Get in the car and head home. We're waiting to hear back from our contact with more info. And, Zeph, hurry. Brack is losing his shit. He needs you."

"This better not be a trick to lure me back. Aidan has unfinished—"

He held out his hand, and she rolled her eyes but relinquished the phone. "Hey, Skye, it's me, um, Aidan. We need an hour, and then we'll be on the road. Tell Brack to hang in there. We're on our way." Aidan placed the phone back in Zephyr's hand and patted her on the arm.

She switched it off speaker and brought the phone to her ear. "Skye? Yes…uh huh…I said, yes…see you soon." Zephyr ended the call and turned to him. "I seriously can't believe this is happening. How in the name of the God and Goddess would Barrington's people get to Ivy?"

"There's only one way to find out. Let's pack up, say our goodbyes, and get back on the road." Aidan wrapped her in his arms and stroked the length of her soft hair. "I'll find Brack's mom and stop whoever is behind this."

Zephyr squeezed him around the waist. "*We—we* are going to stop them. You're on Team Aether now, Aidan Drake."

Chapter Fourteen

Brack

There was no one Brack was closer to than his mother, not even Zephyr or Cadence. She'd given birth to him at the age of twenty, practically a child by Aetherian standards, and they'd grown up side by side. From the moment Brack was born, Ivy had insisted her child was given to her by the God and Goddess, subject closed. He doubted anyone bought her story about him being a gift from the heavens, but she hadn't changed it in twenty-five years.

He turned his silent, idle phone over and over in his sweaty palms. All the texts he'd sent were marked unread, and every call he'd made went straight to voicemail. Brack was two seconds away from a nervous breakdown. Who was Tyler Ward, and why did he have his mom's phone? It wasn't like her to keep secrets from him. Was it possible she had a friend Brack had never heard of before?

"Why don't you sit down? Your pacing is making me dizzy." Cadence leaned back in Brack's favorite armchair, propped his sneakers up on the coffee table, and took a sip from a steaming mug.

"I haven't heard from this Tyler character since yesterday afternoon." Brack dropped onto the couch and sucked in a deep breath. "Why the hell can't you track her phone the same way you tracked Zephyr's?"

"I'm sorry, buddy." Cadence slumped into the cushions. "I tried, but the signal is blocked with some high-level tech I can't break through."

Skye sat next to Brack. "I know you're worried. We all are, but you have to stay focused, or you won't be any help to Ivy." She tucked herself into his side. "Remember, you're a Protector of Aether. *We* will find her, and *we* will put an end to this."

The heat from Skye's body seeped into his flesh, and if Cadence wasn't sitting two feet away, he'd show her how much he wanted to lose himself inside her yet again. The feel of her, the taste of her, the smell of her, and even the sound of Skye's voice was becoming an addiction he had no desire to fight. But not even her allure was enough to keep his mind from returning to his mother.

Brack's empty stomach churned, acid burning his gut. "Not if *we* don't know who the hell has her or where on earth she may be."

"At least, Zephyr and Heller…I mean Cap…oh shit, I mean Aidan. I hope this is the final name change for the soldier. It's exhausting trying to keep up. Anyway, they're on their way home, and I, for one, am relieved," Skye said.

"Give me a break, sweetheart. Ask yourself why you called your sister. What can she do to help? I think you just wanted an excuse to bring her back here," Brack said.

"No, not true. Not true at all. Zephyr is a Guardian with incredible gifts. If Barrington's people really do have Ivy, then we're going to need some serious power to get her back." Skye turned to face him and put her hands on his shoulders. "I admit, I don't like the soldier, no matter what he calls himself, but he may still be able to help us."

"Um, hello, I'm in the room." Cadence waved his arms back and forth. "What's up with you two? The way you've been talking to each other…I…I don't know. Something is different between you. Come on, guys, what's up?"

Brack thought they'd been doing a decent job of keeping things inconspicuous. But denial was a powerful coping mechanism, and it could be a supportive friend or a sneaky adversary.

Cadence gestured toward Brack and Skye. Her hands had done a slow slide down his chest and rested on his knees. They both looked down and then jumped apart in unison.

Their friend stood there wildly jabbing a finger in their direction. "See! That's what I mean. You were…c…c…cuddling and t…t…touching."

"Don't be ridiculous. I can't stand him," Skye said smoothly. "I was only comforting him because, if you haven't noticed, Brack has got one egg too many in his basket, and he's about to drop the whole load."

Brack shook his head. "You've been hanging out with Bear too much."

"And what do you have to say for yourself?" Cadence asked, staring Brack down with daggers in his eyes. "You hate her?"

Brack's voice dropped low, and he gazed directly at Skye. "With a burning passion."

Their friend slapped his hands to his sides. "There it is again!"

Skye and Brack laughed in harmony, but then a strange look came over her, and she stopped abruptly. It was like someone had flipped a switch, and aloof Skye was back. She adjusted her signature braids.

"We're busting your chops, Cade." Skye rolled her eyes. "Seriously, what could possibly be going on?"

"I don't appreciate being messed with." Cadence crossed his arms over his chest. "We're friends, a crew."

Her piercing blue gaze fixed on Brack, and she gave a subtle nod of her head.

"Okay," he said on a long breath. "Something might've happened—"

"Don't make a big deal of it." Skye's cheeks flushed. "It's just sex. We're not getting Joined or anything. There's nothing to talk about…it's not a *thing*."

Cade's eyes popped wide, but Brack's phone blared, startling them all. He lost hold of his cell but managed to regain control before it hit the floor. He'd been waiting for the damn thing to ring, and now he was frozen in fear and shock.

"Quick, give it here." Cadence reached for the buzzing phone. "I'm going to see if I can track it." He flipped open his laptop and set the phone beside it.

"Hurry up and answer before he hangs up!" Brack's panicked voice cracked.

"Put it on speaker," Skye demanded.

Cadence swiped his finger across the screen and then nudged Brack. He realized the voice on the other side of the line had said hello several times, and his friend was signaling him to speak.

Brack cleared his throat. "Hello. This is Bracken Beck. I want to speak with my mother."

"I wish that were possible," the stranger said. "I'm sorry. It wasn't safe to call you back sooner. I'm sure you've been worried, but I want you to know Ivy is all right…for now."

"Enough of this cryptic bullshit." Brack stood, then sat, then stood again. "Who are you, and where is my mother?"

"I told you, my name is Tyler Ward, and I'm—"

"I know, a friend of my mother's." He balled his hands into tight fists. "Listen, here, buddy, my mother and I don't keep secrets from one another, so I can only guess that you're a lying sack of shit since I've never heard of you."

"Life can be complicated, Brack. People have all kinds of reasons for keeping secrets, and when you help me save your mom, you can ask her all about hers. But for now, can we please call a truce, for Ivy's sake?"

His jaw set tight, he spoke directly into the phone. "For the record, I don't trust you."

"Duly noted," the man conceded. "I've been working on a plan to get Ivy out, but I'm going to need your help. Your mom tells me you're strong, and you and your friends have…powers like her. Please, I'm not sure I can protect her much longer."

"What exactly do you want from me?" Brack asked.

****

Skye

Skye's hands fell to her sides. "You're not seriously going to trust this guy, are you?"

"What choice do I have?" Brack paced the room in maddening circles. "He's our only link to my mom."

Cadence stepped in his path, and Brack couldn't avoid bumping into his friend.

"What the hell, man?" Brack's tone held a hint of anger that Skye knew was fueled by nerves.

He placed a steady hand on his Brack's shoulder. "There are always choices. It's important to consider our options and our resources."

Brack shrugged his buddy's hand off and stepped back. "Hmm." He tapped a finger to his temple. "Let's see…we're fucked, we're fucked…oh, and we're fucked."

"Don't be so negative." Skye looped her arm through Brack's and led him to the couch. "Cade is right. We need to take stock of our assets and have a backup plan in case this Ward guy turns out to be a Trojan Horse sent by Barrington's people. Let's call Zephyr and Aidan again. Tell them to meet us a few miles from our rendezvous with Ward, and we'll hatch our own plan. If Tyler Ward is a friend, then great, but otherwise, I'll take care of him." She patted the weapon secured to her thigh.

Brack gave a half-hearted shrug and then turned to Cade. "Um, buddy, I think—"

"Don't bother." Cadence's gaze narrowed. "I know what you're going to say. You want me to stay behind and be your spy. Put my ass on the line and miss all the action. Am I correct in my assumption?"

"I wouldn't put it like that. You're the only one smart enough to help us pull this off. Skye and I both know you're a kick-ass fighter, but your skills at the keyboard are more important to this mission."

"Yeah, yeah, yeah." Cadence positioned himself on Brack's other side and gave him a playful shove. "I just wanted to hear you say it." He opened his laptop and started typing.

"Whatever we do, we'd better do it quickly." Skye picked at her cuticles. "I'm running out of time before Brooke spills her guts to Quill about the vision she had regarding Zephyr."

"Why can't she keep it to herself you may ask? I'll tell you why—love does crazy things to people—that's why." Cadence glared at them and then went back to fiddling with his computer.

She was not *in love* with Brack, and if Cade knew what was good for him, he'd wipe the smug look off his face. "Can we please focus here?" Skye asked.

"Just saying," Cadence mumbled without looking up from his screen.

Brack ignored the comment. "I'll make a list of supplies." He pulled out his phone and began entering notes. "Skye, you should go back to the tower and pack up some clothes and as many weapons as you can. Cade, can you sneak into PH and grab some surveillance equipment and maybe some tools to break into the lab?"

"I'm on it." Cade snapped his computer shut. "I'll be back soon." He was out the door before either one of them could say a word.

"He sure was in a hurry to get out of here. I wonder if it was something we said," Skye joked.

"Now that he and Brooke both know about us, we're going to have to talk about this—" Brack waved a hand between them. "—before the entire village finds out."

"Now? You want to have a heart-to-heart when your mom is in imminent danger?"

"No…well…yes, but I didn't mean this minute."

"I'm going home to pack. We'll have plenty of time to discuss your neurosis on the drive."

Skye headed for the door, but Brack grabbed her hand, stopping her in her tracks. He tugged her until they were face to face, his mouth an inch from her own.

"If wanting to be inside you every minute—" He

pressed his lips to hers and then drew back. "—of every day makes me neurotic then sign me up for *N-A-U*."

"*N-A-U?*" she asked, stunned by his frankness.

"*Neurotics Are Us*," he whispered. Brack ran a finger down her cheek. "You have no idea how much I want you."

"I do." She strained to form words. Skye knew Brack was reacting to all the stress and vowed to be the strong one in this scenario. "I'd better go."

Skye straightened her clothes and turned to leave, but Brack stopped her.

He took her in his arms. "Thank you," he said, kissing the top of her head and then releasing her.

"For leaving you with a boner?"

He laughed. "No, for helping me save my mom."

"No worries," she replied.

But that was a lie. She was worried about everything. Freeing Ivy, learning about Aidan, stopping Barrington's people, but mostly, she worried about her growing feelings for Brack.

A short time later, they were standing beside one of the Protector's specially outfitted SUVs. Hawk was going to kick their asses, but none of them cared. Cadence slammed the tailgate and finished explaining the finer points of the equipment he borrowed from PH. Brack and Skye reached for the key fob at the same time. She looped her finger through the metal ring, and he wrapped his hand around the black plastic cube.

"Let go. I've got it," she said.

"Well, it seems I've got it too, so why don't you let go?" Brack insisted.

"Not going to happen, Beck. You drive for shit." Skye tugged on the ring, and he tugged back.

“That’s a matter of opinion.”

A broad smile crept across Cadence’s face. “Sorry, dude, it’s a fact. You’re like a race car driver on steroids.”

“Wimps,” Brack mumbled, relinquishing his hold on the key.

“I don’t have a death wish. That does *not* make me a wimp.” She opened the driver’s side door. “We’ll be in touch, Cade.”

Skye released the clip on her holster, leaned into the car, and placed her second favorite Glock, Gretchen, in the cupholder. When she straightened, Brack was staring at her. He didn’t say anything, and she wondered what he was thinking.

“Why don’t you hug Cade goodbye already,” she mocked. “And then let’s go.”

“Whatever you say, *sweeeet-heart*,” Brack said, stretching out the word. He tossed his bag in the back seat and got into the car.

She slammed her door and started the engine. It was going to be a long ride and an even longer few days if the sexual tension between them didn’t settle down to a slow simmer.

“Remember who the bad guys are, and try not to kill each other,” Cadence said, tapping the roof of the car.

Skye shifted the SUV into gear, and gravel pinged off the hubcaps as she pulled away. The parking area was quiet, but relief washed over her the moment they were clear of Aether’s magical gates.

“Should we call Zephyr and bring her up to speed on our plans?” Brack asked.

“I guess. Did Cadence connect my Bluetooth?”

“Yes.”

"Here goes nothing." She hit the phone symbol on the steering wheel to place the call.

Her sister picked up on the first ring. "Hey, Skye, we're on our way back to Aether—"

"Sorry, change of plans. We have a meeting scheduled with this guy who claims to be a friend of Ivy's. His name is Tyler Ward. No red flags from Cadence yet."

Brack leaned toward the speaker. "Hey, Zeph, thanks for coming back…both of you. I'm seriously worried about my mom, and we could really use some backup in case this whole thing is a setup. It may be dangerous, and I want you to know that no matter what Skye told you, this mission is strictly voluntary."

"I'm a Guardian, Brack," Zephyr said. "And Aidan is doing amazing learning to control his powers. I love Ivy. She's like a second mother to me. I'd do anything for her and for you."

She clenched her teeth. Of course, her sister would do anything for Brack; Zephyr loved him. It was time Skye woke up and faced that reality. Zephyr would always come in first place in Brack's life, and Skye wasn't willing to be anyone's second choice.

He shifted in his seat. "Yeah, uh, thanks. I appreciate the help. My mom's safe return is the only thing that matters to me right now."

"Oh? What did Hawk have to say about that?" Zeph asked.

His posture went rigid. "Ward insisted my mother wanted to keep it quiet. No Protector or Elder involvement. It was the only way he would agree to meet with me."

"I sure hope you know what you're doing," Zephyr

said.

Aidan's deep voice cut across the line. "Barrington may be dead, but his people shouldn't be underestimated. My memories are still a bit disjointed, but the ones I have are not good. Not good at all."

"Respect," Skye chimed in. "That's why we're going to meet with you guys beforehand. Does tomorrow work?"

"Yes. Tell us where and when, and we'll be there," Aidan replied.

"Thanks again, you guys." Brack's voice lost its luster. "I'll text you the address."

"We'll see you soon. Try not to worry. We'll get her out safe and sound. Love you," Zephyr said.

"Uh, same," Brack answered. "See you tomorrow."

"Bye," Skye said.

Skye knew there had never been anything romantic between her sister and Brack, but once her heart got involved with the sexy and infuriating man, she felt like she had lost several IQ points. Her judgment had become unreliable. She only hoped that Brack proved himself trustworthy in the end. Skye would hate to have to kill the one man she could truly see a future with.

Chapter Fifteen

Zephyr

"Since we don't have to meet those guys until tomorrow afternoon, what do you say we get off the road for the night? Catch a little sleep?" Zephyr asked.

"Great idea. I wouldn't mind closing my eyes for a few hours. Besides, all this driving is making my muscles stiff." Aidan kneaded the back of his neck.

Zephyr unbuckled her seatbelt and got up onto her knees. She stretched across the console to reach Aidan's shoulders and began massaging the tight band of muscles at the base of his neck. The man was large, extra-large, and the smooth feel of his skin covering the thick cord of muscle made Zephyr curious about the rest of him.

He was all about pleasing her, but he still wouldn't allow her to touch him. She'd seen him shirtless, and the man was a sight to behold. But maybe he was scarred below the waist—or something far worse. She didn't care; they'd work it out no matter the circumstances. It was the heart of this man she'd fallen for. There was something in his steely blue eyes; the way he looked at her was hotter than the heat of his Fire.

"W…what are you doing?" Aidan protested. "It's not safe. Sit down and put your seatbelt on."

"You sound like Brack."

The comment slipped out, an automated response,

and when Aidan's expression went slack, Zephyr immediately wished she could take it back. Instead, she retracted her hands, lowered her butt into the cushy seat, and wrapped her arms across her belly.

Aidan's jaw ticked. "So, uh, what's the deal with you two, *really*?"

"No deal, honestly. We've been friends since we were little kids. He's like a brother to me." If the roles had been reversed, she doubted she would've taken the explanation well. "I'm sorry I talk about my friends so much. We're super tight because it's always only been the four of us. You're the first outsider any of us has ever become close with."

"I understand," Aidan said flatly, but his right eye twitched up a storm.

Half of her was secretly happy that the man was jealous because it meant he cared about her.

She smiled. "I can see that you *don't*, but you will in time."

"If you say you're friends and nothing more, I believe you." He returned her smile, but it didn't reach his eyes.

Soon Aidan would come to understand the relationship she and Brack shared the same way everyone in Aether did. Even the smallest of rumors regarding the two friends hadn't surfaced since high school. Zeph planned to dispel the last of Aidan's doubts and put a swift end to his celibacy the minute they were alone.

The jeep veered off the next exit and into the parking lot of a familiar chain motel. Aidan came to a stop under the large portico at the front entry. He tucked Skye's Glock into his waistband and pulled his T-shirt down to cover it. When the gun was secured, he reached back and yanked Zephyr's crossbow out from behind the seat and handed it to her.

"Stay here. I'll go get us a room."

She gestured toward the concealed weapon. "Are you expecting trouble?"

"These days…always."

"No one is looking for us, and even if they were, I'm sure this is the last place on Earth they'd check." She nudged him with her elbow. "Go on, I'm fine."

While he was inside, she typed out a text to Skye telling her they were stopping for the night. By the time she finished, Aidan was back with a keycard in his hand.

"Our room is around back," he said, throwing the car into gear and speeding through the nearly empty lot.

Zephyr wedged her crossbow between her knees and gripped the door's armrest. "What's the hurry?"

"I don't want you out in the open any longer than necessary. We have no idea where Barrington's people may be lurking."

"You worry too much. Are you sure you're not a Protector?" she teased.

A broad smile spread across Aidan's face, softening his rugged features. "I guess marines and Protectors have a lot in common."

"It would seem so." She reached for the door handle, but he stopped her with a gentle hand to the shoulder.

"I'd like to go first. Make certain there are no threats."

Zephyr snorted out a laugh. "You're a Protector, all right."

Aidan didn't reply; he simply stared at her with a blank expression.

Oh, he's not playing. "Fine. I'll stay here like a helpless human," she acquiesced.

He smoothed a hand down the length of her hair. "I do *not* think you're helpless. I, uh, your safety is imperative to Aether…and to me." A ruddy flush rose to Aidan's cheeks, and he slipped out of the jeep without another word.

She watched him through the window, poised to draw his weapon at the slightest sign of danger. He moved like an Aetherian Protector, gliding on silent feet. A door slammed on the second floor, and blue sparks flared at the tips of Aidan's fingers. One of the housekeeping staff emerged from a room, pushing a rickety cart. Aidan shook his hands out, and the sparks dissipated in a swirl of smoke. The housekeeper didn't seem to notice his Fire show and his shoulders returned to their normal position. He swiped the keycard and entered the room. It must have been tiny because he emerged after only a minute and headed back to the car. His gaze locked with hers, and her stomach did a little flip. She wanted this man. It was time to step up her game, stop obsessing, and act on her baser instincts.

Aidan opened her door. "All clear. Are you ready?" He held out a hand to help her from the jeep.

"Ready is a relative term."

"Huh?"

"Never mind," she said, accepting his hand. "I was thinking out loud."

He nodded and pulled her to her feet. "No worries, I'll get the bags."

Zephyr slung her crossbow and quiver over her shoulder and grabbed her bag before he had the chance. "Thanks, but I can take care of my own baggage. You just worry about yours." She smirked and turned on her heels.

Aidan remained silent. Clearly, the guy still required a few lessons regarding the strength and perseverance of a Guardian. Zephyr was up for the challenge. In fact, she was looking forward to it.

****

Aidan

Zephyr's tone was filled with the same challenge flickering in her eyes. Aidan's resistance to this incredible woman waned by the day. The way she looked at him sent his body into instant arousal, but she deserved more than half a man. If he allowed his attraction and feelings for her to screw with his judgment, Zephyr could get hurt. As tempting as she was, he refused to be selfish.

Despite his efforts to tamp down his libido, the small room grew warm. Her luscious curves were on full display in a tiny pair of shorts and a tank. How much could any man be expected to take? Fire tingled down his spine. It was time to make a break for it and cool off a bit before he embarrassed himself.

Aidan tugged his T-shirt over his head and tossed it on the king-sized bed. "I'm dying for a shower. Are you starving, or can you wait a bit to order food?" he asked, hoping to sound casual.

"I'm not hungry…for food," Zephyr replied with an odd lilt in her voice.

"Um, did you need something else?"

"Yes." She closed the space between them, her breasts mere inches from his chest. "I'd like to join you in the shower."

His Fire spread within the confines of his body, and he fought to keep it from escaping. "Zephyr, please, we talked about this."

"You're right. We did. But I still don't understand. Brady said he didn't think you were dating anyone. So, what's the real issue here, Aidan? Why won't you let me see you, touch you? Are you…intact?"

"I'm fine. But *you* need to be protected," he blurted out.

"From what? You?" She reached out and smoothed a hand down his unshaven face. "You'd never hurt me."

He covered her hand with his own, holding it in place. "Not intentionally."

"Intentions are everything." Zephyr stood up on her tiptoes and pressed her lips to Aidan's.

His connection to this woman was pure power in its most raw form. Aidan couldn't fight it any longer. He hesitated for the briefest of seconds and then threaded his fingers into her long, thick hair. All the pent-up desire he'd been keeping under wraps burst loose. His tongue plundered her mouth, and his hands moved of their own volition, caressing every inch of her exposed skin.

A breeze kicked up in the room, and her sweet floral fragrance tickled his nose. Zephyr's signature scent made him hungry to taste her pleasure. The Guardian of Air trembled in his arms. Aidan loved the way she was always in control, except with him.

She pulled back a fraction, her breath coming in heavy pants. "Please, Aidan, I don't need to be protected. Life is full of risks, and this is one I'm more than willing to take." She licked her kiss-swollen lips. "I want you…all of you." Zephyr reached down and stroked the hard press of his cock beneath his jeans.

A moan slipped from his lips.

Zephyr gasped, but then a small, victorious smile

spread across her face. The combination of shock and relief she wore faded in a heartbeat, and she grimaced. “I, uh, have to admit something to you.”

“What’s that? You know you can tell me anything.”

“I, uh, thought you might be, uh, you know, messed up down there,” she confessed, her gaze flickering toward his package.

A laugh ripped through him. “Is that so?”

“Yeah, it’s true.” She covered her face with her hands.

Aidan took hold of her wrists and tugged her hands away from her eyes. “Hey, it’s cool. It’s funny, really.” He kissed the end of her nose. “Besides, now you know all my parts are in working order.”

“Well, I’m still going to need some definitive proof, Captain.” A playful gleam danced in her eyes. “I need to check the status of your equipment. You know, make sure everything is in tip-top shape.” Her face flooded with color again. “Consider this a formal inspection.”

“I’m sorry. I didn’t realize you were in command here.”

Zephyr reached for the button on his jeans. “I’m most definitely in command.”

Her warm fingers grazed the bare flesh beneath his waistband, and Aidan gave up any pretense of a fight. The rasp of his zipper being lowered sent sparks dancing up and down his arms. Zephyr took one step back and raised her palms toward him. His gaze fixed on the Guardian mark embedded in her left palm, the symbol of her Element and her power.

The Air around him swirled, and his underwear and jeans came down in one swift motion, pooling at his ankles. Dumbfounded by her control, he barely registered the fact he'd been completely disrobed by a flick of her wrists. Zephyr's psychokinetic abilities were beyond any display he'd witnessed before, but he tucked his questions away for later. The only thing he wanted now was to take Zephyr the way he'd been fantasizing about. He freed his ankles from the tether of his clothing and tossed them across the room with one foot.

"Oh my." Zephyr eyed his rock-hard shaft. "I can see I was worried for no reason. You're so, so…Aetherian," she said, on a rush of air.

"Pardon me?"

"Aetherian men are known to be well endowed." Her cheeks flamed red. "Not that I've seen many. I mean…I don't have a lot of experience…I mean, I'm not a slut or anything."

He held back a laugh. "Of course, you're not." Aidan toyed with the hem of her shirt. "The only problem I see here is that you're way overdressed for this occasion. Can I help you out of those pesky clothes?"

Her dark pink tongue glided across her lips, and she nodded. Aidan popped the button on her jean shorts and tugged them down. Zephyr stepped out and kicked them aside. A skimpy purple thong accentuated her long slender legs, and the sensation of his Fire tingled at the tips of his fingers. He closed his eyes, counted to five in his head, and called it back. Control over his new power was a constant struggle, but Aidan was determined to be the dominant in his relationship with Fire. Before he completed the thought, flames shot out from his hands and feet. *Guess not.*

Zephyr stayed stock still.

Aidan clapped his hands and stomped his feet, snuffing out the flames. "Every time I think I've mastered these powers, they get away from me, but right now, I want my focus only on you." He slipped his hands beneath her tank top and lifted it over her head. A sheer bra matching her barely-there thong completed his waking dream. "You take my breath away."

Zephyr flattened her hands on his chest and slid them down in a slow caress straight to his erect cock. "And you are the hottest man I've ever seen." She stroked him from root to tip. "I've had many sleepless nights fantasizing about feeling you all wet and soapy against me. How about that shower?"

Aidan scooped her off her feet and carried her into the bathroom. He lowered her to the cool tile floor, but she kept her arms draped over his neck and kissed him. The woman tasted like heaven, the perfect combination of sweetness and fire rolled into one. He snaked one hand around her narrow waist, and with the other, he snapped the clasp on her bra. It popped open, and Zephyr stepped back, allowing it to fall to her feet. Her dark brown nipples hardened under his scrutiny, and he leaned down, sucking one of the stiff peaks into his mouth.

"Sh…shower," she murmured.

Her nipple fell from his lips, and a disappointed little gasp fell from hers.

He smiled. "You can't have it both ways. If you want to take a shower, I need to turn on the water."

"K," was the only word she managed this time.

Aidan reached around the glass door and flipped on the water. When he turned back, Zephyr's fingers were tucked beneath the sides of her sexy underwear. She tugged the thin strings down and shimmied her hips until her thong joined her bra on the bathroom floor. Thick clouds of steam filled the room, but they just stood there in the fog, admiring each other. Her gaze raked over his body, and he grew harder.

"Are you sure you don't want our first time to be in a bed?" he asked, ignoring his intense desire to plunge into her heat.

"Positive," she replied, stepping into the shower.

He followed suit without another word and closed the glass door behind him. Zephyr stood beneath the warm spray, water rushing between her full breasts. Her gaze locked onto his, and she squirted a glob of liquid soap into her hands. She rubbed the light blue gel over her nipples and down her stomach. Aidan leaned back against the cool tile wall and watched the show. Her fingers dipped between her legs, and he nearly combusted.

He moved toward her. "You're too good to be real," he said, running his hands down her smooth, wet skin.

"I can assure you that I am *very* real."

She kissed a path from his neck down his slick body, licking her way to his hard cock. Taking him into the heat of her mouth, Zephyr moaned. The vibrations shot along his shaft, driving him to the brink of madness.

"Honey, please, you'll finish me off before we even get started."

She looked up, batting her water-laden eyelashes, and got to her feet. "We wouldn't want that now, would we?"

His voice went husky. "No, we wouldn't."

Aidan smirked and then dropped to his knees, draping one of her long legs over his shoulder. He flicked his tongue over her sweet bud, and she thrust her hips up to meet him.

"I…I n…need you, Aidan." She gasped.

He stood and lifted her into his arms. She wrapped her legs around his waist, clinging to his slick body. Aidan positioned his cock and slipped inside her tight heat. Zephyr lowered her head and kissed him. They moved together in unison, holding tight until they found their release in a simultaneous orgasm for the ages. Even with his memories evading him, Aidan was sure nothing had ever felt this incredible before and likely never would again.

Aidan didn't remember moving to the bed or how many more times they'd made love. He was caught in a frenzy and feared he'd never get enough of Zephyr. They both should've been exhausted, but the press of her ass against his cock had the potential to stir things up again. He adjusted himself and reminded his body this was the first of many times to come.

Zephyr's raspy voice floated through the darkness. "Aidan?"

"Yes, honey."

"I care about the person you are on the inside. You know, it wouldn't have mattered to me if your, uh, equipment didn't work. Pleasure comes in many forms. We would have found our own way."

His cock jumped at the idea of being left out, and he chuckled. "That's sweet, but there is nothing wrong with admitting you're relieved that I'm…*intact* as you put it."

She cleared her throat. "Fine, maybe a little."

"Little?"

"Ha, ha. I was *not* calling you little anywhere. Male egos, seriously."

"My ego is as *intact* as the rest of me," he teased.

The passing of time warped through the endless hours of their lovemaking. When Aidan opened his eyes, the room was still dark. Zephyr slept in his arms, her floral scent permeating the small room. He drank her in, combing his fingers through her long hair, and she automatically snuggled into his touch.

Aidan sighed into the blackness of night. Would he be able to leave Zephyr if it became necessary to keep her safe? Now that he knew what he'd been missing, he doubted he'd have the strength to walk away. But that was a problem for another day. For now, he would enjoy every minute he got to spend with the woman of his dreams.

Chapter Sixteen

Skye

"What's wrong?" Brack asked. "You've been quiet since we hung up with Zeph."

Skye kept her hands on the wheel and her eyes on the road. "Whatever. I guess I ran out of things to say." The man was a clueless wonder.

"Knock it off, Skye. Everything was fine, and now you're giving me the silent treatment. What gives?" His gaze was burning a hole through the side of her head.

"I'm driving. Just minding my own business."

"I'm not going to let up until you tell me what crawled up your ass," Brack pressed.

Skye refused to relent. "Nothing to tell." She glanced over her shoulder and shot him a saccharine smile before turning her attention back to the road.

"Fine, be that way." He crossed his muscular arms over his broad chest.

A jolt of electricity hit her between the legs, and she squeezed her thighs together. *Don't look at the man. Stay tough.* "There is only one way I know how to be, Beck. *My* way."

"You're acting seriously weird. It's not your usual MO. If I didn't know any better, I'd say you were—"

"Don't you dare finish that dimwitted sentence." A warm flush crept up Skye's neck.

"How do you know it was going to be dimwitted?"

"Please, stop speaking. You're giving me a headache."

"Got it, but the motel we're staying at is off the next exit."

She snorted. "While I appreciate your navigational skills, I've got it under control."

Skye's gut churned with the strangest feeling, and she couldn't peg down its origin. It was like boiling stew left on the stove too long, bubbling and burning inside her. *Stupid emotions.* Skye preferred her tightly controlled Protector's nature, the one where she could pretend she didn't care one tiny bit if Brack and Zephyr loved each other.

"Skye?"

"I thought I asked you not to talk."

"But, Skye!" Brack said her name with a hint of desperation.

"Oh, for Goddess's sake, what is it?"

"You, um, just passed the exit."

"Shit."

Seething at her own incompetence, Skye backtracked while Brack remained uncharacteristically quiet. He stared out the window, making it impossible for her to read his expression. How quiet would the guy be when she told him that they were never having sex again?

The silence in the car stretched on, laden with tension even after she reached the turnabout. The entire time she'd been driving back to the motel, Skye couldn't think of a single thing to say to Brack.

Well, that wasn't entirely true. She'd thought of plenty of things to say to him, but none she'd confess aloud. *I hate the thought of you being with another woman, especially my sister. I want to spend every minute with you, and it's driving me nuts. But most of all, I'm scared of how you make me feel.* Skye honestly didn't understand her own jealousy or her own feelings, for that matter. Deep inside, she knew her sister and Brack weren't in love, but hearing Zephyr say those words to him left Skye questioning everything.

She caught sight of the motel's logo peeking out from behind dozens of overgrown shrubs. This time, she pulled off the highway at the correct exit and followed the bright green signs. The parking lot was half full, and Skye navigated over a series of speed bumps, pulling into the first vacant space. She didn't wait for Brack before she jumped out of the car and into the humid night air. If she had to spend one more second trapped in a tight space with the man, she'd snap for sure.

Ignoring her abrupt exit, he got out of the car. Tipping his chin in one of those nods only guys used, he sauntered off and into the motel office. A few minutes later, he returned with a keycard for each of them and slipped one into her hand. The moment his skin contacted hers, Skye's body reacted with its usual awareness. Heat pooled between her legs, and her nipples tightened beneath her lacy bra. Even if she didn't want to admit it, she'd worn the sexy number in the hopes of eliciting a response from him.

Brack stuck to the hot, brooding vibe he had going on. He didn't speak; he simply gestured toward the rear of the motel, got back into the passenger's seat, and closed the car door. Skye slid in behind the wheel, parked the jeep for the second time, and let out a deep breath. She turned to face him, but he rushed out of the car before she could speak.

Things were way less complicated when they weren't having mind-blowing sex. How was she supposed to explain everything to Brack when she had no idea what was happening inside her own head? It was bound to be a hell of a night no matter which way things played out between them.

****

Brack

Brack popped the SUV's hatch. Skye stayed in the car while it idled in its parking space. The windows were rolled up, but he could still make out the muffled lyrics of her favorite song. The dude in the band droned on about unrequited love and being invisible or some shit. Skye was obsessed with this song. He'd heard her blast it a million times and never thought much of it. This time, as he listened, one thing plagued him. Was it like the song said, and she'd sacrifice everything to be with him, or was he the one making all the sacrifices?

Skye was an impossible enigma to decipher. Brack figured it was best to keep quiet, grab his stuff, and head into the hotel. She'd join him eventually, or so he hoped. Swiping the keycard over the pad, the door made its tell-tale click, and Brack pushed his way into the room. He tossed his duffle onto the king-sized bed and headed straight for the bathroom to wash up. Maybe a blast of cold water in the face would provide some much-needed clarity.

How had everything with Skye shifted? Her demeanor had gone from engaged to silent stoicism in 2.3 seconds. Brack unwrapped the tiny bar of hotel soap and ran it under the tap. He scrubbed his face, raked his wet hands through his hair, and then reached for a towel.

No matter how hard he tried, Brack couldn't shake the notion there was something huge he was missing.

All was well right up until she ended the call with her sister. From that moment on, it had been radio silence. Most women wouldn't hesitate to let a guy know the minute he screwed up, but Skye Anani, Protector of Aether, was not most women. He racked his brain, trying to replay the phone call in his head.

Let me think. We were all talking...making plans...Skye was driving...Zephyr said goodbye and...Nah. Couldn't be...could it? Could she be plain old jealous?

It was an odd emotion to pin on Skye. How could *she* be jealous?

He'd kick his own ass if he could. It was right there in front of his face the entire time. Those three little words had the power to change everything—I love you. Skye thought he loved Zephyr, as in, *loved* her, *loved* her. After all the time they'd been spending together lately, not to mention all the ways in which they'd been spending that time, how could Skye believe he could have that with anyone else, especially her own sister?

Torn between frustration and amusement, he opened the bathroom door and prepared to knock some sense into a certain thick-headed female Protector the minute she returned. He didn't get a chance to prepare any sort of speech because Skye burst into the room. She threw her bag onto the bed next to his and plopped down with an irritated harrumph. Brack was the one who had the right to be annoyed. After all, she jumped to an idiotic conclusion that she knew damn well was a bunch of bullshit.

Skye scowled. "Would you like me to stay outside

so you can call Zephyr back and have the private little chat I know you've been dying for?"

"And there it is." Brack returned her scowl. "Don't hold back, Skye. Tell me how you really feel."

"I feel like you're a player and a half. I feel like the runner-up in some whacko contest."

Anger churned inside him. "Wow." He shook his head. "Just, wow. I can't believe you said that to me."

"Zephyr told you that she loved you, and you said it back."

"Those are just words between friends, Skye. I do love your sister. But not romantically, not sexually, and not in any other way than friendship. I thought you understood that better than anyone." He rummaged through his bag, retrieved a 9mm pistol and an extra clip, and stuffed them into his pockets.

"Are you going to shoot me?" she asked, her tone laced with her typical sarcasm.

"Not right now. I'm going for a walk," Brack said, keeping his voice even. He glanced over his shoulder on his way out. "You may want to lock up. I don't know when I'll be back." He walked out and closed the door behind him with a soft click.

The woman made his blood boil. Usually, it was with lust, but at the moment, he was tamping down some pretty heavy indignation. For Brack and Skye, a fine line had always existed between attraction and resentment, but today, the scales tipped in favor of the latter. He set off at a jog and ran straight for the woods behind the motel. Nothing righted him more than connecting to the Earth.

He broke through the tree line of the unfamiliar forest and slowed his pace. After strolling along for a while, he found a seat on a large, flat boulder set into a wide ledge. Many of the same varieties of plant life thrived here as they did in Aether, and Brack relaxed a bit. Closing his eyes, he leaned back on his hands and communed with his Element. The trees and plants whispered in the gentle breeze. The tension in his body eased, but then a sudden and strong wind kicked up around him, sending dirt and debris swirling in the air. *Skye.*

Brack pushed out a heavy breath and opened his eyes. The woman looked like an angry goddess, and he held back a smile. His own irritation melted at the sight of her. She was incredible: powerful, beautiful, intelligent, a real badass.

Her hands flew to her hips. "Um, hello. Why did you walk out like a child?"

"Says the shrew," he mumbled, loud enough for her to hear.

Skye ignored the jab. "I wasn't finished talking to you."

"Talking *to* me or talking *at* me? I wonder if you ever listen to anything other than the sound of your own voice?"

Skye froze, and her mouth dropped open, but only for a second. "Bite me, Beck." She scoffed.

He stepped into her space. "You know I love a challenge, sweetheart."

Props to her for not lowering her gaze, but Brack couldn't allow things to end with a battle between Protectors. It was time he and Skye came to an understanding. And there was only one way he could think of to make her listen. He raised his palms and twisted one hand over the other. Several thick vines snaked along the forest floor right toward Skye.

She eyed him with a death glare. “I dare you.”

“Challenge accepted,” he said, a wicked grin spreading across his face.

Brack tipped his chin, and two willowy branches came down from the tree above her and wound their way around her wrists. The long vines on the ground followed a path around her torso and between her breasts. She gasped, and her cheeks flushed. At that moment, he knew he had her. The woman was turned on.

“Br-aaack.” She said his name as more of a moan than an actual word.

“Yes, sweetheart.”

“W…what are you doing?” He’d never heard her sound so breathy.

“Trying to get your attention. Is it working?”

She nodded, her chest heaving.

“Great, here’s the deal. I’m going to say this for the last time, and you’re going to listen.” Another nod from Skye, and he continued, “You are the one that I want. There is nothing but friendship between your sister and me. I need you to get that through your thick skull. And when my mom is safe, and all this crap is settled, we are going to talk about our future. Got me?”

Skye licked her lips and nodded again.

“Nothing to say?”

She shook her head.

“Good girl,” he said with a smile. Brack raised his palms again, and the bindings slowly loosened their hold on Skye.

The moment her hands were free, she grabbed him by the shirt and got the strangest look in her eyes. Her cheeks glowed lavender against her beautiful light brown skin. “Wait, um, don’t untie me,” she squeaked out.

He was not the kind of man who needed to be told twice. Brack cinched the vines around Skye’s wrists and ankles and moved in to show this stubborn woman how he felt about her. They were way more in sync than either of them had realized. Convincing her they were going to be together sure was going to be fun.

Chapter Seventeen

Zephyr

Aidan dropped her hand to open the door and then grabbed hold of it again. Zephyr wasn't sure if he was a bit anxious or if he was being a typical overprotective Aetherian male. She could take care of herself, but she loved the feel of his callous skin against her own. Giving his hand a reassuring squeeze, she stepped fully inside the busy diner. She scanned the room, looking for Skye and Brack, but Zephyr wasn't prepared for what she saw.

The two were huddled together in the corner of an oversized booth. They were smiling and laughing. Skye's hand rested on Brack's forearm. Dear Goddess, did he nuzzle her neck? Zeph screeched to a halt, knocking Aidan off balance. Good thing the man's reflexes were better than the average human's because he would've taken her to the ground.

"Hey." He scoped the crowd for threats as he righted himself. "What happened?" His warm hands smoothed over her shoulders and down her arms.

"Sorry, but look over there." Zeph pointed to her sister and her best friend, oblivious to the rest of the world. "They look so…so cozy. I wonder if something horrible happened to Ivy."

"I doubt they'd be sitting here flirting if something happened to Brack's mom. Besides, they would've called us."

"Flirting? They are so *not* flirting. Skye and Brack barely tolerate each other. No way they're—"

Brack leaned over and gave Skye a chaste kiss, effectively cutting off any coherent denial on Zephyr's part. She and Aidan stood near the diner's entryway gaping at the pair.

"You're right. They're not flirting. They're making out." He winked at her. "Are we going to stand here, or would you like to join them?"

Zephyr took a deep breath and nodded. "Let's go."

Skye glanced up and caught Zephyr's eye. She jumped away from Brack as if he was a grenade about to go off. A deep blush colored her sister's cheeks. Skye's I've-got-it-all-together vibe was nowhere in sight, yet by the time they reached the table, she had her Protector's mask firmly back in place. But it was too late; even her sister's cool demeanor couldn't change what happened in front of a room full of people. Zephyr felt as if she had been sleepwalking and woke up in a strange new reality. In the real world, the one in which she presently resided, her best friend and her sister would never share a kiss in a million years.

Brack appeared relaxed and casual, his arm slung over the back of the booth. What was up with that? She decided on the spot that it would be way more fun to watch Skye squirm than to confront them directly. Plus, Ivy's safety was paramount, and they needed to focus. Too bad because Zeph would've really enjoyed this moment.

"You guys are early," Skye said, toying with the end of one of her braids.

"Yeah, no cars on the road." Zephyr shot a

suspicious glare at her sister. "Mind if we join you?"

"Duh, we've been waiting for you all morning." She nudged Brack with an elbow. "Back off and make some room."

Brack leaned into Skye and whispered loud enough for them to hear, "Watch it, sweetheart. You don't want to say something you might have to pay for later."

The look Brack gave her sister was one she didn't recognize. His eyes were shining with their usual challenge, but this time, they held intense desire in their dark brown depths.

He turned back to Zephyr and Aidan, all signs of that other Brack gone. "Hey, glad you had a good ride. Thanks for coming."

"Of course, you're my best friend. I'd do anything for you and Ivy."

"How fabulous for you both." Skye rolled her eyes. "But can we please cut to the chase here? Ivy doesn't have the luxury of time." She threw Brack a death glare. "Why don't you tell them the plan?"

"Well, we don't exactly have a plan per se. It's more of a loose concept." Brack fidgeted with his water glass.

"Got it. That's code for we have no idea what we're doing." Zephyr rubbed her temples. "Great."

Brack propped his elbows on the table. "That's not entirely true. We do have a fair amount of kick-ass Elemental powers among us."

Aidan broke his silence. "I'm afraid those powers weren't much help to Ashlyn when the doctor held her captive. Barrington possesses weapons in his arsenal to combat your powers, and if my restored memories are correct, I have no doubt his team has continued with his work in spite of his death. His people will do anything to control the Elements."

"We're meeting with Ward this afternoon." Brack tipped a chin toward the busy diner. "Here, in a public place. My guess is this guy has no powers, and he's intimidated by us."

Something niggled in the back of Zephyr's mind. "How would Barrington's people know about you, Brack? Ivy would never tell them about her son, about Aether, no matter what." A light breeze swirled around their feet. Her Element agreed with her instincts. "I can't explain it, but my gut tells me this Ward guy is legit. Call it Guardian's intuition."

Brack's eyes went cold, and his nostrils flared. "I sure as hell hope you're right because if he hurts my mom in any way, I'll kill him without hesitation."

"As much as I believe in Zephyr's Guardian gifts—" Aidan turned to her and smiled. "I think I can help with a plan in case Ward turns out to be an enemy. My military training has been flooding back to me recently."

"Thanks. I'd appreciate any expertise beyond our Protector training. Although we are well trained, we tend to rely on our control over the Elements, and as you reminded us, it might not be enough in this case," Brack said.

This humble version of her best friend was as much a mystery as the embarrassed version of her sister was. A strange look passed between Brack and Skye. Zephyr clenched her teeth to keep her mouth from dropping open and put it out of her head until she had time to unwrap whatever was happening here.

A small stack of paper kids' menus sat by the edge of the table. Aidan unfolded one and grabbed a crayon. Somehow even holding a bright orange crayon, which nearly disappeared in his massive grip, the man looked sexy as hell. Zephyr tried not to think about Aidan as a small boy or what their children might look like. *Hello, time, place, Zephyr.*

He flipped it over to the blank side and drew a rough sketch of the building. "You should meet him alone, Brack. This way Zephyr, Skye, and I can keep you covered with conventional weapons. We'll stay hidden. The thick vegetation around here is good camouflage. If any of Barrington's mercenaries are backing him up, we can take them out."

Skye's gaze narrowed. "No way I'm leaving Brack alone with this guy."

What did her sister just say? Zephyr was stunned into silence.

"He wouldn't be alone. All of us would be right outside," Aidan explained.

Brack slid closer to Skye. "I've got this." He slipped an arm around her shoulder. "Besides, you're the best sharpshooter ever, and you'll have my six."

She shoved his hand off. "Of course, but there's no need to get all mushy about it."

For the next several hours, they drank gallons of coffee and ate mountains of pancakes, eggs, and waffles. Aidan drew more detailed plans and handed out assignments like the commander he had once been. Tyler Ward and Brack would meet in a few short hours, and they headed back to the hotel to gather weapons and the materials provided by Cadence. Zephyr said a silent prayer to the God and Goddess that the man could help them bring Ivy home to Aether.

If Zephyr helped to end Barrington's reign and saved Ivy, maybe the Elders would finally see beyond her abilities as a Guardian? *Zephyr Anani, Guardian of the House of Air and Protector of Aether. Keep dreaming and never stop.*

****

Skye

Her stomach fluttered with a sea of butterflies, and not the good kind. The realization that Skye considered Brack's safety above all others, even Ivy's, was not lost on her. She peeked out from behind the prickly shrub Aidan assigned her as a post. The mass of spiky foliage did nothing to block the burning summer sun, and she was beginning to resemble a pin cushion from its three-inch thorns. Dressed in a camo T-shirt and matching cargo shorts helped her blend into the background even if it did nothing to protect her bare flesh from being torn to shreds.

Skye wiped her sweaty palms down the sides of her shorts and practiced taking slow, even breaths. As a Protector, she was used to being in complete control, but as her mind sorted through all the possible outcomes, her stress level skyrocketed. *What the hell is happening to me? You're a Protector of Aether. Get it together, girl.*

When she truly considered it, the notion of Brack being taken out was inconceivable. His fighting skills in both hand-to-hand and with conventional human weapons were highly coveted among the Protectors, but his control over all things botanical was his most impressive skill by far. Brack's gift was rare, only surpassed by Brynn, Guardian of the House of Earth. Suffice it to say, the guy kicked ass when the occasion called for it. In addition, the team, as they'd come to call themselves, would protect each other at all costs. So, why was Skye off balance? It had to be Brack's fault.

Perhaps, he'd put her under some sort of spell, or maybe his penis was magically enhanced. Either way, she feared she was doomed.

She gathered her courage and glanced through the window. To the casual eye, Brack appeared comfortable inside the air-conditioned diner, but when she looked more carefully, signs of his nervousness radiated off the man. The bounce of his body told Skye his legs were jiggling beneath the table. Brack's gaze darted around the diner until it settled on one of the large picture windows. She could feel his steely gaze searching for something. He had the same look in his eyes as when they were tracking prey in the forest of Aether. She sensed his power seeking her out from beneath the cover of her camouflage.

The thorns, which had been scratching up every inch of her exposed skin, retracted until the branches were smooth. *Brack.* Skye's mouth went bone dry, and she froze in place. She parted the now tame greens and sought out his gaze through the glass. He looked directly at her, and the dirty rat had the nerve to wink. Before she could process the annoying yet still somehow sexy gesture, a vine crawled along the ground toward her right ankle. Scowling, she dragged her pointer finger across her throat in a cutting motion, gesturing for him to knock it off. Brack smiled and tossed her another wink.

Too bad the distraction didn't last very long. A car with a single male driver pulled into the lot, and the entire team shifted into high-alert mode. Inside the crowded diner, Brack sat up ramrod straight, his gaze focused on the new arrival exiting his vehicle.

The guy stepped out of a non-descript gray sedan and into the bright sunlight. He glanced over each shoulder at least half a dozen times. Can you say paranoid? Skye stayed low behind her shrub and double checked Gigi, her favorite Glock. Aidan had been remorseful when he handed her back over to Skye. He assured her that he only wanted to borrow the weapon to keep Zephyr safe. There wasn't much of an argument after he confessed and apologized. Besides, Gigi never looked better. Captain Aidan Drake had skills when it came to taking care of a weapon. Not to mention, the former soldier was risking his life to help save Ivy, which was enough of a reason for Skye to forgive him.

She raised her weapon and focused on the new target. It had to be Tyler Ward from the way the man was behaving. Skye couldn't make out the details of his face from her hidey-hole, but he was tall and broad with jet-black hair and light brown skin. He locked his car and walked toward the entry of the diner. His steps were slow and deliberate, as if he could feel eyes on him from all directions. This guy was no dummy; no doubt he was aware he was being watched. Skye had a strong sense that they shouldn't underestimate Tyler Ward.

Fifty yards out was a stretch for Gigi, and every muscle in her body tightened at once. She tossed a glance over her shoulder. Aidan peered out from his post, a thick-trunked oak with not a single thorn in sight. He narrowed his eyes and shook his head at Skye. She ignored the soldier's silent directive. After all, the guy wasn't her superior. He wasn't a Protector or even a true Aetherian, for that matter. Crouching low, she edged her way toward the window. Twenty-five yards, and she'd nail Ward between the eyes before he could blink. The stranger's gaze zeroed in on Brack who was seated in the corner booth that Aidan had selected for its vantage point. Ward moved toward him. If the table hadn't been bolted to the floor, Brack would've toppled it by now.

Even through the glass, it was easy to recognize the unusual way he held himself. For the most part, he was the epitome of cool, but the man seated behind the table did not resemble the Brack she knew in any way. His shoulders were bunched up to his ears, and his knee jerking had reached epic proportions.

But when Tyler Ward came to a stop in front of Brack, all movement ceased, including Skye's. She was able to take in the details of Ward's face for the first time, and a gasp slipped from her lips of its own accord. The man looked like an older version Brack. He had the same skin tone, dark eyes, and hair. They even had the same square-cut jaw, except Brack's was always covered with at least an inch of scruff. Ward was clean shaven and wore a pair of black-framed glasses. He appeared every bit the scientist he claimed to be. But who was this man, and why did he look so much like Bracken Beck?

Chapter Eighteen

Brack

Beneath the table, Brack's knees bounced in an incessant rhythm. He hadn't heard his mother's voice in days, and his mounting fears were taking their toll on his nerves. The chime above the door sounded, and the stranger stepped inside. He was dressed in a short-sleeved button-down that was tucked neatly into a pair of pressed khakis. This guy fit the picture of a lab nerd down to his black-framed glasses. No doubt he was fully human though he was built like the men back home, tall and broad. Stopping in the doorway, he zeroed in on Brack. As he drew nearer, the Protector ran through every scenario in his training but prayed he didn't have to use any of his deadly skills.

"Hello, Brack." The man extended his hand. "I'm Tyler Ward."

A chill ran down his spine. He'd never seen this person before, but somehow, he struck Brack as familiar. Speaking became a lost art as his words clogged in his windpipe. His senses zinged, and he sat frozen in place. He'd been around quite a few typical humans in the past, but this was different.

The man's Aetherian-sized palm hovered in front of Brack for a full twenty seconds before he shook off his bizarre emotional response and accepted the guy's hand.

He gave it a halfhearted shake, but when he tried to retract it, Ward kept a firm hold and squeezed. Brack didn't want to be a jerk, but this was weirdness at its highest level. He tugged against Ward's hold, and the man lost his bewitched gaze, releasing Brack's hand as if he'd awoken from a spell.

"Sorry about that. But I'm really happy to finally meet you." Ward sobered. "Though I never dreamed it would be at Ivy's expense." He tipped his chin toward the bench seat opposite Brack. "Do you mind?"

"Uh, yeah, sure," Brack mumbled as a way of an invitation.

Sliding into the booth, Ward's gaze remained oddly fixated on him. Once the man was settled, Brack had his first opportunity to check him out. He appeared to be in his early forties with coloring similar to Brack's with the exception of his hair which was sprinkled with subtle flecks of gray.

Brack folded his hands on the table. "Let's get to it, shall we? I want my mother out of harm's way immediately. Can you make that happen, or am I wasting my time here?"

"I knew you'd be like this." Ward smiled. "Have a no-nonsense attitude, I mean." He let out a soft, sad-sounding chuckle. "Ivy has told me everything about you, but meeting you in person is a little surreal."

Brack lifted a single brow. "Yeah, well, she hasn't told me a thing about you. So, how about we skip all the kumbaya crap, and you tell me who the hell you really are?"

"I am someone who cares about Ivy Beck more than anything in the world."

Ward reached into his pocket, pulled out a phone,

and placed it on the table in front of him. It was the floral case Brack had gotten his mother as a gift for no other reason than he knew she'd love it. His stomach dropped, and he fought to keep his composure. If anyone hurt her, he didn't know what he might be capable of.

"I realize this must be strange for you. Maybe if you hear it directly from Ivy, you'll feel more comfortable." Ward nudged the phone toward him. "Hit play."

He did as the man instructed, and a grainy video appeared on the screen. A tired-looking picture of his mom came into focus. Her long hair was pulled back into a ponytail, and her eyes were a bit red and puffy. Otherwise, she looked unharmed.

Her voice emerged in a hushed whisper. "Hi, baby. Firstly, I'm all right. I'm sure you're worried, and I'm so sorry. I never imagined this could happen." His mom nodded to a person off camera. "Please, Brack, you have to listen to me. I don't have much time. Tyler is a friend…a very special friend, and I need for you to trust him." She flashed the camera a confident smile, but Brack could tell it was forced. "I love you, and I'm counting on you."

His mother's pretty face disappeared and was replaced by a black screen. The phone slipped from Brack's fingers and clattered to the laminate table. He took a deep breath, straightened, and met Tyler's gaze.

"I'm with you, but if I find out you're lying to me, I *will* kill you."

Ward sat up straighter. "Got it. But I'm not lying to you. I would never lie to you."

"O…okay. Do you have an actual plan, or are we winging it?"

"I have a plan. Ivy guessed there would be more of

you, so I worked off that premise. How about I pay the check, and you go tell your friends hiding outside not to shoot me? I can fill all of you in on my idea at once."

He smiled. Maybe Tyler Ward truly was a friend, like his mom said. Trust didn't come easily to Brack, but it seemed he didn't have much of a choice if he wanted to save her.

"Good deal, but I can pay my own way." He stood and slapped a twenty on the table. "I'll gather the team and meet you outside."

He left Ward to handle the check and headed straight for Skye's self-assigned post. She jumped out from behind her camouflage of bushes before he reached her. Zephyr and Aidan materialized from their hidden positions and joined them as well.

"Well? What happened? What did he say? How's Ivy?" Skye hammered him with a stream of questions.

"Yes, please, answer all those questions at once," Zephyr said.

Brack took both of Skye's hands in his and watched Zephyr go still. His best friend's reaction would have to wait. Right now, the only thing that mattered was reassuring Skye and saving his mother.

"My mom is okay. He showed me a video of her. She says this guy is the real deal…a…a friend of hers. I think we have to trust him because we're useless on our own."

"I have faith in your instincts." Skye squeezed his hands. "And I most definitely have faith in Ivy's word."

Brack turned to the soldier. "Drake?"

"I reserve the right to make my own assessment after meeting the man." Captain Aidan Drake had never sounded more like a marine than he did right now.

“Fair enough.” Brack nodded, not even attempting to hold back a smirk. Things were about to get interesting.

****

Skye

She perched her butt on the jeep’s tailgate and focused on the diner’s exit. The door jingled, and Ward emerged. In the time it had taken for him to walk outside, Skye had convinced herself she’d been mistaken about the strong resemblance between the stranger and Brack. She had to give the guy props. They were a pretty intimidating group, and he made a beeline for them anyway. Most ordinary humans would’ve shit themselves facing the collective power of their team, but Ward’s posture remained relaxed. Skye surmised he was either familiar with Elementals or was too clueless to be frightened.

Aidan stood stiffly, easing Zephyr behind him as Ward drew nearer. Skye was pleased to see the good Captain had his priorities straight. He leaned down to Zephyr and asked in a gentle tone, “Is your crossbow loaded?”

Her sister’s new boyfriend was more Aetherian than she realized, and Skye wrangled in her amusement. The free-spirited Zephyr now had her very own shadow, and Skye couldn’t wait to watch their relationship develop. Poor Aidan was in for the run of his life with The Guardian of Air as a partner.

“Yes, Captain.” Zephyr gave a mock salute. “But can you please chill? Ivy said the guy is a friend.”

“How do we know Ivy didn’t have a gun to her head when she vouched for him?” He looked at Brack, pity in his eyes. “Sorry, but we have to consider the possibility.”

"Believe me, I did consider it, but I know my mother, and I could see the truth in her eyes," Brack ground out.

Aidan nodded in lieu of a response. Brack tipped his chin to the soldier and stepped up to greet Ward. The instinct to protect Brack flooded her system, and Skye strode forward, clutching Gigi to her chest. She eyed Tyler Ward from head to toe. Aidan moved next to Skye and planted Zephyr safely between them.

Ward smiled, and Skye's heart nearly stopped. Tyler Ward was wearing Bracken Beck's slightly crooked smile. It was as if the man stepped through a time machine, hurtling Brack years into the future and spitting him back out again. She swallowed the lump in her throat, and garbled sounds came out of her mouth instead of words. Zephyr gasped, and she knew her sister was on the same page regarding the doppelgangers. On the other side of Zeph, the soldier went rigid, casting an inquisitive glare on their new arrival.

The Protector in Skye seized control of her body, and she walked straight up to Ward, her Glock raised. "Out with it, buddy. Who the hell are you *really*?"

"I understand trust takes time." Ward's gaze zinged from her Glock to Zeph's crossbow and finally to Aidan's double sidearms. "But I assure you, I'm no threat to any of you." He gestured back to Gigi and lifted his hands in surrender. "I promise."

"Skye." Brack took her by the elbow and yanked her backward.

Gaze fixed on Ward, she lowered her weapon but didn't move away.

"Come on." Brack turned to her, his expression pinched. "Take it easy, will you?"

"Whatever," she mumbled, holstering Gigi.

He growled back something inaudible and forced a smile for Ward. "Tyler, this is the team."

The stranger, wearing another one of Brack's expressions, ignored the introduction and made direct eye contact with Skye. His voice was soft and gentle. "To answer your question, young lady, I am a friend who only wants to help Ivy. I hope that's enough because it's the best I can do for right now."

"And *we* appreciate your help." Brack shot Skye a warning look. "Getting my mom out of harm's way is this team's only concern." He joined his friends, sliding into place next to her. "And as I started to say before, this is the team. Drake, Zephyr, and *this—"* He wrapped an arm around her waist, tugging her closer. "—is Skye."

He may as well have added "my" to her name with the possessive way he held her. Skye wasn't sure if she was turned on or if she wanted to slap him across the face. The two of them always managed to walk this sort of tightrope.

Tyler cleared his throat. "I'm pleased to meet all of you."

Aidan's deep voice boomed in the quiet parking lot. "What can you tell us about where Ivy is being held?"

"Barrington was nothing if not thorough. The security measures are extremely high tech, but Brack tells me you've brought some equipment to combat their systems. I have a cabin nearby with all the intel and materials I've gathered. Why don't you follow me, and I can show what I've got, then we can come up with a plan together?"

"Negative." Sparks flared at the tips of the soldier's fingers. "Your location is an unknown factor and therefore not secure," the soldier answered robotically, giving Skye a glimpse of the old Mr. Heller.

Ward's eyes went saucer wide, and he eased back a few feet. Zephyr placed a gentle hand on Aidan's forearm, refocusing his attention. The blue sparks sizzled and extinguished in a tiny puff of smoke.

The soldier gazed down and shook his head. "Sorry," he grumbled to no one in particular.

"You…you make fire?" Ward's words stuttered out as a half question, half statement.

Skye's theory about the guy being familiar with Elementals went straight out the window. Or perhaps, it was only Drake's Fire he'd never experienced before. He claimed to be a special friend of Ivy's, which meant he had to have some knowledge of their people. Brack's mother's gift was part of the collective balance, but it was nothing compared to her son's talents. She had the touch as the Elders would say, and her child possessed uncommon gifts. Ivy could make almost anything grow, in any soil type, but she couldn't control botanicals the way Brack could.

Her sister clasped Aidan's fireless hand. "Yes, he does. I thought you said you knew about us, about Ivy?"

"Ivy is special, and she tried to explain Aether to me, but—" Tyler pointed a shaky finger at Aidan. "—I've never seen anything like that before."

"Yeah, well, try waking up on fire and get back to me," Drake said, dropping Zeph's hand and crossing his muscular arms over his chest.

Zephyr recoiled, and Skye could read the heartache in her sister's eyes. She could appreciate the soldier's anger and frustration. After all, he'd been drugged, kidnapped, his team murdered, and then he'd been transformed into an Aetherian. It was a lot for an ordinary human to take. Although the more Skye thought about it, the more she realized Captain Aidan Drake hadn't been particularly ordinary to begin with.

"I'm very sorry for what was done to you, but I hope you know I had nothing to do with that. It's only been a few weeks since Ivy insisted that I get a job at Barrington's lab," Ward said.

"My mom asked you to get a job at the lab? Why?" Brack asked.

"To help stop Barrington's work from continuing and to protect Aether," Tyler simply stated.

"Why would you care about helping Aether?" Skye asked, her curiosity piqued.

"Because *Ivy* cares about Aether." Ward let out a deep breath. "Please, she needs us. Can't you trust me, for Ivy's sake?"

"Fine," Aidan answered. "But we will do a full sweep of the area when we arrive."

Captain Aidan Drake was a natural leader and inserted himself as commander of their makeshift team. He didn't ask Ward; he told him. Brack bristled slightly. On the other hand, Skye was thankful for Drake's presence, and not for the first time since they'd set off on this mission.

"Whatever makes you feel comfortable is good by me, but can we please go now? Ivy is running out of time."

The soldier nodded, took Zephyr by the hand, and led her to the jeep they'd arrived in. Her sister glanced over her shoulder, catching Skye's eye. Zeph wore an expression only a twin could see through. The one who said, I've gotten hot and heavy with a lunatic. Skye knew it well. She'd started wearing the very same expression the moment she realized she was falling for Bracken Beck.

Chapter Nineteen

Brack

"Enough!" Brack said, sharply. "I can feel your laser eyes burning a hole in the side of my head."

Skye sighed and shifted in the passenger seat next to him. "You honestly don't see it?"

"See what?" he said, his response Pavlovian.

He should've realized something was up the minute Skye handed him the key fob and told him to drive. She required a certain amount of control, and her suggestion should've set off alarm bells in his head. But Brack had been too focused on his mom and her safety to consider Skye's intent.

"I'm not sure how you can be so obtuse. The resemblance between you and Ward is uncanny."

"In your opinion." He huffed out a frustrated breath.

"Hello, in *everyone's* opinion." She leaned in, her tone emphatic. "Didn't you see Zephyr's face?"

He tugged his favorite shield, sarcasm, in place and forced a smile. "I've seen her face a million times. Not sure what you mean." Of course, he'd noticed her reaction, but Zeph was in a weird headspace, and he didn't believe it had anything to do with Ward or Brack.

"Can you say denial?"

"Oh please, Zephyr has been a freak ever since the soldier came into the picture, and you know it. Besides, just because the guy has the same coloring as me doesn't mean we look alike. We…we're… the same type is all."

Skye coughed, doing a poor job of covering a full-blown laugh. "Seriously, Brack, you two look more alike than Zephyr and I do, and we're twins, in case you forgot."

"Your imagination is working overtime."

He gripped the steering wheel a little tighter. Skye was apparently losing her mind. He and Ward didn't look alike. Brack chalked it up to her lack of experience with those outside their world. Most Aetherians weren't used to close contact with typical humans. Perhaps to Skye, they all resembled one another.

"I want to state for the record that you will owe me a groveling apology when this guy turns out to be—" She made a circling motion with her hand. "—some…long lost relative of yours."

"Yeah, whatever." Brack chuckled. "I'll make you a deal. I promise to find all sorts of ways to apologize to you." He waggled his brows. "But maybe you should think about how you're going to pay up once your baseless hunch turns out to be a load of crap."

Skye smirked, reclined her seat a bit, and closed her eyes, all while keeping that irritating expression plastered on her face. Brack had no desire to unpack the baggage her suspicions presented. One dilemma at a time. First, he would save his mom, and then, he'd deal with Skye and her conspiracy theory.

Brack stuck close to Ward's tail. The gray sedan meandered for miles along the winding country highway, and after about fifteen minutes, Ward pulled onto a long, unpaved road. He came to a final stop in front of a small log cabin. Nestled among the trees, it boasted a wide front porch and was perfectly blended into its surroundings.

Tyler parked on the far left, leaving room for him to follow suit. Aidan and Zephyr's jeep arrived a few seconds later and stopped on Brack's other side. The isolated cabin Ward rented was an ideal location to work up their plan. The soldier was out of the car before Brack could blink. He brandished a gun in each hand and was already sweeping the area for threats when Brack turned back to Skye.

She stopped pretending to sleep and removed her Glock from the holster strapped across her chest. Her breasts were wrapped in black bands of material, and keeping his mind in the game seemed an impossible task. It reminded Brack of the vines tied around Skye's body and the way she'd come undone for him. She nudged him with the barrel of her gun, effectively snapping him out of the haze of lust-filled memories.

"Are you kidding?" She glared at him as he tore his gaze from her breasts. "Is that really the first place your mind goes?"

"You don't have any idea where my mind is at," he said. But didn't she?

"Oh, please, you don't think I recognize that look in your eyes by now?" She waved a hand in front of his face. "Your vibe reads horny teenager who can't keep it in his pants."

"Only around you. Every time I look at you, my dick goes instantly hard, and all I can think about is getting you naked. It's a real problem," he said, stepping out of the car and closing the door.

Leaving Skye speechless was becoming one of his favorite things to do—besides making her orgasm, of course. She stayed in the car for a full minute and then emerged red faced. Sparring with her had become a strange sort of aphrodisiac for them both. Brack wasn't sure what that said about them, but he didn't much care.

She pointed a finger in his direction and glared. "We can talk about your problem at a more appropriate time. Until then, not another word. Understood?"

Fighting a chuckle, he raised a hand. "Got it. Protector's honor."

"Have I told you lately you're a real ass?"

"Come on, admit it, you kind of like me sometimes."

The color in her cheeks darkened. "Maybe…once in a while."

Feeling smug, Brack relished the subject change. Skye, on the other hand, rolled her eyes and walked away to join her sister and Aidan in their search. The soldier's posture was stiff as he directed the group to fan out in four directions. The dude had some serious issues to work through.

"Meet back here when you've finished your sweep, and stay frosty," Captain Drake ordered.

Brack's gut told him Tyler had his mother's best interest at heart, and he believed her to be sincere during the short video he watched. Everything about her demeanor had been quintessential Ivy Beck. There was nothing forced about it, but everyone in the group had to be on the same page. Appeasing the soldier with a quick search of the area was easy enough to comply with.

Tyler waited on the cabin's front steps while the team conducted a basic search of the surrounding area. It didn't take long for Aidan to declare the perimeter safe, and soon they were seated around Ward's kitchen table. Tyler put on a pot of coffee, and they sat stoically, trading awkward glances.

Edgy and restless, Brack had to escape, if only for a minute or two. “Um, may I please use your bathroom?” he asked.

“Of course.” Tyler pointed in the direction of the narrow passageway behind them. “It’s down the hall at the back of the cabin.”

“Thanks,” Brack muttered, race-walking toward the bathroom.

He didn’t stop until he reached the stark, white-tiled room. Head spinning, Brack sat on the edge of the tub and took a series of deep breaths. Muffled voices floated in from beneath the crack under the door. Maybe he should’ve stayed in the bathroom, but curiosity gnawed at him. A tiny peek inside the rest of the man’s rental unit couldn’t hurt. Brack crept out of the bathroom, leaving the light on, and closed the door with a soft click.

With his back to the wall, he skulked toward one of the two open doors at the back of the cabin. He slipped inside the first room, which was set up as an office. Large maps and printouts of floor plans covered one entire wall. Photos of faces he did not recognize were tacked to a board in the corner. Tyler Ward had been doing his homework on Barrington’s newest lab, but how did his mother fit into this equation?

Something propelled Brack further, and he inched his way out of the office. What he was searching for, he did not know. On quiet feet, he cracked the next open door. The room was sparsely furnished, with a queen-sized bed in the center and two matching nightstands. Light from the hallway glistened off a silver frame set on one of the bedside tables. He picked it up and gazed down at his mother’s smiling face. A dark-haired, dark-eyed young man had his arm draped over her shoulders. They were both beaming down at a baby wrapped in a pale blue blanket Brack immediately recognized from his childhood.

Hands shaking, he pulled his phone from his pocket and snapped a picture of the framed photo. What the hell did this mean? Brack's stomach did a somersault. Maybe Skye was right about Tyler Ward being a relative, but why the big secret?

****

Aidan

Brack returned from the bathroom with a vacant look in his eyes. His hands were shoved deep into the pockets of his jeans, and he tossed a couple of surreptitious glances in Ward's direction. Aidan's Fire tingled under his skin. Until now, the Protector had been solid under the pressure of his mother's captivity. He couldn't fathom what might've happened to Brack in the time it took him to go to the latrine. Aidan settled his Fire and gripped the handgun balanced on his thigh. Skye must have picked up on Brack's sudden change of demeanor because before Aidan could form a question, she hopped out of her seat and was by the Protector's side.

"Hey, you were gone a while. I was getting worried." The tender concern in Skye's voice spoke volumes about their change in relationship status.

"Yeah. Nervous stomach, I guess," Brack muttered.

Skye shot him a death glare in response to the obvious lie. Aidan almost burst out laughing. He bet Zephyr big money that those two were sleeping together. The entire drive to Ward's, they'd alternated discussing the fact her sister and her best friend were caught blatantly kissing and how much Zeph thought Ward looked exactly like Brack. Aidan admitted the resemblance between the two men was undeniable, but he couldn't get Zephyr to budge on Skye and Brack being together. According to his stubborn Guardian, there was no way they would be hooking up in a million years. Zephyr insisted the whole thing was a prank. *Best prank I ever saw.*

Ward's voice went soft. "Can I get you anything, Brack?"

"I'm fine, thanks. I'd really like to hear about your intel," Brack replied, his tone flat.

"Oh, um, of course." Ward stood. "I have everything set up in the spare bedroom. Follow me."

Aidan got to his feet and tucked his gun into the waistband of his jeans. Zephyr took his hand, and they walked behind the others toward the back of the cabin. The room they entered was devoid of furniture except for an old metal desk and a rickety office chair. The walls were plastered with maps and floor plans. In the far corner sat a whiteboard on wheels with a half dozen photos taped to it and names scrawled in black marker beneath each one. Ward opened several folding chairs propped against the wall and took a seat in front of the desk, his chair turned toward them.

"Wow, this is really something," Zephyr said, scanning the room.

"The more prepared we are, the better our chances are of getting Ivy out safely. Barrington may be dead, but those who are loyal to him haven't given up on his plans." Ward walked over to the whiteboard and pointed to a photo of a woman. "This is Mary Allen."

"And why should we be afraid of some ordinary

human woman?" Skye asked.

"Mary Allen is anything but ordinary. The woman has been Barrington's pawn for nearly thirty years. She was his mistress and is the mother of his son. From what I hear, in her youth, Mary was so enamored with the doctor she became highly vulnerable to his manipulation. Once he had her under his control, there was nothing left of the poor girl except an empty shell. Since Barrington's death, she's grown irrational and dangerous…very dangerous." Ward plucked the picture off the board and passed it to Brack.

The Protector glared at the photo and then handed it to him. Aidan stared at the woman's face, and his blood went cold. Her pale blue eyes leaped from the picture and bore straight through him. She looked familiar, and an eerie chill skated along his spine.

Zephyr leaned into his space. "Aidan? Do you recognize her?"

He swallowed the lump lodged in his throat and nodded. "I think so."

An array of internal fireworks went off inside Aidan, or maybe it was his Elemental powers. At the moment, the *which* wasn't important; it was the *why* he needed to figure out. There was something about the woman in the photo triggering this reaction. Aidan hoped that rescuing Ivy might also lead him on a path to fill in the gaping holes in his memory. If Mary Allen had those answers, he would seek her out whether the others approved or not.

Skye grabbed the photo out of his hands. "Let me see that." She examined the picture. "Looks like a regular old *Karen* to me," she said, handing the photo to Brack.

"Hardly," Ward half spoke, half sighed. "Mary has been running the lab for several weeks now. She's even gotten her pawn of a son, Thomas, under her thumb. The woman is hell-bent on collecting and controlling all Elemental powers, and she doesn't care who gets hurt, Aetherian or typical human. As I said, I haven't been there long, but it's been long enough to see the woman is unstable."

"We'll do our best to avoid her at all costs." Brack stared at the photo in his hands, crushing the edges.

Ward eased the picture from his grip and tacked it back on the board. "Trust me, the last thing we want is a run in with that woman."

"Then our timing will be crucial, but I'm sure we can handle it. Do you know where they're holding my mother?" Brack asked.

"Ivy is in one of the cells on the underground level. Access to her is restricted." Ward stiffened. "I haven't been able to sneak in over the last couple of days, and I'm getting worried."

"Getting worried? We've been insane with worry this entire time," Skye snapped. "Do you mind if I ask you how Ivy found herself in this situation, to begin with?" Her tone was laced with accusation.

Ward returned to his chair and rested his elbows on his knees. "Believe me when I tell you it wasn't my idea." He looked up, his eyes glistening. "Ivy is impossible to stop when she sets her mind to something."

"Don't I know it," Brack mumbled under his breath.

Tyler's lips pulled into a sad smile, and he nodded. "One of Barrington's team discovered Ivy using her powers and reported her to Allen. I had to pretend to be shocked or they would've captured us both. The next day, I managed to steal Ivy's confiscated phone from the security office. I brought it to her, but there's no signal in the cells. She begged me not to call you, but I didn't know what else to do."

Brack approached Ward and clapped a hand on his shoulder. "You did the right thing. We're going to get her out, and then, you are both going to explain a few things to me." Something in the Protector's demeanor shifted, his gaze fixed on Tyler. Aidan wondered what he'd missed.

"Fair enough," Tyler said.

"Um, I hate to interrupt this little moment, but do you have an actual plan to free Ivy?" Skye asked.

"Mostly, but I'll need your help to pull it off," Ward admitted. He reached into a bin on the desk and pulled out four lanyards with clear plastic sleeves hanging from them. "I got these, but we'll need to add photos."

"And what are we supposed to do with those?" Skye sneered at the blank ID badges as if they were poisonous.

"I've taken the liberty of creating aliases for you and your sister. You'll act as my new lab assistants, Dr. Camila Rivera and Dr. Sofia Lopez," Ward said.

"And us?" Aidan asked, gesturing to himself and Brack.

Ward gave them each a slip of paper. One was labeled Nathan Jackson, the other Bradley Smith. "Security guards. If you fill out those forms, I'll have uniforms overnighted." Tyler eyed both Aidan and the Protector with assessing gazes. "Some rather large uniforms." A small smile crept across his lips but was lost as he turned serious again. "I control my own hiring, so I had no trouble adding the women to my department's files, but security is handled by a private firm. Devlin, Barrington's former right-hand man, established it. As I'm sure you are aware, he was killed when your Guardian of Fire was freed. He must have left one hell of a legacy because I haven't come close to breaking into their system to add your aliases to their roster. I thought I knew a lot about computers, but Devlin created an uncrackable line of defense."

"I think we can help you out with any tech issues. We have a hacker with unparalleled skills." Brack smirked.

"Cadence," Zephyr whispered.

Aidan's memories were still pretty spotty, but he was certain he'd never been part of a team quite like this one before, and for the first time in a long time, he felt a part of something special.

Chapter Twenty

Zephyr

The team was on edge. Everyone sat around Ward's table, staring at Brack's phone. He hit send, and the speaker crackled in the silent room.

Cadence answered in a strained whisper, "It's about freaking time. I've been calling and texting for the last two hours."

"Sorry." Brack cringed. "There's a lot going on here."

"Yeah, well, there's a lot going on here too."

"Out with it, Cade. We don't have time to play games," Skye piped in.

"That is one true statement, my friend. Hawk knows you guys are gone, and I don't think I can avoid him much longer." Zephyr could sense Cadence's stress seeping through the phone line.

"Well, maybe you can help us with one last thing before he busts you. I need you to hack into the security company's computers and add two new guards to their team." Brack glanced down at the papers Tyler gave them. "Nathan Jackson and Bradley Smith. I'll email you the details and whatever else we've got as soon as we hang up."

"Consider it done." Papers rustled over the line, and Cadence clicked off without saying goodbye.

“This is not a good sign,” Skye stated the obvious.

“You think?” Brack’s lip curled in a mock sneer.

“Trying to keep it real.” Skye smirked.

“Skye, Skye, Skye,” Brack said, shaking his head. “Do we need to have another little chat?”

Her sister flushed from head to toe but stayed uncharacteristically quiet. Things were getting more interesting by the minute. Aidan’s suspicions were coming to light with each passing exchange between the long-time frenemies, and her soldier tossed Zeph a quiet, knowing look.

“Alrighty, then.” Brack winked at Skye.

Ward did a good job of ignoring their sexually charged banter and handed Brack his laptop. “Everything you need should be right there.” He gestured to the open tab on his screen.

“Don’t worry,” Brack assured. “Cade will take care of it. He’s the best.”

Tyler tipped his chin in the smallest of nods. “I’m not sure what to do now,” he admitted, his voice wavering.

“We wait,” Aidan said, getting to his feet. “There is nothing we can do until tomorrow. It’s late. We should go back to the motel and rest. Let’s meet here at 0700, and we can finalize our plans.”

Zephyr’s belly tingled from the command in Aidan’s voice. Every day Mr. Heller faded from view as Aidan peeled away another layer, revealing more of Captain Drake. Soon Heller and Dr. Barrington would be distant memories to the man she was falling for. She was happy for Aidan but couldn’t help worrying that the more he discovered about his past, the further from her he would slip. What if Barrington’s lab held a drug to reverse what had been done to Aidan? Would he return to his old life, or would he choose Aether—and Zephyr?

And what about the Elders? If things went south, there was no way they'd allow her to become a Protector. Zephyr would simply have to make sure everything went smoothly. Aidan held out a hand to her, and she accepted, tucking her hand inside his. Her inner turmoil would have to wait.

Aidan entwined their fingers, and warmth spread through her. Going back to the motel to "rest" sounded like an opportunity to be alone, but what about Skye and Brack? As much as she wanted to dismiss Aidan's theory of the two being involved, she couldn't deny what she'd seen with her own eyes. Her sister and her best friend had been kissing, and it was no ordinary kiss. There was heat, fire, and off-the-chart passion.

In the car earlier, Aidan asked her if it would be such a bad thing if they were involved, and she considered it. Skye and Brack kissing instead of fighting might be a nice change of pace for their tight-knit group. Being their referee over the last twenty plus years was draining for Zeph. But when it came down to it, Zephyr's opinion didn't matter. Whatever was going on with Skye and Brack had nothing to do with her, and she planned to continue telling herself that until she believed it.

Ward's voice cut into her thoughts. "Goodnight, and thank you all for coming here to help us… I mean Ivy. I'll have coffee and breakfast for you in the morning."

"And we appreciate everything you're doing for my mother, but I need you to understand one thing," Brack said, his tone dark. "Ivy Beck is an Aetherian. Therefore, she is *our* responsibility, and we will do anything we have to in order to ensure her safe return home…to *her* people."

"I do understand." Ward studied his shoes before looking up to meet Brack's gaze and speaking again. "I know where Ivy comes from…who she is…what she is. There is nothing on earth I want more than for her safe return. And *I'll* do anything I have to in order to ensure it happens."

"Harrumph," Skye muttered.

Brack stretched a hand out to Ward. "Looks like we're on the same team."

Tyler accepted the gesture with a warm smile. When their palms met, anyone within a mile could sense the connection between the two men. It brought to light yet another question—what was the whole story with Tyler and Ivy? Because Zephyr and the rest of the group were really missing something here.

"I'll see you in the morning," Ward said. He stood on the porch and watched them get into their vehicles.

The drive back to the motel passed in comfortable silence. Aidan held her hand the entire ride. The constant anxiety he might disappear at any moment made Zephyr relish the closeness. He swept his thumb across the back of her hand, and a gale of goosebumps rose on her flesh. As good as it felt to have him touch her, she worried the moment was fleeting. Aidan was in transition between two worlds—the blissful existence that was Aether and the harsh reality of Barrington's world. Zephyr wished she had more time to convince him he belonged with her, but she only had right now.

She had to be smart. She had to be savvy. She had to be…sexy. She wasn't opposed to using her God and Goddess-given charms to sway his decision. There was no doubt in her mind that Aidan desired her, and she planned to use it to her full advantage. In the short time it took to say goodnight to Skye and Brack, Zephyr had formulated a plan. *Operation Remind Aidan of What He'd be Missing* was ready for action.

The door closed with a soft click, and she pounced on him. Zephyr's lips followed a path straight to the sensitive spot she'd discovered behind Aidan's ear. The sound of his moans filled the quiet room. He gripped her butt and lifted her, inviting her to wrap her legs around him. Satisfaction blasted through her, and she fell into the moment.

No words were exchanged. Clothing flew in every direction, and they dropped onto the bed in a conjoined heap, knocking into the nightstand. The bedside lamp clattered to the floor with a resounding crash.

"Forget it," Aidan groaned in her ear.

His desperate tone sent a spark of need straight to her core, and Zephyr managed to reply, "Forget what?"

He smiled into their kiss and pulled her impossibly closer. "I need you, Zephyr. Are you ready for me?"

"Oh, yes—yes. So very ready."

Aidan entered her in one thrust, slamming the headboard into the wall behind the bed. Thud, thud, thud went the massive piece of furniture with every move they made. The walls in the room vibrated, but Zephyr couldn't bring herself to care, and neither, it seemed, did Aidan. For a fleeting moment, she wondered if her sister and Brack heard them from the thin-walled adjacent room. But Aidan's Fire whooshed over them, heating her skin from head to toe, and all thoughts except the man inside her vanished.

****

Skye

Boom, boom, boom. The motel room wall rattled with a rhythmic beat.

Wrapped in a towel, Skye rushed out of the bathroom, water dripping off the ends of her hair. "What the hell was that?"

Brack sat on the edge of the bed, wearing an identical white towel around his waist. Elbows propped on his knees, he looked up and met her gaze. "I believe it is our overzealous neighbors."

"I don't understand. Are they moving the furniture?"

"Not exactly." A broad smile stretched across his face.

Another boom shook the framed picture on the wall above the bed, and a light flickered inside Skye's head. "Ugh, no way. They're having wild sex in there."

"I'm afraid so."

"Disgusting. What should we do?"

Brack waggled his brows. "We can do better than those amateurs."

"I am not having a contest with my sister in the next room."

He raked his fingers through the damp waves of his dark hair. "Why must you always argue before you agree? You know you want to, sweetheart."

"Don't tell me what I want, and don't call me that." One day soon, Skye might have to admit how much she liked it when he called her sweetheart, but not today.

Brack stood and crossed the room until only inches separated them. Her body flushed with heat, and a tiny breeze floated over their bare feet. He pulled his broad shoulders back, and the muscles in his chest rippled. Fighting the urge to run her fingers over his exposed skin, Skye sunk her teeth into her lower lip. Toying with him a while longer seemed like a more effective plan.

"You're testing me, sweetheart."

"I'm a Protector. I like tests of all kinds. No biases whatsoever."

He broke first. His lips came crashing down on hers in a fierce possessiveness. Skye hesitated for a mere fraction before returning the kiss with equal fervor. Brack's mouth tasted like mint, and he smelled of clean laundry, a delicious combination. She wasn't sure how long they stood there simply kissing with the rest of the world lost in a glorious haze.

Brack slipped his fingers beneath the knot holding her towel in place, and it fluttered to the shaggy carpeting. For the sake of fairness, she returned the favor, and his towel joined hers on the floor. Water still dripped from the ends of her hair and trickled down her bare breasts. He unleashed a sexy smile on her just before he bent low and took one nipple into his mouth. The sensation rushed through Skye and settled between her legs.

Once again, he managed to take her mind off everything happening around them. His mouth worked attentively while his fingers meandered down her stomach and stopped at her small patch of neatly trimmed hair.

"I need to taste you." His voice was gruff and filled with desire.

Skye couldn't manage words but nodded. His wicked smile was back in place as he steered her to the bed. The backs of her legs hit the mattress, and he gave her a gentle shove, tipping her onto the downy surface. He crawled up between her parted thighs, his fingers tracing a path to her core.

The wall behind their bed rocked once again, and the hanging picture clattered on its hook. Much to her disappointment, Brack stopped his erotic exploration. He stood on the bed, removed the picture from the wall, and propped it on the floor.

"Don't want to get blamed if it breaks," he mumbled, making his way back to his position. "Now, where was I when I was so rudely interrupted?" Brack's tongue lashed out, flicking her sensitive bundle of nerves.

"Ahh" was her only communication for quite some time. Brack must have been satisfied with her reaction because soon, his hard cock was poised at her entrance. She grabbed him by the shoulders and pulled his mouth down to hers. Their tongues dueled, twisting and tangling in a familiar carnal dance.

He took his time, advancing in slow torturous increments until he was fully seated inside her. Brack brushed her damp hair back from her face and gazed at her with a look she did not recognize. "You are so beautiful, Skye."

Before she could return the sentiment, his mouth was back on hers. He thrust in and out of her tight channel with a new level of dominance. Skye didn't mind. Though she'd never admit it, she loved the way Brack took control. She was free of responsibilities, free to feel, free to be herself.

Their own headboard slammed into the wall behind the bed, rocking the bedside lamps. Over and over again, it smashed against the sheetrock until tiny pieces broke off and floated through the air. They both ignored it, even as the occasional fleck landed on one of them.

She teetered on the edge, her fingers gripping Brack's tight ass. He stilled inside her, reached down, and stroked them where they were joined. Skye slipped over the threshold, her orgasm breaking free. Brack followed her with a loud cry. They held one another, catching their breaths in a tangle of limbs.

Skye waved her hand and sent the cloud of debris adrift. "I think we broke the wall."

"Guess that means we won," Brack said, placing a kiss on her lips and tugging her closer.

Chapter Twenty-One

Zephyr

They opened the door to Tyler's cabin and were greeted by the smell of fresh-brewed coffee and bacon frying. He was gracious, and if the circumstances were different, it would've been a good time. Instead, they ate in awkward silence. Zephyr studied their host, and when Tyler thought no one was watching, his gaze lingered on his young doppelganger. Brack, in contrast, was riding a huge wave of denial regarding their resemblance. Zephyr and the others had come to an unspoken agreement on how to handle things. The consensus was to follow Brack's lead and treat Tyler Ward as a trusted ally and nothing more.

It was a bit strange, but it was nothing compared to the squinty-eyed stares Skye kept throwing in Zephyr's direction. What was her problem? Could this still be about Aidan? She was under the impression Skye had made peace with the idea of the soldier in her life, but perhaps, she mistook resolve for acceptance? Zeph ignored the scowls and vowed to discuss Skye's attitude when they had a private moment.

After their meal, the group went back to work, ironing out the details of Ivy's rescue. The morning flew by in a flurry of activity. An email appointing the lab's two new security guards had been confirmed. Cadence's expert hacking skills included uploading pictures of the team, along with falsified security licenses for Aidan and Brack. Bogus diplomas and resumes were added to Zephyr's and Skye's files. ID badges were assembled, uniforms acquired, and plans checked and rechecked.

Aidan was the most detail-oriented individual Zeph had ever met. It sealed her conviction that the former soldier would make an ideal Protector. If their little makeshift team didn't get killed and managed to save Ivy, maybe they'd all have a chance to convince the Elders. Even if her own dream of becoming a Protector never came to fruition, she'd be happy for Aidan, and perhaps, it would give him another reason to stay in Aether—with her.

Zephyr brushed her hands over the starched, white lab coat Tyler handed to her. Embroidered letters stitched in black spelled out *Dr. Sofia Lopez* above the pocket. Working the name over and over in her mind, Zephyr traced the lines with her finger. Her stomach tightened. How the hell were they going to pull this off? She and Skye couldn't pass for human scientists. They looked nothing like the ones Zephyr had seen in movies.

In contrast, Aidan and Brack filled out their uniforms spectacularly. The men tried them on to check the fit, and she had to admit she was disappointed when Aidan changed back into his jeans. His ass looked amazing in the pants that were a bit too tight in all the right places, and more than once, she caught herself fantasizing about taking them off with her teeth.

"Guys, come over here. It's Cadence." Brack held up his phone before swiping to answer the call. "Hey, how's it going?"

Cadence's voice was barely above a whisper. "Put

your phone on mute and listen. Whatever you do, don't unmute the call."

Brack complied, and they all gathered around Tyler's kitchen table. Murmured voices and rustling came over the line before Hawk's commanding tone rang out, quieting the assembled.

"Enough chatter. Settle down, and let's get this meeting started." He sounded agitated. "Zephyr and the soldier appear to have taken off, and instead of coming to their lead Protector, Skye and Brack have gone after them."

"This is going to be a disaster," Zephyr offered in a hushed tone, even though they were muted.

"Understatement of the year," Skye chimed in.

Static came over the line or maybe Cadence was adjusting the phone, but a few seconds later, Hawk's booming baritone picked up again. "And to add to our worries, Willow Robbins reports that she hasn't seen Ivy Beck in nearly a week. I doubt this is a coincidence."

The Protectors were a boisterous lot, and it was difficult to discern the specifics among all the shouting. Hawk cleared his throat, and both rooms went quiet, the one back in Aether and the one at Ward's place. The man was not to be trifled with.

"What do you have there, Mr. Wyndham? You know I don't like my Protectors scrolling whilst I'm speaking."

Zephyr imagined Hawk's surly expression while he waited for Cadence to hand over his phone. Their friend's audible gulp came over the line, and they all stared at Brack's screen.

Hawk's tone was laden with indignation. "I know this is you, Beck, and Anani, and I'm sure you and your soldier are with them, Zephyr. I want you to unblock my calls at once and turn your location systems back on. Barrington may be dead, but his disciples are continuing his work. You are in serious danger."

The team remained silent, and the quiet rush of shallow breathing was the only sound in the room.

"Nothing to say, huh? Well, we'll have to see if you're this brave when you face me in person. I'm on my way to save your asses. And as I'm sure you might've guessed, I'm not happy." Hawk cut the call, and no one moved a muscle.

"We shouldn't have blocked him. He sounds extra pissed," Zephyr said, leaning back in her chair.

Brack wore a sheepish look. "What did you want to do, consult him? Somehow, I don't imagine Hawk would have approved of our plans. The Elders are always involved, and they have no concept of time and urgency. We had no choice."

"Like I said before, this is a disaster," Zephyr stated.

"You think?" Skye snorted. "We'd better get this plan of ours in gear, or Hawk is going to show up just in time to ruin everything."

"How long will it take this Hawk person to get here because we need to wait until after hours to go to the lab?" Tyler glanced down at the leather banded watch on his wrist. "There's way too much security during the workday."

Brack stood. "Everyone, do as Hawk ordered. Switch on your phones and unblock our lead Protector before he goes off the rails even more." He turned to Tyler. "It will take them at least eight hours to get here, but we need to leave as soon as possible to avoid Hawk's interference."

Tyler nodded. “Fine, we’ll give it a few more hours. It will be pitch dark by then. Hopefully, our plan will go smoothly, and we’ll be able to rescue Ivy before your people even get here.”

“Everything is going to be fine. I promise we’re going to have my mom back with us soon.” Brack smiled. “Aetherians have a way of making things work. We prevail—always.”

“I’m counting on it,” Tyler said, gazing up at his lookalike.

A light breeze gushed from Zephyr, and no one appeared to notice. But as she pulled it back inside, she caught Skye glaring at her from across the table. The talk she planned with her sister was clearly overdue. If the men detected any tension between the sisters, they didn’t comment.

Zephyr rose and tucked her chair under the table. “Since we have some time, I’m going to get a bit of fresh air. Skye, care to join me?” She narrowed her eyes in her sister’s direction.

“Uh, yeah, sure.” Skye wore a blank expression.

Zephyr held the door open, and her sister walked down the planked steps and headed straight for a set of swings hanging side by side in an oversized oak. The sun dipped low, bathing the sky in a wash of bright orange and red. They both sat, gripped the rough-hewn ropes, and took off swinging in perfect sync.

She waited a full minute before narrowing her gaze on Skye and blurting out a single word. “Spill,” she demanded.

“Not sure what you mean.”

“Seriously? We don’t have time for this.” Zeph couldn’t deal with the mock innocent routine. “What is your problem?"

"Problem?" Skye shook her head. "No problem. I'm just a bit tired, is all. Our neighbors at the motel were making a racket all night long. I believe they were engaged in some raucous sex." She paused. "Oh, wait, that was you."

"Are you twelve?"

"Exhaustion leads to decreased brain function," Skye ridiculed.

Zephyr let out a slow, exaggerated yawn. "In that case, maybe you should talk to your *secret* lover about your late-night antics instead of worrying about mine." She pushed off with her feet and began swinging once again.

Her sister's cheeks flushed a deep shade of lavender. "I…uh…I…don't know what you're talking about."

"Give me a small break, will you? Aidan and I saw you making out in the middle of the diner."

"That was…uh…nothing. A joke. Didn't mean anything."

"Liar." Zephyr dragged her toes on the ground, bringing the swing to a stop. "We heard you last night, too. I may be slow, but I'm not stupid. The way you and Brack look at each other—" her words fell off.

Skye brought her own swing to an abrupt halt and faced her sister. "I'm sorry. I wanted to tell you, but I've been trying to work it out in my own head first."

"I don't know how to process this. You guys have been at each other's throats our entire lives."

"A defense mechanism." It appeared Skye had given the subject a great deal of thought.

"Is that all you've got? Your big explanation consists of three words."

Skye shrugged. "It's not my fault. I think Brack put me under a spell, or maybe his penis has magic powers or something."

Zephyr doubled over in a fit of convulsive laughter. She wiped tears from her eyes and sputtered, "N…nice try."

"Stop. Laughing. It's possible. Strange powers crop up around Aether all the time, and you know it."

"Not magical penises." Zeph began sniggering all over again.

"Brack can make plants grow. Why not his penis?"

"Are you saying his penis got bigger?" Zephyr gestured a stretching motion with her hands. "As in bigger than a normal erection?"

Skye's cheeks glowed. "Well…not exactly bigger…but…oh, shut up. You know what I mean."

"No, I don't know what you mean. Brack's penis doesn't grow any more than any other man's."

"How the hell would you know about Brack's penis?" Skye's expression went dark. "I thought nothing ever happened between you."

"Easy there, crazy pants. Nothing *has* ever happened between Brack and me, but I know he doesn't have a magical penis because *it's not a thing*. What is wrong with you?"

Skye's shoulders dropped. "I'm sorry. I really don't have an answer to that question. I wish I knew what the hell was wrong with me. It's that dipshit. I can't get him out of my head."

Zephyr smirked. "You know you're falling for that dipshit, don't you?"

"Don't be ridiculous. I'm in lust with him. There's a big difference."

"Whatever you say." She got up from the swing and left Skye alone to consider the possibilities. Zephyr continued to hear her sister mumbling about lust and magical penises until she stepped back into the cabin and closed the door.

****

Skye

"I am *not* falling for Bracken Beck," Skye said to the empty swing, her sister left swaying in the warm evening breeze.

What would it matter if Skye was falling for Brack? The whole idea was preposterous. No two people on earth were less suited for one another than Skye and Brack. He was rigid, and she was a risk-taker. He was stubborn, and she was capable of reason. He tiptoed around others' feelings, and she was upfront. But as was bound to happen, they did have a few traits in common. Both she and Brack were excellent Protectors, loyal, tough, and focused. And there was one more thing that couldn't be denied between them…sexual chemistry.

"Skye?" Brack called from the doorway. "We're getting ready to head out. You coming?"

"Yeah, on my way." She took a deep breath and got to her feet.

He waited on the porch, sizing her up as she approached. "Is everything okay?"

"Peachy," she said with a saccharine smile. "Sorry, I was out here for so long. What still needs to be done?"

"Aidan is dressed and has almost finished packing the equipment. The rest of us have to change our clothes, but other than that, I think we're all set." Brack wore his stress on his handsome face. Dark circles rimmed his bloodshot eyes, and his normally well-groomed hair and scruff were a tad disheveled.

She pushed his thick hair off his face. “We’re going to get her back. Try not to worry.”

“I’m not sure that’s possible—” Brack kissed her hard on the lips. “—but I’ll do my best.”

He led her inside, where the rest of the team scurried around the cabin. Zephyr was loading a quiver with bolts, and Skye wondered how she thought she’d be hiding such a conspicuous weapon. Aidan checked a holster at his hip and then another strapped to his ankle. The soldier looked every bit the badass, and for once, Skye was glad he was on their side.

Tyler paced in tight circles around the small living room but stopped when he finally realized they’d entered the cabin. “Oh great, as soon as you two change, we’ll be ready to go.”

The guy appeared as nervous as Brack, which was truly saying something. Tension radiated off both men in waves, and Skye’s own belly fluttered with butterflies. She scooped up the bag of clothing marked with her name from the table and headed into the bathroom to change.

Skye placed the package on the closed toilet lid, stood in front of the sink, and blasted the cold water. The basin filled, and she dipped her hands into the icy pool, splashing handfuls of water onto her face. This would be her second time going into one of Dr. Charles Barrington’s labs to save a fellow Aetherian. It hadn’t been long since they rescued their Fire Guardian, Ashlyn, from the lunatic’s torture chamber, and Skye was more than a little worried about Ivy. Hawk claimed Ash had nightmares from her time in captivity, and after seeing the place with her own eyes, she understood why.

Watching their lead Protector, River, slip away, leaving Lily, his pregnant Adara behind, had been more than enough to give Skye nightmares of her own.

Grabbing a towel off the rack, she patted her face dry. She paused and stared at her reflection in the mirror. With a shake of her head, she snapped the elastic bands off the ends of her braids and began running her fingers through the strands. Scientists likely didn't wear braids. No doubt they were sophisticated and used enormous words that no one else understood. If they managed to fool Barrington's staff and free Ivy unscathed, it would be a true miracle.

She smoothed her hair the best she could and slipped out a neatly folded blouse and a pair of khaki pants from the bag. At the bottom, Skye found black, pointy-toed flats she wouldn't be caught dead in and socks with strange pictures printed all over them. On closer inspection, she noted they weren't pictures at all but symbols, ones like H2O, O2, and CO2. Tyler certainly had an ironic sense of humor.

After donning her nerdy outfit, Skye risked one more glance at herself in the mirror. A shaky laugh fell from her lips. She looked and felt ridiculous. There was no chance this was going to work. If Skye and Zephyr passed for scientists, she'd do a striptease at the next Protector's meeting. She just prayed they had enough smarts and firepower to get Ivy out before anyone got hurt.

Skye stepped out of the bathroom and found Brack leaning against a wall right outside the door. "Are you stalking me, Beck?"

A lascivious grin spread across his face. "I wish I had the time, sweetheart. Unfortunately, this place only has one bathroom. I was merely waiting my turn."

"A likely story." Why was playing with Brack so much fun?

"You truly enjoy yanking my chain, don't you?"

"Whatever do you mean?" Skye batted her lashes.

"You really are a relentless tease."

"I'm not teasing." She tucked her shoulders back. "I'm a scientist."

Brack's gaze raked the length of her body. "Cute."

"It's the new me." She glanced down at her conservative getup.

He took her by the waist and pulled her to him. "It's nice, but I like the real you better."

Heat surged through her from head to toe. It wasn't Brack's words that had her heating up but the sentiment behind them.

****

Brack

One bright spot in this crap situation was watching Skye's expression when she saw her badass-self dressed in conservative garb and a starched, white lab coat. She'd spent ten minutes looking for places to conceal her weapons. Brack entertained several kinky scenarios as a reward when this shit show was over, and his mom was safely back in Aether.

But now was the time for unyielding focus, not hormonal fantasies. He plunged his head under the tap, soaking his hair and rinsing the remnants of shaving cream from his chin. Apparently, Barrington's security team was not permitted to have facial hair. Stepping back, he ran his fingers through the wet strands and dabbed at a small nick on his upper lip. He caught a glimpse of his reflection in the mirror and swallowed the sudden lump in his throat. *Tyler.* Without his scruff, he looked like Tyler. Why hadn't he seen it before?

"Later," he told himself on repeat. "Save mom *now*. Get answers *later*."

His new guard's uniform smelled like dry cleaning chemicals, and his stomach roiled with nausea. Maybe they were making a mistake and should be waiting for Hawk and the other Protectors. He was leading his best friends into a shit ton of danger, not to mention Tyler. It was pure hubris to believe their makeshift team could handle this kind of mission all on their own.

"We can't do this," Brack said, bursting from the bathroom.

Everyone except Skye wore matching looks of surprise. Instead, her mouth stretched into a tight-lipped smile. "Of course, we can." She crossed the room, stopping in front of him. "We've gone over every detail. We'll be in and out with Ivy before anyone even realizes what's happened."

"Skye is right," Tyler said with a confident nod. "I know the lab's layout inside and out, and I've been studying the night crew's habits. We've got this." He picked up a large backpack and slung it over his shoulder. "Now, let's go get your mother."

Brack's words dried up, so he nodded instead of speaking. If anything went wrong with this mission, it would be on his head. It had been Brack who decided the team should go rogue, and he was also the one who agreed to work with Ward. But truth be told, when it came down to it, he didn't care. His only concern was saving his mother and bringing her home safely. He knew it was selfish to put his friends in harm's way, but what other choice did he have?

Weapons were checked and rechecked, along with every bit of the equipment Cadence had provided. Brack inserted a small plastic earpiece, and the team tested their signals. Everything was in top working order, but he still couldn't settle the uneasy feeling lingering in the pit of his stomach. The last time they attempted a rescue of this nature, they'd lost River. Brack had been with Kai, Aether's doctor, as their lead Protector said his goodbyes to the love of his life. Poor River learned he was going to become a father only moments before he passed onto Arcadia. It was one of the saddest memories of Brack's life, perhaps even more than when Landon, a senior Protector, sacrificed his life to save Brack from a cave collapse during the Protector trials.

Brack couldn't waste time reliving past mistakes. The team was coordinated and organized. They were armed to the hilt and had their Elemental powers to boot. Barrington's people weren't going to know what hit them. As Tyler said, they'd be in and out before anyone even noticed.

"I think it still makes sense to take all three vehicles. We don't want to arouse suspicion by arriving together." Ward placed a briefcase on his passenger's seat and slammed the car door.

"Zephyr is coming with me," Aidan stated, leaving no room for argument.

She dropped a hand on his forearm. "We're going to have to separate when we get to the lab. We're not supposed to know each other."

"I'm not happy about that, but I understand." The soldier seemed even more uptight than usual.

They were all feeling the pressure, and Brack thought he might combust if they didn't get going soon.

"Fine. Skye, you're with me. Zeph, you go with Aidan. Tyler, we'll follow you, but we'll space our arrival times in case someone is monitoring security cameras."

"When we arrive, we'll head directly to the security office. We need to place the device Cadence gave us to substitute their live footage with a short loop we'll record. Once we hack into the system, we'll be free to move around the lab undetected." Aidan sheathed a jagged-edged hunting knife and tucked it into his belt.

Brack tipped his chin in a gesture of agreement and triple-checked his weapons, completely out of ways to stall. "Well, then…I guess we should go. Let Tyler head in first. We'll wait down the road from the entrance. Skye and Zeph will have to drive in without us." He was reluctant to add this detail since Aidan's reactions were impossible to gauge.

"Affirmative." The soldier's face remained stoic, and Brack could only imagine what the guy was thinking.

****

Aidan

His disjointed flashbacks unraveled like tiny threads. They burned in a hundred different directions, but the lab was featured in more than Aidan cared to remember. Keeping Zephyr and her friends safe would be his number one priority on this mission, followed by the extraction of Ivy Beck. Once the others were clear, Aidan planned to destroy every scrap of data, every formula, every drug, and any person who stood in his way would suffer the same fate—annihilation. Barrington labs would cease to exist, and the doctor's disciples would scatter like rats in a sewer. No one else would ever endure Barrington's unique brand of torture again.

Fire prickled under Aidan's skin. What if Zephyr and the others got in his way? Her team shared one common goal—to save Ivy Beck. They didn't care about putting an end to Barrington's legacy or about stopping the sick individuals who helped the doctor turn Aidan into…what? What was he now? An Aetherian? A soldier? Perhaps he was a bit of both. Aidan would help them rescue Ivy, but his one-man mission had an agenda all its own.

"You're very quiet." Zephyr's raspy voice cut through the silence. "I'd love to know what you're thinking."

"I'm sorry. I'm running through the plans in my head."

"And that's all?" Doubt diluted her tone, turning the question into a wistful-sounding dream.

Aidan heaved out a heavy sigh. He couldn't lie to Zephyr. "No. It's not. After we rescue Ivy, I'm staying. I'm going to crush whatever is left of Barrington's Aetherian program."

She smiled. "We figured as much. Brack was saying you'd never be able to free Ivy and walk away from the opportunity to take down the lab once and for all."

"I guess Beck is smarter than he looks."

"Apparently so." Her hand fell to his leg. "What can I do to help?"

Zephyr was truly special. Aidan needed to protect her, but he couldn't stop Barrington's people on his own.

"I'm not sure yet." He stroked a hand down the length of her hair. "But I appreciate the offer. We'll need to secure Ivy first, and then we can get to work. If the device Cadence gave us grants us access to their entire network, we'll have the power to introduce an unstoppable virus."

"And I guarantee I'll be there by your side no matter what happens. It's important for you to remember that I'm a Guardian. I've been born with immense power, and I'm asking you to trust in me and my gifts to help you. Bringing down the lab is a goal we all share, including Ivy and Tyler."

"I believe in you above all others." He shoved his hands deep into his pockets. "But I sure as hell hope Hawk and the Elders are in my camp."

The way things worked in Aether was beginning to sink into Aidan's thick skull. He doubted the Elders would agree to allow him back into the village if any of their people were hurt. Aidan would just have to make sure his new team stayed safe. The idea of losing Zephyr scared him more than anything he'd endured under Barrington's control. In truth, he might lose her in the end, regardless of the outcome. Aidan was of two worlds, and he wasn't convinced he belonged in either.

Chapter Twenty-Two

Zephyr

Without a single light on the road, darkness swallowed the team's vehicles. They pulled off the rural stretch of highway and onto the shoulder about a mile from the lab. Zephyr and Aidan stepped out of their jeep at the same time Skye and Brack parked their SUV. Tyler waited, leaning against his car door, wringing his hands. So much was riding on the outcome of this mission. It was a wonder none of them had cracked under the pressure.

Tyler pulled his shoulders back. "I'm going to head in. Remember, space out your arrival times. I'll see you ladies inside." He dropped a hand on Brack's shoulder. "Good luck. Stick with the plan no matter what, and we'll have your mom out of there in no time." He offered a weak smile, got into his car, and drove away.

Skye wrapped an arm around Brack's waist, and Zephyr did her best not to let her shock show.

"We've got this. Ivy is as good as free." Skye reached beneath her starched lab coat and tapped the Glock strapped discreetly in place. "Gigi and I won't let anything happen to her."

"I appreciate the backup." Brack offered a small smile.

This alternate-universe interaction was throwing

Zeph into mental spasms. Who were these people, and what had they done with the real Bracken Beck and Skye Anani? These supportive, cute imposters were freaking her out. Her sister and her best friend hated each, and everybody knew it.

Aidan glanced down at his watch. "We should go."

Brack tipped his chin in acknowledgment.

Skye's other arm came around him, and she hugged Brack tight. "It's all good. No worries, right?"

"Right," he said, his tone unconvincing. "I'll see you later, sweetheart." Brack placed a chaste kiss on her lips.

She glared at him and spoke through gritted teeth. "What did I say about that?"

"I only wanted to leave you with a little reminder of how I feel about you." He smirked and got into the jeep, leaving Skye uncharacteristically speechless.

"Alrighty then," Aidan said, having trouble covering a chuckle. "I'm not going to try to top that goodbye."

Skye leered at the soldier and whispered under her breath, "That's because you have no chance against us."

Zephyr glared at Skye. "Forget about her." She faced Aidan and stroked his handsome face. Staring into his steely blue eyes, she whispered, "Please don't do anything reckless when you get inside. We'll help you take care of everything as soon as we secure Ivy."

"Got it," he muttered. "Now come and kiss me goodbye."

She lifted onto her tiptoes and draped her arms around Aidan's neck. "One kiss coming right up."

Her lips grazed his, and he pulled her close, fusing their mouths together in a mind-blowing kiss. When he eased back, the world came spinning into focus at a million miles per hour. Aidan got into the jeep and slammed the door behind him.

"Whoa," Skye let slip out.

"I'll say." Zephyr straightened her lab coat and smoothed her hair back.

They waited a few minutes and then got into the SUV. Her head should've been in the game, but it was back with Aidan and that kiss. It felt more like he was saying goodbye forever than goodbye for now. Hopefully, after the lab and all of Barrington's work was destroyed, Zephyr would be able to convince Aidan he belonged in Aether.

They drove to the top of a steep hill, and as they descended, a large complex, surrounded by tall, barbed wire fencing, loomed below. Zephyr's stomach lurched. *This is it.* A security shack stood at the mouth of the fortress. Tyler had explained the details, but seeing the small city was nothing she could've prepared for.

Skye pulled up to the booth and rolled down her window. "Hi there." She smiled brightly at the guard on the other side of the window. "We're both starting work tonight. I'm Dr. Rivera, and this is Dr. Lopez."

He didn't smile back. A metal drawer, like the kind at a drive-thru bank window, opened. His staticky voice came over a speaker. "Put your IDs in the drawer," he said flatly.

Skye slipped their newly minted badges into the open compartment, and it closed abruptly.

Zephyr took the opportunity to size up the guard behind the glass. He looked like the mercenaries that Barrington set loose on Aether during Hawk and Ashlyn's Joining ceremony. The guy was broad and well-muscled but had a dull look about him, the type to take blind orders from a complete and total lunatic. Zephyr gazed beyond the gates. Barrington may have been dead, but his legacy sure as hell had survived.

"Welcome to Barrington Labs," said the goon, with zero sincerity. The drawer slid back open. "You're in building three. Follow the signs on your right."

"Thanks." Skye grabbed the IDs, smiled, and waved as she accelerated.

When they were out of eavesdropping distance, Zephyr spoke, "That must have been painful for you."

"Huh?"

"Having to act so nice." Zeph smirked.

"You're a riot."

Their typical banter managed to put a band-aid on the mood, but the moment they parked, silence fell between the sisters. Zephyr reached back and grabbed the steel briefcase Tyler had given her.

"What's with the luggage?" Skye questioned.

"It's my crossbow. Tyler got me the briefcase to disguise it. I told him I couldn't be without it."

"Thinking like a Protector, I see." Skye beamed.

"Just like you and Brack taught me. Be ready for anything and always bring your best." Zephyr patted the case. "This is my best."

"It's good to know I still have some influence over you and that the soldier didn't suck it all out with that kiss."

"Or you and Brack…and his magic penis."

Zephyr laughed, and Skye joined in, but the moment soon faded.

Skye grabbed Zephyr's hand and stopped her from getting out of the car. "Seriously, I need you to promise me you'll be careful in there. I know you can take care of yourself, but these people are merciless."

"Same goes for you, swear?"

They both lifted their pinkies, linked them together, and at the same time, smiled and said, "I sister swear."

The silly childhood ritual fortified them both, and they headed into the building. Tyler waited in front of a tall reception desk, still wringing his hands. Skye glared at him, and he stuffed them into his pants pockets. Revealing themselves with nervous tics was not part of their plan.

"Welcome to Barrington Labs, Dr. Lopez." Tyler nodded to Zephyr and then to Skye. "Dr. Rivera."

He spared a cautious glance at the redhead perched behind the massive desk. She hovered above them like a judge in one of those courtrooms she'd seen on television, but the woman's gaze was fixed on her computer screen.

"Thank you very much, Dr. Ward. My colleague and I are looking forward to getting straight to work." Skye nudged Zephyr with an elbow.

"Oh, yes, let's get started right away," Zeph spit back without thinking.

Tyler did a good job of acting natural. "Great, if you'll follow me." When they turned the corner out of sight, his shoulders lowered from around his ears. "I'm not made for this undercover stuff. I'm a scientist."

Skye cuffed him on the arm. "It's cool. We've got this. Which way to the cellblock, warden."

"Brack was right about you," he said, spinning around and walking down a long corridor.

It took all of Zephyr's strength not to break out in hysterics. She had no clue what Brack had told Ward, but it didn't matter because Skye's expression said it all. Her sister's complexion morphed to a deep shade of purple, but she didn't say a word. Skye turned on her heels and followed him without looking back at Zephyr.

She'd been so focused on Tyler putting Skye in her place that Zephyr hadn't paid attention to where they were going. Each step they took echoed in the barren tiled hallways. The walls were a sterile white, and the whole place gave Zeph the creeps. They reached an elevator bank and stopped.

"I think it's better if we take the stairs. The elevators have security cameras." Tyler gestured toward a door tucked beside the elevators.

"Fine, but let's check out com links before we head below ground," Skye insisted.

Zephyr had completely forgotten about the silent device Aidan had placed in her ear. "Good idea," she said.

"Brack, come in." Skye tapped her earpiece. "Brack, can you hear me?"

A loud burst of static crackled in her ear. "Hey," complained Zephyr.

Skye scowled at her. "You try." Then she rounded on Ward. "You too."

Zephyr and Tyler each attempted to reach Aidan and Brack, but they too, received nothing but an earful of static.

"Shit," Skye grumbled.

"What are we going to do?" Zeph asked. "We need to find those guys."

"We'll have to go get Ivy on our own. Those guys are trained soldiers. They'll be fine. We can catch up with them later." Skye breezed by her before Zephyr could protest. "Tyler, lead the way."

He nodded and held the stairwell door for them. "Lower-level C."

Zephyr gripped the handle of the briefcase containing her trusted crossbow. Of course, it was a bad idea to remove it now, but it didn't stop her from wanting to feel its grip in her hands. Instead, she stayed behind Skye, descending the stairs on quiet feet. Each step brought them closer to freeing Ivy, and Zephyr's stomach quivered with nervous anticipation.

"This way," Tyler whispered, leading them out of the stairwell and down a narrow hallway. When they reached the end, he stuck out an arm, holding them back. "Wait here for a minute while I make sure the coast is clear."

He swiped his ID badge over the scanner, and the door clicked open. Tyler slipped inside, leaving Zephyr and Skye standing there aimlessly. Time dragged on for what felt like hours. Zephyr picked at her cuticles while Skye paced in tight circles in front of the closed door. After a few minutes, the door opened, and they both jumped a mile.

"Sorry." Tyler winced. "Come on, there's no guard on duty."

Tyler gestured for them to go inside, and they complied. The last time Zephyr's anxiety had been this high, Charles Barrington himself was holding a gun on all of Aether's Guardians, and Cassy Sanders had been shot. They passed a series of solid metal doors, and a single bead of sweat trickled down the center of her back. With every barred threshold they walked by, worst-case scenario after worst-case scenario whirled around her head.

"Dear Goddess," Skye blurted out. "Is this a lab or a

prison?"

"Both," Tyler answered.

He walked halfway up the row and stopped in front of a steel door like all the others, but this one stood ajar. Tyler froze for a heartbeat and then pushed it open, his body sagging the moment he stepped inside.

"Ivy!" he cried, pressing a palm to his chest. He turned back to them, and all the color drained from his face. "She's gone." Tyler dropped onto the neatly made cot set in the corner of the tiny cell. "She's gone," he repeated, his voice rough and breathy. He lowered his head into his hands and fell silent.

****

Aidan

Bile rose to his throat. This was it. This was the fortress where Barrington had transformed Aidan Drake from a soldier into an Aetherian. He cinched his grip on the steering wheel. It was time to roll, and his new powers surged with energy. Aidan visualized his Fire receding the way Zephyr had been teaching him, and his Element complied with little resistance. Perhaps he was finally getting control of the Guardian powers he'd involuntarily inherited from Ashlyn.

He pulled the jeep up to a security hut. The one-man structure stood outside a tall gate, topped with razor wire, set on a long rolling track. A guard was stationed inside, and on closer inspection, Aidan could tell the glass was bulletproof. He marked the guy as one of Barrington's mercenaries the minute he saw him.

Brack leaned over the console and smiled at the guard peering out through the window. "Sup? It's our first night," he shouted to the man in the bubble.

"How nice for you," said a tinny voice from a

speaker. "Put your IDs in the compartment." Through the glass, he pointed a meaty finger toward a metal drawer.

Aidan swiped the badges from Brack and placed them in the drawer for Mr. Personality to retrieve. After a quick scan, he sent them back through and directed them toward building two. Aidan found an empty parking space and backed the jeep in the way he'd been trained by the military. Ward told him that his lab was located in building three, and Aidan hated the idea of Zephyr being out of his sight. What the hell was he going to do if he had to leave her at the end of all this?

"Yo, you with me?" Brack asked, snapping him back into the moment.

"Of course."

"When we get inside, we'll check our radio connections. Skye and Zeph are supposed to wait ten minutes before they follow. I'm sure it will take us that long to find a place where no one can overhear us."

"Agreed."

They walked shoulder to shoulder, the Marine and the Protector. The two were an unlikely team, but if Zephyr trusted Brack, so did Aidan. A set of automatic doors opened, and they stepped inside a wide marble lobby. Their rubber-soled boots squeaked across the slick floor, and Aidan's adrenaline kicked up another notch. The place was quiet, but his gut reminded him not to be deceived. He brushed his fingers over the grip of his weapon, checking what he already knew. His gun remained strapped to his side, exactly where he'd tucked it earlier.

If Barrington's people knew what was good for them, they wouldn't force Aidan, or his friends, to use violence of any kind. *All life on Earth has value,* was one of many Aetherian philosophies. Even if Aidan never became a true Aetherian, he planned to respect their ways. Brack urged them to disable instead of to kill. They all agreed not to use their powers or conventional weapons unless one of the team was in jeopardy.

Brack cleared his throat. "Hello."

The Neanderthal stationed behind a long, low desk looked up, an irritated glower creasing his ridged, Cro-Magnon brow. "You the new guys?"

No shit, dumbass, was on the tip of Aidan's tongue, but he bit the inside of his cheek and let Brack do the talking.

"That's us." He pointed to Aidan. "This is Jackson, and I'm Smith."

"The boss is waiting for you in there." He tipped his chin toward a door behind him marked *Security*.

"Great, nice meeting you…?" Brack waited for the guy to fill in the blank, but the jerk didn't look up from his computer screen.

Aidan shrugged it off and nudged Brack toward the door. The Protector grumbled something about ordinary humans under his breath so only Aidan could hear. In this case, Brack made a good point. The guy was a mindless thug, the same as Barrington attempted to turn Aidan into.

Brack led the way inside, and the heavy steel door closed behind them with a loud bang. They entered a neatly appointed reception area. Aidan scanned the space and let out a breath when he realized the room was free of cameras. *Interesting.* The place looked like a dentist's office waiting room. There was a small couch and a few sets of attached chairs. Two doors flanked the long narrow space, one marked *Director*, the other one blank.

The Protector tapped his earpiece and whispered, "Skye, come in."

Nothing happened, not a crackle, no static, no voices.

A thick cord of tendons popped in Brack's neck as he spoke, "Skye, don't fuck around."

Aidan reached up and touched a finger to his own earpiece. He kept his voice soft. "Zephyr? Can you hear me?" He waited a beat. "Zeph, what's going—?"

Again, nothing, not a sound. He looked to Brack and shook his head.

"Mother fucker," the Protector ground out.

"We need to find them stat," Aidan said.

"No. We need to find my mother *stat*. Those guys will be looking for her. I'm sure we'll run into them as soon as we pinpoint my mom's location. Anyway, they can take care of themselves."

Aidan wasn't buying it. The Protector said all the right things, but the soldier in him could read the panic behind Brack's eyes. Besides, it didn't stop Aidan's visions of Zephyr tied to a table by Barrington's lackeys from scorching his synapses. Brack may have talked a good game, but if the way he acted around Skye was any indication of his feelings, the man was about to lose his shit as much as Aidan.

"Fine," Aidan acquiesced. "Let's go meet the new boss, and then we'll search for Ivy."

They knocked, and a muffled voice said, "Come in."

The sound of an electronic lock disengaging clicked, and the door opened with a small pop. Aidan crossed the threshold of the security director's office with Brack on his heels. The room was spacious with a high ceiling. One entire wall was comprised of monitors focused on various locations around the compound. Aidan's throat constricted; they were in way over their heads.

A well-dressed man stood and offered them a broad grin. Unlike the wordless goon who greeted them, at first glance, this guy appeared educated and classy.

"You must be Smith and Jackson." He reached out a manicured hand. "My name is Joseph Romano, but you will refer to me as Chief."

The Protector took hold of the man's hand and gave it a shake. Aidan followed suit, and the moment he made contact, a chill skated down his spine. *Do I know this guy?* Memories bubbled and churned to the surface of Aidan's mind. He stepped back, his gait unsteady. *If I do, he better not recognize me.* He tugged his baseball cap down over his eyes, thankful it was part of the required uniform. Brack shot him a suspicious glare, and Aidan recovered before their new boss took notice.

Just when he thought he'd reeled it in, Aidan glanced down. A blue glow radiated between his thumb and index finger. He waved the offending hand behind his back, working to extinguish the impending inferno. The Protector's brows lifted, and when the guy looked down at his computer, Brack gave Aidan a subtle kick. With a last-ditch effort, he shoved his hands into his pockets and prayed he didn't set his pants on fire. Okay, so maybe he didn't quite have a handle on his new powers.

"I was informed that you two have already been fully trained and briefed before arriving tonight. I don't generally assign new teams to our classified areas, but you both came highly recommended by Mr. Cadence from headquarters."

Brack covered a chuckle with a cough. "Ah, yes, Mr.

Cadence is a good man."

If Cadence hadn't been born an Aetherian, Aidan was convinced he would've been some secret government hacker. The guy was a true genius.

"I'm sure. I don't really know the bigwigs down there too well," Romano said, his cultivated mask slipping.

Aidan's gut was telling him this man was not born of privilege. He reminded him of gold plating, a shiny veneer with the same old rusty metal beneath the thin surface. This guy was no Charles Barrington. Joseph Romano sounded as if he was one step removed from the streets. Perhaps he was formerly known as *Joey the Gent* or *Killer* or some other such name. Unfortunately, Aidan knew firsthand that the Doctor enjoyed transforming people for their potential value.

"Anyway, as I was saying, we need coverage in building three," Romano said.

Aidan's heart leaped. Zephyr and the others were in building three. Maybe luck was on their side after all.

"We're short staffed. My number one, Black, is at the desk. He'll show you to your posts."

As soon as they were on the other side of the door, Aidan sagged. He must have been a masochist for returning to Barrington's house of torture of his own accord.

"Dude, are you all right?" Brack asked.

Aidan bit his lip and nodded.

"You don't look all right," Brack said.

"Don't worry about me. Let's get over to building three and find the rest of the team. Hopefully, they've already located your mother."

"You know, for a guy who looks like he's about to

hurl, you're quite the optimist," Brack retorted.

"And for a guy who's about to get punched in the face, you're very funny."

Chapter Twenty-Three

Skye

"Take it easy, Tyler," Skye said in as gentle a tone as she could manage. She added a pat on his back for good measure.

Tyler's face remained buried in his hands. "It's all my fault," he said with certainty. "I never should have let her talk me into this crazy scheme." He combed his fingers through his hair, muttering, "I'll get a job. No big deal. You worry too much." His voice choked with emotion. "Well, it's a big deal now, isn't it?"

"Shh," Zephyr said in a hushed tone. "Ivy is going to be just fine. Let's keep our heads, shall we?"

"You don't understand." Ward met her gaze, a forlorn shadow in his eyes. "She's my everything."

"Of course I do." Her sister shot him a knowing smile. "But if you want to save Ivy, we need to get out of here and find the others."

Skye tugged on her earpiece, and it fell into her hand. "This thing is completely useless."

Zeph plucked her phone from her pocket and began jabbing it with a finger. "Tyler, is there nowhere we can get a signal?"

"I warned you back at the cabin. They're all about confidentiality around here," he said.

"If we can't reach Brack and Aidan, we need to

handle matters ourselves." Zeph took a seat on the flimsy cot next to Tyler. "Are you sure there are no phones for staff use? Have you ever seen someone using a cell? In a private office, maybe?"

Tyler sat up a little straighter. "Yes, yes." His gaze was clear and focused for the first time since they found Ivy's cell empty. "Last week, one of the lab techs bribed the security guys into letting him order a pizza. They're the only ones with access to an outside line that I know of. But we can't waltz into security and demand to use their phone. Besides, Brack and Aidan's phones and coms are out too, so who exactly would we be calling?"

"First off, I can think of someone we might call," Skye hinted. "And second, you're right. We can't storm the place, but we *can* create a diversion to clear them out."

"The way your mind works is a little scary," Zephyr said. "You know that, right?"

"It's a gift. It's not scary. I'm…resourceful."

Skye winked at her sister, who simply nodded her head listlessly.

"Keep telling yourself that." Zeph got to her feet and faced Ward. "What do you say, Tyler? You with us?"

Tyler stood and pulled his shoulders back. He oozed a sudden confidence that reminded Skye of a certain Protector she was intimately acquainted with. She and Zephyr were standing so close their arms brushed against one another, and when her sister's breath whooshed out, Skye knew she hadn't missed the resemblance either. It was unnerving, and it brought Skye straight to her looming fears. Visions of Brack being wounded somewhere in the massive compound bounced around her head. *One problem at a time.*

"I'm glad you're on board." Zephyr patted Tyler's arm.

"Me too," Skye said.

"Skye?" her sister asked in a saccharine sweet tone.

"Yeah?"

"I just have one question. What exactly will be my role in this scheme of yours?"

Skye gestured toward Zephyr's crossbow, tucked inside the briefcase, sitting beside her. "I think now would be a good time to show Tyler your Guardian Prowess."

****

Brack

They moved the jeep to building three and backed into the space next to Skye and Zephyr's SUV. Tyler's sedan was parked on the other side, and a pang of concern for the man he barely knew rattled Brack. He'd dissect that little nugget when his mom was free and he was with his girl again. Skye was an incredible Protector and an astonishing sharpshooter, but obsessive thoughts regarding her safety clouded his judgment. While he should've been solely focused on finding his mother, pictures of Skye being tortured pushed everything else to the background of his mind.

"Let's find this Mr. Black," Aidan's voice brought him back to focus. "And then we'll get to work locating Ivy and the others."

Brack nodded as if he'd been paying attention to the soldier the entire time. "Good plan."

The two walked in silence until they reached a security podium. An enormous man was perched atop a stool that looked like it may give out from under his weight at any moment. Tufts of dark hair escaped from beneath his tightly buttoned collar and shirtsleeves, giving him the appearance of a gorilla dressed in a suit. The harsh fluorescent lighting reflected off of his sweaty, bald head, leading Brack to wonder if his head was the only part of the guy's body not covered in fur-like hair.

"Chief told me you were on your way. I'm Black."

Brack was relieved when hairy hands did not extend a paw to shake. "It's nice to meet you, Mr. Black. I'm Bradley—"

"Just Black, no mister."

"Sure. Got it. Well, I'm Brad Smith, and this is my partner, Nate Jackson."

"Mr. Romano told us to report to you," Aidan added.

"Chief," Black stated, blank faced.

"Ah, yes, of course, the Chief—"

"No—*the*— just Chief."

"Got it," Aidan said. "Well, we won't take up any more of your time. You can just point us in the right direction, and we'll take our posts?"

Eyes squinted tight, Black consulted a computer screen. "Smith, you're on lower level two, wing A. Take the stairs by the south elevators and follow the signs." He gestured toward the hallway behind him. "Jackson, you're also on lower level two, but you'll be covering wings B and C." He handed them each a radio with a clip attached. "If you have any problems, you can reach me on these. It's channel twelve."

"Yes, sir," Aidan said, fighting his natural inclination to salute.

"Black," he repeated.

This guy was weirder than weird. If Black was an example of Barrington's trusted employees, maybe this mission wouldn't be as tough as they had anticipated.

"See you later, Black," Brack said, giving Aidan an encouraging nudge toward their escape.

Once they were out of earshot, Brack turned to him. "What the hell is wrong with that guy?"

"Barrington," was Aidan's only reply.

Understanding dawned on Brack. "Ahh."

"Come on." Aidan headed off. "Let's get downstairs and find the others."

The corridor was quiet, and his already heightened senses shifted into a new gear. He held the solid metal door for Aidan, and it banged shut behind them. Brack jumped back, his pulse kicking up to overtime. The sound took him right back to the day River, their lead Protector, was murdered in a place eerily similar to this one. PTSD was no joking matter.

Aidan clapped him on the shoulder. "Hey, stay frosty. We've got this."

"Yeah, sure, of course."

Descending to the lower level, their footfalls echoed off the concrete walls and ceiling. The soldier stopped outside a door marked with a giant L2, and an icy chill washed over Brack.

"Wait," he said, grabbing Aidan by the sleeve. "I have a really bad feeling about this."

River was great man, and he would have been a great father, but they'd lost him during Ash's rescue under the same conditions. Brack would be damned if he allowed history to repeat itself.

"We can't stay here. Your mom and the others need us."

"That's not what I mean," Brack whispered. "How do we know someone isn't waiting on the other side of this door? Barrington did it before. His people may be smarter than they look."

"Yeah, that guy Black is a real genius," Aidan said, with an eye roll just like Skye and Zephyr.

"Fine—so not him," Brack acquiesced, on a heavy breath. "But there could be some."

"Fine. What do you suggest instead?" The soldier removed his gun from its holster and pointed it at the closed door.

"We create a diversion somewhere else and then come back here."

"I'm with you. Keep talking." Aidan grinned.

"How are you doing with those Guardian powers of yours?"

"Getting stronger and gaining more control every day, why?"

"What do you say we go make some Fire?"

****

Skye

They relocated to Tyler's private lab. A variety of plant specimens grew on racks running up the walls. Long tubes of glowing bulbs hung above the rows of leaves and vines. Silver metal tables, covered with official-looking lab equipment, filled the empty spaces. Tyler headed straight for a small desk set up in the corner and sat.

"I'll check to see if I can find any information on Ivy," he said. The desperation in his voice was only surpassed by the look on his face. His brows pulled downward, and his eyes appeared cloudy and vacant.

Zephyr removed a quiver of arrows Skye didn't recognize and her crossbow from the case and assembled it in under thirty seconds. As usual, her sister was the most impressive woman Skye knew. If the Elders could see Zephyr right now, they wouldn't hesitate to allow her to participate in the Protector Trials. She was the Guardian of Air, but she was also a Protector of all people.

"It's ready." Zephyr stood with her crossbow dangling from one hand, the quiver slung over her shoulder. "Now, how about you tell us this big plan of yours, or are you making it up as you go along?"

Heat crept up Skye's neck. She had been hoping it would take Zephyr a few minutes, and she'd have some time to refine her plan.

"Yeah, of course, but Tyler seems busy."

Brack's look-alike sat at his desk, transfixed on the computer screen.

Zephyr cleared her throat. "Um, Tyler, did you find out anything about Ivy?"

His voice was so rough; he croaked more than spoke. "Those bastards have moved her somewhere classified." He scrubbed his hands over his face and then peered up at them. "Whatever you're going to do, please, do it soon." Tyler stood. "These people don't mess around. Mary Allen is not known for being gentle with her subjects, and don't ever forget, Ivy will always be viewed as such by that insane woman."

Skye acknowledged him with a tip of her chin and then turned to her sister. "Zeph, do you think you could use your psychokinesis to turn a couple of cameras in the opposite direction?"

"I don't know…maybe. I've never tried anything like that before."

"Did you say *psychokinesis*?" Ward wheezed.

"Yup," Skye replied, hitching a thumb toward her sister. "All Guardians have an extrasensory gift. Zephyr can move things with her mind, and wait until you see her shoot a crossbow."

"Skye is exaggerating as usual," Zephyr insisted.

Tyler shook his head. "I don't think she is. From what Brack told me, you're someone very special."

Her stomach roiled. Had Brack confessed his love for Zephyr to Ward? He had insisted over and over that he wanted Skye, not her sister, hadn't he?

"That's very sweet, but I think he is also a bit biased where I'm concerned," Zephyr said, her cheeks going pink. "We've been best friends since we were kids."

"Any-who." *Subject change, please.* "Here's the plan." Skye paused and gazed directly at her sister.

"Well, go ahead. *You're* the Protector, after all." Zephyr was baiting her.

Skye couldn't allow her sister to provoke an argument at a time like this. She focused on Ward, ignoring Zephyr's comment. "We'll head upstairs to draw the guards as far away from the security office as possible."

"How are we going to do that exactly?" Tyler questioned.

"I'm glad you asked." Skye turned to face her sister. "Let's show Tyler how we handle things Aetherian style."

Zephyr nodded, wearing a tight-lipped smile. "Fine, but how do you propose I walk the halls with my crossbow? Barrington's goons may be dim, but they're not blind."

Grabbing one of the metal carts parked under a grow light, Skye cleared a few potted plants perched on top and brushed the dirt off. "We can use this and cover your crossbow."

"Should work," Zephyr agreed.

Tyler stood by the door, rubbing the back of his neck. "Great, can we please go now?"

Skye checked the hallway before giving Zephyr and Tyler the all-clear. Her sister guided the cart down the wide corridor, keeping one hand tucked beneath the makeshift tarp. Skye unclipped Gigi's holster hidden under her lab coat but didn't take the weapon out. The last thing they needed was to show up on the security cameras looking like an army of bandits, but as a Protector, Skye had to be ready for anything.

Abandoning the cart, they climbed the stairs to the next level. "Zeph, are you ready to do this?"

"There's only one way to find out."

Skye cracked open the door and peered through it. "Coast is clear. Now, see if you can move those three cameras to face the walls." She pointed to the cameras closest to them.

Zephyr scrunched her eyes in heavy concentration. When she opened them again, she wore a look of pure determination. She raised both hands, her Guardian mark on full display, and waved her palms toward the first camera. It wiggled back and forth on its hinged arm but then froze.

"It's stuck. I don't think I can do it."

"Try one of the other ones," Skye encouraged.

Zephyr took her stance once more and heaved out a heavy breath. "Here goes nothing."

She raised her hands again, and with a twisting motion, the Guardian created a tiny vortex of Air. It swirled toward the blinking red light, and the camera spun on its armature to face the wall.

"Well done," Skye said, poking her sister with her

elbow. “I knew you could do it. Do you want to give the other two a go now?”

“Sure.” Zephyr repeated the procedure until all three cameras blinked red lights at the tiled wall.

“Excellent. I think we’re ready for phase two,” Skye said.

“Phase two?” Tyler’s brows knitted together.

“Zeph, see that red box on the wall?”

“Yeah. Why?”

“Because you’re going to shoot an arrow through it.”

“I am?”

“Yup. If you make the shot from the doorway, we can be back by the security office while those dipshits come here to check out the alarm.”

“I’m certain of one thing.” Tyler grinned, giving her Brack vibes once again. “They will be wondering where an arrow came from.”

The trio shared a nervous laugh while Zephyr loaded her crossbow. Tucked behind the stairwell door, the Guardian lined up her shot. Skye had no doubt her sister would hit her mark on her very first attempt. Zephyr placed the stock against her shoulder and drew the string back against her cheek. Pressing her eye to the sight, she let the bolt fly. The instant the bolt hit the mark with a loud clink, a deafening alarm blared.

Skye tugged Zephyr toward the stairs. “Run!”

They took off at full speed.

“Come on. Hurry,” Tyler huffed.

The sound of thundering feet clambered toward them, echoing off the concrete walls of the stairwell.

“This way,” Skye said, directing Zephyr and Tyler through an unmarked door.

The area they entered was pitch dark, and Skye's gut churned. She reached for Zephyr's hand and caught hold of her shirt.

Tyler whispered, "Where are we, and why is it so dark?"

She slipped her phone from her pocket and turned on the flashlight. Skye wasn't prepared for what it illuminated, and from Zephyr's and Tyler's horrified gasps, neither were they.

Chapter Twenty-Four

Aidan

A piercing alarm blared, and strobes lights flashed, filling the stairwell with disorienting sights and sounds. Fire leaped in Aidan's chest.

"What the hell?" he shouted above the resounding sirens.

"Skye," Brack said as if his response was automatic.

"It's a fire alarm. How could it be Skye?"

"Trust me. This has my little Protector written all over it."

"We have to get out of here." Aidan pointed to the door. "I'm sure all the noise has left us a clear path. What do you say?"

Brack jerked his chin up. "Yeah, but let me go first."

"How about we go through the door at the same time?" he suggested.

"Fine," Brack said. "But I doubt we'll fit together with our builds."

An urge to toss the smartass *through* the door struck Aidan, but the radio clipped to his belt crackled to life. "Jackson, come in. Jackson, report to the security office on lower level two. Over."

"You'd better reply," Brack said at the same time his radio went off. "Smith, come in. Smith, can you read me? Over."

Aidan unclipped his radio and depressed the button. "Jackson reporting. Over."

"This is Black. Locate Smith, and you two monitor the security office while the other teams check out the alarm. Over."

"Ten-four. Over and out," Aidan responded, clicking off.

Brack smiled. "Remind me to write Black a thank you note when this is over. He's making this way too easy."

"Please don't." Aidan shook his head. "Things always turn into a clusterfuck when someone says that."

The Protector cuffed him on the arm. "Now you're the one worrying too much. Let's go." He turned on his heels and walked out with a confident stride.

Aidan stayed at his back. He didn't understand how it was possible, but the alarm's bellow was even louder in the corridor.

Brack mouthed the words, "Holy shit."

He wanted to hate the guy on the basis of his history with Zephyr, but Bracken Beck was growing on him.

Together, they jogged down the hall. All of them had studied Tyler's maps back at the cabin, and they found their way to the security office with ease. This time it was Aidan's turn to go first. He nudged Brack aside, cracked the door open, and peered inside. The room looked to have been recently abandoned. Half-filled cups of coffee sat by two stations that were set up in front of an enormous bank of monitors like the ones in the Chief's office.

"All clear," he said, stepping over the threshold.

"This is excellent," Brack said, looking around. "From here, we implement Cade's plan to use their own cameras." He took a seat behind the first station. "He showed me what to do when we were in Aether. It feels like a million years ago." He ran his fingers through his hair. "Dammit, if I can just remember."

Aidan joined the Protector at the next station. The moment he placed his hands on the keyboard, the room began to spin in swirling circles. He braced himself for what was to come, and a wave of memories washed over him. He was in a similar place, doing the very same thing. A trickle of sweat ran down the center of his back. Captain Drake was somewhere dry and hot. Aidan hovered above his own form, watching his hands fly across a keyboard. When he came out of his haze, Brack was staring at him.

"Hey, man, you, cool? I thought I lost you there for a second," the Protector asked, concern etched on his face.

"Yeah, I'm fine, and I remember what to do."

Brack slid his chair back. "Please, be my guest." He gestured toward the console in front of them.

He found the correct panel and used the camera to record footage of the corridor outside Tyler's lab. "A two-minute loop is all we need."

"Good job. After you get this one set up, we can do a few more sections of the building."

Aidan worked with quick efficiency, his actions like muscle memory. He'd done this before…more than once. He was sure of it, and soon they had six different locations sending out recorded images. They would be free to move around the hallways while remaining invisible to Barrington's people.

"Can you switch on the live feed without them seeing, so we can look for my mom and the others?"

Brack asked.

"Yeah, sure." Aidan clicked a few keys, and several screens changed images.

"There!" Brack yelled, pointing to one of the monitors.

Zephyr, Skye, and Tyler were running down a long corridor. The Glock he'd borrowed from Skye was gripped in her outstretched hand. Zephyr had her crossbow and quiver slung over her shoulder. Tyler was unarmed but keeping pace with the women. The trio came to a stop in front of an unmarked door. Skye whipped it open and led the others inside. Once they closed it behind them, they disappeared from view.

"Where is that? Dammit!" Brack appeared over his shoulder.

"I don't see a monitor for that room. We need to find them. Remember that clusterfuck I was talking about? Well, I have a bad feeling this could be it. Let's go."

****

Zephyr

Skye held her phone aloft and directed the beam of light emanating from it around the room. Zephyr was unsure which one of them reacted first, but when the flashlight froze on a long metal table, all the air rushed from her lungs.

Tyler's panic-stricken voice rang out, "Ivy!" He pushed past Zephyr, nearly taking her off her feet.

She steadied her sister with a hand to her elbow and then guided her to the table. A large gash above Ivy's eyebrow oozed, and a few scratches marred her fair skin.

"Is she…?" Zephyr's words clogged in her throat.

He shook his head. "No. Her pulse is strong, and her breathing seems normal." Tyler braced himself against the table. “I think she’s just knocked out.” He leaned over, placed a kiss on her forehead, and whispered, “Don’t you worry, sweetheart, we’re going to get you out of here.”

Sweetheart? Hadn’t Brack called her sister sweetheart? Things were getting more complicated by the minute around here. It couldn’t be any clearer that Ivy Beck and Tyler Ward were in a secret relationship. And where exactly did Brack fit into this little equation?

The lights came on in the room, and the laser focus of the flashlight was swallowed up whole. Skye stood by the door, her hand still hovering over the light switch. Tyler barely looked up from Ivy’s unconscious form, but not six feet away, several more tables were lined up with hers. On the one next to Ivy, a sheet covered a person-sized, motionless lump.

Zephyr’s mouth went desert dry, and she inched her way over to the table. Skye was by her side in one second flat, slinging an arm around her shoulders.

“I’ve got this. Check on Ivy,” Skye ordered.

She wasn’t sure why, but she needed to see what was under the sheet. “No, I want to help.”

Skye nodded, grabbed the edge of the covering, and pulled it back. “Holy shit!” she said, inching back from the table.

Zephyr grimaced and wanted to look away, but she was unable. A beautiful young woman, face bruised and bloody, was secured to the table with metal restraints. Her bright green eyes were fixed open, glazed with horror. Globs of congealed blood matted down a big patch of her thick, dark curls. Zephyr glanced over to where Ivy was still sprawled out and saw Tyler tugging at the same metal cuffs around her wrists and ankle.

The temperature in the room must have dropped because Zephyr felt a chill from head to toe. "We have to find a key or something."

Removing her fingers from the woman's carotid, Skye shook her head. "Not for her. I'm afraid she's gone."

"Who is this poor woman, and why kill her?" Zephyr asked.

"Who knows what experiments they still have in motion. Maybe they wanted to use her like they used Drake?" Skye proposed.

Zephyr's stomach rolled over at the suggestion. "We need to leave this place before we wind up in the same condition."

"Agreed. Let's find something to unlock Ivy's restraints. And figuring out how to transport her until she wakes up is another thing to put at the top of the *do now list*. I'll look around for something we can use to break them open, and you see if you can find something with wheels."

Zephyr forced a weak smile. "I think I can help with the restraints."

Summoning her Guardian power, she rubbed her hands together and then placed them over the metal ring circling Ivy's right wrist. Air swirled around them, and Zephyr closed her eyes. The mechanism clicked open, and Ivy's arm slid off the table. She repeated the process on the remaining locks, and soon Ivy was untethered.

"You don't need to find anything to move Ivy." Tyler stood and lifted her into his arms. "I'll be carrying her."

"Great, let's get moving," Skye said, taking out a second gun Zephyr hadn't seen earlier.

Ivy groaned, and Tyler gingerly placed her back on the metal slab. "Sweetheart, can you hear me?"

She blinked repeatedly and appeared to focus on Ward. "Ty?" Ivy reached up and stroked his cheek. "Knew you'd come." She winced, and her eyes shuttered down again.

"Of course, sweetheart, always." Tyler kissed her temple. "I brought some friends with me," he said softly.

Ivy's eyes popped wide. "Brack?" she asked, sounding hopeful.

Zephyr and Skye approached and stepped into Ivy's frame of view.

"Yes, he's here but not with us at the moment." Skye picked up Ivy's hand. "He's going to be so happy to see you. What do you say we go and find him?"

Ivy's body went stiff, and for a second Zeph worried she had passed out again. But the look of sheer terror that crossed her face was a thousand times worse.

"Sage?" Ivy struggled to sit up and collapsed back onto the table. Her voice dropped to a gravelly whisper. "I need to find Sage."

"What are you talking about, sweetheart? Who is Sage?" Tyler asked.

"She's an Elemental but not an Aetherian. She's…she's, my friend."

Sorrow floated in the breeze that Zephyr had inadvertently kicked up. There was little doubt in her mind that the dead woman was Ivy's friend, Sage.

"Um," Tyler faltered. "Sweetheart, is that her?" He gestured toward the table beside her.

Ivy shifted her gaze for the first time and took in the sight. "Oh, dear Goddess, no. Sage!" she wailed.

She attempted to sit up again, and steadfast Tyler

came to her aid. Ivy swung her legs over the edge of the table, her body sagging with obvious grief. Tyler helped her to her feet and supported her weight, banding an arm around her waist.

"This can't be happening." Tears streaming down Ivy's face, she turned to Zephyr. "You're a Guardian. Can't you help her?"

"I'm so sorry, but I don't have that power. No one does."

"I'm sorry, too, Ivy, but we really do need to get you and Tyler to safety." Skye's Protector persona revealed itself.

"I'm not going anywhere without Sage. She'll have no way to move onto Arcadia if we leave her behind." Ivy's voice grew stronger and steadier. "Please, she was my friend."

Skye nodded. "Fine but we need to go now."

Zephyr found a gurney and wheeled it beside Sage's lifeless body. "Tyler, mind giving us a hand?"

He was reluctant to leave Ivy's side but came to their aid. Ivy's quiet sobs filled the lab as they heaved Sage onto the metal slab with a thud.

With what looked like a sudden revelation, Ivy froze. "Wait, we can't go."

"Um, yes, we can. Watch us," Skye said.

"Where is Aspen?" Ivy tried to stand on her own, and her legs wobbled beneath her.

Tyler snaked an arm around her and helped her to sit. "Sweetheart, you're not making any sense. You said her name was Sage."

"It is. I'm not talking about my friend. I'm talking about her baby, Aspen."

Chapter Twenty-Five

Brack

A room hidden from the view of the cameras could only mean something sinister. Visions of Skye, not his mother, popped into his head. Was it possible to have a heart attack at twenty-five? Shit, he hoped he didn't have to test the theory. He had to get to Skye, had to protect her. Brack jumped to his feet and sprinted out the door behind Drake. The siren's wails drowned out their footfalls.

They'd come to the lab to save his mom, and Brack would do anything to have her back, but his focus had been split. Skye moved into the lead position in his mind—and in his heart. Forget having a heart attack. Maybe he was cracking up?

"Come on. This way," Aidan called over the shrieking din. "I've been here before."

Brack didn't question his new friend, and he wasn't even sure when he began thinking of the soldier as such. Captain Aidan Drake had firsthand experience with some of Barrington's labs, and Brack trusted his instincts. The place was a maze of hallways. Brack could find his way through any forest, but every one of the concrete walls looked identical.

"Is it much further?" he asked, his adrenaline pumping. "Because right about now, I'm on board with your whole clusterfuck theory."

"Yes, almost there." Aidan's breathing was steady and even.

The guy's interpretation of the word *almost* appeared to be quite a departure from Brack's. They raced down at least five more corridors before Aidan came to a screeching halt in front of an unmarked door. Lungs burning, pulse pounding, Brack hovered behind Aidan, fighting the urge to shove him out of the way to get to Skye.

The soldier reached for the knob, but the door flung open before he got the chance. A medical gurney busted through, catching them both off guard. Brack leaped one way and Aidan the other, narrowly missing the hospital equipment charging like a bull on the loose.

He heard Skye's sweet voice before he saw her face. "Brack? How did you find us? When we couldn't reach you, I…we were so worried."

The pressure in his chest deflated, and he sagged with relief. Brack got to his feet and grabbed her around the waist, tugging her against his body. "I've never been happier to see you, sweetheart."

"Me too," she whispered, breathing into his neck.

"Hello, son, thanks for coming for me," a shaky voice called from behind Skye and the gurney.

Brack wanted to hold Skye forever but released her. He walked around the contraption to find his mom, supported by Tyler. She had a deep gash above her left eye and several nasty scratches on her face.

"Mom, thank the God and Goddess," Brack said. He walked toward her and when he reached for her, she fell into his arms. He released her and took a step back, his gaze raking over her disheveled form. "What did those bastards do to you?"

"I'm just a bit banged up is all." His mother smiled weakly, and sadness filled her eyes. With a tip of her chin, she gestured toward the gurney. "My friend, Sage, wasn't so lucky. We're taking her back to Aether for a proper passage ceremony."

"Um, Ivy, I think you're forgetting to mention another very important *little* tidbit of information," Zephyr said, stepping out of Aidan's embrace.

Skye rested a hand on her sister's shoulder. "Now is not a great time. Let's take this chat on the road."

"Maybe we should ditch the body," Aidan suggested.

His mom wiped her eyes on the ratty hospital gown she was wearing. "I promised Sage, if anything happened to her, I'd bring her body back to Aether."

"I hope we can keep that promise, ma'am. Our group is significantly outnumbered, and Barrington's people are extremely well trained," Aidan said, glancing between Ivy and Zephyr. "I'm sorry to seem insensitive, but a dragging body down the hall is bound to draw attention."

Zephyr advanced on the soldier, going nose to chest with the big man. "While I appreciate your desire to protect us, we are *not* leaving here without Sage's body. So, I suggest you give up on any plan that doesn't include that." She stood up on her tiptoes and placed a kiss on his cheek. "In Aether, promises are a big deal, as is a passage ceremony. It's an important part of death in our world. Souls who are denied their rites are said to be tormented."

"Got it. Bring the body." Aidan picked up Zephyr's crossbow and handed it to her. "But can we please get the hell out of here before we get caught?"

"Absolutely," she said.

Zephyr and Aidan guided the gurney back toward Tyler's lab. Brack held tight to Skye's hand on one side while keeping an arm around his mom's waist on the other. Ward had insisted on carrying Ivy, but she cast a veto over his plan, assuring him she could walk with minimal assistance.

Brack's radio squawked, bringing the entire group to a sudden stop.

"Smith? Come in. Over." Black's voice had a robotic quality.

Before Brack had the chance to unclip his radio from his belt, Aidan's crackled to life.

"Jackson? Come in. Over."

Aidan cleared his throat and clicked the button on the side of his radio. "Jackson here with Smith. Over."

"False alarm. No fire. Remain at current post. Over and out." Black signed off, and both radios fell silent.

"Good," Brack said. "They think we're still in the security office."

"As long as Black doesn't come to check on us, we have a bit of time. Let's keep going." Aidan took hold of the gurney and began walking.

"This Black guy sounds like a real warm fuzzy. Friend of yours?" Skye asked, smirking at Brack.

In the middle of this shit storm, Skye was still Skye. It was nice that Brack could count on at least one thing.

"Our new boss," he replied, not holding back his amusement. "We just met, but I can tell how much fun the guy is underneath it all."

"The man appeared to be altered…Barrington style," Aidan said flatly. "They all do."

"Let's not test that theory. We need to get the hell away from this horror show," Skye said.

Zephyr kept pace with Ivy and Tyler. "I think we should get Sage into one of our vehicles. This way, we know her body will be safe." She linked arms with Ivy. "Maybe it would be a good idea if you stayed with her while we take care of things inside."

His mom shook her head. "You kids are always trying to protect me. It's my job to take care of all of you."

"Please, Ivy," Tyler said, bringing his mom to an abrupt halt. "I can't imagine what you've been through, but I know *I* can't stand the thought of you suffering for another minute."

"And I love you even more for that." His mother kissed Tyler Ward right on the lips.

Brack froze mid step and came an inch from crashing into the gurney. He wasn't stupid. He'd figured out his mom was involved with this guy but seeing it up close and personal was a bit much under their present circumstances. When she looked from Ward to Brack, her cheeks flushed with a rosy glow.

Brack shoved away the scene playing on a loop in his head and began moving again. She loved Tyler. His mother loved a man he'd met only two short days ago. Brack felt like he'd entered an alternate universe. The urge to flee took over. He needed air, non-recycled air, grass, and trees.

"How about I take the body back to the SUV?" Brack suggested half out of desperation. "I'll check in with Cade and get a status update on Hawk's ETA. As soon as I finish, I'll come back down."

"What about your mother?" Tyler asked, tugging

Ivy closer while they walked.

"Mom, do you want to come with me and then wait in the car? I agree with Zeph and Tyler. You've been through an ordeal, and you'd certainly be safer."

"I'm not hiding while my family risks their lives." Ivy straightened and took a few slow strides on her own. "I'm going to help stop that crazy bitch, Mary Allen, if it's the last thing I do."

Brack knew better than to argue, but Tyler hadn't gotten the memo.

"You can barely walk. Please, sweetheart, be reasonable," Tyler implored.

Sweetheart? His mother kissed the man, and now he was calling her sweetheart. Brack didn't recall giving permission for the use of his pet name for Skye.

"Tyler, you're fighting a losing battle." Skye smiled. "You and Ivy should go back to your lab and gather anything useful. I'll go with Brack while Zephyr and Aidan head to the security office. We can all meet back at your lab in twenty minutes." Skye took control with such force Brack was caught off guard.

"Smart, well-thought-out plan," Aidan said, wheeling the gurney with Sage's body over to Brack. The soldier dug into his uniform pocket, produced a key fob, and handed it to him. "Here. We'll see you guys in twenty." He took Zephyr by the hand and disappeared down the corridor.

"Please, take good care of my friend," his mother said, resting a hand on the body beneath the sheet. "She was sweet and gentle. She didn't deserve this."

"We will, Mom." He kissed her on the cheek. "You have *my* word."

Tyler wrapped an arm around his mother's waist

again and guided her toward his lab.

Brack was left alone in the empty hallway with Skye and a corpse. What could possibly go wrong?

****

Skye

"Heads or tails?" Skye asked.

"Pardon?" Brack's brows furrowed in that annoyingly cute way of his.

She made a guttural sound in her throat. "The body. Do you want to carry the shoulders or the feet? We shouldn't risk using the elevator, and this gurney doesn't look like it does stairs. So, again, heads or tails?"

"Oh, uh, heads, I guess."

"K, let's go."

Skye pushed the gurney until they reached the stairs. She slipped Gigi from the waistband of her nerdy khakis and then tugged out a second weapon from a holster at her back. Extending both barrels, she swept the area. Their path was clear, and when she turned to tell Brack, he was gently lifting the woman's body and balancing her weight on one of his broad shoulders.

"Hey, what happened to heads and tails?" she asked.

"I've got her. Come on."

Brack climbed the stairs while she continued scanning for threats. Things were unnervingly quiet since the alarm was silenced, and they didn't dare make a sound. When they reached the main floor, Skye paused. Her hair was loose, hanging down her back in long waves, and she missed the controlled feel of her braids.

She flung the offending locks over her shoulder and sidled up to Brack. "I'll go first and signal you when the coast is clear."

He looked like a man who was about to argue, but

Skye closed the door before he could speak. Protector training prepared her for stealth operations, and she moved on silent feet. Weapons poised, Skye crept further and stopped at the abandoned security podium. She doubled back to the stairwell and gently tapped on the door three times. Brack burst out with Sage braced on his shoulder.

They reached the SUV undetected, Skye popped the hatch, and Brack placed the body inside, tucking the sheet around the poor woman. The two made their way back inside the building and headed down to the others without any interference. Something in her gut told Skye this had been too easy, and she trusted her gut more than anything.

Ivy and Tyler were seated in chairs facing one another when they opened the door. The cuts and scratches on her face were already cleaned and covered in globs of ointment. Tyler dabbed the wounds at her wrists with gauze. Ivy's eyes were closed, but she didn't wince or even twitch while he attended to the angry red abrasions.

"Sage's body is safe inside the SUV." Brack came up beside Ivy. "How are you feeling, Mom?"

"I'm all right." Ivy looked pointedly at Tyler. "Everyone needs to stop worrying about me."

"We want to, Ivy," Skye said. "But put yourself in our places. We've been truly afraid for you. Please, try to understand."

"You're sweet, but I promise I'm fine."

Tyler grunted but didn't say anything. Skye liked the guy already, and the way he fussed over Ivy solidified her opinion. She had no idea how things were going to turn out, but she hoped Ivy and Tyler Ward could find a way to be together in the end.

Brack kissed the top of his mother's head. "Let's take things one step at a time, Mom."

A subject change seemed in order. "Have you heard from Zephyr and Aidan?" Skye asked.

"No, not yet," Tyler answered, switching his attention to the wounds on Ivy's ankles.

"Skye and I will go check on them while you finish patching my mom up." Brack stood and gestured for Skye to follow. "Lock the door and dim the lights. I'll knock three times in rapid succession when we come back."

"Be careful. That Mary Allen woman is nuts." Ivy stood on shaky legs to face them. "Please, don't underestimate her."

"We won't," Skye assured. "And we'll be back soon so we can get out of this hell hole together."

Brack stuck to her side like velcro as they made their way to the security office. Maybe her gut feeling had been paranoia because the corridors remained empty. They reached the door, and Brack cracked it open, leading with his weapon. Skye didn't have time to take a breath when he wrenched the door fully open. All the monitors hanging on the wall were dark. The two chairs sat unoccupied in front of a long workstation. Zephyr's crossbow and quiver were propped up on a third chair. Skye couldn't help noticing the strange arrows mixed in with the ones her sister normally used. The Guardian of Air would never leave her prized possession behind. Skye's stomach dropped.

Zephyr and Aidan were gone.

Chapter Twenty-Six

Zephyr

They had the security office to themselves. Zephyr said goodbye to Cadence and placed the phone back in its cradle. Hawk and Quill would be arriving within the next few hours, and she wasn't sure if this was good news or bad. Aidan sat beside her, clicking computer keys and scrolling through the various camera views.

"There is no sign of anyone lurking around out there, and my gut is telling me something is off—way off," Aidan insisted.

"This place is sure to put anyone on edge." Zephyr wanted to say that he was being completely paranoid, and the fact that no one was chasing them was a good sign, but she didn't have the heart.

"I'm sorry, but I've been here before, and it's all coming back to me." Aidan's hands froze on the keyboard, but he didn't look up. "I know the way these people operate. We need to find the servers and implant the virus Cadence created. Then I need to get you and your people back to Aether."

Her people? Zephyr's heart clenched in her chest. "And what about you? Where will you be going?"

"Zephyr, please—"

The door burst open. Her first instinct was to lunge for her crossbow, but it was propped on an empty chair on the other side of the room. Aidan's hand dropped to his hip, but a deep, robotic voice rumbled out a single word, halting his movement.

"Don't," a mountain of a man said.

The Bear Crane-sized guy held a weapon to Aidan's temple. In a mechanical action, he unclipped the holster at Aidan's hip and confiscated his gun. The mute mercenary then repeated the operation with the soldier's backup weapon.

A different male voice mumbled close to her ear, and the stranger's hot breath fanned her hair. "Freeze."

A wave of nausea churned Zephyr's stomach. There was no need to turn around; she could sense the gun pointed at the back of her head. Aidan bristled, but she shot him the side-eye, and he settled. The last thing they needed was to unleash their powers and reveal themselves.

Playing dumb seemed as bright an idea as any. "What's this all about? It's my first night at work here. And as a scientist, Mr. Jackson thought I might be interested in seeing the control room." Zephyr batted her lashes, working up her best innocent look.

"Come," the first goon muttered.

"The woman stays, and I'll come willingly," Aidan said.

"Both," number two announced, pressing the barrel of the gun into her neck.

"Mr. Jackson," she said, softly. "Let's go and see what these gentlemen want. Perhaps they have something of interest to show us."

Aidan stood and surreptitiously tipped his chin toward her crossbow. She could use her powers to bring it to her, but these brainwashed goons would likely get ten shots off by the time she got her hands on it.

"Fine, you first," Aidan said to the massive guy.

The extra-large man didn't speak again. He pulled the soldier to his feet and jabbed the gun into his ribs. Aidan doubled over with a grunt.

While the men were distracted, Zephyr inched her chair toward her abandoned crossbow. She hadn't moved more than a foot when an arm shot out across her chest, sending her wheelie chair sailing backward. Tapping into her Guardian powers, she slowed her momentum until she came to a gentle stop.

The big, hairy goon had his gun shoved under Aidan's chin. "Stop, or I kill."

Something in these men's eyes reminded Zephyr of Aidan when he was still called Mr. Heller. Was it possible Barrington's experiments were continuing even after his death? Neither of these guys had displayed any Elemental powers yet, but the night was still young.

"Are you hurt?" Aidan asked.

She got to her feet. "No."

"You sure?"

"It will take more than that to rattle me. Let's go see what these clowns want." Zephyr spared one last wistful glance at her crossbow, longing for the feel of its power in her grip.

Barrington's mercenaries led them out of the room at gunpoint, her crossbow left abandoned on the chair. The entire situation struck her as odd. It was as if these men didn't recognize her crossbow as a weapon. In fact, Zephyr had a strange feeling these men didn't recognize much beyond what had been programmed into their minds. Their faces were blank and emotionless, their eyes vacant.

"Where are you taking us?" Aidan demanded.

The big hairy guy nudged Aidan with his gun but didn't answer.

"Rude," she mumbled.

"I'm pretty sure Barrington's mind control didn't include etiquette lessons."

"Clearly," Zephyr drawled.

The two mercenaries stayed quiet, occasionally, giving them a shove with a gun barrel to hurry them along. Blue sparks emanated from Aidan's hand and heated her palm. She elbowed him in the ribs. He'd been doing really well keeping his anger and his powers in check, but even Zephyr was having trouble controlling her urge to knock these brainless oafs on their collective asses.

They stopped in front of a set of wide double doors. The goon with the hairy knuckles held one side open while goon two shoved them forward. Zephyr stumbled, catching her balance on a nearby metal table. They were in another lab. This one was much larger than the one where they'd found Ivy and Sage. A glass enclosure stood in one corner of the room, and at least half a dozen medical exam tables, all equipped with metal restraints, filled the empty spaces. Visions of old horror films raced through Zephyr's mind. She gripped Aidan's hand, her knuckles going white.

"Well, if it isn't the elusive Mr. Heller," a chilly female voice denounced. "And you've brought me a gift. How thoughtful."

****

Aidan

A tall, slender woman with blonde hair infused with streaks of gray sat with one knee crossed over the other.

Something hidden in the depths of her eyes gave Aidan pause, and then recognition flared. The photo Tyler had shown them flashed in his head. This was Mary Allen, Barrington's lover. She glared at him from across the room. Fire tingled under his skin but refused to respond to his inner command. He closed his eyes and concentrated, but his powers remained bound.

"No powers in this room, Mr. Heller." The off-kilter woman cackled.

Affronted, he replied, "My name is Captain Aidan Drake."

"We'll have you back to your old self in no time, *Mr. Heller*." The crazy bitch emphasized the name Barrington had assigned him, a name he despised.

Aidan never wanted to hear the name Heller again. Charles Barrington managed to warp and bastardize a name given to him by his brother-in-arms. He would never forget when he deployed on his first tour. His LT dubbed Aidan with a nickname from the get-go. He called him Hellfire because he used to say, "Drake hits like a missile." Barrington may have been dead, but if his threats lived on through this woman, Aidan would eradicate her in a heartbeat. He respected the Aetherians but didn't adopt all of their philosophies on the value of every single living being. The soldier had firsthand experience with some pretty evil people, and he doubted their presence would be missed.

"I'd rather die," Aidan said through gritted teeth.

Mary rose to her feet and approached them. "Oh dear, I certainly hope not."

Zephyr's body went rigid. "I can't summon my powers," she whispered.

Mary's hearing must have been acute because she

responded to Zephyr's hushed statement. "My Charles invented technology to suppress your control over the Elements." Mary studied Zephyr. "So, what have you brought me, Mr. Heller? Another Aetherian, perhaps?"

If she called Aidan by that name one more time, it wouldn't matter if he had powers because he was going to strangle Mary Allen with his bare hands.

"This woman is a scientist who started working tonight. I was trying to pick her up. She doesn't know anything. Let her go, and I'll cooperate."

"Liar, liar," Mary sing songed.

"It's true. My name is Dr. Sofia Lopez. I'm working in the botany lab. The guy is cute, and he offered to show me around." Zephyr started backing her way to the door. "So, um, I'll be going now."

A beefy arm came around Zephyr, yanking her into a chokehold. She thrashed and kicked yet without her powers, she was no match for the mercenary. Aidan jumped for the guy's throat, but a gun crashed down on the back of his head, bringing him to his knees.

"Aidan!" Zephyr screamed.

"Ah, yes." Mary sneered. "For two people who only met tonight… you seem rather familiar with one another. Odd."

A lump was already rising on the back of his head, and Aidan rubbed it while getting to his feet.

Though she was restrained, Zephyr launched a verbal defense. "I suggest you release us before you regret it like your beloved *Charles* did."

Mary's lips tightened into a thin line, and all the color drained from them, reappearing in her cheeks instead. This bitch needed to be taken down a few pegs. Brack and Skye would come looking for them soon, and then Mary Allen would truly understand the meaning of regret.

"Don't you dare say his name." Spit flew from the mad woman's colorless lips as she shouted slurs at Zephyr. "Mutant, filth." Then she pointed a shaky finger at Aidan. "And you, you murderous traitor. That Ivy woman told me you were the one who shot Charles." Her gaze shifted, and she glared at Zephyr. "And if there are to be any regrets around here, they will certainly be yours."

She was unhinged, and although Aidan was half enjoying her reaction, he thought it best not to push her too far. "I'm sorry, Mary, but Charles left me no choice. He was killing people."

"Aetherians aren't people. They are unworthy of wielding the power of the Elements. Charles' vision must be fulfilled." Mary sounded like a zealot.

Zephyr managed to raise a palm in a halting motion. "Now, wait one minute, lady."

Mary's eyes popped wide. "Oh my, a rare treat," she said with a bizarre reverence. "How nice of you, Mr. Heller, you've brought me one with a mark like the redhead. You did well with her firepower. Perhaps, once you have returned to a more cooperative state, I will combine this one's powers—" Mary tipped a pointy chin toward Zephyr. "—with the ones you already possess. I should like to see what becomes of you."

"You're completely insane." Zephyr snarled.

"On the contrary, I'm following the path of a true genius." Mary's tone shifted to that of a person speaking to a very small child. "You wouldn't understand. Charles mentioned how primitive you Aetherians are."

"I'll show you primitive, bitch." Zephyr lunged, but

the silent mercenary held her firmly in place. Without her the use of her Elemental gifts, it was a pointless struggle, but the Guardian would never stop fighting. "Let's see how tough you are when I get you alone without your muscle."

Zephyr slammed a heel down on top of the man's foot, emphasizing her point with a flare Aidan admired. The mercenary's cheek ticked, but he didn't budge. What had been done to these men? Barrington's skills were complex, but Aidan had thought himself to be one of a kind, but the robotic nature of these mercenaries suggested otherwise. He was certain the poor fools had no clue they were under the control of a crazy person.

Chapter Twenty-Seven

Brack

He pounded on the door to Ward's lab three times in rapid succession. The window shade shifted, and a dark brown eye peered out at them. The door swung open, and Tyler tugged them inside, locking the door behind them.

"We're so glad it's you," he said in a breathless rush. "Your mom and I have been worried sick. Every so often, one of the security guards comes by and checks the door. They're definitely looking for someone."

"Yeah, well, they may have found someone," Skye muttered. "Because we found these." She held up Zephyr's crossbow and quiver.

His mother clapped a hand over her mouth. "Dear Goddess, Zephyr and Aidan."

"I'm afraid so. Zephyr would never leave her crossbow behind." Brack approached one of the walls with plants climbing along the floor-to-ceiling trellis. Several leaves rustled and fluttered, moving toward him as he walked by. "We can't stay here much longer. I'm sure they know Zeph and Aidan aren't alone. We need to leave before they figure out that we're holed up in here."

His mother's cuts had been expertly cleaned, and she looked more like her old self dressed in a pair of pale blue scrubs. "You're right, and there's also something you need to know." She crossed to him and spoke in a soft voice. "My friend Sage wasn't alone. She had an infant with her. A little girl named Aspen. Sage saw Barrington's men shoot her husband down, and then she woke up in the lab. Mary Allen took the baby, and I'm not leaving Aspen with that murderous psycho."

"Baby?" Brack thought he was imagining his mother's words.

"You do know what a baby is, don't you? They're little, tiny people who grow up to be big people." Skye smirked.

"Thanks for the science lesson." Brack shot her a playful sneer. "But what I meant was, what does this Mary Allen think she can steal from a helpless baby? Even if the kid is an Elemental, she's way too young to demonstrate any powers."

His mother dropped a hand to his forearm. "*Yet*...she's way too young to display any powers, yet, but they are in her blood. And Mary Allen will extract every bit of it and leave nothing left just like she did to poor Sage." She wiped a tear from the corner of her eye.

"Do you have any idea where they took the baby?" Brack wasn't going to abandon an infant in this torture chamber disguised as a lab.

"I thought we were going after Zephyr and the soldier," Skye said.

"They'll have to manage on their own for a bit longer," Brack retorted.

Tyler glanced up from his computer screen. "You guys, come here and check this out."

They gathered behind Ward, gazing over his shoulder.

"I think I may have narrowed down the possibilities as to where they might be holding the baby. Look at this." Tyler clicked over to another screen. "These areas—" He pointed to one spot on the monitor and then another. "—are no access. You need a special ID badge to get in. I bet they're keeping Aspen in there."

"Great, how do we get in?" Skye asked.

"With this," Tyler said, pulling what looked like a credit card swipe from a drawer.

Brack noticed the little machine had a credit card with metallic tape attached to it. "And this helps us how?"

"This card can duplicate every security badge at the lab," Tyler stated.

"Dr. Ward, I'm impressed," Skye said with a small laugh. "Very sneaky. We won't ask you how many ATMs you've broken into with that thing."

Tyler's cheeks darkened. "Never, I would never—"

"She's kidding." Brack shot her a dirty look. "Skye is just being Skye. Please, ignore her, and tell us your idea."

"We head down to this area first." Tyler pointed to the screen again. "If she's not there, we can check the other area. I'm not sure what we'll find as far as security goes. I've never been in that part of the building."

"It's better than sitting here waiting to get caught." Skye pulled Gigi from her waistband and pointed it at the door. "Let's go save the baby, and then we'll find my sister and blow this joint once and for all."

"Whoa, sweetheart, slow down." Brack caught the visual exchange between his mother and Tyler at his use of their shared term of endearment.

"What the hell for? If Ward thinks he knows where the baby is, I say we shed these disguises—" Skye yanked off the lab coat with her fake name stitched above the breast pocket. "—and get down to business."

"It's going to take a while for my mom's healing powers to catch up. Besides, we can't run in to save the day with guns blazing, a more specific, calculated plan is in order." Brack approached her and kissed her on the cheek. As he leaned in, he whispered in her ear so only she could hear, "I like the lab coat. Don't leave it behind."

Skye punched him in the arm. "You're an idiot."

Brack smiled, and his mom and Tyler were left scratching their heads. Good, he'd show them what it felt like when the people you love kept secrets from you.

****

Skye

Brack's flirting was becoming a battle Skye couldn't fight. She half believed he was using it to defuse his tension. Even in the midst of this crazy situation, the man was relentless. And the identical expressions on Ivy's and Tyler's faces were a priceless bonus. Skye figured Brack was giving them a taste of their own medicine. Curiosity about the relationship between Brack's mother and their new ally had risen to epic proportions among their group. Too bad they were racing to save an Elemental orphan, find her sister and the soldier, and stop Barrington's people. No big deal. They had plenty of time to deal with personal issues.

"I may be an idiot, but I'm your idiot. Unfortunately, we'll have to put all of that on the back burner." Brack kissed Skye on the cheek and then turned to Tyler. "We need a plan to test this theory of yours." He removed one of his weapons from its holster. "I think we should check the cameras in the security office again. Maybe with an assist from Cadence this time."

"You want to go back to the place where they nailed Zephyr and the soldier?" Skye asked. "Can you say, lambs to the slaughter?"

"We won't just walk in there. I can listen in on the radio and see where the other guards are stationed. We may get lucky and get a bead on Zeph and Aidan." Brack wore his confidence well, but Skye could read the worry beneath.

"Have you noticed that your radio has been completely silent? They may be onto you. You arrived with Aidan, and even these bozos can put two and two together," Skye reminded him.

Brack placed his sidearm on the table and fiddled with the switches on the radio clipped to his belt. It screeched and squawked as he ran through the channels until the murmur of disjointed voices grew constant. The four of them huddled around the radio, held their collective breaths, and listened.

"Two intruders apprehended. Over," a man said.

Skye's brain flew to images of Zephyr chained to a table like Ivy, and her stomach lurched.

"Where are they being held? Over." This guy had the strength of command in his husky voice.

"Laboratory B, lower level two. Over."

"Is Ms. Allen with them? Over."

"Affirmative. Over."

"And the small asset? Over."

"Contained. Over."

Ivy grabbed Tyler's hand. Baby Aspen had to be the small asset these psychos were referring to. What kind of animals kidnap an infant and kill her parents?

"Understood. Stay in the security office and keep an eye out for the others. We think one of the scientists may be assisting them. Only shoot if you have to."

The coldness of the man's voice sent a chill down Skye's spine.

"Remember, the boss lady wants them alive, and you don't want to make her angry. Over and out." The scary dude signed off with a click.

Brack turned down the volume and clipped the radio back onto his belt. "Good thing we checked. I guess we go with plan B. We sneak down to the restricted areas and take our chances."

"Good plan. Yet somehow, it sounds vaguely familiar." Skye shot him her best *I told you so*, look.

The wise man ignored her comment and handed her the quiver of arrows. "If you carry this, I'll take Zeph's crossbow."

It was Skye's first opportunity to examine the strange bolts mixed among the others Zephyr generally preferred. Most of them appeared to be ordinary, but three of the arrows stood out in the cluster. One of the arrow fletchings had blue vanes, another a red, and lastly, green. *Hmm? What is this all about?* The secrets among their group were piling up faster than dirty laundry.

Brack swung the crossbow over his shoulder and retrieved his gun from the table. Skye put her arm through the quiver's strap, hanging it across her body. She regripped Gigi and Gert, her twin Glocks. Brack withdrew a second weapon and doublechecked its clip. But when Skye glanced over at Ivy, she swayed slightly before regaining her composure. The woman she'd known her entire life was armed with a 9mm pistol. Her second mom, a person who was all about growing things in soil and nurturing life on earth, was wielding an instrument of death. Charles Barrington still managed to bring out the worst in people, even from beyond the grave.

"There's no reason to hold onto any false pretenses at this point. After the exchange between the guards, it's clear we've been outed. Hopefully, Cadence's handiwork with the cameras will keep us undetected by the goon squad," Skye said.

"We should go. Mom, are you sure I can't persuade you to stay here?" Brack's gaze pleaded.

"Let's go," Ivy said by way of an answer.

Tyler rolled his eyes, exacerbation etched on his face. It was another one of Brack's patented expressions. The similarities between the two men were adding up in a freakish equation. Ivy was lucky the stress of their circumstances kept Brack in check. Otherwise, Skye was sure he would've been all over his mom for answers.

Brack lifted the window shade and peered into the hall. Light flooded through the small opening, bathing his handsome face in a yellow glow. When he turned back to them, his Protector's mask was in place. They all wore the same one. It was the one that told others everything would be fine.

"It looks clear, but I'll go first and then Skye. We'll knock if it's safe to come out." He didn't give his mother and Ward time to argue. He slipped into the hall and closed the door behind him softly.

Skye took a few cleansing breaths and trailed out behind Brack. She blinked several times, adjusting to the brightness but kept a firm grip on Gigi and Gert. Brack had moved down the hall a bit, and he waved her over to his position. She pressed in close to the wall and made her way to him.

"This is one of the passages the guards are watching

on Cade's loop, but I don't want to take any chances," Brack whispered.

She nodded, and he signaled for her to remain in place. He ducked back down to Tyler's lab and knocked three times. Ward came out with a gun in one hand, and Ivy's hand gripped in his other. Ivy's new look said Mother Earth meets warrior. Her long hair was pulled back in a headband fashioned from finely woven twigs, and several vines crossed over her chest, forming a military-style vest. The gun was still throwing Skye off, and she hoped Ivy wasn't forced to use it. The wounds inflicted on her by Mary Allen were fading as her Aetherian healing powers kicked in, but Ivy's wounds on the inside would not fade as easily.

Brack led them along the path they'd set up using the lab's own cameras. When they reached the bottom of the stairs, Tyler gave his gun to Ivy and got out the small device he'd shown them earlier. He wiped his forehead with the back of one hand. The credit card device wavered in his other.

Clapping the poor guy on the shoulder, Brack said, "You've got this." He gave him a little nudge toward the door.

Tyler offered Ivy a weak smile and swiped the card over the scanner. The door clicked, and he pushed it open a sliver. Brack stepped around Tyler, a gun in each hand. Skye moved in behind him, and Ivy and Ward followed. The silence had a heartbeat, and Skye cinched her grip on both of her weapons. Adrenaline shot through her system. Something was wrong with this place.

****

Brack

Getting through the lab was too easy, and Brack

could tell by Skye's posture that she agreed, but they were committed at this point. There was nothing to do except see this mission through despite the apprehension drifting among the group. The restricted area Tyler located was not much further. Brack took point, and the others clustered together behind him, moving like a silent herd.

On this mission, Brack was lead Protector and would sacrifice himself for his team the way he'd been taught. River had shielded them all with his own body, and it cost the man his life. Soon his beautiful Adara, Lily, would give birth to their child alone. At least their baby would have a mother. Sage's baby had no one to fight for her but them. Brack was determined to save Aspen from Mary Allen and her house of horrors at all costs.

They reached a formidable-looking, windowless door made of heavy steel, and Tyler consulted the printout he'd run off. This was the entry to the corridor they suspected of housing the baby. It was unguarded, and Brack's gut clenched. Why were they giving them such easy access to a restricted area? Sirens went off in his head. They screamed danger; *you're being set up*. But he couldn't leave an innocent baby to suffer and die like her mother.

Brack steeled himself and relieved Tyler of the device to unlock the door. If anyone was going to get shot, it would be Brack. It would not be the man his mother loved, and it would most definitely *not* be Skye, the woman he… he what? Brack didn't know how to finish his own thought.

"Are you going to use that thing, or are we just going to stand here and wait for them to come and collect us?"

Skye asked, snapping him back to the moment.

He swiped the card over the glass plate on the wall, and the stairwell door clicked. Brack led with his weapon, nudging it open a little at a time. No guard stood at a post inside. A small breeze kicked up, and Brack confirmed his suspicions about Skye sharing his fears of impending doom. But he couldn't stop. He was compelled as if by an invisible force driving him forward.

They entered a long narrow corridor with a row of ominous steel doors spread out every ten feet on one side of the hallway. The walls were concrete in this desolate area, keeping the air cool and dank. All the doors stood closed, and Brack walked along the row, swiping the card over every single panel. His mother followed him, shoving each one open and then cursing when she found it empty. There was only one cell left. Brack understood Tyler's earlier reluctance to open the door to some horrific scene, and he fought to keep the card steady in his hand.

The final door opened with the same soft click as the others, but this cell wasn't empty. Instead of the usual cot shoved in the corner, there was a small, clear bassinet like the ones Kai had for newborns in the Medical Center. His mother ran over and let out an audible gasp. She gathered herself, wiped a tear from the corner of her eye, and then lifted a tiny bundle wrapped in a graying blanket.

"I've got you, sweet girl," his mom whispered. "We're going to get you out of here like I promised your mother. I won't let them hurt you."

"I'm sorry to inform you, but that's not going to be possible. None of you are going anywhere." Brack recognized Mary Allen from the photo Tyler had shown them, but he wasn't prepared for the evil radiating off the deranged woman.

Chapter Twenty-Eight

Zephyr

Zephyr loathed the idea of ordinary humans keeping wild animals in cages, and their current situation reinforced all the reasons why. Their tiny glass prison put them on display in the much larger room. A bright light shone constantly, offering them no reprieve from the harsh glare. A wide drain sat in the center of the concrete floor, and she shuddered when she imagined the purpose for such a thing.

Aidan ran his hands along the glass, searching for a weakness. He kicked the wall where it met the floor. It didn't budge but sent him sailing back in the opposite direction. He steadied himself, leaving a large, milky handprint on the glass.

"There has to be a way out of this crazy-ass zoo," he huffed.

"There is. That lunatic woman had a remote, but she put it in that drawer over there." Zephyr pointed to the other side of the room. "Face it, we're stuck in here until someone lets us out. Or until Mary Allen and her mercenaries come back and kill us." She slid down the slick glass and plopped onto her butt. "I thought I felt a bit more access to my powers when she locked us in here. Are yours working?" she asked.

Aidan scrunched up his eyes. The man was adorably

sexy, and he had no clue. He snapped his fingers, and a minuscule blue spark ignited.

"Barely," he muttered, taking a seat on the floor next to her. "Why don't you try?"

She stood and rotated her hands, wrist to wrist. A slight breeze floated around their heads, her hair blowing back. "I've got something. Nowhere near my full power, but maybe—"

Zephyr focused her energy on the table with the remote in its drawer. Her psychokinesis skills were about to get a real workout. Aidan hung back and stayed quiet. One of the things she liked best about him was how he didn't push. He seemed to know intuitively what she needed and when she needed it. Zephyr dug deep, coaxing her Guardian gift to the surface through the haze Allen had created.

The metal drawer rattled but then fell still. She lowered her forehead to the glass with a tiny thump. "I can't," she said. "That bitch zapped us or something."

Aidan came up behind her and wrapped his arms around her waist. "You can. You're the Guardian of Air. You can do anything."

"How do you do that?"

"Do what?" he asked.

"Always know the right thing to say." She turned in his arms and kissed him hard on the lips.

He tunneled his fingers into her hair, returning the kiss with equal fervor. Zephyr almost forgot where they were, and when Aidan pulled back, his breath heaved out in heavy pants.

"Talk about proper motivation," she said on a gasp.

A rare smile spread across his handsome face. "Get us out of here, and I'll show you my appreciation in private, far away from this place."

A salacious grin spread across Zephyr's face. "I look forward to it." Closing her eyes, she tapped deep into her powers. *Please, let this work. Please, please, please.*

"You've got this," Aidan encouraged.

"I…am…the…Guardian of Air."

She thrust her palms out and pressed them to the glass, concentrating on the drawer with all her might. Like before, the drawer rattled, but this time, it grew louder and shook more violently until it flung open, its contents spilling onto the floor.

"I knew you could do it," Aidan whooped, placing a kiss on her temple.

"Not to be a Debbie Downer, but it's still on the other side of the room. Maybe you should lower your expectations."

He laughed. "You're the best. Try again."

She nodded and called the remote to her. It spun in a circle. "This isn't working."

"It's moving. Keep focusing. Come on. I believe in you," he said, with complete sincerity in his voice.

Zephyr found a next gear, and the remote slid across the room, coming to a stop in front of her feet. Too bad it was still on the other side of the glass.

"Now what?" she asked.

"You use your powers and hit that red button. Go on, Zephyr."

With one last final push, she fixed her gaze on the remote. It clicked, and the glass wall lifted at a slow, steady rate. Aidan didn't wait. He grabbed her by the hand and tugged her underneath before it finished its ascent. When they were clear of the barrier, he wrapped his arms around her and swung her in a circle.

"You're badass, you know that, right?"

She brushed imaginary lint from her shoulder. "It was nothing."

"I wish we had our traditional weapons, but at least we're free."

"What about those?" She pointed to several long rods hanging from a row of hooks on the wall.

Aidan raced over, grabbed one, and examined it. "Cattle prods," he said, his lips curling back.

"Do they…they use these on people?"

He nodded. "And much worse. We have to find the others." He handed her one of the metal sticks. "Let's go."

****

Aidan

His new Aetherian powers were useful, but Aidan preferred the familiar feel of a gun in his hand. Zephyr reached behind her back more than once, and he was sure she was instinctively going for her missing crossbow.

"We'll get it back," he assured.

He smiled, but the effort it took made it weak. If he was being honest, he would've said, *I'll try to get you and your friends home alive*. Her eyes shone with hope, and guilt raked over him like hot coals.

Zephyr grabbed his sleeve. "Stop it. I know the way your mind works, and normally, I love it, but right now, you're pissing me off. This mission belongs to all of us. You are *not* responsible for my safety or my family's. Got it?"

"I got it." His smile was easy and genuine this time. "Who am I to argue with the Guardian of Air?"

"Damn, straight, Captain Drake." Her vivid blue eyes danced, determination shining in their depths.

They approached Tyler's lab, gliding on quiet feet. The room was dark, and Aidan rapped on the door three times. They waited a beat, but there was no response to their signal. Zephyr stepped around him and repeated his actions but knocked with a bit more vigor.

"I've got this," he said.

Zephyr's brows furrowed, but she strode back to make way for him without question. Trust…she trusted him. Aidan would prove himself worthy of that trust no matter what it cost him.

Since they had gotten away from the lab, Aidan's powers were returning to their full strength. He closed his eyes, concentrated on his Fire, and rubbed his palms together. When he opened his eyes again, the tips of his fingers burned blue. He touched them to the doorknob, and the metal glowed orange. Aidan pushed the door with his hip, and it popped open.

"Skye?" Zephyr whispered. "Brack?"

Silence greeted them like an unwelcome chill.

Aidan snuffed out his Fire. "They're gone," he said, tugging her toward the door. "We have to get out of here. It's not safe."

"Where are we going?"

"To find the others and rescue the baby." Aidan took her by the hand and led her toward the security office. "We're going to check the monitors."

"But what if the guards are in there?"

He brought her to a full stop and shifted her to face him. "We show them who the real bosses are in this place." With a snap of his fingers, his Fire returned in a controlled burst.

Zephyr pulled her shoulders back and nodded. "Right."

The door to the security office stood ajar, and a muted, monosyllabic conversation could be overheard. Aidan tucked Zephyr behind him, but she jammed an elbow into his ribs. He stifled a groan and shook his head at her. The woman was exasperating. She was also beautiful, intelligent, sexy, and powerful, yet at this moment, exasperating topped the list.

He shoved the door open and caught the mercenaries off guard. Goon number one reached for the holster at his hip, but Zephyr's reflexes could not be matched. Fast-moving Air swirled around the man's head, creating a dizzying vortex. He wobbled on his feet and fell to the ground with a loud thud.

Number two's shock was brief, and he reached for his weapon. Before he had the chance to wrench it free, Aidan's Fire surged with fury. Who the hell did these guys think they were taking shots at Zephyr? She was his, even if it was only for now.

Zephyr lunged in front of the flames. "No, Aidan, don't!"

His Fire hit her square in the chest and then extinguished. Her cheeks flushed, and she turned her attention to their remaining attacker. The same tornado of Air rushed the unsuspecting man, sucking the oxygen from his lungs. He collapsed in a heap.

"I had him," Aidan said, injecting more challenge in his voice than he intended.

"I know." She took his still-flaming hand in hers. "You would have killed him."

"Exactly."

"Well, I'm an Aetherian, and I'm always going to look for a non-lethal way. It's something you should consider. These men have been manipulated by

Barrington's drugs…just like you were. Imagine if we had killed you when we had the chance?"

"I'm sorry." His chin fell to his chest. "You're right. It's just…the thought of them hurting you…I can't control myself."

"Try." She smiled.

Aidan laughed. "I will. I promise."

She was better than him and always would be. He could never measure up to the pureness of Zephyr's soul. Aidan was a tainted man. He bent down and seized the guns from both unconscious men. Zephyr held out a hand, and Aidan passed over one of the weapons. She tucked it into the waistband of her slacks and sat at the nearest vacant chair in front of the monitors.

"Now, let's see if we can find the rest of our team."

While she searched the screens, Aidan grabbed a couple of extension cords and tied up the mercenaries.

"Hey, check this out," Zephyr called to him and indicated several blackened monitors. "Why do you think these are dark?"

"I think there are things going on in this place they don't want anyone to see. Not even these guys." He tightened the bindings, securing the men crumpled on the floor.

"Maybe that's where they're keeping the baby?" she asked, sounding hopeful.

"Only one way to find out." Aidan released the clip from the confiscated weapon and slammed it back into place. "Let's roll."

****

Zephyr

She waited at the end of the corridor, her heart thundering in her chest. Aidan hugged the wall and slipped down the hallway, disappearing from view. What was down there? Skye—what if Skye was hurt? She couldn't stand there and do nothing like a damsel in distress. Zephyr was the Guardian of Air, for Goddess's sake. She was a woman imbued with the power of the Elements for a reason. Mimicking the soldier's moves, she followed his path down the mysterious corridor.

Aidan spun on his heels, his weapon poised to fire. "I thought you were going to stay back?" he whispered.

"You thought wrong," she whispered back.

"This is no time to be a wiseass."

"I can't help it. Skye is my sister."

He rolled his eyes, and Zephyr guessed Skye was rubbing off on him too.

"Stay behind me and make sure the safety is off on your weapon. I know you don't want to hurt anyone, but if it comes down to them or us, I hope you'll choose us," he said.

She nodded and grabbed hold of the back of his shirt with one hand, keeping the gun tight in her other. Aidan crept along, and she was hyperaware of the tension in his body. For Zephyr, it was nerves, but for the trained soldier, it was combat mode.

They turned another corner, and she had the distinct impression she'd walked in on a movie set being shot in a prison. A row of steel doors lined one side of an ominous hallway. They stood open wide, and Aidan shoved his gun in ahead of him, going down the line. Every single one was empty, and by the time they reached the final one, Zephyr realized it was hopeless. The soldier kicked the last door in the line and jumped inside, gun drawn.

It swung back, and Zephyr's gaze homed in on the

one thing none of the other cells had—a bassinet. Hands shaking, she approached the clear bin on wheels and peeked inside. *Empty.* Had she truly expected Mary Allen to simply leave Aspen waiting for them? She smoothed her hands over the thin mattress, and something sharp scratched her finger. Reaching in, she procured a plastic ID badge with the name Dr. Camila Rivera printed in bold letters and Skye's picture attached below.

"Aidan, look." She could hear the dread in her own voice, and she didn't like the sound.

He took the ID and met her gaze. "Maybe this means they have the baby somewhere safe."

"Or maybe it means they've been taken."

"In either case, we need to move on and keep looking. We'll find them," he encouraged. "If Mary Allen captured them, I have an idea of where she might've taken them, but I don't think you're going to like it very much."

"Could it possibly be any worse than being locked in that glass prison?"

"Um, well, yeah, I'm afraid so." He winced. "Dr. Barrington liked a good soliloquy, and the man bragged about his plans in gory detail. Your poor friend, Ashlyn, went through a hell of a lot. The cell they locked us in is a preparation area, just like in the lab where Barrington kept me. The real experiments take place elsewhere."

Bile rose in her throat. "I think I'm going to be sick." She bent at the waist, taking in huge gulps of air.

"Try not to panic." Aidan rubbed sweeping circles on her back. "I remember where the munitions locker is, and I bet that's where our weapons were taken."

She stood, feeling a bit more solid. "I want my

crossbow. I'm going to show that bitch it's a bad idea to mess with Aetherians."

"Easy there, tiger. Let's find your sister and the others first, and we'll go from there."

"You were the one who wanted to fight. I'm following your lead, Captain."

"The only thing I want is for you to be safe and for you to be true to yourself. Mary Allen is insane, and who knows what's become of her son, Thomas. Just don't do anything you may regret later on. I can handle the dirty parts of this operation."

As usual, Aidan was right. Tyler had explained the history of Mary and her son, Thomas, so they would all understand who they were dealing with. Charles Barrington manipulated and controlled the young woman since she was barely out of her teens.

One night over margaritas, Brooke opened up to Zeph about the man who raised her, sharing terrifying tales of his emotional abuse and intimidation tactics. Reasoning with a person as damaged as Mary Allen would be a near-impossible task but killing a sick woman would be a sinful act. They would have to wait and see how things played out.

****

Aidan

Being back at Barrington Labs was like wearing shoes that were a bit too small. You could shove your feet into them, but you could never quite get comfortable. The familiarity of this place was unnerving Aidan at every turn. He kept hold of Zephyr's hand and dragged her down to the storage room, which contained a cache of weapons. Before he even opened the door, vivid images flashed in his head. He recalled rows and rows of shelves lining the long narrow room. There were several steel tables covered with a wide variety of knives and some smaller firearms.

"Is this it?" Zephyr asked.

"Yes, stand back, and I'll blast the door with my Fire."

Aidan repeated his actions exactly as he had done with the previous door, and this one yielded just as easily. His vision had been spot on, and the odd sense of déjà vu sent a creepy chill skating down his spine.

"Holy crap." Zephyr gasped.

"Well put." He did a quick scan of the room and turned back to her. "Grab as much as you can carry, and don't forget the ammo."

They hurried, filling their pockets and tucking guns everywhere.

"Oh my God!" Zephyr yelled.

"What is it?" he asked, his heart beating faster.

Her face lit up with sheer joy as she held up her crossbow and quiver. "It's here, and it seems fine." She ran her fingers over the string and counted the bolts.

Aidan held up two Glocks, one of which he was highly familiar with. "Do you recognize these?"

"Skye calls those two Gigi and Gert, I think? Forget the Elders and their rules. My sister is going to kill someone for sure."

He tucked the matching Glocks into the deep pockets of his tack pants. "I've got them for her. Are you ready?"

"I'm good." She showed him the lineup of weapons tucked into her belt, but she held her crossbow in her hands. "This and my powers are really all I need. Now, let's go kick some butt."

"We'll need to follow Cadence's path to stay out of camera shot. It's our only chance to catch Allen by surprise."

"That biznatch isn't going to know what hit her."

Aidan gripped Zephyr's arm, pulling her back. "Please, listen to me. Do not underestimate this woman. Barrington's drugs are powerful, and her mind is warped. She knows why we're here, and she's desperate. People like her are dangerous. If anything happens to you, I'll never forgive myself."

She stretched up on her tiptoes and kissed him gently on the lips. "I feel the same exact way about you. Now, let's work together as a team and stop trying to protect each other."

"You got it, partner," Aidan said.

Chapter Twenty-Nine

Skye

So, this was the famous, or maybe the word was infamous, Mary Allen. She looked like a schoolteacher, not a mad scientist, but the four heavily armed mercenaries backing her up told the true story about this woman. Her soldiers, eyes vacant, spread out with their guns drawn. Brack struggled as they snatched his weapons, and an unarmed Ivy clung to the baby, still wrapped in the ratty blanket. Tyler impressed Skye by showing off the fighting skills of an Aetherian Protector, but Allen's men overpowered him, seizing his guns. The goon with hands the size of trash can lids approached Skye and roughly patted her down.

"Hey, watch it, asshole." Skye shoved back against the immovable wall of muscle.

Brack bristled next to her but kept his head. Blood trailing from Tyler's mouth, he tucked Ivy into the corner and blocked her and the baby from view. Skye prayed the child was uninjured. If Aspen didn't survive, Skye wasn't sure Brack's mom would either. Ivy was tough and strong, but even she had a breaking point.

"Move them into separate cells." Mary Allen jabbed a finger in the air, singling out Skye. "And gag that one if you have to."

Skye called to her Air power, but it remained firmly

rooted inside her, unable to break free. Heat flushed through her entire body. What the hell did this crazy bitch do to her powers?

"Aetherians," Allen said with a creepy chuckle. "These cells have been designed to inhibit your powers, and if you don't behave—" She pointed to a large vent in the ceiling. "—I'll have you rendered unconscious."

It took every ounce of control Skye could muster, but she held her tongue. The braindead thug who searched her missed the knife she'd slipped into her right boot, and the pocket pistol Zephyr gave her for her birthday that was stowed in her left. They were too tightly confined in the tiny cell for Skye to act. She worried the others, especially the baby, would get hurt. It was better to wait for the right opportunity to present itself before doing anything rash.

Brack shot her a look, and as if he could read her mind, he gave a subtle shake of his head. She didn't remember telling him about her hidden weapons, but his gaze dropped to her feet, stopping on her tall military boots.

Ivy's shouts of protest drew Skye back into the fold. "Don't you dare touch her!" she yelled.

Brack jumped into the fray and joined Tyler in forming a human shield to keep the men at bay.

"Relent," Allen commanded as if she were speaking to a pack of trained dogs.

The mercenaries' hands fell to their sides, and they took several steps back from Ivy, Brack, and Tyler.

"I need someone to monitor the subject until I'm finished with it." Mary waved a dismissive hand in Ivy's direction.

"She is a baby, you psycho, not a science

experiment, and you will not lay another finger on her." Rage cycloned through Skye's blood, as did her repressed powers fighting to be released.

"Unfortunately, you are in no position to back up your empty threat. It is my recommendation that you cooperate. If not, I will kill *the subject* making sure you are tied to a chair with a prime view." Mary Allen was warped far beyond Skye's comprehension.

The weapons tucked into her boots pressed against her calves, a tempting reminder of their presence. But they were still outnumbered, and the goon squad didn't appear to value human life, including their own. It was too big a risk to take with innocent people's safety tittering in the balance.

"Fine, I'm backing off," Skye said, holding her hands up in surrender and taking a seat on the flimsy cot.

They ushered the others out at gunpoint and slammed the door shut with a shattering clang. One by one, the disconcerting sound repeated three more times until they were all locked in separate cells. Skye pressed a hand to the thick cinder block wall. Brack had to be somewhere on the other side, and she imagined the feel of his hand in hers. She didn't understand it, but his presence grounded her and made her feel more powerful. Taking in a slow, deep breath, she held it and then let it out little by little. When the mercenaries came for her, Skye would be ready to fight. She unlaced her boots and removed the gun and the knife.

The clank of one of the metal doors opening echoed through the prison hallway. Skye froze, straining to listen. Were they taking someone, or maybe they'd captured Zephyr and Aidan? Her palms grew slick with sweat, and her heart raced. The faint sounds of Ivy's cries leeched beneath the tiny crack under the door.

Being a Protector of Aether, she was not accustomed to the feeling of helplessness. When it was Skye's turn, she would remind Mary Allen and her team of undead soldiers of who they were messing with. Aetherians were endowed with the power of the Elements, and sometimes that included its wrath. Skye had no desire to kill the unhinged woman or the men whose brains had been tampered with but would do whatever was necessary to protect her family.

Time took on a strange rhythm in Skye's windowless prison. Ivy hadn't been returned to her cell, and fear for her friend and the baby became a constant companion. Charles Barrington must have done one hell of a number on this Mary Allen chick to turn her into such a psycho. Thundering footfalls broke Skye from her train of thought and thrust her into Protector mode.

She could shoot with either hand, but her knife skills were far superior when using her dominant hand. Resting the blade on the cot beside her, Skye picked up the best birthday gift she'd ever received. She opened and closed her fingers around the grip to reacquaint herself with its size and weight. *Mouse* was the affectionate name she'd given this little beauty. The pocket-sized gun might have been tiny, but Mouse did not disappoint when it came to accuracy.

The world went quiet. Skye stood poised with a gun in one hand and the knife in the other. She braced herself, ready to spring into action, but her cell didn't open.

Tyler's muffled protests bled beneath the door. "Get the hell off me, you maniacs!"

A body hit the wall, and Skye jumped. The ear-pounding silence which followed the cringe-worthy sound brought her anxiety to a whole new level. She faded back into the corner of her cell. The adjacent cell door clanged shut. Allen's brainless mercenaries must have been set on mute because they didn't make a sound. The mindless purpose with which these men moved was freaking her out more by the minute.

"Skye? Can you hear me?" Brack called to her.

"Yes!" she shouted.

"If you have your blade, try prying the bolts loose from the hinges. Don't worry about your knife breaking because you can always shoot them with that baby gun I know you have in your boot." There was a smile in Brack's tone.

She stuffed Mouse into the pocket of her trousers and began working on the door as Brack suggested. A thick layer of gray paint coated the long pegs holding the hinges in place. Skye wedged the tip of the blade beneath the top and chipped away until the raw metal was exposed. Her fingers cramped, and she stopped, taking a respite from the pain.

"How's it going?" Brack asked.

She rolled her eyes. How the hell did he think it was going?

"Don't roll your eyes," he said.

Either the man was a mind reader, or Skye had become way too predictable.

"I would never do such a thing. Now stop bugging me so I can get this door open."

She worked the first bolt for what felt like an hour, but it only advanced a fraction of an inch. If Skye only had the added boost of her Air power, she would've been long gone from the claustrophobic cell. Wiggling her knife, she managed to nearly free the bolt when the blade slipped, slicing into her palm.

"Ouch, damn it!"

"What happened?" Panic and Brack went together like a fish on a bicycle.

"I cut my hand. It's not bad," she lied, the coppery smell of blood already filling her nose.

"Liar, I can hear the pain in your voice. You'd better put some pressure on that."

Again, her mind went to the question, was it her predictability or Brack's clairvoyance at work here?

"Your suggestions are incredibly helpful. I'm sure I never would have thought of doing that all on my own. Thanks so much."

"Skye," he warned.

"Relax. I'm putting pressure on it." Using her knife, she cut off one of the sleeves of her blouse and wrapped it tightly around her hand. She finished the dressing with a firm knot, wincing from the shot of pain. "If it makes you feel any better, it hurts like a bitch." Skye wiped the hot, sticky blood onto her khakis, leaving a dark red smudge behind.

"Can you still shoot to protect yourself?" Brack's voice dropped low, concern lacing his tone.

"Duh, sharpshooter, hello?"

"Please, don't bite my head off for worrying about you."

"Geesh, men are so sensitive." She snort-laughed and then picked up her knife. "I'm going to work on the bolt. I've almost got the top one free."

More stomping feet crashed down the hallway. Skye stopped fiddling with the hinge and took hold of her gun. Bring it on, goon squad. She and Mouse were prepared for anything.

****

Brack

Mumbled voices traveled the length of the prison hallway and seeped under Brack's door. He looked around for something he could fashion into a weapon. One steel toilet, no lid, no seat, its twin cousin of a sink, and a crappy cot were his only available resources. Brack dumped the mattress onto the floor and broke a piece off the cot's aluminum frame. He was no baseball player, but he wound up for his best swing. The cell's electronic lock beeped, and the door opened with a soft click. Brack braced for the onslaught of mercenaries, but none came. Instead, a very familiar face poked through the crack, her gaze fixing on his makeshift bat.

"Is that any way to greet your rescuer?" Zephyr asked, wearing a broad smile.

Shock slammed Brack. "How? What?"

Zeph nudged Aidan with an elbow. "I think they got to him. He can't even string words together." The Guardian wasn't nearly as practiced in the art of sarcasm as her sister.

Aidan smirked. "You okay, buddy?"

"All good. Skye is one cell over." Brack dropped the busted piece of metal, and it clattered onto the concrete floor.

"Nope, she's right here." Skye appeared in the doorway, lowering her pocket-sized weapon.

Brack was at her side in an instant, picking up her injured hand. He began working the knot on her homemade bandage. "Let me see what you did to yourself."

Skye slapped his hands away. "I'm fine, Dad, and I'm perfectly capable of making a field dressing."

"Wow, you two really are something, aren't you?" Zephyr asked.

Brack replied with an emphatic "*Yes*," and at the same time, Skye responded with a resounding "*No.*" He hadn't realized it was such a controversial question.

"We don't have time for this. We have to get out of here and find the others and fast." Aidan's expression fell slack. "If Allen has taken them to the big lab, they're in real danger. It's the kind of place you don't come back from." The urgency of the soldier's voice was alarming.

"Do you know the way?" Brack asked.

Aidan nodded. "I do, along with a lifetime of shit I wish I didn't have to remember."

Skye sheathed her knife, tucked Mouse into her pocket, and reclaimed Gigi and Gert from the soldier. They also returned Brack's guns, but the best part was seeing Zephyr's crossbow and quiver slung over her shoulder.

"We've got your six, Aidan, lead the way," Brack said.

As much as possible, they stuck to hallways covered by Cadence's camera trick. Aidan moved with the grace of a Protector, keeping to the shadows and dark corners. Brack's limbs tingled, and he choked up on his weapon. Mary Allen better not hurt his mother again or his Aetherian principles might fly straight out the window.

Aidan gave the hand signal indicating they were close to the lab, and Brack's tension ratcheted even higher. The stairwell door burst open, and four men appeared, guns poised.

"Surrender." The mercenary's speech reminded Brack of an automated phone call.

"Um, yeah, fuck that noise," Skye shouted over her

shoulder while she blasted shots at the men's knees.

The same thug who had messed with his girl earlier was writhing on the ground, blood pouring from his leg. But the rest of the robot squad kept coming before Brack could get off a single round of shots. The air around them grew cold. A hurricane-force gust of wind barreled down the hallway, taking the three remaining men off their feet. *Zephyr.* The Guardian of Air was one pissed-off lady.

Skye hovered above the downed mercenaries, a gun in each hand. "Don't move."

Brack and Aidan relieved the men of their weapons. The blank look in their eyes sent a pang of regret through him. These guys had been tampered with, and none of this was their fault. They were unfortunate casualties that had to be stopped regardless of guilt or innocence. This was a matter of survival.

"Hey, look what I found on this one." Skye held up a handful of cable ties. "Handy, right?"

"It depends on what you have in mind." Brack couldn't resist the chance to tease Skye.

"You seriously can't help it, can you?" she responded.

"Apparently not." A wide smile spread across his face.

Once the men were secured, they dragged them into a small office, and Aidan fried the lock with his Fire. They wouldn't be getting out any time soon.

"I don't think it's a coincidence that these guys found Zephyr and me. Mary Allen must've known we were coming. I hope we're not walking into a trap," Aidan said, clapping his hands together to douse his flames.

"It doesn't matter," Brack said, stuffing another gun in the back of his pants. "I'm not leaving my mother and Tyler with that crazy bitch for another minute."

"And don't forget about poor little Aspen." Zephyr winced. "Can you imagine what that woman will do to a baby who can't even fight back?"

"Well, let's not stand here with our thumbs up our asses. Let's go get them," Skye said.

"You really do have a special way with words," Zephyr said, with a mix of amusement and condemnation.

"Thanks." Skye shot her sister a teasing smile.

Aidan came to a stop a few feet short of double doors marked, *Laboratory*. He held them at bay with a hand, and they fell in line behind him. Brack stepped closer, straining to listen to the muted voices coming from inside.

"I'm begging you not to do this," pleaded a young, terrified-sounding male voice. "Please, you're not yourself, Mom. Something's gone wrong with the drugs you've been taking."

"Don't be ridiculous," came a woman's angry response. "Your father wanted this for both of us. He dedicated everything to his work on controlling the Elements."

Brack leaned in and whispered to Aidan, "That must be the son, Thomas. At least it sounds like he's on our side."

"Thomas doesn't hold any power over his mother," Aidan replied. "Charles Barrington was the only one who ever did. I understand that Mary had a baby for one purpose, and that was to give the man an heir."

"Doesn't say much for Brooke, does it?" Zephyr

said.

Something nudged Brack in the back of the head, and he turned to give Skye a warning. But it wasn't Skye; it was a fresh crew of mercenaries. The others must have realized at the same time because chaos ensued.

Chapter Thirty

Aidan

If the mercenaries forced their little band of rescuers into the lab, they would all be done for. Mary Allen likely possessed Aetherian power repressing drugs, and Aidan refused to allow the Guardian of Air to become another science experiment. One of the men grabbed Zephyr by the hair, and a fit of anger unlike any he'd ever experienced before seized hold of his body. All signs of his newly acquired control vanished, and crimson flames erupted from his hands. His Fire rippled in waves, climbing higher and at the same time, inching down his torso, stopping only when it reached his ankles. The rebellious flames burned, transfiguring him into a human inferno.

His words shot out like blasts from a flame thrower. "Get…your…hands…off…her!"

Zephyr belonged to Aether—and to him. But his incredible Guardian didn't need saving. She was far too clever and fierce to let these clowns get the best of her. Zephyr let her body go limp in the mercenary's hold, and the massive man lost his footing. Aidan didn't hesitate. He made his move without the use of any weapons other than his own body. Raising a flaming fist, he smashed the unsuspecting guy in the face. Zephyr gave him a tight nod, turned away, and loaded a bolt into her crossbow.

With Zephyr out of immediate danger, Aidan aimed his focus on Skye and Brack. Raising his gun to shoot, someone jumped on his back and nearly took him off his feet. The man was huge, at least six-five or six, a giant wall of brainwashed muscle. Aidan spun in circles but couldn't shake the unrelenting mercenary. In one last-ditch effort, he ran backward and threw his body full force into the wall, but the guy held on like a dog with a bone.

"Look out!" Zephyr yelled.

He wasn't sure what he was supposed to look out for, but the moment the words left her mouth, the guy on his back went still and then slid to the floor with a loud thud. Straightening up, Aidan caught sight of a thin steel bolt protruding from the man's meaty thigh. Barrington's mind-control drugs were powerful, and he knew it would take something equally powerful to bring this guy down. When Aidan went by the name Mr. Heller and was under the influence of the doctor's pharmaceutical leash, he'd been compelled to continue fighting even at the cost of his own peril. How did Zephyr manage to take down such a massive person with one little arrow?

She came up beside him. "Cadence made me some special bolts a few weeks ago. We haven't had a chance to fully test them." Zeph bent low and removed the arrow in one swift yank. "I hit him with the one we named, The Sleeping Potion. This kind of bolt doesn't penetrate deep enough to do any real damage, but it contains an anesthetic that kicks butt."

"Remind me to buy Cade a beer," Aidan said.

Skye's shouts froze them both where they stood. "Get your filthy hands off me." She kicked and punched a soldier twice her size. "Give me back my gun, you gorilla."

Where the hell was Brack? Aidan sprinted toward the commotion, but something knocked him on his ass. Disoriented, he looked up and watched a tornado fly down the hallway. Zephyr's vortex homed in on the mercenary subduing Skye. The Guardian of Air was on the warpath.

Out of the corner of his eye, Aidan spotted Brack face down on the floor. He propped himself on his elbows, and combat crawled over to his injured friend. Blood trailed down from Brack's temple, and Aidan pressed his fingers beside his windpipe. His carotid pulse was steady, but the poor guy was going to wake up with one hell of a headache.

The air churned in violent gusts, and papers from an open office door swirled around, obscuring Aidan's vision. He pulled Brack to safety and tucked him inside a doorway. Leaving his unconscious friend didn't feel right, but it was his duty to get the others to safety. With one more glance over at Brack, he headed back up the stormy hallway.

There was nothing Zephyr could not handle in any situation. Yet again, the Guardian of Air had rendered Aidan's skills obsolete. By the time he'd gotten halfway to her, the last of their attackers were being bound by Skye. Aidan returned to Brack, who was straining to sit up. He rushed to help his friend to his feet.

"You solid?" Aidan asked.

"Yeah, I'm cool." Brack lifted his shirt tail and dabbed the wound oozing at his temple. It didn't do much to stave off the bleeding, and blood trickled down the side of his friend's face. "Don't worry about it. Let's go."

He had to give the guy credit. Brack had sustained a major head injury, but he was steady as they made their way back to the women. Zephyr loaded a bolt with red fletchings into her crossbow and wore a look of sheer determination on her beautiful face. Skye was double fisting her Glocks, but when she saw Brack, she holstered one and darted to his side.

"What happened?" Skye's gaze flitted around the hallway.

"The asshole with no neck snuck up on me and butted me with his pistol." Brack smirked. "But don't worry, sweetheart, my skull is way too thick to dent."

"So I've noticed," Skye said, returning Brack's flirty smirk with a saccharine smile.

"If you two are finished." Aidan waited for a beat before continuing. "Remember, we may or may not have access to our powers in there. Be prepared for anything."

"They won't catch us off guard again." Skye held up her two Glocks.

Aidan unholstered his backup weapon. "Brack and I will open the doors simultaneously. Zeph, don't hesitate, you hit them with your best shot, and Skye, be ready to shoot anyone who gets in your way. We can apologize to the Elders when Aether is safe."

****

Zephyr

Zephyr wasn't afraid; she was pissed. She planted her feet wide and flexed her fingers, readjusting her grip on her crossbow. Aidan stood on one side of the laboratory doors and Brack on the other. Skye double checked the safeties on her weapons and then tipped her chin up to the guys.

Zephyr kept her voice soft. “On three.” She brought the bow’s stock tight against her shoulder and took a deep breath.

“One, two, three,” Aidan said.

The doors flew open, and Zephyr didn’t think; she reacted. Spying through her sight scope, she pulled the trigger and let the bolt fly. The fletchings spun through the air in a swirl of crimson, and flames erupted from the arrow’s tip. It found its mark in a tall cabinet, and fiery shards of razor-sharp glass exploded on the far side of the room. *Cade would be so proud.* An automatic fire protection system went off, blasting clouds of white chemicals into the air. It suppressed the fire but filled the lab with smoke thick as London fog.

Skye was next to her before she could take a step. “What the hell was that?”

“Later,” Zephyr replied. “Where are the others?”

Her sister grabbed her by the arm. “Dear Goddess, look over there.”

The woman who had been like a second mother to Zephyr was spread out on a slab, her head lolled to one side. They charged across the lab and took up opposite positions beside the steel table.

“Ivy, can you hear me?” Zephyr kept her voice low. She stroked Ivy’s cheek, but she didn’t rouse.

Her sister leaned over and whispered, “Is she…?”

Zeph held her breath and placed her fingers on the side of Ivy’s neck. Her own heart leaped when a pulse jumped under her touch. “She’s alive.”

“That’s something, at least,” Skye said, her relief palpable.

“I’m not sure what they did to her. I don’t see any obvious injuries.”

Skye waved a hand in front of her face. "I'm not sure how you can see anything in here. It's so smoky."

"I think I can help with that," Zephyr said.

She placed her crossbow at her feet and brandished her hands in a circular motion. A steady breeze picked up speed and swept through the lab.

"Guess your powers are working," Skye said. "Another positive."

The smoky haze cleared, bringing an enormous laboratory into sharp focus. Zephyr had never imagined such a place existed. It seemed to go on for miles. Shiny machines whirred from every corner, and long metal tables covered with test tubes, beakers, and all manner of apparatus lined the room. Crowded cages filled with mice and rabbits scaled one wall. Is this the place where Charles Barrington conducted his experiments?

Zephyr couldn't explain it, but she sensed Aidan and homed in on him in the cavernous room. It was odd; she could almost hear him, hear his thoughts. She shook it off as nerves and wishful thinking. Aidan's weapons were drawn on a scrawny young man wearing wire-rimmed glasses and a baggy pair of jeans. Why was Aidan shooting murderous glares and holding some college intern in the wrong place at the wrong time at gunpoint?

"Don't do anything stupid, Thomas," Aidan warned.

Thomas, as in Thomas Allen? Aidan's voice didn't sound like the romantic one Zephyr had come to crave. It took on a cold edge, sending goosebumps skating up and down her arms. She retrieved her crossbow and set her sights on the kid. But a threatening voice called from the shadows, and Zephyr held back a gasp.

"I suggest you and your friends put down your

weapons, Mr. Heller." Mary Allen strode out holding a parcel in one arm and a syringe in her opposite hand. "I wouldn't want to accidentally drop this." She jiggled the bundle, and a tiny hand slipped out from under the dingy blanket.

Aspen. Zephyr lowered her crossbow but didn't put it down. She glanced over at her sister. Skye stood firm, her twin guns at the ready. It was then that Zeph noticed Tyler. He lay prone on the floor not far from Ivy. The back of his shirt was shredded and stained bright red, and he wasn't moving.

Thomas spoke in a shaky voice, "Please, Mom, don't. This isn't you. She's just a baby. The Mary Allen who raised me would never hurt an innocent baby." He held his arms out and gazed at his mother. "Why don't you give her to me?" The kid took a few tentative steps toward her.

The baby's dangling arm wiggled, and her fingers opened and closed over a familiar symbol etched in her tiny left palm. A bold triangle pointed down toward her wrist and was bisected by a line with a dot on the end of the right side. Aspen was not just an Elemental; she was a Guardian of the House of Earth. Zephyr took in a shaky breath. She knew every single resident of Aether, so where did Sage and her baby Guardian come from?

****

Aidan

Aidan shifted his feet and set his sights on Mary Allen instead of her son. He remembered back when Charles Barrington had taken him from the battlefield, Thomas had been a reluctant participant. And now the kid's crazy mother was running the show.

The woman held the infant with a careless

indifference that made the soldier in him lower his weapon. Aidan recognized a mentally unstable person when he saw one. The baby thrashed around in her arms, and Aidan feared Aspen might start to cry. Thomas kept gliding closer to his mother.

"Stop right there, son. Don't make me hurt you or this baby freak of nature," Mary said, waving the syringe in the air.

Thomas stopped and raised his hands in surrender. "I'll stay here, but please, put her down gently and walk away."

"Why would I do that?" she asked, her brows knitted in confusion.

"Because you're a good person, Mom, and if you were…more yourself, you'd see how wrong this is."

"Well, these so-called *people* killed your father, so that makes them the wrong ones." Mary's mouth contorted as if she tasted something bitter. "And you want to protect them?"

"I want to do what's right. This power doesn't belong to us. It belongs to the Aetherians and the Empyreans. Father hurt them and stole from them," Thomas said in a tone one uses when speaking to a petulant child.

Empyrean was not a name Aidan was familiar with, and by the expressions on his friends' faces, neither were they. Was there another Aether out there? Is that why they didn't know Sage and Aspen?

Mary's face flushed bright red against her stark white lab coat. "If you're not with me, then you're against me." She tucked the syringe into her pocket and exchanged it for a semi-automatic pistol.

Thomas paled and backed away. "Mom?"

"Your father's dream was to control the Elements, and I owe it to his memory to continue his pioneering work. And if you were any kind of a son, you would feel the same way." Mary's eyes darted around as if she had just noticed Aidan and the others were still in the room.

"Please, Mom, this isn't your fault. Father, he c…controlled you…and me. He twisted our minds. Father did horrible, evil things to innocent people. He gave you the same drugs he used to create his robot mercenaries. You have to see—"

"Enough of your lies. I don't need your help. You think you're so smart." Her voice rose several octaves, and the baby stirred in her arms. "I'm not under anyone's control. I'm powerful, and soon the Elements will bend to *my* will."

"Mom," Thomas said, more firmly this time. He took a few small steps toward her. "Hand the baby to me."

"No. You stay away from me." She waved the gun around wildly. "All of you, do you hear me? Stay back."

The unbalanced woman was outnumbered, but no one dared move for fear she'd hurt the child. Aidan's Fire crackled under his skin and waited for its opportunity to be unleashed.

"I can't let you—" Thomas flew at his mother.

A loud bang reverberated through the lab, and the young man landed hard, flat on his back.

Mary dropped the gun and stumbled backward with the baby still clutched in her arms. "Why did you make me do that? I told you to stop. Why didn't you stop?"

Aidan couldn't read her reaction. Was she angry or sad? Perhaps she was a combination of both. Her eyes glazed over, and she whispered quietly under her breath.

All he could make out were a few murmurings about stealing Aspen's powers and taking control of the Elements.

"Mom," Thomas croaked. "I'm b…begging you. Don't do this." Bright red blood bloomed across his abdomen.

The syringe wavered in Mary's hand. "I have to. It's my duty. Charles would expect me to go on without him."

While the rest of the group maintained their positions, Tyler moved with stealth. He came up behind the woman and grabbed her by the wrist. The two struggled, and Ward fought to keep the needle away from Aspen. Zephyr moved like the wind and wrenched the baby from Allen's arms. They were so focused on the child they didn't see what happened to Tyler. He staggered back, the syringe sticking out of the side of his neck, its plunger depressed.

"Tyler!" Brack shouted, catching the man before he hit the floor. He lowered him to the ground. "I've got you."

"Give me back my subject." Mary Allen had somehow managed to gain control of her weapon again.

Skye stepped in front of her sister. "Yeah, I don't think so, bitch." The Protector brandished a Glock in each hand. "You see, I never miss…ever, so you'd better drop that gun before anyone else gets hurt."

Aidan joined Skye, raising both of his guns. "You should listen to her. She's not exaggerating. Put the gun down, Mary. It's over."

"Nothing is over until I say it is. Now, you freaks get back." She pointed the gun at Ivy, who was still passed out on the table. "I'll kill her." Mary glided closer to Ivy's unconscious form. "I mean it." She pulled the slide back on her weapon.

Mary Allen shot her own son. There was no doubt about it; this crazy woman meant every word of her threat. Aidan had to do something before anyone else got hurt. His dilemma was getting the gun away from her without getting himself or his friends shot in the process.

Chapter Thirty-One

Skye

Enough of this woman's rambling, Skye cinched her grips on both Gigi and Gert. Her Air power, combined with her Glocks, had never let her down before, and her gut told her they wouldn't fail her now.

The baby's cries reverberated through the lab. Skye spotted the little one safeguarded under a nearby table and Zephyr stepping away. Her sister, ever the Guardian, refused to hide behind Aidan and Skye. Holding her crossbow, Zephyr used her body as a shield between Ivy and the gun-wielding lunatic. Ivy struggled to sit up, but Zephyr kept her focus on Mary. One of the strange new bolts Skye recognized from Zeph's quiver sat in the flight grove of her sister's crossbow.

"Put the gun down, or I will shoot you with this arrow," Zephyr stated in a calm, flat tone.

"Gun versus arrow? And they said you Guardians were supposed to be intelligent." Mary's gray, wavy hair stood out in every direction, making her appear even more deranged.

"This isn't an ordinary arrow, Ms. Allen. It replicates the powers of the Guardian of Earth, like the infant you kidnapped."

So, that's what those fancy new arrows did. This had Cadence written all over it.

Her sister glared at Allen, her voice still steady, "I have another that simulates the powers of our Water Guardian. You remember Brooke Barrington, don't you? She goes by Brooke Sanders these days."

Mary's cheeks flamed crimson. "Another vile traitor…an abomination."

"I'm not going to tell you again. Drop the gun," Zephyr said, with a bit more bite this time.

"Mom, please," Thomas said, his voice a strained whisper. "Give up this insanity."

Aidan snatched a pile of chucks from the counter and pressed them to the gushing wound in Thomas' gut. The kid winced but offered the soldier a grateful smile. Aidan grabbed a discarded sweatshirt, tucked it under the kid's head, and turned to the woman who called herself his mother.

"You shot your own son, Mary. We need to get him to a hospital, or he's going to bleed out," the soldier implored. "Look at him."

"Causalities are a consequence of war. He shouldn't have interfered." Mary's words were strong, but she seemed unable to make eye contact with her son.

"It's only a war if you make it one," Aidan said.

Thomas coughed, then grimaced in pain.

"You don't understand," Mary said, the gun oscillating as she moved like a drunk leaving a pub. "Plans have to be carried out. You don't deserve these powers."

"You're giving me no choice," Zephyr said. "Stop."

The woman either did not hear the Guardian or did not heed her warning because she kept heading straight for Ivy, now on her feet. An arrow with deep green feathers flew from Zephyr's crossbow. The bolt hit its mark about a foot in front of Mary. The tile floor cracked, opening a three-foot fissure. The room shook, and a stunned Allen lost her footing but somehow managed to hang onto her gun. Skye and the others were far enough from Zephyr's demonstration to avoid any real damage.

"Hey, Zeph, nice work." Brooke Sanders walked through double doors, along with Quill, Hawk, and Ashlyn. "I've got some Water power over here if you'd like me to add a little something, something."

Mary scrambled to her feet, a small gash running along her brow line. "What are *you* doing here?" She sneered at Brooke, venom oozing from every word she uttered.

"I see we're going to dispense with the niceties. Fine then," Brooke said. She faced the woman shooting daggers with her eyes at the Guardian. "I've come to save my family and to stop my father's work from destroying any more lives."

"Charles Barrington wasn't your father," Mary said, pointing her gun at Brooke. "Your mother was a lying whore, and she deserved what she got."

Quill raised a SIG Sauer and directed it at the raving woman. "Watch it, lady, because I have zero qualms about blowing your head off."

"I am in charge here." Mary's tone was unconvincing, her voice cracking. "I will extract all of your powers and add them to Charles' brilliant formula. I'm going to continue his legacy and create an army of perfect soldiers."

"Yeah, well, most of your perfect soldiers are toast, so what now?" Skye couldn't resist taunting the woman even though she knew it was a dumbass move.

"Those men are inconsequential experiments. They

weren't enhanced with Elemental powers. I can control their minds with a handy formula Charles developed to make people more susceptible to suggestion." Mary ranted on, still waving the gun haphazardly. "Where is the child? She bears the mark, and I must extract her powers."

The room went quiet. All eyes were focused on Mary Allen. Now steady on her feet, Ivy stood beside Tyler and Brack with Aspen in her arms.

"Over my dead body," Ivy said, her voice strong.

"That can be arranged," Mary said in a vicious tone.

A shot rang out. Mary Allen jolted backward and crumpled on her side. She did not flinch, and she did not stir—and Skye was confident the woman never would again. Blood pooled on the floor around Mary's body, and her eyes were wide with shock. Thomas dropped to his knees. The gun he'd been holding clattered to the floor. Aidan rushed in and caught the kid before he hit the ground.

Brooke ran to Thomas' side. "Oh, dear Goddess, what happened?"

Thomas offered the Guardian a weak smile. "Charles Barrington." A single tear rolled down his cheek. "My mother—not always like this."

"I wish I'd known you were Charles' son—" Brooke fell off, her own eyes filling with tears.

"Couldn't have helped me." Thomas coughed, and a trickle of blood trailed from the corner of his mouth. "Glad you got away."

Brooke took his hand. "We're going to get you out of here and to a hospital. You're going to be fine."

"Too late." Thomas struggled to sit up but collapsed back to the floor.

"Please, let us help you." Brooke brushed his hair back from his face.

"No—I help." Thomas' voice grew softer. "Captain?"

Aidan crouched down next to him. "Right here, kid."

"F…front pocket. Keycard." Thomas lifted his arm and winced.

Swift as a pickpocket, Aidan produced a black plastic card from the front of the kid's jeans. "What's this all about?"

"Server room—level three. D…destroy everything." Thomas grabbed Aidan's sleeve, leaving a smear of blood. "So sorry—hurt you."

"It wasn't your fault, kid. Everything is going to work out." The soldier gazed directly at Zephyr. "I have the Aetherians now."

"Baby and mother—Empyreans—"

Thomas' head lolled to the side, and Aidan reached over, manually closing his eyelids. The kid looked like he could've been sleeping, but Skye knew he was gone. The room was quiet. Everyone was focused on Thomas' lifeless body. The poor guy had no chance with two lunatics for parents, and yet, he had given his own life to save them all.

****

Brack

The baby's cries reverberated through the lab. Brack looked up at his mother. She swayed back and forth, soothing the infant with soft whispers. "Can someone please take Aspen from me? I need to see to Tyler."

He moaned at her feet, emphasizing her point.

Zephyr handed her crossbow and quiver to Aidan.

"Give her to me, Ivy." She stepped up and reached for the baby.

"We need to get Tyler back to Aether," Aidan said to Hawk. "Kai saved me, and I'm sure he can do the same for Tyler. He's a good man. We couldn't have rescued Ivy and the child without his help. Please, let Brack take him back, and I promise I'll stay and destroy the servers."

"Correction." Zephyr appeared at the soldier's side. "*We* will destroy the servers."

"Very well, kids," Hawk smirked. "Here's what's going to happen. Brack and Skye, you take Ivy and our new friend back to Aether. My crew will take the child with us so you can focus on keeping—"

"Tyler," Brack filled in.

"Yes, of course, Tyler. It's easy to see that he is important to all of you." Hawk's gaze shifted between Brack and his mother. "Get going. We'll take care of everything here."

Skye holstered her weapons before joining Brack to hoist Tyler up. They half dragged, half carried him through the deadly quiet building, his mother never losing step. When they reached the car, he and Skye worked in tandem to ease Tyler into the backseat of the jeep. Ivy slid in beside him and rested his head in her lap.

Brack went around to the driver's side door, but Skye stopped him with a tap on the shoulder. She smiled brightly and held out her hand, eyeing the key fob he was holding. Brack didn't have the energy to argue, yet he didn't relinquish the keys. When her fingers brushed his own, he grabbed her and pulled her toward him. Brack brought his lips to hers and kissed her softly.

"Thank you for everything you did in there to save

my mom."

"It's my job as a Protector. It was nothing." Skye's cheeks flooded with color.

"Whatever you say, sweetheart." He tossed her a wink and got into the passenger side without another word.

Skye shook her head, but her lips curved into a small smile. She got in, started the jeep, and they were off back to Aether.

His mother didn't speak. She alternated between stroking Tyler's hair and staring out the window. The silence in the car was the loudest of his life. When he thought he might explode from the tension, he nudged Skye. She glanced over at him and raised her eye brows disapprovingly. In Skye-speak, that was an encouraging gesture, meaning get your head out of your ass and talk to your mother.

Brack cleared his throat. "Um, Mom?"

"Yes."

"How's he doing?"

"His pulse is really fast. He seems to be in pain, but he's not really awake."

"Since Tyler is resting, maybe you can tell me how it is you two know each other." Brack turned around in his seat to face Ivy. "I think it's time, don't you?"

Tears pooled in his mother's soft hazel eyes, and she nodded. "You deserve the truth after all these years."

"Is it weird for you with me here, Ivy?" Skye asked.

"No, not at all. You and your sister have always been like my own kids. Besides, everyone in Aether will know soon enough." Ivy ran her fingers through the length of her hair and glanced down at Tyler before meeting Brack's gaze. "I'm so very sorry, son."

"It's a little late for apologies, Mom. I have a pretty good idea of what's going on here, but I'd rather hear it from the beginning."

She wiped away a few stray tears. "Dear Goddess, it all started so long ago. I haven't thought about the beginning in ages." The corners of her lips curled into a secret smile, and she leaned back against the leather seat. "When I was young, I was obsessed with being surrounded by nature. The freedom to explore the plant life in the forest intrigued me more than just about anything. My parents were old fashioned and didn't allow me to go off on my own until my sixteenth birthday. I remember being so excited I was jumping out of my skin. It was Autumn, and the air smelled of pine." His mother's eyes glazed over with an unfamiliar wistfulness. "I walked and walked and walked, no plan, no destination in mind. I was ecstatic to be away from Aether. I'd never felt so free in my entire life. Which is why I didn't realize how far I'd wandered. I was beyond Aether's borders, and I had no clue. That's when I saw him for the first time."

"Tyler?" Skye asked, not bothering to keep the shock from her voice. "You've known him since you were sixteen?"

"Yes." Tears rolled down his mother's face. "I thought I imagined him, a boy around my age, sitting on the forest floor, a magnifying glass in his hand. He was as surprised to see me as I was him. For a full minute, we both just stared at each other, not saying a word."

"What did he do to you?"

"Nothing, dear Goddess." She pushed Tyler's hair back from his face. "He was…is special."

"What are you trying to say, Mom?"

"I'm trying to explain about Tyler…and me."

"Ignore your son, Ivy. Keep going. We're listening." Skye glared at him over her shoulder.

His mother's eyes were clouded with tears, and he felt like a total jerk.

"Sorry, Mom, I know this can't be easy for you. Please go on."

"If you're sure."

Brack reached across the seat and took his mother's hand. "I'm one hundred percent sure." His stomach churned in anticipation.

"Tyler lived in a town about thirty minutes away. We had so much in common, and we became fast friends. I didn't tell him about Aether or my powers for a long time. He thought I was an ordinary girl until one day, he caught me using my powers to heal some trampled flowers. I'll never forget the look on his face. It was half intrigue and half terror."

"So, you told him about Aether?" Skye asked.

"I did. We'd known each other for a while by that time, and I trusted him. We met every day in the forest for several years, and we grew close—very close." His mother's fair complexion went scarlet. "Tyler wanted to take me out on a proper date, show me off to his family and friends, but he understood the ramifications of me being discovered. No one in Aether knew about our relationship, and I was terrified about what would happen if the Elders found out. I knew they would never allow my relationship with Tyler to continue."

"What did you think they'd do, kill him?" Brack asked.

Ivy shook her head. "No, I never thought they'd hurt him physically, but I feared they'd forbid us to see each other, and that concept was inconceivable."

"Ah, yes, the Elders and their ancient ways. So, you decided to keep it on the down-low?" Skye added with flair.

"I wasn't willing to take any chances when it came to our relationship. I couldn't." The dreamy look in his mother's eyes returned. "I fell in love with Tyler, and he was all I cared about. He scrimped and saved until he could afford to buy a secluded hunting cabin in the woods. Every time I claimed I was going off to commune with nature, I was spending time him. That cabin has been our home together for over twenty years."

"And?" Brack gestured with a hand for her to state the obvious, but he needed to hear it from his mother's lips.

Ivy swallowed audibly. "Tyler Ward is your father, Brack."

"Duh, I didn't truly believe I was an immaculate conception, and I'm pretty sure no one else bought it either," Brack said, unable to keep the snide tone out of his voice.

His mother ignored his rude comment. Skye, on the other hand, pinched him hard on the thigh.

"Tyler kept an apartment in town and attended the local university. He studied to become a botanist and an engineer. He has a double Ph.D." Ivy's face lit up with pride. "You get your smarts from him…and your looks."

"Um, yeah, we all kind of noticed the whole doppelganger thing." Skye caught Ivy's gaze in the rearview mirror and smiled.

"This is a lot to process, and I'd like to ask you one more question. Why, Mom? I get you keeping it from everyone—but *me*? How could you keep this from *me*?"

Tears streamed down her cheeks, her eyes puffy and red. "I didn't want you to have to lie for me. I thought I was protecting you. I'm so sorry, Brack. I hope someday you can forgive me. I never meant to hurt you."

"Ivy?" Tyler groaned.

"I'm here, Ty, don't worry. We're taking you to Aether. Kai is the best doctor in the world. He'll help you."

Tyler reached for Ivy, and she leaned down to him. He spoke softly, but Brack heard him clearly.

"I've always wanted to see Aether with you, sweetheart. If I don't make it, spread my ashes over that beautiful lake you talk about so much." Tyler closed his eyes, and Ivy broke down in sobs.

****

Skye

The remainder of the ride flew by in a blur of emotion and tension. They handed Brack's father over to Kai at the Medical Center, and Skye sagged with relief. Ivy, of course, refused to leave Tyler's side but insisted Brack and Skye both go home to rest. When Brack planted a kiss on his mother's cheek, Skye knew her favorite mother-son duo would work things out sooner rather than later. And if Tyler managed to pull through, everything would be perfect for the Becks. With a promise to call the minute she knew anything, Ivy followed Kai into the exam room, leaving Skye and Brack alone in the waiting room.

"You must be exhausted. I'll walk you back to the tower," Brack said.

Skye didn't reply. Instead, she wrapped her arms around his waist. He pulled her in tight, let out a heavy breath, and kissed the top of her head.

"You know you don't need to be brave *all* the time," Skye reminded him. She gazed into his dark brown eyes. "Tyler is your father. You care about him. It's only natural to be worried."

"I'm definitely not brave *all* the time," he replied. "I was terrified when that crazy bitch took you away from me. I thought I might never see you again. Or kiss you—or feel you—or make love to you."

"Brack, I—"

But then he was kissing her, and she lost the will to argue. Brack's tongue stroked hers, and she had to stop herself from wrapping her legs around his waist in the middle of the Medical Center. They broke apart, their breaths coming in heavy pants.

Brack smiled. "Come with me." He took her by the hand. "I want to show you something."

"Seriously? I've seen it. Don't get me wrong, it's pretty great, but I'm kind of tired at the moment." Skye smirked.

"Not what I had in mind, but I like the way your mind works. The *something* I want to show you is a surprise you've never seen before."

He held her hand and didn't let go while they walked in silence. Curiosity bloomed inside her. What was Bracken Beck up to now? She told him she was tired, but in truth, she was never too tired to be with him. Admitting how much she wanted him…needed him, wasn't easy for Skye, but maybe the time had come to tell him how she felt.

"Hey, um—"

Shock hit her like a bolt of lightning. She dropped Brack's hand and stared. Framework had been set on a large foundation for a house in the woods, and Skye glimpsed the East Tower in the distance.

"What do you think?" he asked, sounding more uncertain than she was accustomed to hearing.

"I think I'm confused. What is this?"

"I kind of figured that was obvious. It's a house, or at least it's going to be soon."

"Thanks, the merely obvious aside." She popped a hand on her hip. "Who does this belong to, and why are they building it in my backyard?"

Brack's cheeks flooded with color. "It's mine. I asked the construction crew to build it for me…and…well, I…I—"

"Oh, for Goddess's sake, out with it already."

He barked out a laugh and picked up her hand again. "Man, you really aren't going to make anything easy for me—ever."

"Harumph." Teasing Brack had become an obsession of sorts and a bit of an aphrodisiac.

"I thought you might like to live near your sister." He tugged her to him. "I commissioned this house because I was hoping I might convince you to move in with me. Long before Mary Allen locked you in a cell, I knew, with my whole heart, that I didn't want to spend my life without you at the center of it. You're the one for me, Skye Anani. I'm sorry it took me so long to get my head out of my ass and realize the truth."

Warmth spread through her, and her heart thundered in her chest. Skye had expended so much energy trying to prove herself as a Protector that she almost forgot about the importance of being a woman first. She was a woman with feelings—a woman with desires—a woman who wanted this man with everything inside her.

"You know, rumor has it, I can be a bit difficult."

"We can work on it," he said.

"Are you sure you want to do this?"

Brack's smile lit up his handsome face. "Positive. Clearly, *easy* isn't my jam."

She looped her arms around his neck. "What is your jam, Mr. Beck?" She waggled her brows.

"Wait a sec, so, is that a yes?" He pressed his lips to hers before she could answer.

When they finally came up for air, Skye whispered a soft "Yes."

He took her by the shoulders and held her back. "Yes? As in, you want to move in with me?"

"We're really going to have to work on your poker face."

"I can't hide from you. I never could, and I don't ever want to." He pecked her on the lips.

"Fine, on one condition. I'm sure you must know what I want," she said, heat rising to her cheeks.

His brows knitted in confusion. "I'm afraid you're keeping me guessing because I have no clue."

This was turning out all wrong. Skye was no good at telling people what she wanted, not even Brack.

"Hm. What could it be?" He feigned contemplation, tapping his temple.

"Don't tease me." Her gaze fell to her feet.

"I would never tease you…well, that's not entirely true, but you get my drift." He lifted her chin and looked into her eyes. "You can tell me anything, especially when it comes to your needs."

"Fine." She huffed. "I…I want you to…to…call me…sweetheart."

Brack gazed at her with eyes that resembled melted chocolate. "My pleasure, *sweetheart*. I hope you know that I love you, and I'm going to spend the rest of my life proving it to you."

"Well, that's a relief because I love you too." Skye kissed him with all the love in her heart, and nothing had ever felt so right.

Chapter Thirty-Two

Aidan

Time must move at a different rate when you're over four hundred years old. Three days had gone by since their return from the lab, and still no word from the powers that be regarding Aidan's status. Barrington's facility had been reduced to a mere shell, its infrastructure obliterated. So, where did a former soldier fit in the eyes of the Elders now?

Fighting alongside the Aetherians, he'd been part of a team again. It was an experience he'd relished. The connection he shared with his new friends was rare, and he was smart enough to appreciate their unconditional acceptance. The Fire Guardian's powers lived inside him, something coveted by even the most powerful of Aetherians. From the moment Ashlyn's DNA had been fused with his, he understood the reasons why. Only one thing more powerful existed in the world—his feelings for Zephyr.

He may have been confused throughout his journey to Aether, but he had never been confused about her. Zephyr deserved the very best, and Aidan could only dream of measuring up one day. Captain Aidan Drake had been a man of valor and honor. As to who was Aidan Drake, the Aetherian, that remained to be seen.

Zephyr burst through the front door, her pretty face

flushed from the summer heat. She had on a pair of those tight, black bike shorts he loved so much and a matching jogging bra thingy. He didn't know what she called it because all he cared about was how hot she looked while wearing it.

She plopped onto the couch next to him and blurted out an exasperated, "Hi."

"I take it your meeting with Hawk didn't go well?"

"He told me to be patient." She sat up straighter. "In case you hadn't noticed, patience is *not* one of my virtues."

"I'm sure everything will work out as it was meant to."

"Wow, you sound like an Elder." Zephyr mock shuddered. "Soon you'll be saying weird stuff like Bear." She cleared her throat. "Well, my young Guardian, you are in a real pickle, but you were the one who threw yourself into the brine."

Damn, she was cute. He absently reached for a strand of her hair and twisted it around his finger. "I'm sure it won't be that bad. Why don't you tell me about your visit with Ivy and Tyler instead?"

"It was great." Zephyr's eyes sparkled. "Kai says Tyler handled the transition well. He'll be going home with Ivy in another few days. He'll be weak for a while, but he's going to make a full recovery. Brooke and Kai agree it's too early to tell if he'll manifest any Elemental control, but either way, the Elders have granted permission for him to stay in Aether."

"And the baby?"

"Once Kai clears her medically, the Elders will decide who is best suited to raise her."

He tipped his chin in acknowledgment. "That makes

sense. I'm happy to hear Ward is going to stay. Tyler, Ivy, and Brack make a great family. Maybe it's a good sign for us?"

Zephyr smiled. It was her naughty smile, the one she saved only for him. She looped her arms around his neck and kissed him. As if on instinct, his hands moved to her waist, pulling her close. Nothing fit together the way he and Zephyr did. He poured himself into the kiss, brushing his tongue gingerly against hers. She responded with a cock-hardening moan.

Aidan couldn't get enough of this incredible woman. She climbed into his lap and wrapped her long legs around his waist. The thin layer of her shorts kept little between them, and his erection pressed against the heat of her core. There was a fair chance they weren't going to make it to the bedroom.

"Where are Skye and Brack?" he asked, kissing his way up her neck, her sweet floral fragrance filling his nose.

"Not home," Zephyr groaned and ground her pelvis against his, making sure he got her meaning.

She slid back onto his thighs and slipped her hands beneath the waistband of his basketball shorts. Gripping his erection in her warm, soft hand, she began stroking him up and down. The guttural sounds he made surprised them both, and they laughed like teenagers.

A loud knock sounded on the front door. It swung open and then closed with a bang. They weren't expecting anyone, and Aidan froze in a state of momentary shock.

A booming voice rang out, "Hello, is anyone at home?" Bear stepped further into the room, coming within a few feet of the couch.

Zephyr yanked her hand out from his shorts, and the elastic band snapped against his skin. She jumped to her feet and slapped on a fake smile. But it was far too late.

"Oh, hi. I didn't realize you were stopping by," she said in a smooth, easy tone.

Zephyr's beautiful, dark hair appeared raked through, and her lips were bee-stung red from kissing. Bear would have to have been blind to mistake the situation because Aidan had no doubt that he had gotten an eye full. And if by some miracle he didn't, then the massive hard-on Aidan was sporting said it all. Zephyr tossed a throw pillow to him, and he placed it on his lap. Heat rose up to his neck and filled his cheeks.

This is one of these situations where I ask myself, hmm, should I say something here or pretend the Elder didn't just catch us about to have sex?

"I, uh apologize for barging in." The Elder stumbled over his words. "I fear I have interrupted a private moment."

Aidan had never seen the Elder flustered before. It was amusing, but he tempered his reaction out of respect for Bear.

"It's fine, we were just…talking. Please sit." Zephyr ran her fingers through her hair and sat down next to Aidan on the couch.

The Elder glared at a spindly wooden chair across from them but chose the loveseat next to it instead. It was a chair for two, but Bear squeezed in, end to end. Zephyr chuckled under her breath, but Aidan didn't miss it. He didn't miss a single detail when it came to her. The way she moved, the sound of her voice, the feel of her skin, Aidan memorized them all in case the Elder had come to say the former soldier was no longer welcome in Aether.

“I do not require an explanation.” Bear brushed it off with a wave of his hand. “Let us discuss the matter at hand. I have come to speak to you on behalf of all the Elders. Our fact gathering has concluded, and it appears we owe you both a debt of gratitude.”

Zephyr’s grip tightened on his hand, but she remained quiet. Too nervous to speak, Aidan nodded in acknowledgment. An inferno of Fire tingled beneath the surface of his skin.

“And, as a reward of sorts, we would like to offer you both a unique opportunity. If you wish, you may participate in the next running of the Protector trials. Captain Drake, your decision is not contingent upon your staying here in Aether. It is clear you are one of our people. You risked your life to save your fellow Aetherians, and you destroyed Dr. Barrington’s hold on our world. Take some time to think it over.”

“Thank you, sir. I’m honored.” Aidan rose and extended a hand to the Elder.

An enthusiastic shove from behind knocked him off balance. As he righted himself, the reason for his sudden clumsiness became clear. *Zephyr.* She’d leaped up from her seat and launched herself at the giant man.

“Are you serious? Oh my Goddess!” she shrieked, kissing Bear’s cheek with a loud smack.

The Elder’s roaring belly laughs filled the room. “I am pleased you are happy, my young Guardian.” A hand the size of an oven mitt stroked Zephyr’s cheek. “Soon you will be the first to combine two roles among the Aetherians, but I believe you to be up to the task.” The Elder cleared his throat. “I shall leave you to your um…celebration.”

****

Zephyr

"That was simultaneously the most embarrassing and coolest thing ever." Zephyr's heartbeat raced a mile a minute. "I still can't believe it."

Aidan lowered his hands to her shoulders and gazed into her eyes. "Believe it. The Elders get it now. You are capable of so much more than they've given you credit for. You were the one who saved everyone. Aspen owes you her life."

She wrapped her arms around his waist and buried her face in his chest. "*We*, we saved Aspen, all of us."

"I guess we make a pretty good team, huh?"

"Definitely." She looked up at him and smiled.

"So, um, would you mind very much if I hung around here?"

"You want to stay—in Aether?"

"Yes, but only if it's what you want too. I understand if…you…you know, don't—"

Zephyr raised her marked palm. "Stop!" She shook her head. "You're giving me whiplash. Please, just tell me what it is that you're thinking."

"I think what I've always thought…you're far too good for me."

"Guardians are people, too," she joked. But hope reigned inside her, and she found the courage to open herself up to this man she'd fallen for. "Seriously though, is it because of the Elders' offer, or is there another reason you want to stay?"

He leaned over and gave her a chaste kiss on the lips. "The minute I met you, my life changed. Even from beneath the veil of Barrington's mind control, I sensed you, and you've been saving me in one way or another ever since." Aidan stroked his hands down her arms, goosebumps rising under his touch. "You never gave up on me, not once. You taught me to be an Aetherian and opened your heart to me. You are the number one reason I want to stay. But it's important you understand that when I fell in love with you, I also fell in love with Aether."

"Aidan," she whispered on a long sigh.

"No more hiding. I need you to know the way I feel. And while I'm confessing here, I want to admit that for a long time, I thought you were in love with Beck."

"I told you, he's like a brother to me."

"Yeah, I get that now, and of course, once I witnessed the crazy attraction between your sister and the guy, I got over it pretty quickly. But no matter how hard I tried, I couldn't wrap my brain around the idea of ever measuring up to a Guardian—"

"Please, don't—"

He stroked a gentle hand down her hair. "Let me finish."

She nodded.

"Hawk came to see me yesterday when you were out. We had a long chat."

"Oh?" A rush of adrenaline tingled through her body. "I didn't realize you and our lead Protector had become so chummy."

"Neither did I." He chuckled. "Hawk's a good guy, and his heart is in the right place. I'm sure growing up with Bear as a grandfather must've had quite an impact on him."

"Bear has an impact on everyone." She laughed.

"Anyway, Hawk told me the story of how he and Ashlyn got together. He explained about coming to terms with his inability to measure up to a Guardian. You see, it's not the point."

"The point?" she asked.

"To measure up."

"You've lost me."

"What I'm trying to say is, I know I'll never be good enough for you, but I will love you enough to make up for any of my shortcomings. According to Hawk, being the Kanti of a Guardian is a very important job. He considers it to be even more important than his role as lead Protector of Aether. And I…I would like to apply for the position in your life." His cheeks flushed. "I love you more than anything in this world, Zephyr." Aidan got down on one knee. "Will you marry me?"

Her brain froze for a second and then kickstarted. "Oh, you mean, *Join* with you."

"Yes, yes, that's exactly what I mean." Aidan beamed.

"In that case—" She dropped down in front of him and threw her arms around his neck. "—I'd love to."

Damn, I should've gotten her a ring. Do Aetherians even give each other rings?

"Don't worry about it," she whispered. "It's not a thing here."

Aidan pulled back, the flush in his cheeks fading. "I…I didn't say anything. I was just thinking that I should've gotten you a ring."

He was right. It was the oddest feeling. Aidan claimed he had not spoken aloud; his words were in her head. What the hell was going on here?

"Are you sure? That doesn't make any sense." Zephyr paused and tried to collect her thoughts. They'd been through an ordeal together, that was all. They were having some kind of joint hallucination.

"I did not say a word. I swear it."

"Hm, if you didn't speak, but I heard you—" She grabbed him in a bear hug and then released him. "I think I understand."

"I'm glad one of us does. You want to share it with the rest of the class?"

"You have Ashlyn's powers."

"I recall," he said, sounding skeptical but giving her some leeway.

"Ashlyn's extrasensory gift is telepathic communication with her Kanti. The moment they committed to each other emotionally, they were bound." Her lips spread into a wide grin. "I guess I'll never have to doubt your sincerity."

"You'll never have to read my mind to know how I feel because I'm going to show you every day of our lives. I love you, Zephyr Anani."

"*And I love you, Aidan Drake*."

"*Life sure is going to be interesting with a wife who can read my mind.*"

"*Adara, and you're not kidding.*"

"*And I'm also the luckiest man, my beautiful Guardian.*"

Epilogue

Brynn Reed, Guardian of the House of Earth

"Just because I can communicate with animals, and they tend to follow me around does not make me a cartoon princess. I'm a badass Guardian. Come on, Ash, you're a Guardian, you have to understand," Brynn said, pleading with her eyes.

"Oh, I understand." Her friend's shoulders sagged. "And I'm the last one who needs to be reminded of what a Guardian is capable of, but I *will* be the first to remind you that the mark you were born with comes with more than just powerful gifts. It comes with responsibility and obligation. You were chosen for a reason."

"I know, I know. But this isn't the same. I love babies as much as the next person, but I'm supposed to guide the future Guardian not raise her. Someday, I may want kids but not for at least one hundred years. For Goddess' sake, I'm only twenty-nine."

"Aspen is the Guardian of Earth, Brynn. Where else does she belong?"

"With Ivy? She was friends with the kid's mom. They're practically family," she said, desperation lacing her voice.

"Ivy has her hands full with Tyler's recovery. She wanted Aspen, but Tyler needs her right now."

"Well, um, is there really no one else?"

Ashlyn picked up the sleeping infant from her stroller and handed her to Brynn. "You are the best suited for the job even if you don't realize it yet."

The baby squeaked, and Brynn jumped. "What was that? What does she want?"

Her friend laughed. "You need to chill. She's probably just waking up from her nap. I put a bunch of bottles in your fridge. Let's go warm one in the microwave. Babies are often hungry when they first get up."

"See, this is a huge mistake. I have no idea what I'm doing here." She followed Ashlyn into the kitchen, the baby squirming in her arms. "What if I screw up and something bad happens to her?"

"Babies are resilient. Aspen has been through a lot. I'm sure you can relate." Ashlyn shot her a knowing look. "It will be a good experience for you both."

"Do the Elders think she and her mother were from that Empyrean place Barrington's son told you guys about?"

"Possibly."

The microwave beeped. Ashlyn removed the bottle, twisted the nipple on, gave it a shake, and shoved it at Brynn. "Here."

Brynn pulled back the wrapping tightly swaddling the infant and held the bottle out to her. "What if they come looking for her?"

Aspen's hand came up, and she grabbed for a lock of Brynn's curly hair. Her tiny fingers opened and closed, and she caught a glimpse of the baby's miniature Guardian mark. Every line and curve matched her own. Aspen truly was the next Guardian of the House of Earth.

"The Protectors are working with the Elders to come

up with a plan. It may take some time, so what do you say? Are you in?"

The baby's bright green gaze locked with hers, and warmth spread out from the center of her chest. The connection she fought against could not be stopped. Aspen smiled up at her, and Brynn realized that this child would be a part of her forever.

"Yes, I will." Brynn brushed a hand over Aspen's soft tuft of dark hair. "We'll figure it out together. Right, Kiddo?"

The baby squealed with delight.

"And so it begins," Ashlyn said with a smirk.

A word about the author...

M. Goldsmith has been publishing her stories since 2018, but her love of romance fiction goes back to her childhood. Married to her college sweetheart, she lives on Long Island and cherishes visits from her three grown kids and enormous extended family.

Thank you for purchasing
this publication of The Wild Rose Press, Inc.

For questions or more information
contact us at
info@thewildrosepress.com.

The Wild Rose Press, Inc.
www.thewildrosepress.com

www.ingramcontent.com/pod-product-compliance
Lightning Source LLC
Chambersburg PA
CBHW072303020726
47501CB00002B/380
* 9 7 8 1 5 0 9 2 5 2 6 8 8 *